BLOOD
AND
SAND

ELIZABETH HUNTER

BLOOD AND SAND
Copyright © 2013
Elizabeth Hunter
ISBN: 978-1489523419

Cover Design: E. Hunter
Edited by: Anne Victory
Formatted by: Elizabeth Hunter

For information about the Elemental Mysteries series, please visit:
ElementalMysteries.com

TO KRISTY

An amazing writer,
An amazing reader,
And a better friend than I deserve.

This one is for you.

ALSO BY ELIZABETH HUNTER

The Elemental Mysteries Series

A Hidden Fire
This Same Earth
The Force of Wind
A Fall of Water

The Elemental World Series

Building From Ashes
Waterlocked (novella)
Blood and Sand

The Cambio Springs Series

Long Ride Home (short story)
Shifting Dreams

Contemporary Romance

The Genius and the Muse

ACKNOWLEDGEMENTS

Thanks, as always, to my wonderful family and friends who put up with me while I am writing, especially the Small Boy who makes me laugh. Thanks to my pre-readers, Kristy, Sarah, Kelli, Gen, and Natalie. Thank you for forgiving my mental instability at odd moments and sacrificing your time and attention to this book. Thanks to Florence + The Machine, whose album, Ceremonials, was my almost constant soundtrack while writing this book.

Thanks to the many reviewers and bloggers who promote my work and spread the word online and in person. I am constantly amazed by the level of professionalism so many of you exhibit at what is usually a volunteer job. Many, many thanks.

And thanks to Johnna for the last minute catch on the egregious Doctor Who error. (I'm still a little embarrassed.)

Thanks to my editing team, Anne and Sara. *Such* a pleasure working with you!

Thanks to my agent, Jane Dystel, and all the team at Dystel and Goderich Literary Management.

Thanks to my girls. (You know who you are.)

And thanks, always, to my readers. Thank you for being enthusiastic about this world. Thanks for your encouragement and kind words. I hope I will always do justice to the confidence you place in me as a storyteller.

PROLOGUE

San Francisco, 1884

DON ERNESTO ALVAREZ strolled through the streets of Chinatown, his favorite daughter on his arm. The scent of human waste mingled with exotic spices and cooking fires. On the evening fog, he could smell the ocean and the scent of fish from the bay. The mist swirled around him, teasing his energy with its call. At his side, he felt his daughter's blood pulse.

"What is it?"

Her fangs dropped. Paula was only twenty years immortal and often had a harder time controlling her cravings.

"Blood." Her nose lifted in the air. "Fresh. There's a fight somewhere."

Ernesto gave her an indulgent smile. "Shall we? The opium was disappointing. We might as well see if there are other entertainments before we return to our lodging."

Their safe quarters that night were with a trusted ally of Ernesto's, Ekaterina Grigorieva, a water vampire who controlled much of the Pacific Northwest. While her headquarters had recently moved to the growing city of Seattle, Katya still chose to meet with allies in San Francisco. Ernesto had traveled up the coast of California with Paula, looking for amusement in the lively city along with a more favorable price on lumber for his ships.

Ernesto let Paula lead him down the alley, which smelled of fish and laundry soap, to see a surprisingly interesting sight.

It was a human, a Chinese man, which was not surprising as they were in the section of the city overwhelmed by the foreigners. What *was* surprising was the flurry of activity surrounding him. It looked like the

1

human had been thrown out the back door of a gambling hall. He must have displeased the proprietor somehow. But instead of the beating that would have been common from the four other men surrounding him, Ernesto watched, intrigued, as the human held off his four attackers with swift punches that almost appeared to flow at immortal speed.

Punches turned into kicks. The four humans who had thrown the man out were not without their strengths, and blood was flowing. He heard Paula whine at his side, eager to taste it, but Ernesto put a hand on her arm, stilling her. He wanted to watch a bit longer.

The human was abnormally fast. He did not try to hold off his attackers, but let them draw close, then used swift punches to knock them back. And throughout it all, his face was a mask of impassive focus. He seemed almost bored, despite the bruise that was forming on one cheek, another on his eye, and the blood that dripped from his mouth to his chin. His face said one thing, but the coiled tension in his body said something entirely different.

What exquisite anger.

Ernesto felt his fangs drop, and he took Paula's hand, slowly walking closer to the fight.

The humans didn't notice, so focused were they on their own bloody feud. Despite his skill, the lone human was starting to falter; four opponents were simply too much for him. Still, he fought on, showing no signs of capitulation. Ernesto wondered whether the other humans would kill the man. That would be a shame. He was a fine specimen, and his blood was rich with the smell of the ocean.

"Paula," he said quietly, reluctant to interrupt the fight.

She hissed, "Yes?"

"Stop them."

He could feel her trembling in anticipation. "May I drink, Father?"

"Drink your fill from the four, but leave the fighting one for me."

In the space of a blink, Paula was on them, dragging one human back to a dark corner and piercing his neck with her fangs. The copper smell of blood filled the alley, drowning out the smell of garbage and fish. The three remaining men did not notice the loss of their friend; they were more focused on the slowly weakening Chinese man. The lone human *did* notice the absence of one of his attackers, and he scanned the alley, all the while holding off the three other men as best he could. Finally, his eyes paused on the mist-clad form of Ernesto and he blinked.

One of the attackers knocked him to the ground at that point, but within seconds, that man was gone as well. Paula had grabbed him and latched on to his neck, letting his sounds of struggle fill the air.

"Paula," Ernesto chided. "We do not wish for attention."

Immediately, the man grew limp in her arms and fell silent. By this point, the two remaining humans who had been beating the Chinese man had turned to see what the commotion was. Their eyes grew wide and their mouths dropped open in horror as they watched their fellow human crumble to the ground. One darted for the door of the gambling hall, but Paula was already there. He didn't even have time to scream. The other made for the mouth of alley, his voice pitched high as he yelled for help, but Ernesto caught him by the hand and squeezed. The man fell silent, his mind flooded by Ernesto's powerful amnis.

He stepped closer to the Chinese man, handing Paula the human's hand as she finished drinking his comrade.

"What are you?" the human asked in perfect English.

"You speak very well." It was true. He had a distinct accent, but his words were clear. "What is your name?"

"What are you?" the human asked again, wiping the blood from his eyes and inching toward the dark street.

"How did you learn to fight like that? It was fascinating and very effective."

The man never took his eyes off Ernesto, but he straightened a little. "My father taught me to fight."

"He would be proud."

"No." The man was inching along the grimy brick wall. "He wouldn't."

There it was again, just a flicker in the human's eyes. Such *exquisite* anger. What would it be like with immortal power behind it? What would it take to leash the power of such a creature? Ernesto's blood pumped in his veins and he bared his fangs at the thought. The human saw his opportunity and ran out of the alley, silently fleeing the vampires and disappearing into the night. Paula appeared at his side half a second later.

"You didn't drink, Father."

He turned and smiled, patting her cheek and taking his handkerchief from his pocket to dab at a spot of blood on her chin. "I'm not hungry for blood tonight, *mi querida*. Did you enjoy yourself?"

"*Sí, Papá. Gracias.*"

"Good. Now that you've had your fill..." Ernesto finished tending to his child, then his eyes grew cold as he turned to the foggy night. "Find the human, Paula. And bring him to me."

CHAPTER ONE

San Diego, 2013

THE LIGHTS OF THE CLUB pulsed red and gold as he swirled the ice in the glass in front of him. The frozen water turned and twisted, spinning the liquid in his glass into a small whirlpool that splashed over the edge of the cut crystal. His amnis caught the drops that fell to the table and quickly slid them back in the glass, leaving the polished wood unmarked. The music, the abysmally loud techno and pop that the patrons preferred, flowed around him as he sat in the black leather booth, watching.

Baojia was always watching.

Humans danced in a mass like one pulsing organism. Skin. Heat. Sweat. The mingled scents of blood and alcohol filled his nose, but he had already fed that night, a pretty young co-ed who would have no memory of his teeth in her neck. He would have indulged in more, but the girl had too much alcohol in her blood, so he pushed her back toward her friends, who only giggled and winked at him.

Idiotic humans. Baojia was painfully bored.

The club in San Diego, *Boca*, was his sire's pride and joy. It had been recently remodeled, thanks to Baojia's presence. He had nothing better to do, after all. He was stuck in San Diego, having a time-out like a rebellious toddler. The first year had been deserved; he had taken his exile with stoic grace. After all, it had been his failure that had led to the death of Ernesto's kinsman and his negligence caused Ernesto's favorite granddaughter grave injury. Beatrice De Novo had been under his protection, and he had failed in his mission.

No, the first year had been well deserved.

The second year as well. Perhaps.

Baojia had been in San Diego for three years. Beatrice De Novo had recovered—rather admirably—and had settled with her mate in Los Angeles. She had probably forgotten about him. Forgotten the years he had watched over her while the damnable Italian had been jaunting around the world. It wasn't Giovanni Vecchio who had protected the young human, it was Baojia. For four years, she had been his assignment. Her safety hadn't been his only job, but it had been a priority. It still stung that she had no idea the lengths to which he had gone.

History. He took another sip of water. It was history. He had more important things to worry about. Like how to relieve this excruciating boredom and convince his sire to release him from the hell on earth of college children who thought they ruled the world.

"Boss?"

He turned at the sound of his assistant's voice. "What is it, Luis?"

"Do you know a woman named Natalie Ellis?"

He frowned. "Human?"

"Yeah."

"No."

"Okay, I figured." Luis patted the back of the booth in the VIP area of the club, which took up the balcony. "I'll tell her to take off."

He shrugged. "Let her stay and keep drinking as long as she's not causing a scene."

"Okay. She's at the bar if you want to look. Redhead in a black dress. Cute, if you like freckles."

His mouth turned up at the corner. "How sweet."

"Yeah…" Luis chuckled. "Something tells me… not. Oh, and here's the report from the casino. Jared dropped it off earlier. You still meeting with Rory at two?"

He nodded. "Make sure my office is clear and show him in as soon as he arrives. What time is it?"

"Eleven."

He stretched his neck to the side in a completely habitual gesture. He didn't need to stretch any more than he needed to drink the water in front of him. Still, those little signals all put the humans around him at ease. "Wonderful. It's busy tonight."

"Back to school, Boss." Luis grinned. "A fresh crop of newly legal eye candy."

He often forgot how young Luis was. The human was only twenty-five, the son of one of Ernesto's longtime human employees. The don of Los Angeles was nothing if not loyal. He kept the fealty of his human servants for generations, which had served him well in the rapidly changing atmosphere of Southern California.

"Get back to work being charming, Luis. And keep an eye on the new bartender. I think he's pouring a little heavy for the more attractive female patrons."

Like the redhead in the black dress who was definitely not a co-ed.

As soon as Luis had mentioned red hair, his eyes had searched for her. From his perch in the corner, Baojia could observe three of the four doors in the club. A monitor in the corner watched the other. He could see the bar, and the mirror behind it let him see each and every movement of the humans tending it. The DJ's booth was elevated and also monitored by a camera that fed into a small screen he could see from his seat.

The dance floor took up most of the main level, lined by booths that were reservation only. The VIP area in the balcony was even more exclusive. *Boca* had become the premiere nightclub in downtown San Diego, and Baojia had remodeled it with security in mind. If he had to be stuck in a tiny corner of his sire's kingdom, that corner would be the most secure in Ernesto's territories.

Baojia stood at the balcony and watched the redhead, who was sipping a clear cocktail with two limes. Her hair was a tumble of red waves; very attractive, he had to admit. Her pale shoulders were bare, but the rest of her dress hugged her curves. She was of medium height and had an athletic build. Not slight and girlish like the children on the dance floor. She was around thirty in human years if he had to guess. She stood out for that alone. Her dress and makeup fit the club; the intelligent eyes that scanned the room and ignored the males surrounding her did not.

Natalie Ellis.

He didn't know her, but she was intriguing. She'd asked for him, specifically? He'd have to ask Luis. Very few humans knew his name.

Who are you, Natalie Ellis? He narrowed his gaze as she checked her mobile phone, punched something in, then slipped it back in her purse. It was a large purse, the kind a professional woman carried, not a girl out clubbing. Right dress. Right jewelry and makeup. Wrong purse.

"You're a pretty liar, aren't you?" he murmured, his hands hanging in the pockets of his perfectly tailored black suit. Baojia abhorred ill-fitting clothes. "And how do you know my name?"

He saw Luis approach and touch the woman's shoulder. She turned, her polite smile slowly turning down. She was annoyed. Her eyes flicked up to the balcony and met his. He cocked his head as they held. Curious. Most humans wouldn't hold his gaze for long; some instinct always told them to look away from the predator. Not her. Her eyes kept right on his. Challenging. Tempting.

Very curious.

She kept watching him as she reached back and grabbed her cocktail. She tilted the glass up, and her throat undulated as she swallowed, the pale skin glowing in the red lights of the club. Never taking her eyes off him, she finished her drink and set the glass down, then finally turned back to Luis. She reached in her too-large purse, handed Luis a card, then stood. Baojia watched her until she left through the crowded front doors. Then he turned and sat down again, pulling out the report about the casino in the desert near El Centro.

Baojia stifled the groan when he opened the file and saw the first column of numbers that filled it.

He had to get back to LA.

Rory McNair was already sitting in a chair and drinking a glass of blood in his office when Baojia escaped the still-lively club at two. His sister Paula's husband was a casual man. He and Baojia had been turned within twenty years of each other and always had a good relationship, though Rory's allegiance was to Paula first. The two had been mated for over one hundred years. Of all Ernesto's children, it was Paula, Rory, and Baojia whom their father trusted most. Well, until the Chinese disaster, as Rory referred to it.

"How you doing, brother?"

Baojia shrugged. "I'm bored. Watching college kids and redecorating nightclubs gets old. How are you?"

"Overworked and living with an annoyed wife." Rory's grey mustache twitched. "How did you manage all this shit and still have a life?"

Since Baojia had been exiled, the majority of the security for Ernesto's large territory had fallen to Rory's hands. Paula was the businesswoman. Baojia had been the security. Rory was mostly a man of leisure, so the sudden weight of responsibility for a region stretching from Northern Mexico to Central California was not a welcome addition to his life.

"I *didn't* have a life, remember?" He smiled. "I suppose I should be grateful for the vacation, but I just find myself obsessing over all the problems that could be cropping up in my absence." He raised a quick hand. "Not that I don't trust you. I just know that it's a lot. Have there been any more problems in the mountains?"

"Nothing much." Rory twisted the tip of his mustache and leaned back in his chair, blood forgotten. "They're still growin' up there, but the gang activity has been contained." Marijuana production in the Southern California mountains was hardly something Ernesto usually worried about, but the infiltration of gangs from Northern Mexico was. It was not uncommon for other vampire leaders to send in criminal gangs they controlled to test the resolve of their neighbors. Problems out of the ordinary had to be dealt with swiftly and decisively in order to maintain a leader's position and authority. Baojia worried that Rory wasn't taking it seriously enough.

"Let me know if there's anything I can do to help."

Rory snorted. "From San Diego?"

Baojia ignored the sting. It wasn't intentional and it was hardly something Rory could help. Until Ernesto decided to let him out of his virtual prison, he was stuck.

"Sorry." His brother looked contrite. "You got the casino numbers?"

"Yes." He pulled out the file. "I'm warning you, everything appears to be in order."

Rory's eyes twinkled. "Not a single head we can crack for missing money or booze?"

"Sadly not," he said with a smile. "But the employee pension fund needs a new manager."

"Embezzlement?"

"Retirement."

"Damn."

By three in the morning, Rory was gone and Baojia was leaving the club. Luis would take care of the few after-hours patrons they entertained so Baojia could return to the home he had secured on Coronado Island, a few steps from the beach. It was a modern house with exactly the right number of windows and a very secure location. His driver dropped him off before dawn and returned at nightfall. Was it his comfortable warehouse in downtown LA? No, but it was modern and had a good area to train, so he was as content as he could be. He was just about to step into his car when he heard the voice.

"Are you Baojia?"

He smiled, somehow knowing it was Natalie Ellis before he turned. "Where did you hear that name?"

"Took me a while to figure it out once I saw it written," she mused, stepping closer. "*Bow*—like the bow of a ship, *jeeah*. It's cool. Chinese?"

"Perhaps." Baojia spun around and regarded her. "Where did you hear it?"

"Does it matter?"

"Very much so." He noticed that she had taken off the heels she'd been wearing and put on a pair of thin, black shoes, but her dress and makeup were the same. "You brought the wrong purse, Ms. Ellis."

"How—?" She frowned before raising the very practical black handbag. "I guess you see a lot of college kids, huh? Not the usual?"

"You stood out. That's not a bad thing. Where did you hear that name?"

She stepped closer. "Did your errand boy give you my card?"

"No. And I wouldn't let him hear you call him an errand boy."

Her lips wore a slight smile. "But he is."

Baojia stepped closer. "We like to allow children their illusions, don't we?"

Her eyes were blue. A clear blue that reminded him of old memories of the sky reflecting on the water. She was a creature made for sunlight—a dusting of freckles covered her nose and dotted her shoulders. Though her skin was pale, it was flushed with life. The unexpected curl of arousal surprised him. Human women rarely held his interest.

"Listen, I don't want to waste your time. I'm looking for Baojia because someone told me he could help me with a story I'm writing."

"Oh? You're a writer?" In his experience, humans usually abhorred silence and would fill it with useful information, given the chance. One rarely had to question them. Just remain silent and they would tell you what you needed to know.

"Yes." The woman remained silent, too. One hand was placed on her hip and the other clutched her too-large purse. He couldn't stop the smile. Apparently, they shared the same sentiments about silence. Finally, he shrugged and turned away.

"I'm sorry, Ms. Ellis. I can't help you."

"You *are* Baojia, aren't you?" She was persistent; he'd give her that. "If you won't help me, I guess I'll have to go talk to Ivan myself."

He spun so fast her eyes swam.

"Hey, how did you—"

Within seconds, Baojia had her tucked in the back of his sedan and told his driver to circle the block. Closing the privacy screen, he held her hand and watched her. She was completely out, rendered unconscious by the shock of his energy. He tried not to curse at his clumsy handling of the situation, but the sound of the other immortal's name on her lips had startled him. What did this soft sunshine girl want with Ivan? And how the hell did she know to come to him for an introduction? She clearly did not know about their kind judging from her reaction to his speed.

"Ms. Ellis?" Still holding her hand, he called her name softly to rouse her. He lessened the electrical current that ran over his skin and onto hers. "Natalie?"

"Hmm?" Her eyes blinked open but still swam with confusion. "Where am I?"

"In my car. I'll make sure you get home safely. Where did you hear the name Baojia, Natalie? Who gave it to you?" His amnis eased into her mind, loosening her tongue. At this level of influence, she would tell him anything he wanted.

"Dez did, silly." She sounded drunk, her cerebral cortex awash in amnis. "You know, Desiree Riley... Well, Desiree Kirby now. I think she changed her name when she married Matt."

"Desiree Riley?" Beatrice De Novo's best friend was also the wife of Matt Kirby, who ran security and other sensitive assignments for the

Italian fire vampire who had taken somewhat permanent residence in Southern California. Giovanni Vecchio was Beatrice De Novo's husband and a wary ally of his sire's. Desiree Riley was, to put it bluntly, a human who knew things. Also, a human who wouldn't have given out his name without reason, from what he knew of her. "Why did Dez give you my name?"

"Badgered her." Natalie laughed. "Poor thing. Kept at her until she cracked. It's an important story, she knows that. Needed information. My editor…" The woman drifted off again and Baojia realized he had lost control of his amnis for a moment.

"Natalie?"

She was a lovely rumpled heap in the back of his car. Her red hair tumbled around her, falling into her face. Her nose wrinkled at the ticklish strands, causing Baojia to smile as he brushed it away.

"Need to talk to Ivan. Name keeps coming up." Her forehead was wrinkled now. "So many gone. Can't… can't continue. 'S wrong, you know?"

"No." He didn't know. Didn't know what she was talking about, but the mention of Ivan's name was not something to be taken lightly. And there was no way this girl should be going to speak to the leader of Ensenada on her own. That was out of the question. He'd have to call Dez and investigate tomorrow night, but until then…

"Natalie," he whispered.

"Yeah," she whispered back.

"Where do you live?"

She told him her address without question, along with a rather amusing anecdote about her neighbor Mr. Sanchez and his new Chihuahua. Finally, he had to interrupt.

"I'm going to take you home now. Forget about Ivan."

She smiled mischievously. "I don't forget anything, buddy."

"You will this time. Trust me." He pulled her up and she slumped against his side, her head rolling to the side. Her neck was bared to him, beckoning him despite his earlier meal. Baojia felt the pressure increase as his fangs pressed down and the earlier curl of arousal turned into a jolt. He wanted this woman. Eyeing her neck, he considered what he knew about her.

Natalie Ellis was a writer, a persistent one. She was also a friend of Dez's, and possibly, Beatrice's friend as well. Did she know them from school? He searched his memories of Beatrice's time at university but could find no mention or memory of this woman. She seemed to be the right age to have been in grad school with Dez and Beatrice.

"Who are you, Natalie?" He brushed away another strand of hair, twisting it around his finger for a moment. "And why did you come looking for me?"

She grinned, even though her eyes were closed. "Knew you were Baojia." They flickered open and met his. "You're really handsome. How did you move so fast?"

"I'm magic."

She giggled uncontrollably, throwing her head back in delight and sending a wave of her scent toward him. He growled at the back of his throat, which caused her to stop short and look at him with sleepy calculation. "You're not magic," she said. "But you're something."

She had good instincts.

"Something?"

"Something… different." She leaned closer and pressed herself against his chest, one hand going to his mouth. Her blue eyes looked up into his, then she looked down at his lips and traced around them. His teeth throbbed in his mouth and his lower lip dropped down on an exhale, revealing the tips of his fangs to her gaze.

A tentative finger reached out and stroked along one. "Cool," she whispered.

"Natalie," he said, his voice low and hoarse, "you are not to contact Ivan in any way. Do you understand? Forget about him."

He increased the pressure of his influence on her mind until she slumped against his chest.

"Okay," she sighed.

"Never. Never speak to Ivan."

"Sheesh." She curled her lip. "Bossy."

"I'm serious."

"I can tell. In fact, I bet you're *always* serious." Natalie rolled her eyes and pulled away. He let her go and tried to ignore the suddenly cool spot on his chest where she had rested. "Baojia?"

"Yes?"

13

"You're taking me home?"

"Yes."

"Okay. I'm tired. And I have work tomorrow. And my editor's boss… Ugh. I know he doesn't like me. He puts up with me because of the drug-bust story, but it pisses him off. And I need to meet Kristy tomorrow. Did I put that in my phone? I better put that in my phone." He cocked his head, watching her as she chattered. Suddenly, she looked down. "I can't believe I wore this dress."

He smiled, oddly amused and sad that this interesting human would have no memory of their encounter. "You look lovely in it."

She smiled back, her eyes sparkling. "Even with the wrong purse."

"It made you stand out."

"True."

She fell silent after that, his influence and the late hour lulling her into a peaceful slumber. He relayed her address to the driver, then sat back, pursing his lips as he looked at the human woman in his car.

"A writer," he muttered. Writers took notes. Notes that might contain Ivan's name. It wouldn't do for her to find those and start getting curious again. He didn't have time to search her apartment before dawn, but he'd definitely be asking Dez some pointed questions tomorrow. Why had she given his name to a reporter? What was Natalie talking about when she said it had to stop? Why did Dez trust her?

He sat up a little straighter and silently cheered when he realized he had something to investigate other than disappearing bottles of the top-shelf vodka. Then he glanced back at the human.

What if she started looking for Ivan before he could find out why she knew about him? What would happen if she ran into the wrong people while he was in day rest?

He frowned. She was just a woman. Why was he so concerned?

Baojia let out a frustrated breath. Stupid, curious humans. They could be irritatingly persistent. But it was more intrigue than he'd had in months; he was actually looking forward to solving this mystery, even if it *was* regarding a mortal. Natalie's leg moved against his, and he followed the line of her ankle up until the pale curve of her thigh disappeared under the edge of her dress.

She was attractive and curious. What if she went looking for Ivan? She had no standing in their world. The name of Desiree Riley certainly wasn't going to mean anything to more than a few. She didn't *belong* to anyone. If she was an employee of his sire's, she would fall under Don Ernesto's general aegis and be protected against another vampire's influence or use. If a vampire kept her for blood or sex, she would fall under his personal aegis and would be even more protected.

But Natalie was under no immortal aegis at all, which meant she was fair game. He tapped his foot as he watched her sleep. The question wouldn't leave him alone.

What if she went looking for Ivan?

Her head rolled to the side, and his eyes traced over the smooth, unmarred expanse of her neck. He felt his fangs lengthen and he leaned closer. Slipping one arm around her back, he brought her body close to his and her eyes blinked open.

"Hey, handsome."

"Hey."

"Whatcha doin'?"

He took a deep breath, enjoying her scent, which held hints of the ocean and the sun. "I'm putting you under my aegis."

"What does that mean?" She frowned. "You're kinda weird."

"You have no idea." He leaned closer and heard her sigh when his lips brushed against her pulse. Was he doing this for her? Or for himself? He tried to stop thinking and enjoy the anticipation of the bite.

"What are you doing?" she asked again.

"I'm going to bite your neck and drink some of your blood," he murmured. "You won't see the bites, but others will. And it will offer you a measure of protection until I can figure out what's going on."

"I didn't hear that right." She blinked rapidly. "You're going to... what?"

His amnis washed over her skin, and Baojia felt the damp coastal air draw close as his energy wrapped around her. He closed his eyes and slid his fangs into her neck. The rich taste flooded his mouth, and he felt Natalie arch her back.

"Ohhhh, that feels really good. Holy... W...what are you doing to me?"

He took only a mouthful before he grunted and forced himself back, licking the last bit of blood from his lips before he pierced his tongue and healed the delicate wounds in her neck. He closed his eyes, trying to will away the natural reaction of his flesh to hers. The sight of his marks in her neck gave him too much of a primitive thrill.

"Natalie—"

He was cut off when she kissed him. She grabbed his face with both hands and threw herself into it, moaning into his mouth as he gently pushed her away.

"Natalie, you're under my influence. It's—" He cleared his throat. "This is not appropriate."

She was dazed, staring at him in confusion, hands still on his cheeks and arousal bringing a delicious flush to her pale skin. "Why not?"

"Trust me. I have a feeling if you ever remembered this, you'd be more than a little pissed off."

She did the adorable wrinkling thing with her nose again. "I'm not going to remember this?"

"No." He gently pushed her back and buckled her into her seat belt.

But I believe I will. For quite some time.

CHAPTER TWO

NATALIE ELLIS DIDN'T SLEEP IN. So when the sun hit her face, she sat bolt upright in bed, looking around in confusion. Glancing down, she saw she had somehow fallen asleep in her bra and underwear and she had an odd feeling in her head. Not a headache exactly…

"Ugh." She groaned and swung her legs over the side of her bed, almost tripping over her black ballet flats. She shook her head to clear the sleep from her eyes and pulled on a long T-shirt, then put her unruly red hair into a messy bun at the back of her head. She'd just had it cut, and the stylist had snipped off a bit too much. As a result, it was constantly falling into her face. She curled her lip in annoyance and decided she needed coffee.

"Coffee," she whispered as she made her way to the kitchen of her small duplex in Hillcrest. She could hear Mr. Sanchez's new Chihuahua, Pippy, yapping already. "Coffee, coffee, coffee," she chanted, trying to ignore the high-pitched barking. It wasn't that she didn't like dogs. She'd grown up with a German shepherd, for goodness sake, but she wasn't totally convinced that Chihuahuas were actual dogs. Her brain was still fuzzy, as if she'd taken a sleeping pill. Not that she ever did. Natalie didn't need much sleep, but when she finally crashed, she went out like a light. Hitting the counter, she managed to pull out the filters and grounds, pouring in the Kona blend she treated herself to on payday.

After the coffee was started, she looked around her house again. The small living room flowed out onto a whitewashed wooden deck that was the real reason she had leased the place. It was her second house in San Diego, but the one she hoped to stay in. Close enough to downtown to ride her bike, she was within walking distance of cafes, a good market, and lots of boutiques and restaurants. The fact that she also had a friendly, grandfather-ish landlord helped too. Mr. Sanchez thought being a writer was slightly more glamorous than it actually was, but then she was fairly sure she'd heard *His Girl Friday* playing more than once from her side of the wall.

As if on cue, her phone rang. Where was her phone? She always knew where her phone was. It was practically glued to her hand. Natalie looked around in confusion, noting the general disarray for the first time. Her nice black dress was hanging on the back of the dining room chair. Her heels were tossed by the couch. Her purse... was ringing.

Picking it up from the coffee table, she dug around, hitting answer just in time to hear her editor, Kristy, muttering.

"—least have the decency to call if she's not coming in like she said. Don't know—"

"I'm here, Kristy." Shit, she sounded annoyed. It was Saturday, wasn't it? Natalie rubbed her eyes. It had to be. She wasn't supposed to go into the offices of the *Tribune* on Saturday.

"Hey! Where are you? We were supposed to meet for lunch at the Hash House, remember?"

"Oh shit," she groaned. "What time is it?"

"How late were you out last night? Did you find him?"

She wrinkled her forehead. "Find who?" She racked her brain. Where did she even go last night? Her dress said nice restaurant or club, but she didn't remember. She blinked, the scent of coffee starting to clear her head.

She didn't remember?

"I don't know. Whoever you were supposed to be meeting. Dan thought it sounded like a guy. Weird name though."

"Kristy, I don't..."

"What? Are you okay?"

Natalie cleared her throat. "I'm not sure."

All annoyance fled her friend's voice. "Hey, what's going on? Do you want me to come over?"

"I, uh... I remember leaving work last night."

"You left late. You told Dan you were following up on a lead for the coyote story."

"Right." Where had she been? Pushing down a swell of panic, Natalie walked to the kitchen and poured a cup of coffee, drinking it black. It burned her mouth, but she swallowed anyway, desperate for the jolt of caffeine. "I remember coming home. Mr. Sanchez was here. He made me a pan of enchiladas." She opened the fridge. The metal pan was there, missing two enchiladas from her dinner last night.

"You have the best neighbors. Loud and Louder never make me anything." Kristy lived next to the most vocal married couple in history. Natalie would think her friend was exaggerating except she'd tried to watch a movie at Kristy's one time and they'd actually given up after round three was louder than both rounds one and two.

"Okay, enchiladas here," she muttered to herself. "Think, Nat. Where did you go?"

"Do you really not remember what you did last night? Because that's not good."

"You're telling me. It looks like I went out, but…"

She looked around, taking in the evidence she could see. Dress thrown on the chair. Shoes kicked off. Purse thrown on the table with her phone not plugged into the charger for the night. If she didn't know better, she'd say she'd gone out with friends to a club or a bar, drank too much, and came home to crash. But if she'd gone out drinking, Kristy would have been there.

"Kristy…" She took another drink of the scalding coffee. "I don't remember what I did last night. Like, no memory. At all."

"You didn't meet anyone, did you?"

She laughed a little. "No evidence of amorous encounters. Sorry."

"I can always hope."

As soon as she said it, her stomach dropped. Could there have been?

Kristy said, "Oh shit." The thought must have hit her at the same time.

"Are you thinking—"

"Natalie, you are one of the most level-headed people I know. This is not like you at all. You have never blacked out. Ever. Even in college. Someone might have drugged you. You need to go to the hospital right now. I'm coming to pick you up."

Her heart began to pound. "I'll get dressed."

"Don't shower. Don't do anything else. Just throw on some loose clothes and meet me at the door. I'll be there in ten minutes."

"'Kay." Natalie set down the coffee, willing herself not to puke. This wasn't happening. This didn't happen to her. It happened to the people she wrote about. "Kristy, drive fast."

"I'm right around the corner."

"And you are in fantastic health, Ms. Ellis." The doctor seemed a little too cheerful for someone who was doing a drug screen on a panicked thirty-one-year-old woman. "All the tests came back negative. There are no drugs in your system. In fact, everything appears to be in good working order, though you are a little anemic, but that's relatively common. Do you not eat a lot of red meat? There are other sources of iron or supplements if you—"

"Wait, wait, wait." Kristy interrupted the doctor. "So you're saying there are no drugs. At all? She just lost hours of her life for no reason at all?"

Natalie tried to calm her friend. "Kristy—"

"No! That's ridiculous." The doctor gave her friend a condescending look. "Look at him. He thinks you drank too much, can't you tell?"

"I probably did drink some. I told you I was going out. Maybe I tried something new and it just hit me harder than normal." Natalie had been at the emergency room for hours at that point. She just wanted to go home and take a shower.

"I know it seems very serious, but you would be surprised by how common sudden memory loss can be," Dr. Sun said. "Often stress combined with a poor diet can trigger it."

Kristy frowned. "What about a stroke? Could she have had a stroke?"

"Kristy!"

Dr. Sun held up a hand. "We did screen for that. There would be evidence in her blood work."

"A tumor? Does she have a tumor?"

"Oh my gosh." She rubbed her face with both hands, wishing she was at home with her laptop.

"Again, there is no evidence of that, though if your friend would like more extensive MRI work done, that is an option. However, since this has not happened before, and there *may* have been alcohol involved..."

"Seriously, Kristy, just let it go. Dr. Sun—" She held out a hand and shook the doctor's quickly. "Thank you. Unless there's anything else, I'll get dressed."

"No problem at all. Now," He turned serious. "If this happens again, please see your regular physician. While a one-time occurrence is probably no more than your body telling you to take a break, repeated loss of memory—"

"I got it." She began to gather up her clothes. "It's probably a massive malignant brain tumor. Or brain-eating aliens. One of the two."

Kristy rolled her eyes as Dr. Sun smiled. "Will you take this seriously, Nat?"

"Yes, mom. Now, will you drive me home please?" She stood and grabbed her purse.

Her purse...

You brought the wrong purse, Ms. Ellis.

She glanced down at it. The wrong purse. Who told her that? It was just her regular purse, packed with her wallet, a notebook, pens, too many pencils, and lip gloss... It wasn't wrong.

You stood out.

The smooth male voice popped into her memory again. A male voice. But the doctor had said there was no harm done to her person. No evidence of sexual activity. No drugs.

"It's just my purse," she whispered, tucking her phone in the side pocket. She had a sudden flash.

Lights pulsing. A cold gin and tonic. Where was he? Why all the mystery? She grabbed her phone from her purse and fired off a tweet before she stuffed the phone back in her purse. Ugh, this music was impossibly loud...

"Natalie?" Kristy was standing there, keys in hand. "You ready? The nurse said you could just check out at the desk in front."

"Yeah, yeah, yeah." She waved her hand at Kristy, pulling the phone out of her pocket and opening Twitter. She quickly clicked on the tab for her own profile and checked her last tweet.

21

Eleven hours ago. *At #Boca and bartender isn't light on the gin. Looks like this dress was a good choice after all.*

Boca. The club downtown. She'd been at Boca in her nice dress, drinking gin and tonics. "Kristy, what did I say I was doing last night? What did I tell Dan?"

She frowned. "He said you were going out to follow up on a lead for the coyote story."

The coyote story. All her notes were at home, but she'd look through them. It sounded like she'd gone out the night before, hoping to meet someone about the piece she was working on. "Why would I have gone to a nightclub for that?"

Kristy shrugged. "No idea. Would you have written it down?"

She pulled her notebook out and flipped to the last page she had written on as they walked down the hospital corridor. There were a series of Spanish names and phone numbers. The address for the Mexican Federal Authorities in Ensenada. Another phone number for her police source out in El Centro. She remembered all of them.

"There's nothing new here. I'll have to check at home."

"Well, if it's important, you'll have it written down." Kristy patted her shoulder. "You always do."

Natalie tucked her notebook away and hoped like hell her friend was right.

She sipped the coffee she'd reheated as she looked through notebooks, scanned the scattered sticky notes attached to her desk, and looked on the back of computer printouts for any clue as to why she'd been at a fancy nightclub in downtown San Diego the night before.

Since the mid-90s, reporters and others who followed crime in the Southwest had been aware of the startling frequency of young women being abducted near and around Ciudad Juarez. Authorities seemed reluctant to look into the matter too deeply. Some said it was a serial killer. Others said it was a result of sociological and cultural factors that led young working women to be targeted. Corruption. Drug cartels. Organized crime. NAFTA, for goodness sake. Everyone had a theory, but Natalie didn't care. She'd seen evil. Looked it in the face at an early age.

She just wanted it to stop. Hundreds of women had been killed and no one seemed to be able to do anything about it.

And when isolated reports began trickling in about the bodies of young women being found in the desert on the California-Mexico border, Natalie couldn't ignore it. Some of the reports speculated the women were victims of a *coyote*, a human smuggler, who was tricking the women into paying him, only to abandon them in the desert. Many of the bodies had been found in extremely remote locations and all were Mexican citizens. Others said whatever was hunting in Juarez had moved west, ready to wreak havoc on the women of Tijuana and Baja California.

The reports from both sides of the border were troubling. The pictures were gruesome.

When Natalie had sought permission to pursue the story from her editor, she'd been given the go-ahead, but only if it didn't interfere with her regular assignments. So far, most of her work on the case had been gathering police reports from Mexico and the outlying desert towns in Imperial County, looking for any names that repeated, any patterns that hadn't been noticed. Most of the work had been done at night, so most of her notes were here at home.

She threw down her pencil in frustration and rubbed her eyes. She still had a strange feeling in her head. Not a headache, necessarily. Just a vague fuzziness that wouldn't go away. Most people probably would put it down to exhaustion, but Natalie rarely tired, even when others were falling down. This just wasn't like her…

Leaning back in her desk chair, she heard her phone chirp, signaling a text message. She went to the kitchen to pick it up.

"Dez?"

Natalie frowned. She hadn't spoken to Dez in ages. Not since her old friend had quit the university library and gone to work for that private foundation in Pasadena. They'd met when Natalie was doing research on a story for the college paper. Dez and her best friend had both been helpful —librarians really were the best researchers—but Dez had been the one she'd kept in touch with the most.

How did it go last night? The message bubble glowed on the screen.

"How did what go last night?" A burst of excitement flooded her and she flipped to her call history. There it was: a forty-minute conversation with Dez Kirby at seven o'clock in the evening. She'd initiated the call to

Dez. Dez, who had given her a lead that must have led her to Boca in her best dress.

Natalie hit the number to call her friend back just as she saw the sun slip over the horizon. She stepped out on the patio to enjoy the cool night air.

"Hey!" Dez picked up. "I hope that helped. I wasn't even sure whether he'd talk to you, but—"

"Who? Who the hell did I talk to, Dez, because—I'm gonna be honest —today was really, really weird. Hi, by the way. There is a whole big chunk of last night that I do not remember at all, and I'm really confused."

"W…what?" Dez said as she moved around, and Natalie remembered her friend had a daughter now. It was probably bedtime or bathtime or storytime or something. "What are you talking about?"

"Why did I call you yesterday?"

Dez laughed a little. "Why did you say you called? Or why did you really call?"

"Both."

"Well, you said you were calling to catch up since it had been months since we talked last. Matt says hi, by the way. He invited you up for a visit anytime you want."

"Oh, that's sweet. And I'd love to see Carina. The pictures are just… She's adorable, Dez. So amazing that you're a mom now."

"Weird, right? Anyway, so we chatted for a bit, then you started asking me if I knew anything about the murders in Juarez, which I did."

She let out a breath. "That's right. You helped Dr. Givens when he was working with Amnesty that summer."

"Yep. So I'm pretty familiar with the history, but I didn't know about the stuff happening down by you. Did you say you don't remember any of this?"

"Nope. Nothing. The doctor seems to think it's stress, but I'm not so sure."

There was a long pause on the line. "Well… stress will do weird stuff to you. I know it's been really hard with work and being a new mom. Sometimes I feel like sleep is just a happy memory, so it could definitely be stress. I wouldn't let it worry you, because that would just make it worse, right? You're probably tired. Have you been sleeping normally? If I remember, you never really slept all that much, and if you're following a story—"

"Why are you rambling like a loon?" Natalie rolled her eyes. "Whatever it was, the doctor said it was probably nothing to worry about, though I think he thought I had way more gin than I actually did. But what were we talking about on the phone last night? You asked if I'd talked to someone. Who did you mean?"

"Um… Well—" Dez's voice broke up a bit.

"Dez?"

"Hey, can I call you back?"

"Dez, I really need to find out what happened. I mean—"

"I know. And I am going to call you right back, but I have a call coming through right now, and I really think I ought to take it."

She sighed. "Okay. I guess. But can you get back to me later tonight? I'm at home."

"I definitely will."

"Thanks, Dez. Appreciate it."

"You got it. Okay, gotta go."

"All right. Say hi to—" Dez had already hung up. "Matt."

Natalie looked at the phone. "That was weird."

CHAPTER THREE

BAOJIA WOULE HAVE PREFERRED to meet with the Kirbys in person, but since that would have taken too long, he contented himself with a speakerphone while he practiced his forms. He stood in the center of his first-story studio, which had been customized to suit his particular needs. Weapons hung in neat rows along the eastern wall and a quiet fountain burbled in the corner. A long mirror hung along the north wall, ensuring precision as he practiced the ancient forms his human father had taught him.

He practiced every night. It centered him physically, emotionally, and spiritually. At just over 150 years old, he was young for one of his kind. Vampires took care not to make too many children, and he was one of only four living vampires his sire had created. He had been turned for his skills and human strength, which were only amplified by his sire's amnis. And the discipline that made him such an effective fighter in his mortal life allowed him to master his elemental strength at a young age. He was young, but he was also unusually powerful.

Baojia sensed a change coming. Some shift in his immortal life beckoned him, though he had no idea what it could be. But it was there, teasing the corners of his mind and filling the vivid dreams he still had during his day rest. Practicing the *wing chun* forms he had learned as a child was his own form of meditation.

Currently, the patience he was so known for was being tried by the woman on the other end of the phone.

"Well, what do you want me to tell her?" Dez asked. "She's going to expect a call back."

"Then delay her until I can find out more, Mrs. Kirby."

"Please, call me Dez. I feel weird with you being so proper."

He paused, slightly uncomfortable at her informality. "Dez, I don't know how much Matt has told you about Ivan, but—"

"I haven't told her anything about Ivan." Matt broke in. "This is the first I've heard about all this." Baojia could tell Matt Kirby was annoyed with his wife. He could also tell Dez didn't really care.

Dez said, "This is the first I've heard about Ivan, too! She did *not* mention that name to me. She asked me about the murders happening along the border because I worked on a documentation project down in Juarez when I was in college. Nat remembered I'd had some experience with that case, so she called to ask me—"

"What murders on the border? Did you say Juarez?" Baojia stopped mid-extension. His arms hung perfectly still, but he felt his heart thump once. "Dez, what murders?"

There was silence on the other end of the phone. Finally, Dez said, "I… I thought you would have known about it. I mean, it's on the edge of Ernesto's territory. That's why I gave her your name. I really wasn't trying to cause problems, but I thought if anyone would have information…"

Baojia heard Matt talking to his wife as his mind raced. "Honey, Natalie's a reporter," the human said. "A really smart, persistent one, if I remember correctly. Why on earth did you think giving her an introduction to a vampire would be a good thing? She's going to figure out something's not what it seems, and the last thing Baojia or Ernesto need is someone really smart and really curious poking around!"

"Don't talk to me like that! You didn't see what happened in Juarez. I did. And looking back with what I know now, I'm almost positive there is some sort of tie-in with a vampire. None of the human authorities could make sense of it. And there were hundreds of girls, Matt. Hundreds. And if what was happening in Juarez is moving into California—"

"Desiree," Baojia said. She stopped as soon as she heard his voice.

Dez still sounded annoyed. "What?"

"Thank you for making me aware of this."

That seemed to surprise her because she fell silent.

Matt said, "I'm sorry your name was brought into this, Baojia. I know you keep a low profile, even in LA."

"I'd rather be informed than anonymous. It's fine. I'll deal with it."

Murders along the border. He'd tracked the activity in Juarez for years, and he had to agree with Dez. There was probably a vampire or a group of them that was responsible for the deaths of so many young women. But since Juarez, Mexico, was clearly out of his sire's territory, there wasn't much that he could do about it. It was horrible, but not his concern. Murders along the California border, however…

"When did she start following this story?"

"Natalie said it started a few months ago. There were isolated reports out in Imperial Valley about farmers finding bodies, but the police investigations went nowhere. Then the Border Patrol reported that nine bodies were found out in the middle of the desert two months ago. They guessed that a *coyote*, a smuggler, had taken the women's money to get them across the border, then led them out there and abandoned them. There were no visible signs of death. They thought the women had just passed out from dehydration and died of heatstroke. But Nat had been following the cases down in Imperial, and she thought the Border Patrol's story didn't really check out."

"Why not?"

"All the women were found together, within a few yards of each other. If they'd been left out there, they would have walked. Probably some would have fallen behind. They would have been spread out, at least a little. But the bodies looked like they'd been dumped in one location."

Smart human.

"And there were no visible signs of death or struggle?"

"No bruises or wounds. Could they have been—"

"Drained?" He hated to think it. "Yes. A vampire could have drained them and sealed the wounds. It would be unusual, but it's possible."

Most of their kind didn't need to drink much blood. To drain a human was wasteful. Gluttonous. Like killing a chicken to get the eggs. Only the youngest and most immature would do it, and a responsible sire wouldn't want to attract the attention. No, vampires only drained when they were out of control or intended to kill an enemy. How could nine young women in the desert have become a target? Dez was right. The similarities to Juarez were disturbing.

"And then she started to get in touch with some of her contacts in Mexico," Dez continued. "When she called me… Baojia, I'm sorry if you feel like I exposed you in some way, but if this is like Juarez, then it has to be stopped. The killings down there have been going on for years. They're still going on, despite what the Mexican authorities say. If this is a vampire in Ernesto's territory—"

"I'll look into it." He came out of his frozen stance, continuing in his practice as his mind started to catalogue the information he'd been given.

"You will?"

"Of course I will," he said, slightly annoyed. "Did you think I was going to let some vampire run rampant in the desert?"

"Well, no, but—"

"It would look incredibly bad for my sire if I allowed something like that to continue." The fact it had happened in Ernesto's territories at all was bad enough. Did Rory know about this? Why hadn't he come to him for help? He felt the water from the fountain draw to his chest as he resumed practice. Cross. Thrust. Center. Draw back. Center. Sweep. His loose practice pants brushed silently against his legs.

"There's the whole innocent-people-being-slaughtered thing, too," Matt said.

"That too." His thoughts tripped back to the curious redhead. "How did your friend get Ivan's name?"

"I have no idea," Dez said. "Honestly, I've never even heard of him before. But Natalie… she has a way of finding out things. She didn't mention Ivan to me. Who is he?"

Matt said, "Not anyone you're ever going to meet. That's for sure."

Baojia took a deep breath, willing himself to be patient toward the human man. Really, did he think keeping his mate uninformed was to her benefit? "Ivan has a similar job to mine, Dez, but he works for the vampires who control most of Mexico and Central America."

"Who is that? Are they in Mexico City? I thought you said something about Ensenada."

"Who runs Mexico is not important. Yes, Ivan runs things in Ensenada, and he's the one who I'll have to talk to if there's a vampire out of control in Northern Mexico."

"Ensenada's only a few hours away. Shouldn't he be taking care of something like a vampire on a rampage?"

He tried not to roll his eyes. "He *should* be. But Ivan often does what he wants. I'm curious how your friend got his name. She shouldn't go talking to him. Can you persuade her to leave this alone?"

"Natalie?" Dez snorted. "Not likely. And she never mentioned his name to me, so I can't warn her without making her even more curious."

"You're going to have to stall her."

Now it was Dez who sounded exasperated. "Look, you don't know this woman. She's like a really friendly bulldog. If she gets her teeth into something, she's not going to let go. And she has very little sense of self-preservation."

He frowned, unaccountably irritated with the human reporter. "Is she stupid?"

"I thought you said you met her. Did she seem stupid to you?"

No, she seemed clever. Persistent, obviously. Funny. Tempting. He willed away the image of the reporter stumbling into her little house and immediately stripping off her dress before he could escape. The light dusting of freckles on her pale skin was scattered… everywhere. He cleared his throat. "No, she didn't seem stupid, but she needs to stay away from Ivan. Other than his mistress, he has no regard for humans. They're food and entertainment, that's all."

"Wow. He sounds like a peach."

"She needs to stay off his radar, Dez. Give me some time to investigate this without having to worry that your friend is going to trip into something that will get her killed."

"But, Baojia—" Dez sighed after Matt whispered something to her. "I'll do what I can. I'll try to distract her, but if she finds out, she's going to be pissed."

"Better pissed off than drained in the desert."

"True," Matt said. "And if there's anything we can do on our end, let us know."

"I will." He wasn't going to pass up that offer, not while he was stuck in San Diego. Matt Kirby could be a good ally in Los Angeles. "And Matt, I'd appreciate your discretion in all this, if that's possible."

In other words, don't tell Vecchio.

A tentative alliance existed between Matt's employer, Giovanni Vecchio, and Baojia's sire, Ernesto Alvarez, mostly because Vecchio was married to Ernesto's favorite granddaughter. But like most in-laws, there was tension. A vampire of Vecchio's age and reputation didn't exist in any city without tension. He was a fire vampire and a powerful one. It was only through Beatrice's influence and her mate's desire for a low profile that Giovanni and Ernesto could exist in the same city without killing each other. For Ernesto to look weak to Beatrice's husband would tilt the alliance in Giovanni's favor, which would throw off the delicate balance of power.

Matt heaved a sigh Baojia could hear from 120 miles away, even without the phone connection. "I swear vampires are like kids in high school some days."

Baojia chuckled, knowing exactly what Matt meant. "Some of us act our age, human."

"That's because you're the guy who has to clean shit up when things get messy."

He smiled. Matt was human, but Baojia still considered him a peer, and a competent one at that. He'd tried for years to get Matt to work for him, but the human preferred his more low-key role under the fire vampire's aegis.

"We have to make sure Beatrice doesn't hear about it," Dez said. "She and Natalie were friends, too. If B hears that Natalie may be in trouble—"

"She and Gio will step in," Matt added. "And if they step in—"

"I won't have to worry about being stuck in San Diego anymore," Baojia said. "Because Ernesto will kill me."

"You said it, not me."

"All right. Let me dig around down here." He walked to the giant windows that looked over the water and crossed his arms. How was he going to poke around without raising Ivan's ire? Or Ernesto's? And why was he still concerned about that annoying human woman who had complicated his life? "Just distract your friend, Dez. However you can."

"I'll do my best," Dez said as a baby cried in the background. He'd forgotten Matt had recently become a father. "I gotta go." There was a slight pause. "Baojia?"

"Yes?"

"I know I've kind of made a mess of things, but Natalie's a really great person. And she's really dedicated to helping people with her work. Just... keep that in mind. I couldn't stand it if anything happened to her. If she gets in trouble, will you help her?"

He squeezed his eyes shut and tried to ignore the weight of obligation she was thrusting on him. Damn woman. Once he was given a job, he was incapable of not seeing it through.

"Baojia, *please*."

He shook his head in resignation. "I'll do what I can to keep her safe."

Shit, shit, shit. Why couldn't he just say no?

"Thank you. I won't forget it."

Neither will I. In fact, Baojia had a feeling there was a lot about this situation he wouldn't forget anytime soon.

Despite the new complications in his life, Baojia walked into Boca that night in a better mood than he'd enjoyed in months. Maybe years. He ignored the boring pulse of music and the human women who tried to catch his eye. He nodded once to Luis, then ducked into his office to call Paula, trying not to smile. For the first time in almost two years, he wasn't bored out of his mind.

He dialed the old-fashioned rotary phone and swirled the ice water the waitress brought back. He was watching the ice cubes tumble when his sister answered.

"*¿Cómo?*"

"*Paulita.*" He slipped into Spanish. "What are you doing tonight?"

"*Hermanito*, Rory complained all last night about spreadsheets and résumés. What are you doing to my husband?"

He smiled. One of the things he disliked most about being in San Diego was missing the company of Paula. There were few vampires or humans he liked spending time with, but Paula was one. "It's not my fault he doesn't have your keen appreciation for numbers. What's going on at home?"

"Oh, the usual. Lots of meetings with the accountants as we get ready for the end of the fiscal year. And there's a trade meeting with a Japanese company that Father seems anxious about."

"Any security concerns? Human or vampire?"

"Human. And not that I know of," she said. "It's more financial. Their earnings reports don't seem to match their investment activity…" She started in on a litany of business information he would catalogue and examine later. Ernesto's shipping interests had shifted in the past forty years to focus on Asia, which created new balances of power and influence that Baojia had to keep track of. He had a hard time getting excited about the business side like Paula did, but the political and security ramifications were interesting.

Power followed money in the vampire world, and both fed into the influence that individual immortals wielded. An immortal in power only lasted as long as he could support those under his aegis. And what had been the status quo for hundreds of years could shift in the space of a heartbeat if the balance of power became tenuous. Considering most immortal business empires were run like combinations of corporations and organized crime, it had never been a boring job. Paula handled the business end, and Baojia had been in charge of security and information. Up until he had fallen out of favor with his sire, the balance had worked beautifully.

"Paula?"

"Hmm?"

He could tell she was distracted by something. She was probably looking at financial papers the same way he read police reports or watched security tapes. "Have you heard anything about humans being killed along the border?"

"You mean Juarez? You know Father told you to stay out of that. It's none of our—"

"Not Juarez. Closer. On our border, *hermana*."

There was a pause on the line. "What? *Our* border? With Ivan?"

"Mmhmm. I heard a disturbing rumor that humans were being found out in the desert."

"Ivan's side or ours?"

"Both. I need to investigate more. I may need to set up a meeting with him."

He heard her mutter. "Well, don't let Father get wind of it. He's still… you know."

"Trust me, I know."

"Want me to mention it to Rory? I think technically that's his job while you're gone."

"Mention it to him. Have him call me when he can."

"*Hermanito*…" Her voice was soft. "I don't know why he's being like this. I've tried to talk to him."

"It's not your fault," he said, unexpectedly homesick. "It's mine. I fought alongside Vecchio. I knew it would make him angry, and I did it anyway."

"Why?" she groaned. "I still don't understand—"

"It was the right thing to do, Paula." When he closed his eyes, he could still see the bodies of the dead monks. The blood pouring out from under Beatrice's body on the riverbank where Lorenzo had stabbed her. "Even if he doesn't understand."

"You were supposed to protect his human, not join a war."

"I know." His thoughts flicked to the reporter and his promise to Dez. "Right and wrong are subjective in our world. We both know this."

"Be careful," she said. "I don't want you hurt."

He smiled. "I'll be fine."

The following night, he had Luis put in a call to Ivan's human staff, laying the groundwork for a meeting between the two vampires. In all likelihood, it would take weeks to actually happen. The night after that, he was following a smartly dressed redhead into the cheapest bar in downtown San Diego. She crossed 5th Street and headed into the dimly lit club that clung stubbornly to its cheap neon beer signs and even cheaper beer while the rest of downtown San Diego reveled in aspiration.

Slipping into the dim bar, he tried to ignore the floor that stuck to his handmade leather shoes. The barstools were cracked red vinyl and occupied by a curious mix of patrons, but the old Chinese woman behind the bar nodded at him and pointed her chin toward an empty stool. It was well away from where Natalie Ellis was sitting, but he preferred that. He wanted to observe the woman. For now.

He watched her as she slid onto a stool and dove into the conversation at the end of the bar, obviously familiar with the group of older men who looked like regulars. Their voices drifted to him as he ordered a vodka tonic and settled in to watch.

"Hey hey! There's our girl," one of the men called. "About time you let us take you out to celebrate."

"You guys..." She shook her head while plopping onto the empty barstool in the middle of the group. "It was months ago."

"Biggest drug bust in county history and you act like it's no big deal?" another man said. "Your story practically broke that case for those knuckleheads in the DEA."

"Hey, Marty, isn't one of those knuckleheads your nephew?"

"Doesn't mean he's smart."

She grinned. "Pretty sure that means he's *not*, actually."

The men around her burst into laughter.

This was her natural environment, Baojia decided. The perfectly coiffed woman at Boca had intrigued him, but the friendly girl who joked with the old men and sipped a beer almost came close to charming. She was relaxed here, despite her professional attire, which did not stand out as much as he would have expected. The gritty bar was filled with all manner of humans. Businessmen in suits mingled with working men in coveralls, both watching a baseball game that was on the television in the corner. There were more men than women, but not so few that Natalie stood out. There weren't many students, but then it was Thursday night, not Friday or Saturday. Strangely, though the dive bar was completely opposite of his own club in numerous ways, the smell was remarkably similar. Alcohol. Sweat. Skin.

Blood.

He hadn't eaten since he'd taken Natalie's blood days before. It was probably a bad idea to see her again without feeding, but he trusted his self-control enough to chance it. This was the human who had provided him with some level of intrigue. He was grateful for that. And since he'd promised Dez anyway...

He watched her with the old men at the end of the bar. Almost all of them were grey-haired and wrinkled—men who would be her father's age or older, if he had to guess. They watched her with a paternal protectiveness he could respect. She told stories they laughed at. They told jokes that made her groan.

She was happy. Bright.

His eyes slipped to her collar; he could see the pale, freckled skin where he had bitten her. He knew instinctively that, should she ever discover he had marked her, she would be angry. He took a sip of his cocktail and mentally shrugged. There was no need for her to know unless she came to the attention of another immortal. And if she did, annoyance with him was the least of her problems.

"I'm gonna pee my pants unless you stop." She burst out laughing. "Okay, okay. When I get back, we're changing the subject."

"Spoilsport," one man said.

"Yeah, yeah, yeah." She laughed and stood up. "Hey, Howard, can you order me another beer?"

"Sure thing, Nat."

He watched her as she rolled her eyes and ducked down the hall leading to the bathrooms. Baojia picked up his drink and wandered closer, pretending to watch the baseball game. As he approached, he ignored the sounds of the television and tuned in to the old men's conversation.

"—anyone called her dad?"

"Would she ever forgive us if we did? She didn't even call him when she was getting threats during that last story."

There was scattered muttering. "I'd feel better if she at least had a dog. She lives all alone."

"She travels too much for a dog. She needs a nice guy. Marty, I thought you was gonna set her up with your nephew."

"She heard he was a cop and wouldn't give him the time of day." They all laughed. "Says she'll drink with us, but that's as far as it goes."

"Eh," another one said. "My Tricia's the same way. No cops. No firemen. Probably wouldn't want her dating one of these young guys, anyway."

So Natalie's father was a police officer, as were the men she was drinking with. Retired, he was guessing. He smiled. She was smart. Old cops kept their noses in their old precincts. If she wanted sources for stories, these men would know who to ask. Plus, it was evident she had a genuine affection for them. Then he frowned. They were also, evidently, worried about her.

He heard her leaving the restroom, her step already familiar to his ears. He subtly moved into her path, letting her brush up against him and spill his drink.

"Oh my gosh!" she said, looking up with an embarrassed smile. "How clumsy am I? I'm so sorry. Let me get you another one."

He looked down at her, more intrigued by the minute. Her scent was distracting, a mix of salt, honey, and the jasmine that grew around her house. "It's fine. Sorry I didn't see you."

"No, it was my fault. I wasn't paying attention." She looked down at his black suit. "It got all over you, too." She pulled him toward the bar. "Hold on, I have some napkins here…" She dug into her familiar purse and brought out a stack of brown napkins he recognized from a local coffee chain. "I always take too many when I get coffee, but I keep them 'cause you never know, right?"

He tried not to laugh as the man named Marty spotted them.

"Nat, you mess up the guy's suit? You gotta stop trying to run men over. A simple hello works."

"Hey, shut it." She slapped the old man's arm as she dabbed at the spot of vodka and tonic water on his chest. "Poor guy was just trying to watch the game and I ran into him. I'm so sorry," she said again.

He cocked his head, amused at her fussing. "It's fine, really."

"This was probably just dry-cleaned, right?" She did the nose-wrinkling thing she'd done in the car the other night. "You look very… well-pressed."

"I'm not sure if that was a compliment or not."

She laughed, a pleasant sound that he decided he wanted to hear more often. "It is! Just 'cause I hang out with these jokers doesn't mean I can't appreciate a man in a nice suit," she said with a wink.

"Hey," another one of the old men spoke. "You wear a suit when you're dead."

"Or you work in a cubicle," Marty said.

"Same thing," Baojia added, and all the men laughed.

"Natalie, I like this guy." One of the old cops slapped his shoulder. "Sit down and let our girl here buy you a drink."

"Oh thanks for offering." Natalie turned to Baojia and said, "Sorry for the peanut gallery. Join me for a drink? It's the least I can do since I messed up your suit."

He smiled. This was far easier than he'd expected.

"I'd love to."

CHAPTER FOUR

YOU LOOK WELL-PRESSED? Are you kidding, Natalie?

She mentally kicked herself. First, she ran into the incredibly attractive man who'd been sitting at the end of the bar, then she spilled his drink, then she started dabbing what was probably a thousand-dollar suit with cheap coffeehouse napkins and calling him "well-pressed."

She really needed to get out more.

Natalie was beginning to think Kristy's assertions that hanging with "the old guys" did not, in fact, constitute a social life might be right. Still, Incredibly Attractive Suit was smiling at her, so that was something. He hadn't run screaming from Marty and Howard, either. And he was gorgeous. Black, black hair and brown eyes you could fall into and never find your way out. You wouldn't want to. He was taller than her, but not by much. She'd put him at five ten or eleven, maybe. And his body... Well, if the suit made the man, then this suit—nice as it was—didn't have much work to do, in her opinion. The man was all there.

He said, "I'd love to."

"Love to what?" She blinked, coming out of a daze. Was her hand still on the front of his chest? Yes. Yes, it was. She pulled back and mentally cursed when she realized her hand had been resting on his muscles like she was grabbing a new toy. She could already feel the blush staining her cheeks. Damn her pale skin. Now Attractive Suit was looking at her like she was crazy.

"You asked me to join you for a drink."

"Yes." She shook her head a little and smiled, motioning to an empty stool at the bar. "I did. What were you drinking?"

"A vodka tonic."

She held a hand up to grab Connie's attention. "So, I make it a point to know the names of everyone I drink with. What's yours?"

Natalie noticed the slight hesitation before he said, "George."

Liar.

"George, huh?" She only smiled and sat down next to him. "I totally pegged you for a 'George.' Come on, is that really your name?"

He shrugged and leaned an arm on the bar, angling his body toward hers. "My given name is Chinese and really hard to pronounce. So I go by George."

"Chinese, huh? Are you from China originally? What part?" She finally caught Connie's attention. "Hey, can I get a Grey Goose and tonic?"

"Sure thing, honey." The middle-aged woman turned to mix the drink. Connie didn't put up with crap, and she treated her regulars right. George-who-wasn't-George would get a good drink.

She turned to see him giving her a look. Natalie shrugged. "Was that right? You look like you have premium tastes. I guessed."

"You guessed correctly."

"I'm smart like that." She sipped the beer Marty handed down to her. Luckily, the guys were keeping their opinions to themselves, for once. Their attention had turned to the game. She glanced over her shoulder. "Sorry. You were watching the game. You don't actually have to talk to me."

"I thought you were smart," he said. She narrowed her eyes, but he looked like he was about to laugh. "You seem far more interesting than a baseball game."

Smooth. That was almost *too* smooth. Almost.

"Thanks, George. Same to you." She took another sip of beer.

"And what is your name?"

"Natalie."

"Natalie, it's nice to meet you. Do you come here much?"

She couldn't stop the snort. *Okay, maybe not so smooth.* "Um… yeah."

"Sorry." He had the grace to look embarrassed and shook his head. "That sounded like a bad line, didn't it? I'm genuinely curious, though. It's my first time here. Is it always so…" He looked around. "Diverse?"

She nodded. "Mostly. More younger kids on the weekends, but during the week, it's a pretty regular crowd. Connie and her sister have owned this place forever. They've pretty much kept it the same. I know the decor's a little dated, but the glasses are clean and the company's good."

"Something tells me you don't much care about the decor."

"No." Then she tried her best for a flirtatious look. "Not that you don't class up the place in that suit, George."

It must have worked, because he leaned a little closer. "Class can be overrated. And I don't have any complaints about the decor, not with you sitting there."

"Is that so?" She couldn't think of anything else to say. He was actually flirting back. Maybe her luck with guys was changing.

Connie brought his drink and he took a sip, raising his eyebrows a little when he tasted it. "She certainly doesn't pour light. Are you trying to get me drunk?"

Natalie laughed. "Maybe? I haven't decided yet."

"I'm on to you now, Natalie."

"Damn. There goes my dastardly plan to take advantage of you." She wanted to bite her lip as soon as she said it. *Too soon!*

George's smile dropped and a distinct, hungry look came to his eyes. "Where would be the fun in that?"

She blinked in surprise.

His smile returned, but this time, it had a slightly wicked edge. "I'd much prefer to be sober when you take advantage of me."

Okay, maybe not too soon.

Natalie could feel herself blushing again, but she ignored it. "Well, you're certainly not shy."

"Neither are you, despite that rather attractive blush." His voice was a little lower, a little rougher. Natalie squirmed in her seat. Was she actually getting turned on by a complete stranger in a bar with the Padres playing in the background?

A shout rose from all corners, providing a much-needed distraction.

"Damn that ump!"

"Frickin' blind is what he is."

"If that was a strike, then call me Bunny."

"Get me a beer, Bunny."

The shout and the annoyed muttering broke the tension that had been building and Natalie sat up in her seat a little, taking another drink of her beer. "You a Padres fan?"

He smiled like he knew exactly what she was doing. "I'd be a fool to admit otherwise in this crowd."

"Tell you a secret?"

George leaned closer. "Please."

"Oakland A's."

He pulled away. "Blasphemy."

She shrugged. "Don't tell anyone or my life is forfeit."

He sipped his drink again, tracing his finger around the rim of the glass. Her eyes were playing tricks on her, because it almost looked like the ice in his glass followed the path of his finger. She shook her head. *No more beer, Nat.*

"Can I tell *you* a secret?" he asked, staring at his drink.

"Of course. I'm very trustworthy." *As long as you're not a dirty politician or a bad cop.*

His dark eyes focused on hers. It was ludicrous to say a spark jumped between them. No, it was more like… a pull. She wanted to lean closer, so she did.

"Giants."

Natalie gasped. "That's worse than me!"

"You hold my life in your hands."

"I do." She took another drink. "Great blackmail material."

"I should have known. It's always the pretty ones who are the most vicious."

She laughed. "So, what do you do, George-who-isn't-George?"

"Other than run into pretty girls at bars?"

"You're being nice. I ran into you."

"Maybe I bumped into you on purpose." His dark eyes danced and his smile took her breath away for a moment. "And I'm in private security work."

"Really? Mysterious."

"Not nearly as much as it sounds." He shrugged. "Mostly for clubs and other businesses. Casinos. Things like that."

"So, your own business?"

"No, my boss is in LA."

"Ah."

"But I live here. Well, have lived here for the past three years or so. I'll probably be moving back to LA eventually."

"That's interesting."

"What do you do?"

Natalie smiled to herself. "I'm a reporter. A crime reporter for the *Tribune*."

"So you make those lurid headlines they blast over the front page?"

"Ha!" She shook her head, pleased he hadn't recoiled like many men did. Reporters didn't exactly have the best reputation, especially among those in any kind of law enforcement or security work. If her dad hadn't been a cop, the guys at the end of the bar would never have even given her the time of day. "No, it's someone else's job to do headlines. I just write the stories."

"A writer, huh?" He looked thoughtful. "Hard job. Dangerous?"

"It has its moments." She shrugged. "But it's very rewarding. I'm working on a story right now about some girls out in the desert who were murdered. It's kind of like the Juarez case. Are you familiar with it?"

He turned serious and the mood shifted. "Sure I am."

She took another long drink of her beer. "It's not as bad as Juarez. Not yet, anyway. I'm hoping to coordinate with some colleagues on the other side of the border. Find out what's going on before it gets worse."

"Is that a good idea?" His smile had fled. "To go looking into that? What about the police?"

"Clueless." She shook her head. "Not clueless, exactly. It's just that it's happening in multiple jurisdictions. Multiple countries, even. There's so much protocol and paperwork they have to do. Journalists have more freedom than police in some cases."

He put his hand on her arm and she felt a tingling sensation where his fingers touched. "Natalie, do you really think you should—"

"You know…" She pulled her arm away immediately. "I get this funny feeling you're going to be really presumptuous and say my work is too dangerous. Maybe that I should leave it to law enforcement and find something else to occupy my pretty head?" She wrinkled her nose in distaste. "You weren't going to do that, were you, George?"

"Nat—"

"Because you seem like a smart guy, but you don't know me well enough to have an opinion about what I can and can't do."

"I wasn't—" He stopped himself and there was a long pause. "I was. You're right. I don't know you well enough to make assumptions."

"Thank you for not being an ass."

"You're welcome." He didn't sound happy about it, though. That was fine. Far more important people in her life had problems with her chosen career and she ignored them, too.

"Need help?" He raised an eyebrow. "Security work, remember? You need a bodyguard?"

Her heart sped as she imagined all the ways she'd be happy to have him guard her body. And there went the blush again. "It's not really—I mean, I don't need a bodyguard. Thanks."

"No harm in offering."

"You—" Natalie cleared her throat but couldn't hide the smile. "How did you get started in security? Are you from LA?"

He let out some sound that was amused and irritated all at the same time. Interesting.

"No." He did the thing with his finger on the glass again. And again, it looked like the ice followed it. It had to be a trick of the light. "No, I'm from San Francisco. Well, I was born in China, but lived most of my life in the US. My boss hired me in San Francisco. Trained me. Put me to work in his business. He does international work too, so having someone who speaks as many languages as I do is useful."

"You don't have an accent."

He shrugged. "I don't consider myself Chinese. I became a citizen long ago."

Natalie laughed. "Well, not *that* long ago." He couldn't have been any older than her. In fact, if it wasn't for the serious expression and knowing gaze, she'd say he was younger.

"I'm older than I look." He slid closer. "I just have one of those faces. And how did you become a reporter? Did you always want to be?"

She pulled back a little and took a sip of beer. "Yeah. Ever since I was a teenager. I grew up in Oakland. Went to journalism school at UCLA."

"No kidding?"

"Yeah. Moved down to San Diego for work. But I like it. You?"

He gave a rueful laugh. "Some nights I miss LA. Other times…" He looked at her. "I don't."

"I miss Northern California." She frowned. Why had she told him that?

George blinked, obviously surprised. "I do, too."

"Do you have family?"

He looked confused. "What?"

"In San Francisco?" She cleared her throat. "My dad still lives in Oakland, but we're not close."

"I… I do have family there, but I'm the same way. We're not close."

"Just a couple of strangers in a strange land, then." She squinted out the windows of the bar. "It's so bright here. I miss fog sometimes. Miss the smell of the ocean. It smells like the ocean here, but not the right way. That probably doesn't make much sense."

He was looking at her, his mouth hanging open a little. "That makes complete sense."

Natalie shrugged, feeling strangely exposed.

"May I call on you?"

"Uh…" She almost spit out the beer she'd been drinking. "Call on me?"

"Call. Call you. I'd like to see you again, if you would like."

And there was the blush again. Damn automatic reaction. Curse her Scottish ancestors and their milky-pale skin. "I'd… Sure. You can call me." She tried not to be flustered as she reached for her mobile in her purse. George leaned away as soon as he saw it. "Why don't we just exchange phones? I'd… like your number, too."

"I can give you my phone number, but I don't have a mobile."

She frowned. "Don't have a mobile what?"

"Phone." He looked amused. "A mobile phone."

Natalie blinked, confused. "Y…you don't have a mobile phone?"

George smiled. "Nope."

"Are you… a time traveler? Alien?" She shot him a crooked smile. "Unexpectedly hitching a ride in a blue police call box?"

He burst into laughter. Thank God he was a *Doctor Who* fan. "No. I just don't have one. Landline only, I'm afraid."

"But your work… How do you get by without one for work?" She clutched her iPhone like it might run away into the attractive, phone-less man's hands. "Mine is practically glued to me."

"I can see that." He was still laughing. "It's probably because of work. Mobile phones are unsecured lines. Anyone can listen to your phone calls if they know what they're doing. People store too much sensitive information on them. Especially smart phones."

"Paranoid much?"

He raised an eyebrow. "It's not paranoia if they're actually after you, Natalie."

She tried not to smile. "You know... you're kinda weird."

For some reason, that was really amusing to him. "I've been told that before." He laughed, and something about his smile, the angle of his head, jostled her memory.

You're kinda weird.

You have no idea.

"Natalie!" Kristy called her name from the door. She'd almost forgotten she was supposed to meet her friend for the movie later. "What are you—Oh, hi there." Kristy's eyes bugged out when she saw George. "Hi. You're not Marty."

"Hey!" Marty yelled from a few seats away.

Kristy yelled back, "Not that I don't love you, Marty! Hi. Natalie, introduce me to the pretty man."

George cocked an eyebrow. "Pretty?"

"Oh, sexy eyebrow. Can I just call him sexy eyebrow?"

Natalie snorted. "George, meet Kristy. Kristy, George."

"George..." She frowned. "...does not do you justice. I think I'm going to stick with Sexy Eyebrow."

Luckily, George laughed at her crazy friend. "Kristy, it's very nice to meet you. I was lucky enough to have Natalie spill a drink on me earlier."

"Oh, you poor thing." She stroked George's arm, mouthing "wow!" behind his back when he turned to grab his vodka tonic with the magic ice. "Do you want to join us? We're going to a movie, and not even a chick flick."

"Unfortunately, I can't tonight. Maybe another time, though." George grinned at Natalie while he reached for a napkin, then the pen in the inside pocket of his shirt. "No chick flicks, huh?"

Kristy said, "Natalie prefers things bloody."

She rolled her eyes. "Thanks."

"It's true." It was also true that her friend was still stroking George's arm.

The poor man didn't even seem to object, he just handed Natalie the napkin. "I prefer things bloody, too. My number. There is an answering service if I'm not there." Then he pointed the pen in her direction and handed her a napkin. "Yours? Before you escape to your bloody amusement."

"Haha." She took it and quickly scribbled her name and number on the napkin. "I feel so twentieth century, exchanging paper."

"I'm old-fashioned like that."

"Should I burn this?" She handed him the napkin and got up from the bar. He stood as well. Kristy, luckily, had backed away, but was blatantly staring. "After I memorize the number? Just to be secure, Mr. Paranoia?"

"Just keep it safe." He ducked down and for a moment, she thought he was going to kiss her.

Her breath caught, but he only murmured in her ear. She could feel his cool breath on her neck when he said, "I'd really hate for you to forget me."

"Wow."

"I *know*."

"You never meet men like that!" Kristy was practically jumping as they walked toward the theater.

"I do… Okay, I don't." She laughed and thought of the phone number tucked carefully into her wallet. "He was really great."

"Was he smart?"

"I didn't get the professor vibe off him, but definite street smarts." Which she preferred, being the daughter of Detective Mark Ellis.

Kristy continued, "Funny?"

"Dry sense of humor, but definitely funny."

"That's your favorite kind!"

"I know. Can you stop bouncing?" She was starting to feel like they were attracting attention. She got the crawly feeling that someone was watching. Luckily, she was fairly sure it was just directed at her friend's antics.

"Oh, and *hot*. So freaking hot."

"I was kinda getting the impression that you thought so, considering you wouldn't let go of his arm."

"Did you feel it? It's a really nice arm." Kristy sighed. "My trainer has arms like that."

"You still holding that crush? Dan has nice arms. You need to go out with Dan."

"I can't." She pouted. "We work together."

"He's nuts about you and has been for years. And you love the geeky kind."

"Can we talk about you and George-who-should-not-be-named-George some more?"

"Why shouldn't he be named George?"

"He doesn't look like a George." Kristy finally stopped bouncing. "No offense to the Georges of the world, but he just doesn't look like one. I don't know, there was something…"

Despite her bubbly appearance, Kristy had a very keen eye for detail. Natalie's instincts tripped again. "What?"

Kristy said, "That's not his name."

Which was the same thing she'd thought before she'd been distracted by Mr. Attractive Suit and Witty Banter. She'd caught the hesitation before he introduced himself. Was he telling the truth about having an unusual name? Or covering something else? "You know, there *was* something—"

"Ugh!" Kristy cut her off. "We're reading too much into this. What possible reason would he have to lie about his name? We need to stop being so suspicious about everything, Nat. We're both starting to get paranoid. It's this business, I tell you. And this case."

"It's not paranoia if they're actually after you," she muttered.

"What?"

"Nothing. Let's go watch things explode."

She was up until three that morning again. Natalie knew it wasn't healthy, but she had spent the entire movie distracted by her week. The weird trip to Boca, the memory loss, the case…

This case.

It was eating at her. She stared at the list of names again.

Consuela Castillo

Alma Florez

Ana Romero

Reina Ortiz

Maria Covarubias

And those were only the ones who had identities. Most of the bodies dumped out in the desert they were still trying to identify. The ones with ID on them were from the odd cache of nine bodies that had been found north of Brawley. She glanced through the notes she'd taken about the five girls.

Born in Guadalajara. No criminal record.

Born in Guanajuato. No criminal record.

Born in Monterrey. No criminal record.

"Reina did, though," Natalie whispered as she paged through her notes. Reina Ortiz had been arrested for public disruption outside a club in Ensenada last summer. The club was named Bar El Ruso, a nightspot she'd never heard of before, but then, she had friends who were far more familiar with Ensenada than she was. She fired off a quick e-mail to her friend Manuel, hoping he'd get back to her in the morning.

"El Ruso, El Ruso…" Why did it sound familiar?

She shuffled through the stack of papers, chasing a memory. "Got it, got it, got it! Sticky note. Where's the sticky note?" She could see it in her mind. It had been on a bright green sticky note. The name. She knew she'd heard that name before.

"Ah ha!" Natalie pulled out the paper. It was just peeking out of the edge of one pile, attached to another file from a girl who'd been found near Imperial, one of the few the Border Patrol had been able to identify. She was twenty-two, another Tijuana native who had found her way to Ensenada. Lourdes Miranda had been on the outs with her family, but her younger brother did tell the police she had been working at a bar in Ensenada and sending money to her parents to help pay the bills.

"Bar El Ruso," she said, skimming over the file.

Tacked onto the first sticky note was another one in yellow. A name she'd jotted down, but Natalie didn't remember why. She had to get more organized.

Ivan Balankin. For some reason, simply reading the name to herself made her slightly ill.

"Who are you, Ivan?" She hoped Manuel got back to her quickly. "And what do you have to do with Bar El Ruso and these girls' deaths?"

Chapter Five

BAOJIA THOUGHT he had perfected patience in the previous 129 years, but his brother-in-law was trying it.

"Rory, ignoring the dead humans for the time being, this needs to be looked into for two reasons. One, it will look very bad for Ernesto if there is an out-of-control vampire draining women and leaving them for the human authorities to find. It's sloppy. Two, it's bad for business."

He sat at his desk, idly tapping a pencil next to the driver's license picture of Natalie Ellis as he spoke to Rory on the speaker phone. It was not a sufficient picture. She looked pale and unsmiling, nothing like the vibrant young woman he'd spoken to that night at the bar. Rory was huffing and puffing on the other end of the line, probably more irritated than concerned that Baojia was thrusting another task on him.

"I just don't understand why—"

"Nine human women found out in the desert creates headlines, Rory. Headlines that might be picked up by more than local news."

Her words from the other night rankled him. *You don't know me well enough to have an opinion about what I can and can't do.*

Oh how wrong you are, pretty human.

Baojia continued gently lecturing his brother-in-law. "National news would be the worst. The last thing that our sire's very profitable clubs and casinos need is a drop in tourism because the national news is speculating about a serial killer in San Diego. It's not there yet, but if this isn't dealt with, it could be. Now..." He paused. "If you'll ask Ernesto, I'd be happy to look into it. It's closer to me, and the club—"

"I'll take care of it," Rory broke in. "I can deal with this. I don't need your help."

Great. Now he'd pissed off Paula's husband, too. He was never getting back home. "Fine. I was only offering because I know you're busy."

"Yeah, well…" Rory sounded slightly mollified. "It's fine. Thanks for the offer, but I'll get some guys on it."

"There is an earth vampire who lives outside Brawley. He goes by Tulio. He's a bit of a hermit, but he can be helpful at times."

"Money?"

It was always hard to tell with Tulio. The immortal was quite old and very temperamental. "Just feel him out. He doesn't have much use for human money, but he likes favors. Often just knowing you'll owe him one is enough. He's highly territorial, so if there's been an incursion near him, he won't like it."

"Does he recognize Ernesto?"

"As much as he recognizes anyone. Remember, he's a hermit. He has no interest in politics. But he's cautious, too."

"Okay." He heard Rory shuffling papers. "Thanks for the tip."

"You're welcome. And let me know if I can help."

"I heard you called Ivan's people."

It was easy to forget how fast news traveled. "I had some questions for him. Nightclub business."

"Anything to worry about?"

"I'll take care of it."

"Good," Rory said. "None of us wants trouble with Ivan."

"Understood." He heard the odd beeping sound the phone made when another call was coming in. He frowned. "Rory, I need to go."

"Talk to you later." Rory immediately hung up, which meant the phone switched over to the other call. There was a slight clicking sound, then he heard Dez's voice.

"—don't know how long it will take her, Matt. The traffic down there —"

"Dez?" Why was Dez calling? This couldn't be good.

"Baojia! Natalie's on her way to Mexico!"

"What?" His fangs dropped and he stood up at his desk, already in motion. "When? Why?"

"I don't know! She didn't call me, or I would have tried to talk her out of it. She's probably pissed at me because I'm still giving her the runaround about our conversation last week."

He shook his head. "So how do you know she's on her way to Mexico?"

"She tweeted a picture of the border traffic. I guess she's stuck there. It's Friday night—you know how bad it gets around San Ysidro, even on the US side."

"She's stuck in traffic?" He strode toward the door and waved for the first waitress he saw. "Get Luis now," he whispered.

"She was, but I don't know how long—"

"I'll take care of it."

"Do you think she's going after Ivan?"

Baojia's heart thumped. He had a feeling it was only a matter of time. He'd gone to her apartment, but the pile of papers scattered over her desk before had been gone, and there was no sign of her notes anywhere. He suspected she had taken them to her office or put them somewhere safer. Part of him was glad she was becoming more cautious, but the other part was just annoyed.

"I don't know. I'll do what I can."

Dez sounded like she was almost in tears. "Baojia—"

"I'll do what I can, Dez." He waved Luis over when he saw him coming down the hall and threw a set of keys at him. "I'll call you later."

He immediately picked up a pencil and dialed her friend and editor's number. He heard Kristy pick up.

"Hello?"

"Kristy." All pretense of the polite man was gone. "This is George. Natalie's friend from the other night."

"Oh, hey! Wait, how did you get this number?"

"I need to know whether Natalie is going to Ensenada tonight."

"What?"

"Ensenada, Kristy. I need to know if she's going to a club in Ensenada."

Silence. The friendly girl was gone and a cautious woman answered him. "I don't know what she told you, but as her editor—"

"My job is in private security, Kristy. In nightclubs. I have information that tells me whoever she is meeting—" *Please don't say Ivan.* "—could be dangerous. Very dangerous, Kristy. I need to know if she went there, and I need to know if she's alone."

Kristy's silence told him she was taking the situation seriously, at least. Finally she said, "She called an old friend of ours in Ensenada. Manuel said he'd meet her down there, but she said she needed to go to this bar where a couple of the girls had worked. She was just going to check things out. Maybe talk to a few waitresses. She knows not to—"

"What was the name of the bar?"

"Bar El Ruso. She was following up a lead about some guy named Ivan."

He was settled into the back of Luis's car, mentally taking inventory of the situation, but Luis kept interrupting.

"Boss, this is a bad idea."

"I know, Luis."

"We've already started the wheels to have a formal meeting between you two. If you just show up at Ruso, it'll look like you're being impatient or are dissatisfied with his people. It's not gonna look good."

"I know, Luis."

He shifted in his seat and looked out the window, watching the passing lights of Tijuana. They were still over an hour away. Thanks to Luis's connections at the crossing, they'd made it through in far less time than he guessed Natalie had, but he suspected she would still beat them there. Why the hell had he promised Dez he would look out for her friend? Why the hell had he put his marks on her? This was turning into a giant headache.

"It's gonna look like you're trying to push the meeting up and we haven't really specified what it's even about, so he's going to be suspicious and it's just the two of us. Why are we doing this?"

"None of your business. Just drive."

His assistant gave a strangled laugh. "Right. Fine then, what are we going to *tell* him we're there about?"

"I'm going to tell him the truth." *Somewhat.* "I'm there fetching an errant human. We'll be fine."

"This is such a bad idea."

He tapped his foot in the back seat and tried not to think about Natalie's laugh. Or her quick wit. Or the smell of her blood. He was forced to admit the damn woman had crept under his skin. The last time that happened, he'd lost focus. People had died. The girl he was supposed to protect had been hurt. Almost killed. And this car ride was taking far too long.

He cursed under his breath and muttered, "I should have just swum."

"Yeah, because showing up soaking wet to a casual meeting where you're just going to fetch your girl-toy is so likely."

His quiet voice didn't need any emphasis to be chilling. "You are never to refer to Ms. Ellis as a toy of any kind. Do you understand, Luis?"

The young man was silent at first. Finally, he said, "Yes, Boss."

By the time they had pulled up to the entrance of Bar El Ruso, it was almost eleven o'clock. Baojia had formed no less than seven plans to deal with the situation when they found her. It would all depend on who she was talking to and whether or not Ivan had noticed her. Luis parked the car and followed him in through the VIP entrance. The one where weapons were not checked. Two fourteen-inch, German-made butterfly swords were strapped to his thighs under his slacks, within easy reach if things became interesting. He hoped he didn't have to use them, but better safe than sorry. Ivan would expect him to be armed because Ivan would be armed, too. Ivan, however, would not be as subtle.

The guard at the VIP entrance, a tall immortal whose energy registered young, paused for a moment when he saw Baojia, holding up a hand to stop him and Luis. Baojia gave him a suitably disdainful look before he stopped.

"Is he expecting you?" the guard asked in perfect English.

"No."

"Very well." He waved someone over, whispered in his ear, then nodded at Baojia. "Welcome to Bar El Ruso."

As he walked through the black curtain, he blocked out the flashing red and blue lights that pulsed and lit the club like eerie lightening. He searched for her, finding her by the bar holding another clear cocktail and watching. She hadn't seen him yet. He pulled Luis closer. "Go. Find Ivan and make our apologies for intruding. I'll be right behind you."

"Boss—"

"Go. I don't think she's caught his attention yet." It was a miracle she hadn't. There appeared to be a cruise ship in town, or some other event, because the bar held more than the average number of Americans. Luckily, Natalie wasn't the only pale, redheaded girl in the place. He walked toward her casually, pausing when a cocktail waitress passed. His instincts tripped and his fangs fell down.

Blood.

The girl's pulse called him. *Blood. Blood. Blood. Drink.*

His mouth dropped open and he growled low in his throat, though he'd already fed that night. His mind raced. What was causing this reaction? He was angry, but that normally didn't rile his instincts the way this girl had. Then he noticed another waitress. Common enough looking, but her blood also whispered to him.

Feed.

Another cocktail waitress passed by, her blood as delectably scented as the first two. Through sheer force of will, his fangs retracted. He blinked and forced himself to look for Natalie again. She was still at the bar, but now she was talking with one of the waitresses. The girl looked nervous, and he could see a vampire—one acting as bartender—watching the two from a distance. They were well within hearing range and Baojia knew the other vampire would hear anything Natalie was saying. There was no time to lose. If the ruse was to work, he had to get control of himself. He also had to not kill the bartender who was eyeing Natalie's neck. He felt wild and edgy. The instinct to tear Natalie away from prying eyes and clamp his mouth to her vein was almost overwhelming.

In a few short steps, he was standing behind her.

"—Rosa, I just want to know a little more about Lourdes. How long did she—"

He slid his hand along the back of her arm, letting his amnis flood her mind. Natalie stopped talking and looked over her shoulder with a dazed expression. "You?"

"Natalie." He leaned down and kissed her neck possessively, then looked up at the waitress, his fangs falling again at the combination of the girl's scent and the smell of Natalie's skin. "You may go."

The frightened girl shot a look at the bartender, then darted away. Baojia pulled Natalie into his arms and held her close, brushing back her hair and whispering in her ear as she clutched the front of his jacket.

"You're standing out again, Natalie. They've already noticed you asking the waitress questions."

"I knew there was something… What are you—?"

"You need to be quiet and let me talk." He slowly walked her away from the bar and toward the VIP lounge. It would be nice to think he could escape without talking to Ivan, but that was not going to be an option. She stumbled along with him. He tried to balance the influence he was using so she was unable to talk, but could still walk at his side. His arms stayed around her waist. "We're going to meet some very dangerous people, Natalie. And you're going to do exactly what I tell you. Exactly. You're going to play along because if you don't, you'll die. Do you understand? I'm going to lessen my influence now and you need to answer me."

He paused near the stairs and cupped her face as he saw her eyes blink into focus.

She whispered, "Who are you?"

He stroked her cheek and brushed a kiss along her jaw, playing the part of the indulgent lover as he lessened the energy that flooded her mind. "Questions later. Do you understand what I told you?"

"No. What do you mean, play along? I know these are dangerous people, but I was only—"

"Please don't make me use my amnis again. I need to know whether you can be trusted to play along or whether I can't allow you to speak."

He saw the fury in her eyes. "Can't allow—?"

"Again, Natalie, I need to know whether I can trust you. Do you want to die?"

He saw her pause and think. Baojia continued stroking her cheeks, which had flushed with anger. It gave her a lush, tempting color he knew the other vampires would notice. He had to make them believe she was his. If he couldn't, they were both in very serious danger.

"What's your name?" she finally asked. "Your real one."

He heard the edge of compromise in her voice. "My name is Baojia."

Her mouth dropped open, a round, tempting "O" that he leaned down and captured with his lips before she could speak again. His fingers grasped the nape of her neck and he pulled her closer, letting the edge of his tongue touch hers before it danced back. Her mouth was soft and warm, her taste... The smell of the blood pulsing around him made his fangs throb. A frustrated growl left his throat as he pulled away from her mouth to whisper in her ear, his hand still tangled in the riot of red waves at her neck. "And you won't forget me again. But I need to know if I can trust you, Natalie."

"Okay." Her breath was hot on his neck. "But I want answers later."

"That's unavoidable at this point. Now play along and pretend to be dumb for a while." There was no more delaying; he had to go up the stairs. Tucking Natalie under his arm, he strode up to the VIP balcony, so much like the one at Boca. He knew video monitors were watching. Knew that his appearance and Natalie's was being catalogued. Even as they walked, her picture was being sent to spies in Tijuana, San Diego, LA, Mexico City. It was a matter of hours before her identity was known.

One of Luis's cautions in the car leapt to his mind again. *"You know you might be creating the vampire equivalent of an international incident, and all over a girl, right?"*

Nope, he was never getting back to his life in LA. They reached the top of the stairs.

"Ivan." Baojia didn't try to be overly friendly. Ivan would only be suspicious. "I offer my apologies for arriving unannounced like this."

The black-eyed Russian looked him over but did not offer a seat. Ivan, despite his name, was Mexican by birth, son of a Russian emigrant to Northern Mexico who was turned at the beginning of the twentieth century, if Baojia's information was correct. His face had been scarred in human life, giving the young man a vicious-looking grin that made humans and vampires around him cringe, even without his reputation. He sat on a red velvet couch with a girl on each side, the very picture of every vampire cliché Baojia could imagine. He had to force himself not to roll his eyes.

"Baojia. It was a surprise to see you this night. What brings you to Ensenada?" Ivan's eyes had latched on to Natalie, who was leaning into Baojia's side, being suitably silent.

"It's rather embarrassing, to be honest. I hope Luis filled you in."

"Your human said you were here for a girl?" Ivan's unnatural grin widened, and Baojia felt Natalie stiffen. He sent a creep of amnis over her. Just enough to relax her so she didn't look surprised. "How times have changed. I don't recall you being fond of human women."

"I'm not, but there's not much to do in San Diego." Baojia glanced around the club. "I'm sure you understand. Where's Constantina?"

The name of his longtime mistress seemed to trip Ivan up for only a second before he said, "Some ridiculous illness. Not sure." He shrugged. "You know how they complain."

Ivan's mistress was one of the most formidable women Baojia had ever met. A human fiercely loyal to her immortal lover, she possessed keen intelligence and sensual beauty in equal measure. She was integral to Ivan's businesses. If Constantina wasn't at Bar El Ruso, something was definitely up.

"Hmmm." Baojia tried to look bored. "Well, as I said, I offer my apologies for the unexpected visit."

The vampire motioned Baojia to a seat. He relaxed infinitesimally as he sat down and pulled Natalie onto his knee.

"The things we do to alleviate boredom, eh?" Ivan said with a nasty glint in his eye. "She's pretty. Very... American-looking."

"I'm fond of her. She's kept me more entertained than most."

Natalie tensed as the two men continued on as if she wasn't there. Baojia absently played with a piece of her hair, hoping she would relax on her own and play along.

"I'm very curious what you wanted to meet about, but first, can I offer you a drink?" Ivan leaned over to a girl at his side, brushing her hair to the side as he licked her pulse, then bit. Luckily, Ivan was too busy to notice Natalie's reaction. The woman went stiff in his arms, a protest about to burst from her lips. Baojia sent more amnis over her. She was going to want to kill him. She wouldn't, of course. But she'd want to. He grabbed the back of her neck possessively and pulled her down to nuzzle her neck.

"No reaction," he took the opportunity to murmur, then placed a gentle kiss on her neck as the girl across from Ivan moaned. Natalie was trembling. Not anger, he finally realized. She was scared to death. He looked over at Luis, who was standing in a corner, also looking terrified. "Luis." He caught his assistant's eye and motioned him over. He waited for Ivan to finish drinking, which he did, licking the last of the girl's blood from his lips, his fangs bared as the human slumped at his side. "Ivan, I wonder if I might send my humans to wait in the car so we can speak more openly."

"Of course. Tio will see them out."

A large brute of a vampire sped to Luis's side while Baojia rose. He slid an arm around Natalie's waist for a moment, squeezing her hand and sending another wave of calm over her. "Take a nap, darling. You've had a long night."

Natalie only blinked and nodded, but he could see the tears forming at the corners of her eyes. "I'll wait in the car," she whispered.

"Luis will see to you if you need anything."

His assistant held out an arm and Baojia put Natalie's in his, reluctant to let her out of his sight, even if it meant getting her farther away from Ivan. Just then, Ivan's man stepped a little too close to Natalie, and she cringed as the strange vampire bared his teeth and took a threatening sniff.

Baojia's tightly leashed control, strained by the tension permeating the club, snapped as Luis was forced to pull Natalie behind him. He reached for one of the short swords. A slight rip at the edge of his pocket was the only warning Tio received before he was pinned to the wall by Baojia's blade through his neck. The vampire scrambled, pulling at the sword that was lodged an inch from his spine, as Ivan laughed and Baojia darted in front of him, tugging Natalie along. He danced on the edge of violence, sorely tempted to end the life of the presumptuous brute.

"See that?" He flipped the hair away from her neck, baring the bite marks he'd made the first night he met her. Natalie couldn't stop the whimper that left her throat when Baojia pulled his blade from Tio's neck and wiped off the blood on the vampire's shoulder, baring his teeth in his face. "Do you know who I am? You do not sniff what is mine. Do you understand?"

"Learn some manners, Tio!" Ivan was still laughing. "Carlos, see to the humans."

"Yes, Boss." An older vampire Baojia recognized stepped out of the shadows and motioned Luis and Natalie to the stairs.

"Carlos is far more controlled. Your humans will be safe with him."

"Thank you." He took a deep breath, ignoring the wild adrenaline scenting the air. "Luis, take the girl to the car. I'm sure I'll only be a few more moments."

"Of course." He held out his arm for Natalie again. "Shall we?"

Before she took it, Baojia caught her eye. Her terrified gaze only said one thing.

Monster.

Chapter Six

THE BLACK MERCEDES was parked close enough to the club to be safe from vandals, but far enough away that it wouldn't be caught by traffic in case its occupants needed a quick getaway. The man named Luis kept his hand on her arm the whole way there, guiding Natalie as she stumbled in a horrified daze.

Fangs. The one named Ivan had bitten the girl's neck and he had fangs. There had been blood and fangs and the horrible crunching sound of the monster's neck as he was flung into the wall by Geor—Baojia's... sword? Knife? Who the hell carried a knife that big? The one who smelled her had fangs, too. She'd seen them. He hissed at her like a snake. And then...

See that? You do not sniff what is mine. Do you understand?

The tears she'd held at bay started to roll down her cheeks and she felt Luis's hand tighten on her elbow.

"Just a few more minutes, Natalie."

Nausea rolled through her, tightening her stomach as Luis unlocked the car. She heard a terrible gasping sound and realized it was coming from her. Luis, to her surprise, laughed.

"A few too many cosmos, huh, Nat?" He guided her behind the Mercedes and put a hand on her back. "Better get rid of it now; he's just gonna be more pissed if you mess up the car."

She lost it, leaning over and emptying her stomach as the insane man stood next to her. She realized he was still talking with someone.

"—stubborn little thing. Someone's companion at Boca was raving about the DJ here and she couldn't get enough. The boss said he'd bring her, but I guess she got impatient. She's new."

"I don't think it's a big deal. I'm sure they'll work it out."

"Hope so. Baojia was pissed on the drive down here, that's for sure."

Natalie fumbled for her purse until she realized that Luis was holding it. Damn. If she could just get her keys…

She felt him nudging her up and waving goodbye to the man… monster… whatever he was… that had walked them out of the club.

"Few more minutes," Luis whispered. He opened the door and gently helped her inside. Then he got in the front seat and immediately locked the doors.

"Okay," he said, turning around to hand her a box of tissues and a bottle of water. "He's out of hearing range, so unless they had guards I didn't see, we're safe to talk. You okay?" He did look concerned. He looked scared actually, as if he was waiting for her to collapse or explode or suddenly sprout antennae.

Which, considering what had just happened, was entirely possible.

Natalie glared at him, took the bottle of water, swished some in her mouth, then tried to open the door. She cocked her head silently at Luis, who turned to roll down a window so she could spit it out. She took another long drink of water, dabbed at the tears still staining her face, and turned to her… protector? Kidnapper? Chauffeur?

"What. The *fuck*. Was that?"

Luis let out a long breath. "Yeah… This is gonna be interesting."

"Interesting?" Her angry tears dried and she felt the rage boiling up. "Interesting is not the word for what that was! Horrifying. Bizarre. Unreal —oh!" She gasped. "They spiked my drink. That was a hallucination."

"Um, no it was—"

"Wait," she said with a frown. "I didn't drink anything. I specifically didn't drink anything because I thought the bartender looked sketchy. I didn't drink anything, so it couldn't have been drugs."

"Natalie—Ms. Ellis—I'm not sure which one you like, but—"

"Oh! No…" Her eyes widened. "It was some kind of airborne hallucinogen. They had those fog machines going and—"

"Natalie!"

She looked up, having almost forgotten she had an audience. "What?"

"You weren't drugged. You weren't having a hallucination. I saw the same thing you did in there."

Her stomach plunged, and she felt the bile rising again. "Luis, open the door."

"I cannot let you out, Nat—"

"Gonna puke again."

"Oh." He unlocked the door just in time for Natalie to lean out of the sedan, leaving the last of her lunch on the sidewalk in Ensenada. When she pulled her head back in, Luis was there with another bottle of water and a worried expression.

"I'm sorry," he said.

"For what?"

"That you had to see that."

"And what…" She swirled and spit again, fairly confident there was nothing left in her stomach. "What the hell was *that*, Luis?"

"That, Natalie Ellis, was a vampire pissing match, and you were in the middle of it."

"Vampires."

"You've said that, like, five times now."

They had been in the car for at least ten minutes and there was still no sign of Baojia. She was fairly sure that she could take Luis in a fight, though, so Natalie wasn't all that worried. And she was pretty sure Luis was normal. Well, mostly. He did wear too much cologne.

"Still trying to wrap my head around that idea." There was no such thing as vampires. Or werewolves. They were in the same category as Big Foot and the Chupacabra.

"I forget how weird it can be to someone who doesn't know. I mean, I grew up around it so—"

"You grew up around it?" Her mouth dropped open in horror. "Around that?" She pointed at the club she could still hear music pulsing from.

"Huh? That? Oh no. Nooo." He shook his head in horror. "Are you kidding? My mom—"

"Your mom knew?"

"Of course she did! I mean… No, not that. She would have freaked if we saw anything more violent than *Tom and Jerry* growing up. We were never—"

"Then why the hell did you just say—?"

"Listen!" The young man took a deep breath and closed his eyes. "Natalie, what you just saw was… awful. We like to think that kind of stuff never happens, but—"

"Luis!" Panic welled up and her eyes darted around the car. She had to get out of there. At any moment, one of them could come back. "You have to get me out of here. Just give me my keys. Tell them I got away."

"I can't. It's not safe. Will you just listen?"

"It's not safe in *here*. I can tell you're normal like me." She tugged on the door handle, but it was locked again. "You have to help me. Whatever those things are, they're dangerous. Leave with me before he gets back. I know people who can help you. You don't have to—"

"It's not like that!"

She stopped tugging on the door and moved closer to him. "Then tell me. You can tell me what's going on."

"I'm trying to explain." He glanced out the window, but there was still no sign of anyone approaching the car. "You have to stay here. You have to let him protect you."

"Protect me? *Him*? He's one of them!"

"Listen, you're a crime reporter, right?"

"Yeah?" What the hell did that have to do with vampires and fangs and monsters named Tio?

"So, you see all kinds of horrible stuff, right? Things humans do to other humans."

She blinked, trying to make sense of what the young man was trying to say. "There are bad people everywhere, Luis, but—"

"And there are bad vampires, too. That's my point. It's just like the regular world in most ways. There are good guys and there are bad guys. Those guys? Ivan? Tio? They're the bad guys. The *really* bad guys. But Baojia? He's a good guy."

She could hear the sincerity in Luis's voice. Natalie had a pretty good sense of when someone was lying to her, and Luis wasn't. At least, he didn't believe he was.

"And he went to a lot of trouble tonight to come get you. Trust me, it was really risky coming here alone, but if Ivan had found out you were connected to Baojia and were in his territory—"

"But I am not connected to Baojia! This is insane. I met him once and he told me his name was George, and we had a drink and that's all. And it was—obviously—all an act. I'm not *his* like he said. I don't even know what all this is about. I'm just investigating a story."

Luis looked as confused as she was. "Well, trust me, you're connected somehow. Otherwise, there's no way he would have done all this. You're not under Ernesto's aegis, as far as I know, and that's the only other reason he would go to all this trouble. He doesn't really have a human-chick thing. I mean, he likes women. But he's not a vampire who gets attached, so—"

"Stop!" she finally screamed, squeezing her eyes shut. "Just… stop! There are no such things as vampires. This is crazy!"

Luis fell silent, and when Natalie finally looked at him again, there was no trace of the lighthearted young man who had been trying to comfort her.

"You saw it yourself, Natalie. *Felt* it yourself. You saw Ivan feed from that girl. You felt it when Baojia touched you. Admit it or don't, but you would have done anything he asked. You wouldn't have been able to help yourself. Are you gonna be one of those delusional people who tries to believe their eyes are lying to them? Or are you going to accept that there just might be things in the world that you didn't know about before? The truth kind of hit you over the head tonight, but it's still up to you. You gonna fight it or roll with it? You don't seem stupid."

Just as she was trying to process what the young man was saying, there was a tap at the window across from her. A dark outline stood motionless as Luis unlocked the door. Then Baojia opened it and slipped into the car with barely a whisper. The vampire glanced at her with an unreadable expression before he spoke quietly to Luis.

"Luis, watch your tone when you speak to Ms. Ellis. And drive home. As fast as you can."

"Where are you taking me?" she finally asked as they left the lights of Ensenada behind them. "My car—"

"I will arrange for someone to pick up your car and return it when we reach San Diego."

Luis had raised the privacy screen so it was just her and George-who-wasn't-George in the back seat of the car as they drove north. At least all the highways were familiar, so she didn't think he was lying about going back to San Diego.

Vampire.

The word, the twisted reality of it, hung in the air between them. A part of her couldn't accept the idea. The other part—the part Luis had spoken to—knew it had to be true. Baojia was quiet, but the tension in his shoulders told her he was not relaxed in the least.

"If you just give me my keys, my friend Manuel—"

"Ah yes, your friend, Manuel." His voice was soft and almost frighteningly calm. "Where was he tonight, by the way? A couple might not have been quite so conspicuous. Did Manuel have more important things to do than see to your safety while you ran stupidly into the lion's den to ask questions about his teeth?"

Natalie's mouth dropped open. "Are you… Are you mad at me? You? Mad at *me*? Are you kidding?" He remained silent, but by then, she could practically feel the waves of anger pouring off him. "I don't think you have any right to—"

"I told you not to go to Ivan!" he burst out. "I told you, 'Never. Never speak to Ivan.' And you didn't listen!"

The privacy screen rolled down a few inches. Natalie could see Luis's saucer-eyed stare. "Um, Boss—?"

"Put the screen back up, Luis!" The screen immediately went up, but Baojia was still fuming.

"I have no idea how my directions could have been more specific. 'Don't speak to Ivan' is pretty damn clear. How many Ivans are there?"

She was as confused as she was angry. "What are you talking about? When did we ever talk about Ivan? I met you *one time* and then you show up—"

"I should have known. Should have kept you under house arrest after I met you the first time."

"The first time?" Oh… Those weird flashes of memory suddenly made sense. "We met before, didn't we? You're the reason I can't remember that Friday night."

She could tell from the look on his face she was right. It wasn't an apologetic look in the least. Baojia was still angry.

"I told you not to go to Ivan, Natalie. Why couldn't you just listen?"

"Oh, I don't know," she yelled. "Maybe because I couldn't remember it, you bastard! What else did you do to me? Was it the same creepy shit you did back there that made me practically unable to speak? What the hell was that? Do you know I thought I'd been drugged? I thought I had a brain tumor, for God's sake!"

"No, you didn't."

"I might have! I spent hours in the emergency room. Kristy wanted me to have a cat scan!"

"Which you didn't have." He crossed his arms. "You did, however, go to speak to Ivan when I told you not to."

"Baojia. It was *your* name Dez gave me, wasn't it? Why did she lie about it? Does she know what you are?" Natalie suddenly gasped, terror clutching her throat. "Is she in some kind of trouble? Oh, my God! Matt. The baby! Is Dez okay?"

His head rolled back as he groaned. "Of course she's okay! She's the one who called me and told me you were on your way to Mexico, Natalie. She's the one who sent me after you."

"How did she—"

"You tweeted some picture at the border crossing." He paused. "And someday, someone is going to explain to me what the hell Twitter is."

She frowned. "Oh, it's this microblogging site where you're limited to one hundred forty characters and—why? Why the hell did Dez call *you*?"

"Because she asked me to protect you," he said under his breath. "She felt responsible because she gave you my name in the first place and got you caught up in all… *this*. And she knows the case you're investigating has something to do with our world—"

"The vampire world."

"The *world* world." He looked at her from the corner of his eye. "It's the same world. You haven't fallen into another dimension. There are just things you didn't know about before that you know now."

She swallowed audibly and didn't miss the fact that he glanced at her neck. "You're a liar," she said. "And a monster. And I want to go home."

The line of his jaw tightened. He was silent for a long moment, arms crossed, a black enigmatic outline as the night sped past. "I never lied to you," he finally said. "And you're not going home."

"You can't kidnap me."

"Yes, I can. And I will if you don't cooperate. You can call Dez when we arrive at my house."

"I'm *going* to call Dez as soon as we get to *my* house." She only got angrier at his amusement. "What?"

He started laughing, the kind of rueful laughter people resort to when things were just that bad. "You're quite…"

"What?"

"Interesting. For a human. And stubborn."

She curled her lip. "You're pretty stubborn too. But since I don't know many vampires, I can't compare."

"You've probably known more than you realize."

"What's that supposed to mean?"

"And you'll know even more if you return to your house." His smile faded. "Ivan knows who you are now; he won't be shy about sending spies. He's going to be curious. I don't take up with human women, as a rule."

"Am I supposed to feel special?" They were approaching the border crossing. Natalie knew if she yelled for help, the border patrol agents would stop them. They'd help her. There was no way—

"If you're thinking about making a break for it, I wouldn't suggest it, Natalie. I'm quite serious. It's not safe for you to go home. You're going to my house for the time being until we can figure out some other, more suitable, location for you. I'll have a better idea tomorrow evening after I wake and can make some calls."

"I'm not going to your house. And what? You really sleep all day?" She put a hand to her neck as mental pictures from the club assaulted her. "You're going to bite me and drink my blood, aren't you?"

"Already have. And you should take off your heels. Get comfortable."

"What do you mean you already—wait, why should I get comfortable?"

Her heart caught in her throat when he appeared at her side. It was as if he teleported; it was that fast.

"You should get comfortable because…" He threw an arm around her shoulders before she could protest, drawing her to his side as he stroked soft fingers along her arm and the drowsy haze started falling again. "Time for a nap, darling."

"Don't call me darling. You're a liar. I…" She fought to stay conscious, but her eyelids fell. "Ha…ate you."

"I think you might actually mean that." Was it her imagination, or did he sound sad? The heaviness fell over her like a warm blanket. It was almost as if the fingers on her arm feathered over her whole body, bringing with them a gentle pressure. *Sleep. Sleep. Sleep.* She imagined a kiss on her forehead as the car slowed at the border crossing, and she thought she heard him whisper.

"I never lied."

When she woke, she was in a warm, windowless room, still in her dress and lying on luxurious silk sheets. She blinked and sat up, shaking her head to clear the weird and sadly familiar hazy feeling from her head. She pinched her eyes shut, shook her head, then opened them again to see a crisp white note sitting on the edge of the night table. Near it, a duffel bag from her closet was sitting next to her shoes, which were lined up perfectly with her old white sneakers. She looked back at the note, which in clear, precise letters read:

It was not a dream.

"Well, shit." She unfolded it to read the inside.

> *Natalie,*
> *You are not a prisoner here, but you're not free to go, either.*

"That's pretty much the definition of a prisoner, asshole."

> *I will wake at dusk. Please make yourself at home in my house. I packed a few items from your closet...*

"Are you kidding me?" She stood, tempted to rip the note to tiny shreds. "You went through my stuff?"

> *...And some extra shoes. Anything missing, I will be happy to procure for you.*
> *Baojia*
> *P. S. Your butler is waiting.*

Natalie stormed out of the room, surprised the handle turned on her first attempt, only to be met with the most stunning view of the Pacific Ocean she'd ever seen from inside a house. It stretched wide, a solid wall of glass framed by sleek modern pillars in white marble. Turning in place, she saw that her room opened up to a huge living room with a small kitchen in one corner. It looked like the guest suite of a very fancy hotel. And on one soft leather couch sat Luis, paging through a copy of the *Tribune*.

"This report on the hotel robbery is good. I don't really read the paper, but I noticed a stack of them downstairs, so I picked one up. You're a good writer."

"Thanks. Are you supposed to be my butler?"

"Haha. Such a sense of humor the vampire has," Luis said. "But yes. I'm stuck in here as long as you are. 'See to her wishes, but don't let her leave.' I believe that was the job description."

"Don't let me leave, huh?" Natalie cast her eyes around the room. "We'll see about that."

Chapter Seven

BAOJIA WAS PRACTICING his forms to the melodious background noise of Natalie banging on the door of the guest suite, calling him every vile name she could think of. As suspected, she had a rather vivid imagination.

Cross. Thrust. Center. Draw back. Center. Sweep.

Center.

Center.

Center.

He took a deep, meditative breath, trying to still his mind from the flurries of information all begging for attention.

Rory had called at dusk.

Then Paula.

Then Ivan's people.

Luis had called from the house phone to tell him Natalie had spent all day inspecting windows and air-conditioning vents for means of escape before she had taken to simply banging on the door incessantly until she was let out so she could go home. His assistant had also been subjected to a rather thorough interrogation about the vampire world.

I thought she was going to waterboard me!

He was insane. There was no way any of this was going to end well.

Cross. Draw. Center. Sweep.

Humans were dying in the desert and he had no idea who was behind it. His sire was still angry with him and wanted him cooped up in San Diego. A human reporter had discovered not only that vampires existed, but also that San Diego's premier nightclub was owned by them. The same reporter was locked in his guest suite, and the electronic lock system keeping her there was due to release in—he glanced at the clock—five, four, three, two…

He heard the click followed by the tumble, followed by the rush of feet that ran down the stairs to—

"Who the *hell* do you think you are?"

Center.

Baojia turned, swiveling in his stance until he faced her, still practicing his forms in nothing but a pair of loose pants. She noticed.

"Good evening, Natalie." He'd picked excellent clothing for her. The dark jeans hugged her hips and the blue-green shirt matched her eyes.

Focus. There was an angry human in his practice room.

"I said, *who*—"

"I am Baojia, oldest son and chief of security for Don Ernesto Alvarez, immortal leader of Los Angeles and its territories." The corner of his mouth lifted as he stood in a rigid stance. "And sometimes known as George. Welcome to my home." He finished the combination, took a deep breath, and closed his eyes for a moment. Seeing her awake in his home put him in an oddly good mood. He tried not to wonder why. His introduction had taken a bit of the wind out, but he could tell she was still angry. "I apologize for not giving you a tour last night. You were rather exhausted."

"Probably because you did that creepy shit with your vampire power to knock me out."

"I didn't actually use very much." He opened his eyes and strolled over to her. "You shouldn't have been unconscious. Have you had any extra stress in your life lately? Suffered from exhaustion?"

"Are you asking about my health?"

"Yes. I promised to keep you safe. If you have any health issues, I should be made aware of them so I can tend to you properly."

"Tend to me?" Now she was just blinking. "I… I'm healthy as a horse. Can we please—?"

"That's such an odd expression. You look far healthier than any horse I've ever seen." He couldn't stop his eyes skimming over her figure.

"Oh… wow." She shook her head. "You actually just did that. You kind of made a pass at me after you *kept me prisoner* for a whole night, you ass!"

He shrugged and lifted a hand, flicking a finger so that the water bottle on the bench flew to his hand. Natalie's mouth dropped open.

"It was an observation, not a proposition. And I kept Luis prisoner, too. I didn't want you to feel singled out."

"How…" She sounded out of breath. "How did you…"

"Didn't Luis explain that part?" He let the smug smile peek out. "He said you interrogated him very thoroughly. Something about bright lights and metal chairs."

"Nothing…" She took a step back. He followed. She took another. "Nothing about… floating stuff. That was—"

"It's the water." He opened the bottle and freed it, feeling his element's excitement at his presence. The water in the bottle flowed out and swirled around his neck, circling him like a snake. Natalie watched, not with horror, but with awe. She reached a hand out before drawing back. "Don't be afraid to touch it if you want. There's nothing special about this water. It's the same stuff you drink." He glanced at the blue bottle. "Direct from the spring, in fact."

"But how—"

"Immortals, vampires—whatever you choose to call us—all have a connection with one of the elements. For me, that connection is water. I control it, and it gives me strength." He called more water from the fountain that ran toward him in a floating river. He sent the water to circle her legs before he created a shimmering waterfall before her. It danced and shone between them, a living wall that reflected the lights of the harbor. Her anger fled and he saw the wonder take over. Natalie reached her hand through the waterfall and he saw her face break into a smile.

"It's beautiful," she said. "Magic."

Her hand hung in the air, covered with the water he had called. Baojia reached out and touched her spread hand, fitting her fingers with his. Her smile dropped, but she did not pull away.

"It only seems like magic," he said quietly. "But it's all quite natural, I promise. No spells or incantations."

She stepped to the right and so did he, the water still rippling between them and her hand still linked with his. "But you're a vampire. You drink blood?"

"Yes. I eat some food, but I have to drink blood to survive. Human or animal. Either one will suffice, but I don't kill unless someone threatens me."

"What does blood have to do with the elements?"

They continued to circle each other, the water still hanging between them, and he didn't let go of her hand. "What is the body but the sum of the elements? Water, Earth, Air. The fire of human energy and heat. We were all once human. We are the same as you. Only more… durable."

"Immortal?"

"Oh, we can be killed." He had to smile. "But you might think of us as death-resistant."

There was a long pause as they continued to slowly turn through the room. "You lied to me."

"Not about everything."

"Why can't I remember the night we met? The first night?"

Slowly, he let his amnis creep up her arm, being careful not to use too much. "Do you feel that?"

"Yes. Please don't—"

"I won't take your memories away again. I already told you that. I was trying to protect you. I told your friend I would do my best to keep you safe, and I don't break my promises. I was hoping you would stay out of this completely. I planted the suggestion for you to forget about Ivan, but you must have found his name anyway."

"It was in my notes. I almost got sick. The first time I read his name. There was something about it."

"It was my suggestion. But you're very bright and very stubborn."

"I'm not going to apologize for that."

"I don't expect you to."

"What is it?" She glanced at their linked hands and he let his amnis dance along her skin. The tiny hairs along her arm reached toward him. "How do you do that?"

"What you're feeling is called *amnis* by some of us. It's an electrical current—energy, just like what fires in your brain and animates your nervous system. It runs under our skin." He carefully pulled it back and used it to push the water away from their hands so a circle opened between them and he could see her face clearly. "It's what connects me to my element. It's what animates me. Amnis is what lets me alter human thought by affecting your cerebral cortex."

"Short-term memory." Her forehead was wrinkled in thought, and he knew he had tempted her curious nature.

"Among other things."

"Speech?"

"Yes."

"Consciousness?"

"Obviously."

Her eyes narrowed. "Emotions?"

"Your emotions are your own. Vampires can't influence those." He let his eyes fall to their hands. "Other than by normal means, that is."

Natalie pulled her hand away and the water fell, splattering on the ground until he swept it up and returned it to the happily gurgling fountain in the corner. "None of that."

"You liked George well enough." He was surprised by the stab of envy toward his human facade she had been so at ease with.

"George was a liar."

He felt his fangs drop but was careful to conceal them from her. "No, he wasn't. Only about his name because I thought you might recognize it."

"Were you following me?" She was relentless. "Were you following me that night? Did you follow me after? Why bother meeting me in the bar? What was the point? Were you just messing with me?"

Why did the woman get under his skin so? Baojia stifled a growl. "I had an assignment. I needed to know more about you."

"So, I'm an assignment?"

He couldn't decipher her tone of voice. It was angry, but there was a hint of something...

"You have friends in my world—people I respect—who would like me to keep you safe. I have promised to do this. As I said before, I keep my promises."

"Have a *vampire* keep me safe?" She threw up her hands, suddenly sounding resigned. "Have a vampire keep me safe from other vampires? I guess that makes sense, right? Or I'm going to wake up in the psychiatric hospital soon and this will all be over."

The key was to appear as normal as possible. He knew it must have been a shock. He was still young enough to remember his own horror and incredulity when faced with what he had thought were only horror stories meant to terrify a child. The *jiangshi* of childhood nightmares had come to life on the streets of old San Francisco to kill his attackers and eventually claim him.

"Maybe you'd like to call Dez now."

"Maybe you could tell me what all this has to do with those murdered women? It was a vampire who was killing them, wasn't it? But I'm supposed to trust you?"

The frustration began to rise. "I think you should call Dez."

"I think you should answer me!"

"Well *I* think—" He clenched his teeth to stop yelling. Why did she cause him to yell? In the car the night before, he'd thought Luis was going to drive off the road. He'd probably never heard Baojia raise his voice in anger. Or raise his voice, period. "I think lots of things. But right now, I want you to call Dez. She will be able to explain this better than I can. And you trust her. So why don't we just call your friend so we can get this cleared up and get back to finding some answers about dead bodies turning up in the desert? That sound like a plan, Natalie?"

Her face was flushed and her eyes blazing, but at least she didn't look scared anymore. "Fine."

"Fine."

"We can call from my house."

"Nice try. We'll use my office here."

"Asshole."

"Stubborn brat."

"Kidnapper."

He couldn't stop the smile. "You could do this all night, couldn't you?"

"Yep." She spun around to stomp away, but then turned back. "I don't know where your office is."

The office in the house had been specially equipped for immortal use. There was a rotary phone with a speaker attachment and an old-fashioned answering machine.

"Wow. You guys are really into the retro thing, aren't you?" Natalie eyed the phone with disdain.

"It's our amnis. Because our energy is electrical in nature, we tend to short out more modern equipment. Old cars are okay, but new ones we need drivers for. Rotary phones are fine. Mobiles? Nope."

"So that's why you don't have a mobile phone." She looked around. "Computer?"

He shook his head. "There *is* some voice-command software that an… associate of mine is working on that would enable our kind to use computers without breaking them, but it's still in the trial stage. She was a bit of a computer nut as a human, so she has a hard time living without one."

Natalie was still examining his office with a frown. "I thought you said you were in security. Surveillance. That kind of thing. How could you possibly… Oh, was that a lie, too?"

"Not a lie." He opened a cabinet to reveal video monitoring equipment. "I have humans who set it up, then all the monitors are put behind insulated glass for me. I can see but not touch. It's the hands-on work and intuition that I use the most. I've been doing security for a long time."

He heard her pause. "How long?"

"Over one hundred twenty years." Why did that suddenly seem so old? "And I'm relatively young for a vampire."

"Wow."

He looked over his shoulder so see her gaping at him. She might also have been checking out his ass. He tried not to laugh. *Not bad for an old man, eh?* "I told you I became a citizen a long time ago."

"Are you really from San Francisco?"

"Yes. All that was true." He lifted the phone and dialed the Kirbys' number. "I told you I didn't lie."

"And why should I believe you?"

He raised an eyebrow as the phone began to ring.

She said, "I'm not being obnoxious or stubborn. Logically, what reason do I have to trust you? You have to see where I'm coming from."

"I do." He heard Matt pick up the phone. "And I respect your caution. It bodes well for your survival. Matt?"

"Baojia, is that you?" The man's voice was frantic. "Dez is going out of her mind. Is Natalie okay? Please tell me she's with you. Is she safe?"

At the sound of Matt's voice, he saw tears well up in Natalie's eyes and her shoulders relax as the underlying tension left the room. She collapsed in the chair behind his desk, taking a deep breath and covering her face.

"I'm here, Matt." She swiped at the tears on her cheeks and rested her elbows on the desk, leaning forward and taking a deep breath. "I'm okay. Tell Dez I'm okay." Then she met his eyes, and Baojia saw a seed of trust take root. "I think I'm gonna be okay."

"So you *do* think it's the same MO as the Juarez case." Natalie was in full investigative mode on the phone with Dez, and Baojia found the whole experience of watching her while she took notes on the yellow legal pad… oddly stimulating.

Dez was talking through the speaker phone. "As soon as I learned about the existence of vampires, I had to think of Juarez. There was so much that never fit. Sure, some of the cases were solved, but it was such a weird pattern. And to have it go on for so long—"

"But there were a lot of theories, Dez. I'm still not sure that we're necessarily dealing with a super—I feel like I'm on *X-Files*—*supernatural* murderer." She doodled in the margins of the paper, small circles that grew into larger patterns. "I mean, it's still possible that what we're dealing with is human, as sick as it is."

"It was odd to me that the Mexican authorities never devoted the kind of time and resources to the case that they ought."

She lifted her shoulders, gesturing to her friend who wasn't in the room. "Bribes? Back-door deals? Good ole boy network? A disgusting lack of concern for female victims?"

"Or amnis? Vampire influence? Powerful people not wanting to shed light on secrets?"

"It's too soon to tell whether the murders in the desert are isolated incidents or something that could be linked to Juarez," she said. "I don't want to jump to conclusions that leave out other avenues of investigation."

"I agree," Baojia said quietly.

Natalie offered him a small smile and said, "Unfortunately, we may not be able to make any links until more women are murdered."

"Or more bodies show up."

She nodded. "It's possible there are a lot more out there."

Matt spoke up. "Baojia, have you asked Ernesto about this? Can he make inquiries?"

"If things were normal, these murders would give me the excuse to reach out to my peer in Mexico City the way I couldn't with the Juarez case. That never affected us or our border; this does. But Rory is in charge right now, so I'm having to go through him."

"Will he be as persistent as you?"

He hesitated, hating to speak ill of his sister's mate, but he knew Matt would keep his mouth shut. "Probably not. He's up to his neck in my job, and I don't know how well he's doing, to be honest. If I were still in charge in LA, this would have been dealt with a while ago."

Natalie must have picked up on the subtext. She said, "So you're on the outs with your boss… father… whatever. So he put your brother-in-law in charge, and officially you can't do much, but you're still the one with connections and the know-how, so your brother-in-law can't do much either?"

Perceptive little thing. "In a nutshell, yes."

"Ugh." Her head fell back in the chair. "This is so much like dirty politics, it's scary."

Baojia muttered, "You have no idea."

There was a curl of hair that kept falling into her face every time she took notes. She'd blow it away with a gust of air, then it would fall back into the exact same position. He wondered why she didn't tie her hair back, but found he rather liked watching the stubborn lock of hair, even though it annoyed her.

Persistent and annoying. How apt.

She and Dez started going over facts again. He would have to find a way to get her notes for her. She seemed as bright as Dez reported, and Baojia could use any extra help on this case. Plus, if she kept busy with him, Natalie was far less likely to be off putting herself in the middle of dangerous situations she was unequipped to deal with. It would make his assignment to keep her safe far easier if she just stayed close.

She was repeating a list of names from memory when he reached over and tucked the errant curl behind her ear. She shot him a quick smile but then returned to her scribbling.

"Okay, *if* it is the same perpetrator as in Juarez, that means someone moved." She turned to Baojia. "Is that something he would... I don't know, need permission to do? Or would tell anyone?"

He nodded. "Theoretically, if a vampire moves into another's territory, he should make the other vampire aware. Seek tacit permission, even if they live on the outskirts. The American Southwest is still very new and not as regulated as some other parts of the world. In this area, an immortal wouldn't necessarily have to swear any kind of allegiance, but he'd have to at least acknowledge the authority of whoever controlled the area."

"So, if this guy was living in Juarez, but moved—"

"He would probably let Ivan know, since Ivan is the point man in that area for the cartel that controls Mexico. Or he'd tell Ernesto, if he lived on this side of the border."

Natalie sat up straight. "Wait, cartel? As in drug cartel?"

"Something like that. It's complicated."

She frowned but turned back to her notes. "You're explaining that later."

He muttered under his breath as he started to pace the room. "Of course you *think* I am."

"What does—?"

Dez's voice broke through the line. "Listen, Natalie. I know you want to follow this story—and I think we all agree whoever is doing this has to be stopped—but can you accept that even if you find out the truth, you may never be able to publish the results?"

She snorted. "Why not?"

A heavy silence fell over the room and Baojia turned to her. "Are you serious?"

"Hey, whoever is killing these women—human or vampire—they deserve justice." She stood to face him, arms crossed. "These girls deserve to have their killer put away. I'm not going to be part of a cover-up. Forget it."

"When we find who this is, he *will* get justice. I'll kill him myself, but if you publish this story—"

"What? You're just going to kill him?"

His voice rose again. "That's the way it works in our world."

"You just decide? No courts. No trial."

He pointed to her notes. "What kind of trial do you think this monster deserves? If you're right and he's killed over fifteen women—"

"The world deserves to know!"

"The world deserves nothing!" he roared. "Those girls deserve nothing. They are dead. They are past caring. And if you publish a story that exposes our kind to the world, then you will be dead, too. You will be ridiculed by your own press and then someone, somewhere, will come and kill you. I am not threatening; I am predicting, Natalie. And you cannot die. It is not acceptable."

She had turned pale as a sheet so the freckles stood out on her face and the color drained from her pursed lips. Still, her eyes didn't waver. "It's my job to find the truth."

Baojia stepped closer. "And it's my job to keep you alive."

He finally heard something from the other end of the line. Matt said, "Then the two of you better figure something out. You both want to stop this, so compromise. But Natalie, I have to second what Baojia was saying. If you publish this, someone will come for you. Most vampires around the world just want to live in peace and be left alone, but if they're threatened, they will protect their interests. And they won't take kindly to any human who tries to expose them. Do you think you're the first to try?"

Baojia didn't back away. He couldn't. Despite the fear in her eyes, he saw the resolve, too. She had a mission—a clear one—and part of him envied her that. He was a soldier by nature; he needed a purpose. It was just Natalie Ellis's bad luck that his current mission conflicted with hers, because he was going to keep the stubborn human alive, no matter how her behavior set him on edge. From the corner of his eye, he saw Luis push through the office door with a note. He held his hand out and the human brought it to him.

Glancing down, he read it quickly, knowing as he reached the end that things were only going to become more violent before this was over.

"Matt, Dez, we need to go."

The anger fell from Natalie's face and she looked at the note in his hand. "What's wrong?"

"Another body's been found in the desert. And this time the location is no accident."

CHAPTER EIGHT

THE ONLY ILLUMINATION was the yellow headlights of the old black Camaro as they sped into the desert. No lights on the dashboard. No radio hummed. Even the clock seemed to have stopped. She glanced at the shadowed face of the driver, a vampire. A vampire her friend swore would protect her. A vampire who could make water behave like a pet. A vampire who was really good at being quiet.

She slipped her hand in her pocket and pressed the button on her phone, quickly scrolling through her playlists to find the appropriate accompaniment to driving through the desert with an undead, bloodsucking creature of the night. He looked over when he heard the music.

"Elvis?"

She shrugged. "Elvis is always appropriate."

"I was wondering how long it would take you," he said.

"Hmm?"

"Most humans hate silence."

"Oh." She glanced at her phone. "Do you mind?"

"Not at all. I saw him in concert a number of times."

She tried, but she couldn't stop the snort. "George, are you familiar with the term 'mindfuck'?"

"Very familiar," he said with a low laugh.

"This night—the last week, in fact—I've been swimming in one."

"You'll get used to it."

Would she? She looked at his profile, barely discernible in the dark car. Glancing around, she asked, "So, all the lights and stuff in the car…"

"Shorted out at one point or another." He shrugged. "It's the only car I can drive without messing up the engine. I'm amazed the headlights still work. I don't need the other lights or dials, and I didn't want to bring Luis. Besides," he said and ran a hand along the dashboard, "this is a pristine 1968 Chevy Camaro. Far more character than that Mercedes Luis prefers."

"My dad would kill for this car." She said it without thinking. Why had she brought up her dad?

His voice was a low growl. "How do you know I didn't?"

Her stomach dropped.

"Kidding, Natalie. I bought it new."

She breathed again. "You can't joke about that kind of stuff."

"Why?" His face was invisible in the darkness. "Too soon?"

"Because you can't. And we need to talk about this whole judge, jury, executioner thing you think needs to happen. Whoever is killing these women, they're still a—"

"Human being? No, they're not. If it's a vampire who is doing this, he is a monster and deserves to die."

She bit her lip to stop the angry retort. If she was going to have any chance, she had to reason with him. "You're a vampire. Are you a monster?"

"I am a vampire who controls himself. Who feeds in small, non-harmful amounts from donors—most of whom are willing—"

"Most?"

He ignored her and continued. "I work very hard to keep my baser instincts in check, not only for my own self-interest, but for the safety of the humans and vampires around me. You would not want to see me unfed. That said, even if I was ravenously hungry, I would not be so far gone that I killed indiscriminately in large numbers like this vampire is doing. This is not hunger. This is something else. He is not a person, Natalie. Killing this vampire would be like putting down a rabid animal."

Silence fell as both of them stopped talking and the song switched. A ballad came on then, something beautiful and achingly sad.

"Natalie."

"What?"

She heard him shift and wondered why. Did vampires get cramped? Did they ache after sitting in the car for two hours? And where the hell were they going anyway?

"When the vampire bared his teeth at you in the bar—do you remember?"

Her pulse picked up and she flashed to the grotesque grin of the monster they called Tio. "Of course I remember," she whispered.

"What were you thinking in that moment?"

She blinked. Why was he asking this? "I… I wanted to run, but I knew I wouldn't be able to escape. I wanted… I just wanted someone…"

"Wanted what, Natalie?"

She shrank in her seat. "I wanted someone to get it away from me."

"And you didn't care how. If I had killed it, you wouldn't have felt remorse or guilt. Not in that moment. You would have been relieved. Those were your instincts talking. The same instincts you're going to have to learn to listen to if you want to survive in this world."

"I'm not sure I want to."

Natalie could feel his eyes glaring at her. She wasn't sure how, but she did.

"That's a stupid thing to say."

"Wha—?"

"Don't say you don't want to survive. Don't *ever* say that."

"That's not what I meant." She sighed. "I meant I'm not sure I want to be in *this* world. *Your* world."

"Too bad." His voice was harsh. "It's your world now. You don't have a choice."

You should always have a choice. She blinked back tears that threatened to spill from the corners of her eyes and stared straight ahead at the cracked road. Finally, she said, "Where are we going?"

"A casino."

"Oh yeah, 'cause there's only one of those in the state."

"It's the one out by the Salton Sea. My father owns it."

"I thought that was an Indian casino."

"It is." He added, "They might have needed a very private backer to get started."

"Ah. And your father is… you said something about Don Ernesto."

"Don Ernesto Alvarez is the immortal leader of Los Angeles and much of the Southwest. He used to control most of Northern Mexico, too, but he ceded control of that territory to the new cartel some time ago."

"Why?"

"He says economic interests had waned for him." Baojia shrugged. "I did not question him."

"And he's your father?"

"In the immortal sense, yes. He sired me."

"How?" She wondered when he would get tired of her questions. He had way more patience than most people she met.

"He found me, drained my blood to the point of death, then fed me his own."

He said it so matter-of-factly. "So, he killed you."

"No. He *sired* me. I was not unwilling."

"Why?" She turned toward him. "Why would you do that? You'll never see the sun again. You'll never have a family. You'll have to drink human blood for the rest of your life." Luis had filled her in on the particulars. Immortality definitely had its downsides.

He glanced at her. "He offered me something, and it was worth the trade."

What had been the trade? Power, surely. And she could tell Baojia liked the power. He would never age or grow weak like a human man. But she didn't get the sense he was vain, despite his handsome face. Fastidious, maybe. He did seem to like things in their proper place. His house had been immaculate. And he'd changed from the rather delicious practice pants he'd been wearing earlier into an immaculate black suit with a white button-down shirt. He'd left off the tie so it hung open at the throat. His shoes were expensive. His neatly cut black hair didn't have a strand out of place.

But vain? No, she didn't think so. He was a creature of habit who took his human facade very seriously. If she hadn't seen him practicing his martial arts with water whipping around him like it was an extension of his own limbs, she'd never have believed he was anything but a very handsome, very successful executive.

"Do you ever regret it?" she asked.

A lone street lamp lit up the car as they turned at an abandoned intersection, and she saw him blink. Then she felt the whisper of his fingers as they tucked a curl of hair behind her ear.

"Occasionally."

The neon lights of the casino still glowed. Cars still populated the parking lot. And Natalie could hear the telltale sounds of the electronic slot machines drift from the casino doors as they parked the Camaro out on the far side of the lot. She could see a few men gathered near a group of dumpsters, and most of them were smoking. She got out of the car and looked at her phone. It was three in the morning already.

"Are we going to have enough time before sunrise?"

Without warning, he was at her side. "I'll manage."

She'd never thought about it before. The sun rose when it rose. But Baojia had to know exactly how much time he had. His life depended on it. They started walking toward the men and she got out a camera that was stuffed in her purse. It was a compact digital with high resolution that could shoot in raw format. The best camera she could get for the size. It had come in handy more than once.

"You really don't need that," he said.

"Why not? And they haven't called the police yet?"

"I have really good eyes." He nodded toward the men. "And they know to call me first."

As they approached, the men glanced at them, then looked away. Without a word, the men stubbed out their cigarettes and walked away from the dumpsters; none of them looked at Baojia twice.

"Why are they going?"

"They're not needed."

Natalie put a hand on his arm and he halted immediately. "Baojia, if this isn't related to the other girls—"

"Then I will tell the casino manager to call the human police, who will investigate thoroughly and receive full cooperation from all employees of the casino and everyone else in our organization." His face was still severe, but she noticed a slight softening around his dark eyes. "Further, if this is an employee—Luis said no one recognized her, but I will check—her family will be well taken care of."

It was the best she could hope for; she knew it. "Okay."

"But if this is what I think it is, we're not calling the police." He glanced at her phone. "Don't even think about it. I'll lock you up someplace very secure. You know I will."

Her eyes narrowed and she shoved her phone back in her pocket. "Fine."

"Now, stay here while I take a look first."

"Don't take too long."

He smiled. "Bossy. And trust me, I'll be fast."

Natalie could have sworn he just disappeared. One moment he was standing in front of her, the next he wasn't.

"That's so weird."

"I heard that!" He was standing near the dumpsters, looking at something on the ground behind him. "Stay back for now. I need to… get a sense of things."

He darted around, a blur that slowed occasionally so she could make out his form. Trailing around the parking lot. Disappearing into the desert only to appear as a flash under a streetlight again. Natalie glanced around nervously. Wasn't he afraid of others seeing him?

As if he could read her mind, he appeared at her side, straightening the cuff of one black sleeve. "I don't worry about people around here. They see what they want to see."

"Is it a vampire? Did a vampire kill her?"

"Yes." He looked at her with a hint of trepidation. "You've seen dead bodies before?"

She walked toward the dumpsters. "I'm not squeamish."

"Natalie." He was still standing near the car as she turned to face him. "This was not your fault."

Her eyes widened and her heart raced as she turned back to the dumpsters. She started running. By the time she'd reached them, he was already there, bending over the girl. Natalie recognized her immediately. It was the waitress from Bar El Ruso, the one who had been so nervous, the one Natalie had pressured to talk.

"Oh, dammit." The waitress could have been sleeping. There wasn't a mark on her that Natalie could see. But her lips were blue and her skin was ghostly pale. "Her name was Socorro," Natalie said hoarsely. "She said her name was Socorro."

"This was not your fault."

"Well, we definitely know Ivan has something to do with all this."

His eyes were grim. "I guess we do. And he left the body on Ernesto's property for me to find. Which means he knows I'm aware of it, too. I suspect he's done his own digging into your background, so he'll have found out what you were working on."

She shook her head, walking away to stare down into the girl's lifeless face. "I need to get back to the city. My notes are at the office. I need to—"

"You're not going back to the city." His voice was clipped. "Not until this is over."

Natalie spun around, glaring at him. "Listen, mister. I know you think you're protecting me, and I know Dez and Matt said you were trustworthy, but you're not my boss. You're not my father. And you have no right to tell me what I can and can't—"

"Look at her," he said, his iron control slipping. He spun her around again, pointing at the dead girl on the ground. The grip on her arms wasn't bruising, but it was firm. "You were talking to this girl a little over twenty-four hours ago. Now she is dead. Do you think they would think twice about doing this to you? Do you see what can happen?"

"I knew this story was going to be dangerous when I took it on," she said. "Don't lecture me, I'm not a child." She pulled away and turned to face him.

"No, you're not." His voice was low and fierce. "You're an infuriatingly stubborn woman who has no survival instincts. You need to drop this and let me—"

"You need to not tell me what to do." She stepped closer, her chin jutting out as she got in his face. "Because trust me, that never goes well."

"Why won't you listen to me?" The anger dropped from his voice; it was pure confusion. "I don't want to have to force you or coerce you. I don't want to have to use my amnis to keep you safe."

"Then don't."

"I will if I have to."

His eyes raced over her upturned face and Natalie realized her heart was pounding. Fear. Anger. And an unmistakable hint of arousal. A faint memory of his lips teased her. Had they kissed that first night? Was she imagining it? Her body responded to his proximity; Natalie could feel the hair on the back of her arms rise and reach toward him.

Baojia's voice was hoarse when he said, "Natalie…"

She swallowed hard, looking away from him and to the dead waitress as she said, "Baojia, there are some things more important than my safety. Finding the truth about who is killing these girls is one of them."

He started to say something, only to stop and cock his head to the side. His eyes narrowed, then looked off into the distance toward something she couldn't see.

"What?" she asked. "What is it?"

"Remember when you said about mindfucks?"

"Yeah?"

"Get ready for another one." He grasped her hand in his and angled himself slightly in front of her as he squared his shoulders toward the edge of the desert.

"What are we—Oh, whoa." She felt the earth tremble beneath her. She should have known; apparently vampires were like dogs who could sense when earthquakes—

"His name is Tulio and he's mostly friendly."

Natalie blinked. "What?"

Instead of dying off, the earthquake was only growing stronger. And the sound...

"What is it?"

"Elements, remember?" His hand squeezed hers. "Not everyone controls water."

Elements. Water, wind, fire... *earth*. "Oh, shit!"

The air was knocked from her lungs when the ground opened up and a giant of a man emerged. He was six feet tall, at least, with straight black hair and a smudged face that bore distinctly Spanish features. A broad forehead and heavy brows hung over eyes that looked black in the night. He wore a pair of what looked like canvas work pants and the rest of his body bulged with muscle. No shirt. No shoes. The man took an arm and swiped at the sand that covered his face as he continued walking toward them. The earth that had opened up closed behind him when his feet touched the pavement.

"Baojia."

"Tulio."

The vampire bent down and scooped up the dead girl, cradling her in his arms like a child before Natalie could protest.

"Hey!"

Tulio paused for a moment, glancing at her before he looked back to Baojia. "Come to my place. You can bring your human if you want."

"We'll be there in a few."

"There's more."

Then Tulio walked back into the desert and disappeared beneath the sand.

"Holy cow." That's it. Natalie couldn't think of anything weirder than that.

"Holy gopher might be more fitting."

"How'd he do that?"

Baojia shrugged and tugged her hand, leading her back to the car. "He's an earth vampire. That's what they do."

They were back in the Camaro and bouncing over dirt roads when she finally asked, "What did he mean, 'your human'?"

"Caught that, did you?"

She rolled her eyes. "Well, I knew you were playing at something like that at Ivan's, but I assumed that was just to get us out of there."

"That's partially true."

"What do you mean partial—?"

"Humans in the vampire world have very important roles." He interrupted her, turning the subject, if not changing it completely. "We employ you more and more to deal with computers and technology that we cannot. You are necessary for those of us who have professional obligations during the day, like Luis works for me. And you are also…"

"Food."

He frowned at her. "Human beings are often our companions, as well as being employees. They provide company and yes, sustenance, too."

"Like a pet?"

"Trust me." His voice was suddenly hoarse and she glanced over to see the tips of his fangs peeking out as he watched her. "Not like a pet."

Natalie could feel the blush hit when she saw them. Apparently, fangs were stimulated by more than just hunger or violence, and suddenly, they seemed a little more interesting and a lot less scary. "Oh."

"Were you just looking at my fangs?"

"No!"

He laughed, a low, knowing chuckle that made her heart take off at a gallop. "Liar."

The rest of the trip to Tulio's was filled with silence as Natalie began cataloguing the questions she had for the odd man who had taken the girl's body without a murmur of protest from her vampire.

There's more.

More bodies? More to tell? There had to be more to tell, because he hadn't told them anything. She was assuming Tulio was not the murderer for several reasons. One, Baojia had seemed at ease with him, and he would probably know if Tulio was in league with Ivan. Two, the giant man —vampire—had picked up the dead girl with exquisite gentleness, not like someone who could kill and leave the body out by the trash. Three, Natalie had a gut reaction to the man, and it didn't say dangerous.

Of course, she'd trusted Baojia when she met him at the bar, and he'd turned out to be a liar, so maybe her gut wasn't as accurate as she thought. Or... maybe George was closer to Baojia than she was ready to admit.

She glanced at him in the moonlight. He was so determined to keep her safe. Maybe she was just an assignment to him. Or... maybe her first impression of him in the bar wasn't all that far off.

I never lied.

She didn't know what to believe anymore.

"Where does this guy live?" She hadn't seen a light for miles.

"Away."

"From what?"

"Everything." He smiled. "He's a bit of a hermit."

"A bit?"

Just when she thought she'd never see a sign of civilization again, Natalie spotted the shadow of an old truck and a barn leaning near some old sheep pens. The boards were broken-down and the barn was breaking apart, but the truck, though old, appeared in good condition. And when the car's headlights landed on it, she realized the barn was in better condition than she'd thought.

"Is this where he lives?"

Baojia smiled. "Sort of." He stopped the car and before she could open her door, he was there, opening it for her and helping her out. Then he nudged her against the car and stepped closer, leaning down as if he were going to tell her a secret. But he didn't say anything; instead, she felt his breath blow cool on her neck and the skin of his jaw brushed against hers.

"Hey." She tried shoving him back, but he didn't move. "What are you —"

"Shhh," he whispered. "Quietly. Tulio thinks you are mine. This is good and will protect you. But you don't smell like me, which he will notice unless I mark you."

She couldn't speak; the unmistakably erotic images the feel of his skin on hers brought to mind choked out rational thought. "But—"

"I'm not going to bite you." Baojia's voice was a low growl. He had never sounded less human. She shivered when his lips brushed her neck. His fingers teased the tiny hairs at the nape of her neck. "I am only going to mark you."

She let out the breath she'd been holding and managed to speak. "If you lift your leg on me, I'm gonna kick you in the balls."

He laughed again; she could feel his lips smile against her skin. He pulled back for a second and his face was illuminated by the dim moonlight. Eyes dark and focused on her neck. Fangs long and gleaming. She could see the edge of his tongue when he flicked it against the tip of one tooth, but he only bent down to her neck on the other side, stroking his cheek along hers like...

A cat, she thought with a sudden smile. He was brushing his skin along hers like a cat looking for a friendly pat. Without thinking, she lifted her hand and stroked along the back of his neck, feeling the thick black hair under her fingers as his body shuddered, then stilled.

Before she could blink, he pulled back; his jaw clamped shut and his nostrils flared.

Okay. Not a cat.

He let out a slow, even breath and said, "Careful."

"Right." Her voice was high and she could feel herself blushing again. "Stop that."

"What? Blushing?"

"Yes. The scent on your skin becomes more enticing."

"The more you talk about it, the worse it's going to get. I don't exactly have control over it. Trust me, I wish I did."

He muttered something else she couldn't hear, then tugged her away from the car and toward the barn. "Let's go see Tulio. You'll be fine. Last time I checked, he had his own woman."

She rolled her eyes. "How very caveman of him."

He only laughed. "You have no idea."

Chapter Nine

BAOJIA TRIED TO IGNORE Natalie's scent as they approached Tulio's strange house. The blush made her cheeks heat and her blood-scent stronger. He couldn't help wondering just how much of her body that blush would cover if properly encouraged. He was betting a lot. Perhaps that was something else the clever little human would like to help him investigate.

He took a deep breath and focused on the reason they had come to the hermit's home.

"Tulio likes to be left alone, but in his own way, he considers this whole area his territory." He grasped Natalie's hand a little tighter and walked toward the low rise of hills behind the barn. "Not that he would ever challenge Ernesto—he has no interest in business or politics—but he doesn't like strange people or vampires wandering around."

"So he'd notice someone dumping bodies on his front lawn?"

The woman had the most amusing way of stating things at times. "Exactly."

"So when he said 'There's more.' You think that's what he was referring to? More bodies? If Tulio doesn't like vampires wandering around and there are more bodies—maybe some that the police haven't found but he has—why hasn't he stopped them? It sounds like it would be characteristic of him, from what you've said."

He grimaced. The human was becoming more attractive with every intelligent observation. "Yes, he would stop them. If he knew where they were. But I also noticed there was no strong vampire scent around the girl's body."

"I thought you said she was killed by a vampire."

"She was." He saw the entrance and stood back, letting their host become aware of them in his own time. Baojia glanced at the dark, empty horizon; he was beginning to worry about the sun.

"But you said—"

"There was vampire scent all over the body." Tulio's voice broke through the night. Good, he wasn't wasting time on power displays. He hardly needed to; they were on his turf. The vampire's head popped up from the crease of hills where his home was buried. "But there's no scent of our kind leading to or away from the bodies."

"They were dumped during the day," Baojia said, nodding at Tulio and still holding on to Natalie's hand.

Natalie's eyes widened in understanding. "Left by humans, not vampires."

"Yes." The big vampire waved them over. "Come on in. Bring your woman. Cirilda has some food made for her."

He climbed up the hill and then over to see a small door, barely visible if you weren't looking, tucked into the sandstone rocks and partially obscured by a convenient stand of mesquite bushes. Tulio was disappearing inside.

"Wow. It's like a dugout," Natalie said.

"It *is* a dugout. Earth vampires like to live underground."

"Well, that makes sense… inasmuch as any of this makes sense."

He smiled. "You'll get used to it."

Baojia ushered her over the hill, ducking inside before her out of caution. It was a spacious room hollowed out of the sandstone hills, far cooler than the air outside. Smooth walls had been decorated with beautiful woven clothes and pictures he suspected Tulio's human had painted. Two dark passageways led farther back in the hill, but the room was lit by gas lamps and a few candles, creating a cozy, welcoming home. Their host was sitting at a large wooden table with his woman, a Tarahumara Indian from Copper Canyon in Northern Mexico, who was pouring a mug of something from a clay jug. He motioned to the two chairs across from him as Cirilda moved back to the small kitchen area in the corner.

"My woman will get you some water."

It was more than just a friendly gesture from the vampire. Since Baojia was a water vampire and could use any water as a weapon, an offer of it was a gesture of trust, so he nodded in thanks. "I thank you, Tulio."

"No need to be formal. What's your human called?"

She spoke up for herself. "I'm Natalie."

"Natalie, you may help Cirilda if you like."

"Excuse me?"

Baojia grabbed Natalie's hand, squeezing before she exploded at the man. Cirilda, who looked to be in her early fifties, barked something over her shoulder that made the other vampire smile, and Baojia knew Tulio was teasing in his own odd way. "My woman's skills don't lie in the kitchen, Tulio. But thank you for the offer."

Natalie made an odd whining sound that told him she was biting her tongue.

He cleared his throat and dove into the issue at hand. "There are more bodies."

Tulio nodded. "Thirty-four. All dropped off during the day. Usually in groups of three or four. Sometimes more. I buried them; Cirilda said words so their spirits could rest."

"Thirty-four?" Natalie whispered, as horrified as he was.

"Are all of them marked as she was?" Baojia asked.

"Marked?" Natalie said. "I didn't see anything. Marked how?"

Tulio looked to him, letting Baojia explain. "There were multiple bite marks on the girl, Natalie. They had been healed by vampire blood, which can mend surface wounds. That's why you couldn't see them, but they are visible to our sight for some time."

He saw Tulio lift an eyebrow in his direction and knew the other vampire had spotted the faint bite marks that were still visible on Natalie's neck. Luckily, the man didn't say anything.

"So more than one vampire drank her blood," she said. "Is that normal? It seems like you all don't share very well from what I've seen."

"Smart girl," Tulio said. "No, it's not normal. But then something in her blood isn't all that normal, either."

Baojia looked at him. "So it wasn't just me?"

"No. And the other girls were the same. There's something… sour about their blood. What's left of it. Smells fermented almost."

"That's what I thought, too." He didn't know how old Tulio was, but it was far older than him. "Have you ever—?"

"No. Never smelled anything like it."

Natalie said, "Could there be something different about these girls? Something about their blood that makes the vampire feeding from them lose control?" She looked between Baojia and Tulio. "Like a drug or something? Alcohol? Speed? And are you sure it's more than one vampire, or could it be multiple bites from the same one?"

Her constant questioning may have been irritating at times, but Natalie Ellis asked *good* questions. He supposed that's what made her so successful at her job.

"Human drugs don't do anything to us," Tulio said. "It's something else."

"And it's definitely more than one," Baojia said. "The bite marks were different sizes and widths. This isn't a single vampire. It's more like a pack."

"Is that normal?" Natalie asked. "To… hunt that way?"

"Depends on the vampire," Tulio said. "Most earth vampires like me are more social. So sometimes those who hunt animals hunt in packs for fun. But humans? I would say no. Not for ages. It takes a depraved sort to hunt humans like that. I'm not saying it never happens, but I wouldn't call it normal. Not these days, anyway."

Baojia could see Natalie shudder and knew she was imagining it. Perhaps bringing her to Tulio's wasn't the best idea after all. The man could be overly blunt. Still, she gathered her resolve and continued to question him.

"But you said they were brought in by humans, so there had to be someone organized enough to arrange it. And how would they even—"

"Trucks." Tulio was looking at him again. "I've noticed there are tracks near a lot of the dump sites. Big rigs. Could be a container truck or something like that."

Baojia hummed. "There's certainly no lack of those out here. A container truck would blend in more than an out-of-place pickup."

Their host nodded and Baojia sipped the water Cirilda had placed in front of him. It refreshed him but also reminded him they were running short on time. "I don't want to cut our visit short, Tulio—"

"You're not going to make it back to the casino by dawn," he said, as if reading Baojia's thoughts. "You'll have to stay here. I have secure rooms that lock from the inside. You'll be safe."

"Thank you." It was probably the best they could do. He wondered where Natalie was going to sleep.

"You share a day chamber with your woman?"

Natalie's face colored with that damn blush again. "You know, I'm not his—"

"No, I don't. Is there someplace for her to rest, as well?" He'd have to make sure to keep the keys with him so she didn't escape during the day. As for safety while he was sleeping, there was a shotgun hanging over the door and he knew for a fact Cirilda knew how to use it. It was all the guarantee he'd get. Luckily, they were out in the middle of nowhere, and all the truly dangerous things would be sleeping while the sun was up. Baojia doubted anyone could find this place, even if they were looking.

"Wait." Natalie was already protesting. "I'm just gonna be stuck out here all day while you guys… hibernate, or whatever you do?"

He heard Cirilda laugh.

Baojia said, "I'm sure Tulio has a library."

"Forget it! I'm not staying out in the middle of nowhere all day!"

"Fine." Baojia nodded toward the door, knowing she wasn't stupid enough to actually leave. "Good luck finding your way back. Hopefully, I'll be able to find you at nightfall. Try to watch out for the roaming packs of vampires."

"Jerk," she muttered, grabbing her purse and standing. "Do I at least get a room with a lock? Is there a bathroom?"

Cirilda walked over and patted Natalie's cheek, muttering something in her native tongue that made Tulio laugh. Baojia didn't speak Tarahumara, but he smiled anyway. "Sleep as much as you can. You might be surprised how late you rest with no sun to wake you."

Angry eyes met his. He was sure she'd try to get him back in some way before this was all over. Oddly enough, he was amused by the thought. He wondered just what tortures Natalie Ellis could dream up in her busy little brain. Then his thoughts wandered off into other, more dangerous, territory as he watched her follow Tulio's woman down a passageway. Her rounded hips swayed as she walked, and she tossed him one last furious glance over her shoulder.

Yes, that kind of revenge was certainly worth imagining.

"You'll have your hands full with that one," Tulio said quietly. "You've bitten her, but she's not yours."

"Yet."

"Looking for a challenge?"

Baojia shrugged. "I hate being bored."

The earth vampire just laughed.

When he woke the following night, the first thing he heard was her voice.

"Nobody knoooooows… the trouble I've seen…"

He frowned for a moment until he placed the song. Then Baojia had to bite his lip to keep from laughing.

"Nobody knows my sorrowwww…"

He rose from the small pallet in the narrow room with multiple locks and stood, arms crossed, listening to her sing the jailhouse ballad. Despite everything going on and the mess they'd both landed in, she made him smile.

"Noboooody knows the trouble I've seen. Glooory, hallelujah."

He slipped down the hall to see her lying on a sofa, swinging one leg over the edge as she stared at the earthen ceiling. Her eyes lifted to his.

"Good evening, Natalie."

"Evening, jailer. If'n I had a metal cup and bars, I'd be rattling my cage, but sadly, I do not."

Baojia couldn't help it, he burst out laughing. She rolled her eyes, then stared back at the ceiling. He approached, eyeing her stretched out on the couch, the pale sliver of her stomach peeking out from the edge of her T-shirt and her red curls spread around her face. Her fury from the night before had fled. She looked relaxed and decidedly more well-rested. Even more, there was no hint of fear in her expression.

Which was good, because he wanted her.

Baojia sat on the end of the couch where she had laid her head and picked up a curl of her hair, twisting it around one finger. "It couldn't have been that bad."

"Cirilda doesn't speak English. I'm fairly sure she understands it, but she doesn't speak it, so when I finally woke up—I have no idea what time it is, by the way—I tried having a conversation with her, but she just smiled and nodded and fed me soup. It was really good soup, I'll give you that. Did you take my phone?"

He hummed, still twisting that curl around his finger. Her phone was history. He'd buy her another.

"Oh, and Tulio does have a library. A huge one, in fact. But the only books in English are some mining manuals and a travel guide to Barstow. Who the hell wrote a travel guide to *Barstow*?"

She was amusing. And she smelled wonderful. He was hungry. He hadn't fed for days and he knew he was dancing on the fine edge of control, but he didn't want to stay away from her. He dropped the curl he'd been playing with and picked up another, just as unruly. She was still rambling, but her pulse sped every time his fingers came close to her skin, so he knew his presence was affecting her. He smiled to himself when her nervous rambling continued. He could smell the flush on her skin.

"Are we leaving soon? If you're awake, then it must be nighttime, right? I'm so completely turned around. You took my phone, didn't you? Dammit, George, I had stuff on that phone. Are the pictures even retrievable at this point or did your vampire magic fry it?"

"Natalie," he whispered.

"What?" she asked in an irritated voice. "You took my phone, didn't you? That was *my* phone, Baojia. Not yours. Have some respect for—"

He put his hand over her mouth and took a deep breath. "Better."

She shoved it away and sat up, her color high and her mouth open in shock. "Do *not* cover my mouth like I'm a child! That's just—"

Baojia slid a hand to the nape of her neck, tugged her forward, and covered her mouth with his own. Her lips molded to his on instinct. She was delicious. Far better than his memory of the first night they'd met. She tasted of chiles and cumin and wine. Her body was stiff with shock and he took full advantage, sliding his other arm from the back of the couch up the curve of her spine to send her tumbling off-balance and into his chest.

"Much better," he said, pulling away for a second. Natalie's mouth opened in protest and he tugged her full lips back to his, biting lightly on the lower one until she opened her mouth, then he slid his tongue inside, teasing along hers until she was panting. She straddled his legs on the couch, her hands trailing up his biceps to grip his shoulders as her nails dug into his skin. The tiny bites of pain triggered a primitive thrill. He could feel the heat where he held her at the small of her back and his fingers slid into her riotous hair, twisting and tangling those red waves until her heart was pounding. He could feel it against his chest.

Alive. She was so alive and Baojia felt as if he'd been cold for so long. He could hear his own silent heart thump once against hers. He wanted her. Needed her.

Needed her?

The low growl built in his throat, and his fangs fell down, nicking the edge of her lip.

"Ow!" She gasped and pulled away, her mouth red and swollen. His eyes narrowed on the tiny trickle at the corner of her mouth.

"Let me…" He pierced his tongue and licked up, sampling the heady flavor of her blood and the salt on her skin as he healed the tiny cut. He wanted more. "Natalie—"

"Stop," she whispered, placing a hand on his chest. "Are you going to bite me?"

He stilled immediately. "Do you want me to?"

"I… I don't…" Her eyes were round and uncertain. "I don't know."

He groaned and pulled her close, leaning his forehead against hers as he tried to gather his control. She was frightened. This wasn't the way it should be.

"One day," he said in a low voice, "I want you to crave my bite."

She blushed again; he stopped breathing. Her scent was too tempting.

"Does… I mean, doesn't it hurt?"

As if on cue, a low satisfied moan of female pleasure echoed down the hall from Tulio's chamber. Baojia looked at Natalie, who had turned toward the noise, her mouth falling open a little.

"No," he said. "It doesn't."

"Oh. I didn't think…" She backed away, untangling from his arms, distancing herself. "I mean, she's so much older than him."

Baojia cocked his head in confusion until he remembered that Cirilda was probably in her fifties. "He is far older than her, Natalie."

"Oh." She shook her head. "Of course. I just… She looks older, so it's kind of confusing."

Humans were often strange about age. They put so much stock in appearance. "Remember to not judge their relationship by human standards. They have been together many years. I know he's very fond of her. I doubt her age troubles him except as a reminder that their time is limited."

He saw her look thoughtfully down the hall as the sounds of carnal pleasure turned to more intimate, muffled conversation. He heard a low laugh from Tulio, then another quick exchange between the vampire and his lover.

"He wouldn't make her a vampire?" she asked quietly.

"No. If he did, it would change their feelings toward each other. It is a different kind of relationship and would break their connection as lovers."

"Someone else, though?"

He shrugged. He doubted there were any immortals Tulio trusted enough to change Cirilda. Any vampire who sired her would have her loyalty and an unbreakable bond for eternity, possibly interfering with her loyalty to him. "She may not want to become a vampire, Natalie. I don't know."

"What will happen to her?"

"I imagine he will take care of her until she dies, unless she wants to leave. He is an honorable man." Why was she so troubled? "Are you worried about her?"

She shook her head and moved farther away from him, which displeased him. "No. It's none of my business."

"But you are worried about something."

"I, uh…" She stood up and grabbed her purse. "I'm worried about the case. What's our next step? Are we leaving soon?"

She was lying, but she did have a point. They had little time to waste. He needed to drive to Los Angeles, find a safe place to keep her, then speak to his father. Ernesto wouldn't be pleased, but there was little he could do about that. This problem of the murdered humans had landed on his father's back porch, courtesy of a visitor from the south. It could be an isolated challenge to Ernesto's authority from a rebellious underling, or it could be a more dangerous test from the cartel. Either way, the time for sentiment was over. His father would have to deal with this, and he'd have to speak to Baojia.

"Wow." Her laugh was tense and nervous. "Whatever it is we have to do tonight, it doesn't seem like you're looking forward to it."

He stood up and walked to the kitchen to leave a note for Tulio. Who knew when the vampire would leave his bed? "Let's get on the road. We have a long way to drive tonight, and I have a meeting that can't be put off. Our host won't mind if we see ourselves out."

She was quiet in the car all the way to Los Angeles. She was quiet as they exited the freeway in Pasadena and headed toward Matt and Dez Kirby's house. She was just… quiet. Baojia almost wished she would start the incessant chattering again. His mind raced back to their kiss. That was when her behavior had changed. But she wanted him as much as he wanted her. Though she had backed away from his bite, she had been as affected by it as he had been. He was certain.

But perhaps he had been wrong. Perhaps she still feared him in some way. The thought sickened him. He had never taken a woman who was unwilling.

"Natalie?"

"Hmm?" She turned her head toward him, a polite distance in her eyes, and he realized what was wrong. Their kiss on the couch in Tulio's cave *had* affected her. But then came the questions. And if he'd learned anything about Natalie, it was that she didn't ask needless questions.

What will happen to her?

She hadn't been asking about Cirilda; she'd been asking about herself.

She was human. He was not. And she was pulling away from him before she got too close. If he was human, she would have taken him as a lover, perhaps more. But he was not human, and she was not a vampire. His eyes left hers and turned back to the road.

He had been wrong. Despite appearances, Natalie Ellis's survival instincts were very well honed.

Chapter Ten

HE JUST LEFT.

Baojia dropped her off at Dez and Matt's house, spoke a few words to Matt, then disappeared into the night. She should have felt relieved. For the first time in days, she didn't feel like she was being kept. And she was free of the annoying vampire who bossed her around, stole her phone, and kept her as a prisoner—albeit a very well-treated prisoner. She was at her friends' house, sitting in their kitchen, enveloped by warmth and light and people with pulses. But… the feeling of unease bombarded her as soon as his car pulled away.

"I feel like I'm going crazy," she said as she collapsed at the table. Dez sat across from her, rocking a sleepy Carina as Matt made her some tea.

"Welcome to my world." Dez reached across and squeezed Natalie's hand. "I'm so sorry you got pulled into this."

"I'm not," Matt said. "Well, I mean if you were going to pursue this story, I'm glad you got pulled in on this end and not when you were a body found out in the desert."

"Thanks, Matt."

"You're welcome." He set down the tea. "I'm not going to lie—you're not in a good position, Natalie. You know about the vampire world, but you're not employed by a vampire and you're not under anyone's personal aegis. You are—by your own admission—pursuing a story that could expose a lot of very dangerous secrets. And you've attracted the attention of a very unpredictable representative of the Mexico City cartel."

"Mr. Mysterio called me 'his' in front of the other vampire out in the desert. And the ones in Mexico. That mean anything?"

Matt shrugged. "Unless he's actually been biting you, that doesn't mean much." Suddenly he narrowed his eyes. "Has he?"

Natalie flushed and Dez slapped Matt's arm. "Matt!"

"What?" He stood and went back to the kitchen, still frowning. "It's a fair question."

"No. No biting. But Baojia promised to keep me safe." She swallowed the lump in her throat and asked the question that had been circling for days. "Can I trust him? Really?"

Dez nodded. "Totally trustworthy, Nat. He's the one who guarded Beatrice for years, and he guarded her grandparents. He's one of the good guys. If he promised to keep you safe, he'll keep you safe."

"As much as he can," Matt muttered.

"Hey!"

"Dez, you're used to hanging around Gio and Beatrice, both of whom are immortals answerable only to themselves. Baojia is not his own man. He's under Ernesto's aegis. If Ernesto wanted Natalie—even if Baojia has put her under his protection—he'd have to hand her over."

"Hand me over for what?" She lowered the mug she'd been about to drink from.

"Have your memory erased, most likely." Dez reached over and took her hand. "Ernesto is a very civilized guy." She shot her husband a glare when Matt snorted.

"Baojia said he wouldn't erase my memory again," Natalie said. "I don't want—"

"It wouldn't matter what you wanted," Matt said quietly. "Ernesto's a decent enough vampire, but he has one priority: Ernesto. If it doesn't serve his interest to protect you, then you'll be on your own."

"No, you won't," Dez said firmly. "Because you have friends."

"Dez…" Matt's voice was a warning.

"I know what you and Baojia talked about, but it's ridiculous for her to be staying here and not tell Gio and Beatrice."

"Wait, Beatrice?" Natalie put two and two together. "B? That's… Gio and Beatrice?" She felt the curl of panic in her stomach. "Who's Gio? And are you telling me?" Her voice was getting louder by the minute. Her heart was racing, and the room started to close in on her. Natalie tried to quiet down when she heard the baby start to whine, but Matt and Dez's comments from before suddenly hit her.

He's the one who guarded Beatrice for years…

Gio and Beatrice, both of whom are immortals…

Natalie whispered, "Are you telling me Beatrice De Novo is a vampire?"

She took Dez and Matt's silence as an affirmative.

Dez was pale. "Um… yeah, about that—"

"A vampire?" Natalie scooted back, looking around a kitchen that suddenly didn't seem so familiar, owned by people she thought she knew. Only those people didn't work for vampires or have best friends who turned into vampires. "She's a *vampire*?"

Matt said, "Dez, give me the baby. She's freaking out."

"She didn't used to be a vampire!"

Matt took the baby and Dez walked over to Natalie, putting a hand on her shoulder.

"Natalie, breathe." Dez's voice sounded like it was underwater, and Natalie jerked away from her touch.

Not real. Not real. *Not real.*

Every time she thought she had a handle on this crazy new reality, something else slapped her. She thought she knew these people, but she didn't know anything. Suddenly, she was desperate to see the one person in this weird new world who seemed normal despite everything. But he was gone. He'd left her. Was he coming back?

"Baojia…" She took deep breaths. "Where—?"

"He had to go to Ernesto's, Nat."

Breathe. Breathe. Breathe. He wouldn't abandon her. He'd be back. He promised. And for some crazy reason, she believed him. When he was there, she felt like herself. Even when the crazy happened, he made her feel like everything was going to be okay. He had to come back.

"Don't panic. You're going to be fine. It's all going to be fine."

"It's not going to be fine!" she screamed. "I don't want to know all this. I want to go home!"

The baby woke and started to cry. Matt took her out of the room while Dez put her arms around Natalie and made soothing noises in her ear.

"It's okay, Natalie. It's going to be okay."

"He needs to come back right now and take me home. And… and he needs to tell me what happened that first night."

Dez blinked in confusion and pulled back. "What are you talking about?"

"The one I can't remember. Every time I bring it up, he changes the subject. And I don't... I need to trust him." She was shaking, but at least the tightness in her chest had eased. "I feel like I'm losing my mind, Dez. I feel like this is a really bad dream I've been having for days, and I need... I just need to know I can trust him, because—"

She broke off. Why was it so important that she trust him? She was here, with her friends, but she wanted him. His silent, steady presence that made the impossible real.

Natalie remembered the feel of his hands teasing her hair on the couch at Tulio's. The dry, amused laughter when she made a joke. His fierce protectiveness. The sensual promise in his kiss. Running through it all was the current of desire that had caught her. If she was honest with herself, it had swept her up days ago when she'd bumped into him at the bar. How much was a lie? How much was the truth?

I never lied.

"I'm falling for him," she whispered, sitting down in the chair again. "And I can't."

Dez sat across from her. "For Baojia?"

"I can't. I can't. I'm so stupid. Of all the... He's not even human. I don't—"

"Just stop. One thing at a time." Dez pulled her into another hug. "I don't know what to say. I wish I knew what to say. Beatrice knows him better, but he and Gio don't get along, so—"

"Who's Gio?" Her voice sounded numb. "Why don't they get along?"

"Do you ever stop asking questions? It's a long story. And Gio is Beatrice's husband. They met back when she was in Houston, but then he left when she came out here for school. And... a bunch of stuff happened. They were married a few years ago."

"And Gio is a vampire."

"Uh huh."

"And so is B."

"They both are now."

Natalie let her head fall to the table and the tears come to her eyes. "I give up. Logic has no place in this world anymore. I'm falling down the rabbit hole. Taking the blue pill. Or the red one. Whatever."

Dez started rubbing small circles on her back. "You'll get used to it. I remember being pretty freaked out when Beatrice first told me. Want some wine?"

Wine sounded… like a pretty good idea, actually. "How many bottles do you have?"

As it turned out, just one bottle and Natalie was feeling significantly better.

"Wait, wait, wait…" She and Dez were sitting in the guest room on the second floor in their pajamas. Matt had already put the baby to bed and made a couple of phone calls before he gave Dez a kiss and retired for the night. "So, Beatrice De Novo is a *water* vampire now—"

"Uh huh."

"And she's married to a *fire* vampire?"

"He's kind of a badass."

"Fire and water." Natalie wiggled her eyebrows. "*Steamy*."

Dez burst into laughter. "And you're a little drunk."

"Not nearly enough, trust me." She closed her eyes and the pleasant buzz made her sigh. Wine made everything better. "He's a really good kisser."

"That's what I hear," Dez said, pouring another glass. "Oh, wait. You're not talking about Gio, are you?"

"Who's Gio?" She frowned. "Oh, right. Fire dude. No, not him."

"Baojia?"

She sighed and fell back into the pile of pillows. "Yes. I hate that he's so sexy."

"Why not just enjoy it? A good kisser, huh?"

"Very good. Very… thorough. I mean, when he kisses you, you feel *kissed*."

"That makes…" Dez laughed. "…complete sense."

"Hush. It does to me." Her head was spinning now, but she wasn't sure if it was from the wine or the memory of a very skilled mouth. With fangs.

"He has fangs. Am I going to cut my lips every time I kiss him? I'm not sure that's a good idea…"

Dez ignored her. "I saw him sparring with Beatrice once. No shirt. The view was very nice."

"Uh huh." She nodded. Maybe she needed to stop; it was getting a bit swirly up there. "That's right, B always did the martial arts, didn't she? I wonder if I should take some."

"Probably. It's good self-defense. And you might be able to convince someone to give you some one-on-one lessons." Dez grinned.

"Don't encourage me. You know this can't be healthy." She groaned and sat up again. "I should drink some water and go to bed. It's been a very long few days."

"You should." Dez stood up and collected the glasses while Natalie pulled back the covers and slipped into bed. "Sleep as long as you can. Trust me, with this bunch, sometimes sleep is hard to come by."

"Thanks for everything, Dez."

"No problem. You'll feel better in the morning."

"Yeah?" She shook her head. "Probably not. Because… he's still going to be a vampire, and I'm still going to be a human."

Dez walked to the door and opened it. "Hey, Nat?"

"Hmm?"

"I have no idea how he feels. He doesn't seem like the kind to wear his heart on his sleeve or anything. But… don't rule anything out, okay?"

Natalie had to fight back the urge to cry. Stupid wine. "He's not like us."

"No, he's definitely not." Dez's eyes suddenly took on a depth that the friendly blond woman rarely revealed. "But I've seen some pretty amazing things the past few years. And I know we're more alike than we're different."

More alike than different? Maybe.

Natalie nodded. "I'll try to keep that in mind."

When she dreamed that night, she was sitting in the sunlight next to him, and he was laughing.

"You're ridiculous," he said.

"You love it."

The smile made the corners of his eyes crease and his teeth flashed in the sun. "I do."

He leaned forward, brushing her mouth with his. Her arms opened to welcome him and he embraced her. His skin was warm from the hot summer sun. Brown and smooth under her fingers. He kissed her again and again, teasing her lips apart as he played with a lock of hair at her temple. They were on the beach; she could hear water in the background and the sand was warm under her legs.

He pulled away, put his hand on her shoulder and shook her. "We have to go."

She frowned. He wasn't laughing. He looked deadly serious, and he said it again.

"We have to go."

Natalie blinked awake. The moon was still visible from the corner of her eye and the room was dark. Baojia was standing over her, a hand on her shoulder, shaking her awake.

"Natalie, we have to go now."

Chapter Eleven

BAOJIA WAS STILL FEELING a sense of unease as he drove away from the Kirbys' comfortable, secure home. Matt was almost as paranoid as he was about safety, and the human had just become a father. The house had the best security money could buy, complete with surveillance, motion and heat sensors, and an armed guard that Mrs. Kirby probably didn't know about. It was obvious Matt took no chances with his family. There were only a few places more secure in the city of Los Angeles, and those had systems Baojia had designed himself.

No, it wasn't Natalie's safety that had him uneasy. It was the distance in her eyes. It set his teeth on edge. Her silence in the car had annoyed him. Her eagerness to leave his presence at her friend's house had annoyed him. And the fact that he was so irritated about her mood annoyed him.

"I'm brooding more than the Italian," he muttered, steering the car toward Long Beach. He hadn't called or announced his presence in LA. He knew from talking with Rory the night before everything fell apart in Mexico that Ernesto was staying in the house in Long Beach. When Baojia showed up, he'd just have to talk to him. He saw the guard's eyes widen when his car pulled up.

"Good evening, sir. Is Mr. Al—"

"Open the gate, Jim. He's not expecting me, but I need to talk to him."

He stared the human guard down. It only lasted a few minutes. Sad. That was far too easy. The man would have to be replaced. As he parked the car and walked into the house, he noticed all sorts of areas that needed improving.

"Outside perimeter is weak," he said quietly. "Not enough lighting or guards."

He brushed past the humans at the door. "Too many humans; not enough vampires." What the hell was Rory doing?

Baojia knew the minute the real security caught him. Thank God someone was actually working. He was halfway to the library before a real impediment emerged.

"Baojia." His second-in-command, Nicholas, held up a hand. "Please wait."

"Ridiculous." Baojia snorted. "If I was trying to break in and harm him—"

"You're preaching to the choir on that one," his former assistant murmured. "But you know there's not much I can do."

"I'm glad *you're* here, at least. Let him know it's me and I have to talk to him."

"You know he won't be pleased."

"Of course I do. Which should tell you how serious this is."

Nick nodded for two younger vampires to come stand on either side of him. "I'll go announce you."

"Fine."

"Please don't kill the boys if I take too long. They're new, and I'm still training them."

He rolled his eyes. "Just go, Nick."

The younger vampire disappeared toward the library and Nick's two foot soldiers stared at him in silent awe. At one point, he leaned toward the library, just to see them jump. He was still wearing the twin blades he had taken to Mexico. Nick had forgotten to check him for weapons, which was foolish. He'd have to speak to him about that. A few minutes later, he heard steps coming down the hall and a familiar energy reached out.

"Paula."

"*Hermanito.*" She made a quick motion and the two guards departed. "What are you doing here?"

"I have to see him. Is he in the library?"

"What happened at the casino last night? Jared called me in a panic. There was a young woman killed?"

"That's what I need to speak with him about."

She looked flustered, which didn't seem right. "Well, why didn't you call Rory? If you'd gone through him—"

"Paula, I need to speak to my sire." His words became clipped. "Is he in the library? I'll deal with his temper."

Nick's voice broke in. "Baojia?"

"Yes?"

"He's waiting."

Baojia frowned as Paula stepped away from him. She did not follow him, but turned and walked in the direction of her office. He smothered the fleeting hope he'd felt for a moment when he'd seen her face. He hadn't been face-to-face with his sire in almost three years. Baojia had hoped for months the invitation would come. Had hoped he would be forgiven and welcomed back. But he knew whatever eventual homecoming happened, his father would not forgive this impertinence. Baojia had been sent away; it was up to Ernesto to set the terms of his return. By appearing like this, he might never be welcomed back as an honored son.

He took a calming breath. His sire's reputation and safety were more important than Baojia's own position. He walked toward his fate with resolve.

When Nick opened the door, Baojia saw him. The rush of affection was natural, the blood in his veins recognized the immortal who had given him life. But layered upon that were years of devotion and respect. "Father?"

Ernesto did not look up from his seat behind his desk.

"Father, I ask your forgiv—"

"Why do you come to my home when you have not been called?"

The sting was immediate and ripping. He swallowed the hard lump in his throat. "I must tell you—"

"There was a human murdered and her body dumped near the Salton City casino. Your brother has already informed me. What did you do with the body? The human authorities should have been contacted. This is not a concern of mine."

"But it is."

"I am told it is not."

Baojia frowned. "Who has told you this?"

His father finally looked up. "What have you done with it, Baojia? Why are you going against protocol? The human police should have been called."

"There is something very wrong here. I did not take her body, Father. Tulio did, along with the others."

He heard his sire start to grumble. "That meddling hermit. I should kick him out of my territory."

"I would not advise that."

"And what would you advise?" His voice rose. "Going down to Ensenada after foolish women? Attacking a rival organization's guards? Confiding in a *newspaper reporter*?"

It was worse than he'd anticipated. "If you would let me explain—"

"Explain what?" Ernesto's anger was legendary, as loud as his child's was silent. His voice echoed through the house, and Baojia could hear the guards scurry to the door.

"There are humans being murdered in the desert by vampires," Baojia said, keeping his voice even and calm. "Bodies have been dropped on your land like some dog pissing on a tree, marking his territory. Whoever is doing this is threatening you, your reputation, and everyone under your aegis. Father, you have to listen—"

"Do not call me your father as you stand before me, insulting me with your presence!"

Baojia could not breathe. The pain radiated from his chest as Ernesto rose to his feet.

Ernesto continued on. "Do you think I am incapable of seeing what is before me? Do you think I need you to tell me what is and isn't a threat?"

He forced himself to speak. "Someone in the cartel—it might only be Ivan, but it could be more—is testing you."

"Stop trying to justify yourself and leave my presence. Maybe someday I will forgive this disrespect."

"There is something very wrong with the bodies of these girls." He looked at the floor, swallowed back the lump in his throat, and kept talking. "Packs are feeding from them—"

"Get out."

"—and their blood is tainted by something that makes it—"

"I will have your own men remove you, if I must."

"You must listen to me!" Baojia roared, raising his voice to his sire for the first time in over 120 years. He raised his eyes and met Ernesto's shocked stare. Slowly, the shock fell away to be replaced by a cold expression.

"You will bring this reporter—the woman from Mexico—to me. Leave her here and return to San Diego."

His own temper, so long buried, roused itself. "I will not."

Ernesto stared at him, his eyes narrowing as he bared his fangs. "You will do this, or I will have it done."

Baojia let his lips curl back, his own fangs long in his mouth. "No, you will not."

Slowly, his sire's face fell, shock returning as he stared at his child. "Baojia?"

His silent heart thumped in his chest as he stared back. His sire would not listen to him. Ernesto had tied his hands behind his back, crippling Baojia from safeguarding those he had vowed to protect: Natalie, his sister, even Ernesto himself.

He had only one recourse. "Ernesto Alvarez, I have been your loyal child for one hundred twenty-nine years—"

"Do not do this."

"—I have served you faithfully and without question for all that time, as honor demanded."

"You cannot take this back," his father hissed. "Once this is done, it cannot be undone. *Think*."

"I have," he said, the pain flooding his chest as bloody tears came to his eyes. "I ask to be released from your aegis this night."

"Foolish boy." Ernesto shook his head. "You foolish, foolish boy. After all I have done for you."

He ignored the tears that tracked down his cheeks and lifted his chin proudly. "Sire, do you release me as I have asked?"

Ernesto let out a long breath. "I release you, Chen Bao Jia, as you have requested. Leave my aegis this night."

It hurt. Even knowing it was the only way, it ached to hear his father say the words that cut him off from the only family he had known since boarding a boat a world away.

With an air of finality, Ernesto said, "I owe you no protection. You owe me no fealty. Leave this place and do not come back."

He forced his lips to form the appropriate words. "Thank you, Don Ernesto Alvarez. May honor sustain you, even as I leave your clan."

Baojia's eyes rose to Ernesto's one last time. Then he turned and left the room.

He did not stop at the door. He did not stop at the gate. Ernesto would have to tell his sister she was not his sister anymore. Baojia drove aimlessly through the black streets of Los Angeles, suddenly realizing that for the first time in over one hundred years, he had no mission. None. No protection. He was fair game for any challenger. No human under his aegis could seek refuge or help from Ernesto's clan. No backup was coming if he got into a fight.

The woman from Mexico.

Natalie. Ernesto knew about Natalie. She was the only one directly under Baojia's aegis, the only human he had publicly claimed, and now her safety was at risk, not only from Ivan and whoever was working with him, but possibly from Ernesto himself. He didn't think his sire would physically harm the human unless she threatened him in some way. And Natalie wasn't likely to threaten a vampire…

Never mind. He closed his eyes in frustration. She'd threaten him.

Ivan was bound to hear that he wasn't in Ernesto's clan soon, then he'd make his move, backed up by the cartel. As a newly independent vampire, Baojia had no confirmed allegiance or established allies. And custom dictated he shouldn't linger in Ernesto's territory for longer than was necessary to get his personal business in order. Added to that, he had a human woman he had become responsible for. The idea of disappearing into the night to start a new life on his own was no longer an option.

Baojia raced through different scenarios, most of them ending with Natalie and him both dead, until he settled on one that had a chance of working. It wouldn't be pleasant, but he'd at least survive long enough to make sure Natalie would be safe. Turning back toward Pasadena, he gritted his teeth and prepared for the night to get even worse.

He parked a block away, knowing that approaching on foot would be less threatening. As he neared the gate, he heard the fluttering sound overhead and the slight smoky smell that permeated the grounds. By the time he was in sight, the Italian was already leaning against a brick pillar, his guard vampire perched on top with her legs crossed under her and an enormous smile on her face.

"I told you," she said.

Baojia halted across the street, hands hanging in his pockets as he stared at the fire vampire who stared back.

This was going to suck.

"Giovanni Vecchio," he said. "I need your help."

"Natalie, we have to go now."

He hated to wake her, but it was close to dawn and though Vecchio's house was only a few blocks away, he needed to make sure Natalie was secure and out of Matt and Dez's house before he could rest for the day. The last thing he wanted on his conscience was the human family coming into harm's way because of their presence.

"Natalie."

She murmured something and rolled over. "In the sun. Can't be in the sun."

She saw her eyes flutter open and an unexpected warm rush filled his chest. She was so vulnerable. And beautiful. He brushed the hair out of her face.

"You need to wake up. You can go back to sleep soon, but we have to move first."

"You're handsome when you smile, you know."

Baojia felt the corners of his mouth turn up. "And you're beautiful when you're sleepy. But you need to wake up."

He rose and began tossing her things into the duffel bag he'd taken from her house. Had it only been three nights ago?

"What are you doing?" She finally sounded more awake.

He tried to make his voice as businesslike as possible. "I have been forced to leave my father's aegis. We need to move. I have found a safe place for us to go right now. I don't want the Kirbys to come to any harm because of us being here. It's not far away, and I upgraded the security on the house a few years ago, so I know it's very safe."

"Baojia—"

"Dez will be able to come and visit you there with no problem, but the Kirbys are not vampires, so I don't want to put them in a bad position.

It's complicated. Political. The place we're going… It's neutral territory. Sort of."

"Why did you leave your father's aegis? What does that mean?"

The unexpected question caused him to halt. "It means I am no longer his son. Please don't ask me why right now. Please just wake up and get dressed and cooperate, Natalie." He turned around when she didn't make a smart comeback. She was looking at him with eyes that saw far more than he had intended to reveal. "I'm just trying to keep you safe."

She finally nodded. "Okay."

He left the room so she could dress. Within a few minutes, she had pulled on a pair of jeans and a T-shirt along with her running shoes.

"Are you cold?" he asked. "Do you need a jacket? I didn't get you a jacket."

"I'm fine."

She held her duffel bag, which he grabbed from her hand. As she started toward the stairs, he pulled her back and laid a searing kiss on her mouth. He felt her hands reach up to his cheeks, gripping his cool skin as he kissed her ravenously, almost desperately.

I will keep you safe. I made a promise, and I do not break my promises.

Finally, he broke away and wrapped his free arm around her, burying his face in the soft skin of her neck. He took a deep breath, inhaling her scent. It centered him. Her hands remained on him, stroking his hair and playing with the collar of his shirt. For a brief moment, he felt her warmth seep into his skin and allowed himself the luxury of her touch.

"Do you need to drink?" she asked quietly.

"No. Matt had some bagged blood he gave me earlier. I'm fine."

"Okay."

"We should go." He pulled away and grabbed her hand, walking her down the stairs and out the front door. Matt was there to lock up behind them; Baojia paused at the door. "Matt, my thanks. If there is any assistance I can offer you or your family in the future, it is yours."

The human smiled. "Thank you. Good luck. Be safe. And don't kill anyone I like."

Despite the grim situation, Baojia had to smile. "I'll do my best."

CHAPTER TWELVE

WHEN NATALIE WOKE, she was resting on dove-gray sheets in another room she could barely remember entering. She was still in her T-shirt from the night before, though her jeans had been pulled off and her hair fell loose around her face. A note with her name written neatly on the front lay next to her, illuminated by a shaft of sunlight from the window.

> *Natalie,*
> *Hopefully, you will get enough sleep. You are safe here, and I'll see you as soon as I wake. Please make yourself at home here, but do not leave the house. There are humans and vampires here who can see to any need you have while I am resting.*
> *Baojia*

She took a deep breath and tried to remember the previous night. Waking had been a blur. She hardly remembered getting dressed or packing. He'd kissed her—she remembered that. He'd been... upset. It was hard to tell with him, but she would have sworn he was deeply, deeply troubled. When he'd kissed her by the stairs, it had almost seemed desperate, and her only thought was that she wanted to comfort him. Probably ridiculous when she'd been such a basket case herself.

She'd been barely conscious when they pulled up to the luxurious home only a few blocks from Dez and Matt's. She had faint memories of thick hedges and a wrought-iron gate. A fountain and a dimly lit kitchen. At some point, Baojia had picked her up in his arms and simply taken her to a bed—it must have been the one she was sleeping in—because she couldn't remember much else except his whispered voice in her ear.

Rest, Natalie. I'll be close by.

Where was he? Where did he sleep? In a bed like this in a room with no windows? Did he breathe? Did he need to? He was so... inhuman. So how had he become so familiar?

Natalie groaned and rolled over, burying her head in the cool sheets. They were safe. For now, at least. She needed food and a shower, maybe then she could get her feet under her. Sitting up, she surveyed the room she'd been sleeping in. It had sage-green walls with warm mission-style furniture. Her mangy duffel bag was sitting on top of a dresser with a bottle of water and fresh flowers placed next to it. She saw two doors, one of which she hoped was a bathroom. Rolling out of bed, she walked to the window, enjoying the sunlight streaming into the room.

Her room was on the second floor of what looked like a luxurious, Spanish-style house. Mansion might be a little too grand of a term, but not by much. The grounds were surrounded by a wall and a hedge she could just barely see over, and fruit trees and roses dotted a yard with ponds, fountains, and a large swimming pool.

"Beautiful." She blinked. Where on earth was she? Lifestyles of the Rich and Fangy? This couldn't be Baojia's sire's house, so where had they landed? She looked around the room again and walked to the painting that hung over the dresser.

"Georgia O'Keefe. I think... that's not a reproduction." She moved her duffel bag farther away from the priceless painting, somehow thinking it might explode and spray her bargain wardrobe all over it. "Holy shit. Holy shit, Natalie." Baojia's house in San Diego had been nice, but simple. This place...

She peeked in the bathroom. "Marble tub. Of course there's a marble tub." She let out a deep breath and surveyed her surroundings. In the past three days, she'd woken in a strange oceanfront house, what could only be called a cave, and now this. She shrugged. "Nicest prison so far. I must be moving up in the world."

Grabbing her bag, she made sure the other door was locked and went to the bathroom, mentally taking stock of how her life had changed as she showered with the Italian-labeled bath products she found.

First order of business, call Kristy. Her editor was used to her disappearing for a few days, but by now the woman was sure to be frantic and had probably called Marty and the boys. Maybe her dad, even. She tried not to wince at that. Also, she needed to get ahold of her notes. They were at the office in a locker down by the fitness center, but Kristy could get them. And she knew there was information in there that would mean more to Baojia than it had to her. Between the two of them, they might be able to find out more about Ivan and his connection to the women Tulio had buried in the desert.

Speaking of Tulio, she'd like another conversation with the strange vampire. He'd buried the bodies, but had he looked at them? Had there been any identifying documents? Any evidence that might have been destroyed? And where, precisely, had he found them? Was it even important? From what they'd discovered two nights ago, it sounded like the girls were being killed somewhere else and transported to the California desert, possibly by truck. Where had they been killed? If Ivan was behind it—and it seemed he was, judging by the death of the waitress from the bar—then Mexico was the most likely scene of the crimes. Were there any vampires in Mexico who might be friendly, or did they all owe allegiance to this mysterious cartel?

Natalie had a sudden vision of the vicious vampire Tio and others like him, chasing girls through the desert, feeding on them and killing them as if the girls were no more than prey. She shivered even in the steaming water. This was so much more dangerous than anything she'd ever investigated. She'd fallen into a world that barely seemed real, filled with creatures that looked human but were decidedly not.

And putting aside the physical danger, there were layers of history and grudges and politics she could only guess at. Forget human feuds, vampires seemed to take family dysfunction to a whole new level.

She dried off, patted her hair dry, and pulled it into a quick ponytail. She didn't have any of her normal hair products, so it was the best she could do with the wavy mop. She remembered Baojia sitting next to her on Tulio's couch, playing with stray curls as she chattered nervously. He seemed to like her hair. She smiled despite herself. Then she remembered his kiss and felt her face color.

"What the hell are you thinking, Nat?" She sighed and poked her head out of the larger door, curious to see more of the grand home she'd landed in. There was a long hall filled with more doors, but at one end, she could see a staircase. She crept closer and cocked her head when she heard it.

Apparently someone in the house liked *Mario Brothers*.

Wide-eyed, she peered around the doorway into a den filled with deep couches, bookcases of DVDs and games, and two people staring at an enormous flat-screen television.

"You got it. You got it… Watch out, Ten—"

"Be quiet."

"You're coming up on a really sharp left—"

"Shut up, Benjamin."

"Just…" The teenage boy leaned over a small Asian woman, who was staring at the screen with grim focus, gripping a white plastic wheel.

She batted his hand away when he approached. "I know how to do this. Go away."

"Will you just let me help?"

"I am thousands of years older than you. I think I can figure it out, you brat."

Natalie must have let out a squeak, because the boy turned.

"Oh, hey! You're awake." He tapped the small woman—vampire?—on the shoulder before he stood. "Tenzin, she's awake."

The vampire didn't turn around. She was wearing what looked like pink driving gloves as she continued to stare at the game, leaning to the left as the wheels squealed on the surround sound.

"She's been awake for half an hour, Ben. She took a shower with that shampoo that smells like figs, and I think she's hungry. Damn it!"

The vampire threw the white wheel to the ground and grabbed a box from a stack next to the coffee table.

The boy paused on his way toward Natalie. "You kill another one?"

"Yes. And I was just about to beat Yoshi. I hate that stupid little dinosaur."

Natalie said, "Everyone likes Yoshi."

Ben grinned at her. "Tenzin's not everyone. You must be Natalie." He held out his hand, and Natalie shook it. "I'm Ben."

"You're human."

"One hundred percent," he said with a laugh. "Did you get enough sleep?"

"Uh huh. And she's a..." Natalie nodded toward the small woman Ben had called Tenzin.

"Vampire. Immortal," he said. "Video game addict. Pain-in-the-ass, also known as Tenzin."

"You should talk," the woman muttered, trying to extract the new wheel from the stubborn box. Finally, she held the box up. "Ben?"

The boy walked over. "Why don't you just bite through the plastic?"

She bared her teeth and long, curving fangs gleamed in the low lights of the windowless room. "I got a piece of plastic stuck right here last time I did that. That stuff is horrible. Why do they put everything in it?"

"Oh my God," Natalie swore under her breath. The vampire's teeth were the most vicious thing she'd ever seen. Long and curving, they looked like white blades in the woman's mouth.

Tenzin's eyes flicked to her. "Baojia said you knew about our kind. Don't pass out."

"I'm not going to pass out." *Hopefully.*

"Your heart rate says otherwise. Take a deep breath."

Ben finished opening the new wheel with a pair of scissors, inserted another game controller, and handed it to Tenzin before he walked over to Natalie. "You'll be fine. Why don't we go get you some breakfast? Well, more like lunch right now."

She took a deep breath and nodded, still eyeing Tenzin, who was completely ignoring her at that point and watching the game again. Ben ushered her toward a spacious living room with a slate fireplace and more mission-style furniture.

"She's a little different, even for a vampire."

"How is she awake? I thought they slept during the day."

He shrugged. "The older they are, the less sleep they need. They just have to stay out of the sun. And others... Well, they're kinda like us. Everyone's got their quirks, you know?"

"Is she a water vampire?"

"Wind, actually." He frowned and looked over his shoulder. "I hope she doesn't mind me telling you that."

"I don't!" Tenzin's voice was faint, coming all the way down the hall. "She's hungry, Benjamin."

He smiled over his shoulder, then nudged her toward another door. "Let's get you fed, then."

Ben led her through a dining room and into the kitchen she barely remembered from the night before. An older man was cooking behind a large, professional range and an elderly woman was sitting at a breakfast table, surrounded by a newspaper she appeared to be reading.

"Ah," the man said. "Our guest is awake. What can I get you to drink, dear? Mineral water or juice? There's still some coffee if you'd like some."

"Coffee would be great, thanks." Natalie followed Ben to the table and sat down across from the old woman, who had the most vivid green eyes she'd ever seen. "Hi."

"Hello." The woman smiled, her face crinkling as the morning sun shone on a cap of neatly cut silver hair. "You must be Beatrice's friend, Natalie."

"Beatrice?" She blinked. "Is this her house? No one told me. Wow."

The woman nodded. "I'm her grandmother, Isadora. This is my husband, Caspar."

"Hello." The older gentleman smiled as he set down a cup of coffee and gave his wife a soft kiss on the cheek. "I understand you and Baojia have had a rather interesting few days."

She sipped her black coffee. "You could say that."

"He's such a dear man," Isadora said.

Natalie blinked, surprised by the obvious affection in the woman's voice. "How do you know Baojia?"

She heard Ben rifling through the refrigerator, but Caspar came and sat next to Isadora.

"We've known him for years. He upgraded the security in the house a few years ago when we first moved here. Then last year—"

"Beatrice and Gio had to go to Italy for some time," Isadora broke in. "Baojia stayed with us until they returned. Then he had to return to San Diego. But he still calls occasionally to say hello and asks after us."

"Very fine individual," Caspar said, his English accent giving the words a crisp, dignified tone. "I'm so glad he felt comfortable coming here when he needed help."

Isadora gave her a mischievous smile. "And I do believe he and Gio might get along better now that you're here, Natalie."

She frowned. "Uh… why would they—"

"Roast beef or turkey?" Ben called. "You want a sandwich?"

"Turkey would be great." She sipped more coffee. Apparently everyone here thought well of her vampire, even if she still had her doubts. "By the way, is there a phone I can use?"

Caspar and Isadora exchanged guarded looks.

"I really need to call my editor and let her know I'm alive. I don't need to tell her where I am—she's used to me being vague—but if I don't call her by today, she'll be calling the police to report me missing. We kind of have a three-day rule."

Caspar visibly relaxed and nodded toward the counter. "There's one right there."

"And I don't even know where I am, so it's not like I can call the cavalry to come in."

Isadora let out a tinkling laugh. "My dear, I believe you'll discover the cavalry is already here."

Natalie poked her head into the library. The windows were shuttered and gave off no light, but a few dim lamps were scattered around the room. Overall, it had that weird, musty smell she associated with libraries and old bookshops. She swallowed audibly. "Uh… B?" She stepped farther in the room. "Beatrice?"

A low voice came from the far corner of the room. "Natalie Ellis, why do you trespass on my inner sanctum?"

Natalie rolled her eyes and flipped a switch, flooding the room with light. "Really?"

Her old friend's laughter burst from the far corner of the library. "Oh my gosh, your face, Nat!"

"Get the hell over here and give me a hug, you weirdo. And no biting. I heard you like that now." Beatrice rose from the chair where she'd been sitting and crossed the room, just slightly faster than should have been possible.

"Hey, you." Beatrice gave her a hard hug. "How did you end up in my guest room?"

She tensed for a moment when she felt her old friend. It was Beatrice, but the difference was there. The cooler skin. The stronger arms. Natalie forced a smile to her face. "Long story. So you're really a dark and mysterious creature of the night now?"

Beatrice pulled back and grinned, her fangs dropping down as Natalie's stomach also took an instinctual dive. "Yup."

"Well." She blinked and shook her head. "You never really were one for sunbathing, I guess."

A wistful smile touched Beatrice's mouth. "Not so much. It's good to see you. Despite the circumstances. I have to stay away from most of my old friends, so… It's really good to see you, Nat."

"It's good to see you."

"Dez filled me in a little this morning. Dead women in the desert, huh? Are you sure it's like Juarez? I remember you always followed that case."

They walked over to a table and Natalie could already see news reports and clippings from the previous crimes littering the table. "I'm not sure of anything anymore. There are definitely dead women, but I don't know what it has to do with Juarez. It's possible there's no real connection, and this Ivan character is using those events to mask his crimes here."

"Get everyone thinking it's the same serial killer or gang and use it to cover his own actions?" Beatrice said. "I guess it could work. And you're sure it's Ivan?"

"Fairly sure." They both sat down and Natalie spread her hands over the news clippings. "There was a body dumped night before last, out at one of Ernesto's casinos near the Salton Sea. It was a girl I'd just been talking to down at Ivan's bar the night before."

"Jeez, Natalie. You went down there alone?" Beatrice's eyes widened. "What were you thinking?"

She threw up her hands. "This is me! I was following the story. I thought it was maybe gang-related, but nothing about it said supernatural, immortal killers. How the hell was I supposed to predict this?"

"You couldn't," said a voice by the door. The voice was followed by perhaps the most handsome man Natalie had ever seen. He was art on legs with an Italian accent and a seductive stare.

"This is your husband?" she murmured to Beatrice.

"Yep."

"Nicely done, my friend." Natalie held out her fist and Beatrice bumped her knuckles with hers.

"I like him." Her friend gave the handsome man an adoring smile. "Hi, honey."

The man bent down to brush a kiss across Beatrice's cheek. "Good evening, *tesoro*." Then he stood and held out a hand to Natalie. "And Ms. Ellis, may I say how very nice it is to meet you? Welcome to our home. I hope everyone has made you comfortable."

"Very. Thanks." She stood and shook his outstretched palm, noticing that unlike Beatrice and Baojia, this vampire's skin was warm. Almost feverish. "You must be Gio. I've heard a lot about you."

"Giovanni Vecchio. And if it was from Baojia, I'm sure it was very flattering."

Her eyebrows lifted in amusement. "Dez actually."

"Ah. No wonder you're not running away screaming." He smiled again and pulled out the chair next to Beatrice.

"Be nice." Beatrice gave him a playful slap on the leg as he sat. "You two are too much alike. That's why you don't get along."

He lifted an eyebrow. "You think that's the reason, do you?"

"Getting back to the current problem…" Beatrice gave him a pointed stare before she turned back to Natalie. "It seems like there are still too many questions. And the Ernesto situation makes it all more problematic."

"Can someone tell me what, exactly, the Ernesto situation is?" Natalie asked.

"I think it would be best if Baojia shared that with you," Giovanni said. "I am not sure of the details and I don't know how much he wants to tell you."

Her lip curled. "Please tell me you're not one of those 'don't worry the little woman' types."

A self-effacing smile crossed his face. "My wife has taught me the absurdity of that notion. I just know he's a very private person, and I have too much respect for Baojia to speak out of turn. Besides, he'll be awake soon. In the meantime, our resources are yours. What can we help you with?"

She took a deep breath and folded her hands. "Well, I just talked to my editor and, after she got finished lecturing me about making her worry, she promised to send a box of my notes to a FedEx office here in

LA. I'm not sure where we are, so I just gave her the name of one near Union Station."

"I'll arrange to have someone pick it up and bring it to the house. What's in your notes?"

"Maps of the locations where the bodies were found. Victim profiles I'd worked up." She shrugged. "A few police reports from Imperial Valley and notes. Lots of notes from phone interviews. I have some e-mails, too. It's just kind of a jumble, to be honest."

"Ooh!" Beatrice grinned, her fangs on display. "Does it need organizing? I love organizing."

Giovanni smiled. "Natalie, I believe you came to the right place."

Natalie was lying on the bed in the guest room, catching a quick nap before the night truly started, when she heard him. The door creaked, just a little, and she looked over to see a sliver of his solemn face.

"You can come in, Baojia."

He pushed the door open and stepped inside, shutting it behind him. "How are you?"

"Better." She watched him. He was so careful with her. As soon as he entered the room, she saw him subtly check the surroundings, paying particular attention to the windows and the door to the bathroom. "I don't think you need to worry. It's like Fort Knox here."

"No." He couldn't help himself. He looked in the bathroom and checked behind the door. "The security here is better than Fort Knox. Are you rested?"

"Yes."

"And they fed you?" Satisfied that no intruders had crept into her bathroom through the tiny window, he moved to the closet.

"Yes, I've been fed, watered, washed. All shiny and new, George."

He looked over his shoulder and smiled slightly as he looked inside the small walk-in closet. "We're safe, Baojia."

"I know." Still, his eyes scanned the room and tension radiated from him.

"Will you come sit down, please?" Natalie patted the edge of the bed. "You're making me nervous."

He sat near her feet, studying her.

"Now," she finally said after he'd looked his full. "Let's talk about the first night we met."

CHAPTER THIRTEEN

"YOU BIT ME?"

Baojia sighed. "After everything I just told you, that is what you focus on?"

She was angry. "You *bit* me. Without my permission—even my kinda-drunk permission—you bit me and drank my blood." She hadn't left the bed, but she was glaring at him with one hand covering her neck. He leaned over and pulled her fingers away.

"That bite saved your life in Mexico after you went to speak to Ivan. After I told you not to." He leaned over her, holding her wrist in his and stifling the satisfied growl that wanted to surface every time he saw the pale, silvery scars. "Those marks on your neck were the reason I could come after you and no one would question it. Without them, you would have been fair game. Would that have been preferable, Natalie? Would you rather be dead? Or Ivan's plaything in Ensenada?"

He could tell the minute righteous anger turned to fear. Her face grew pale and her eyes widened. His anger fell away. "Don't cry."

Tears gathered at the corners of her eyes. She'd been so strong; the sight of her crumbling tore at him inside. He gathered her in his arms, rocking her back and forth.

"Don't cry. Natalie, you're safe. Don't cry."

"Too much," she whispered against his shoulder. "I feel like everything changed in one moment. And I'm starting to wonder whether I'll ever be able to go back. Is it always going to be this way? Will my life ever be normal again?"

He held her for a few more minutes as she calmed down. Finally, he said, "It won't be the same. It can't be. And for that, I am sorry." But a bitter taste filled his mouth, and a guilty voice in his head whispered that he wasn't sorry at all.

She pulled away from him and narrowed her eyes, still sniffing a little. "Not going to apologize for the bite though, are you?"

"Are you going to apologize for going to Ivan's?"

Natalie wrinkled her nose the same way she had in the car that first night. "I don't even remember that. How am I supposed to apologize for not taking advice I don't remember, you dork?"

He couldn't help it, he smiled. She was not amused.

"Stop."

"Can't."

"You're not allowed to smile. You didn't apologize for biting me."

"And I'm not going to."

"Urgh!" she growled, flopping back on the pillows as he leaned over her. "You're so damn stubborn."

He had to laugh. "Look who's talking."

She didn't even respond, only lifted one eyebrow and asked, "What else?"

"What else, what?"

"What other embarrassing stuff did I do that I don't remember? I always remember things—I hate this."

He debated about telling her she had kissed him. "You... ah—"

"I kissed you, didn't I?"

He blinked. "How did you know?"

"I tend to get affectionate when I'm drunk. I figured amnis-intoxication might be the same."

"I'll remember that." He smiled again when she punched his arm. "And I might have seen an eyeful when I took you home."

Her mouth gaped open. "I *was* in my underwear that morning! I'd forgotten that part."

He held up his hands. "It wasn't me. I opened the door and you started stripping."

"Oh no!" She covered her face. "And you looked?"

Of course he had. Did he look like an idiot? He decided she didn't need to know everything. "I made sure you were safe and no one was in the house, then I locked up and let myself out."

Her hands were still over her bright red face. "That's all?"

"Disappointed? I'm not going to lie and say I didn't enjoy the view."

She punched his arm again, then rolled over and buried her face in the pillows. "Dying. I'm dead."

His hand trailed down the exposed nape of her neck and over her shoulder. "You most definitely are not. Nor will you be anytime soon, Natalie Ellis."

She took a deep breath that he matched. The human gesture seemed to soothe them both and he could feel the tension start to leave her shoulders. He continued to run a hand over her back, up and down, enjoying the meditation of listening to her steady heart and rhythmic breathing. She was so full of life. She made him feel alive, despite the pain of loss that still throbbed inside him.

Baojia couldn't decide what he felt. For the first time in his immortal life, he was directionless. He had no family. His sire had cut him off at his own request. He was heartsore and confused. But he didn't regret his actions. Nor did he second-guess himself. And oddly enough, he wasn't lonely. Looking at the strange woman on the bed, he realized he hadn't felt lonely since she'd appeared. Odd. And unexpected.

"Baojia?"

"Hmm?"

"What were you and Beatrice?"

His hand stilled. "We… were nothing."

She rolled over and looked at him. "I'm not stupid. I know her husband doesn't like you. I know she gets a weird look on her face when your name is mentioned. So whatever it was, it wasn't nothing."

How could he possibly explain? He still didn't quite understand it himself. "Beatrice was an assignment."

"What kind of assignment?"

"I watched her for Ernesto. She is his blood relative, and she was unguarded by Giovanni. For five years, he left her here. I don't fully understand why, but I know they've made their peace about it. And while he was gone, she needed protection, so Ernesto asked me…"

"To watch her." Her usually open expression was cautious. Wary.

"I guarded her. That was my assignment. And then later, I helped to train her. Before and after she became a vampire. I was her weapons instructor. And also her bodyguard."

Natalie's eyes narrowed. "You had feelings for her."

"I…" He took a deep breath. "I watched her for *five years*. Watched her grow and mature. She's a fascinating woman. I had feelings… for the *idea* of her. But by the time I had the opportunity to truly know her… She was Giovanni's. She was always Giovanni's; I can accept that."

"But you didn't like it."

"Natalie—"

"Hey, you're a hundred and twenty years old." She rolled over again, facing away from him. "I'm sure you've had plenty of women who caught your interest in all that time. I shouldn't even pry. It's none of my business, but she's my friend, and—"

"You have…" His voice dropped. "…every right to pry. And it is your business."

Silence fell between them as he lifted his hand again, slowly running it down her back. He could feel her skin heat beneath his touch.

"Natalie?"

"I'm not mad."

"You asked me once whether I ever regretted becoming a vampire."

"And you said 'Occasionally.'"

The feel of her skin soothed and excited him. He let his amnis touch the surface and it prickled in awareness. "The night in the bar downtown. When I made you bump into me."

"Confessing that too, huh?" she said, a smile in her voice.

"I wish… I wish *that* had been our first meeting. When I left you that night, after you and your friend went to the movie, I wished that I was a normal man, and I had simply met you at the bar. That I could have joined you for the movie and talked with you more."

She said nothing, but he could hear her pulse begin to speed.

"Because you were smart and funny. I wish I could see your hair in the sun. You said that the smell of the ocean was wrong. And I've thought that every night for a hundred years, I think, but I didn't recognize it until you said it."

Then there was silence. Until she finally whispered, "George?"

"Hmm?"

She reached over her shoulder and tugged on his hand as he leaned closer. "Lay down with me. I think I need a hug."

"Um… okay."

She rolled and scooted over on the bed, pulling him close and wrapping his arms around her like a blanket. He tensed for a moment, unsure of what she wanted. His body roared to life as his senses filled with her scent and heat. But when she put her head on his shoulder and sighed, he forced himself to relax.

"Baojia?"

Did she have any idea how that breathy voice whispering his name affected him? He felt his fangs throb. "Yes?"

"What are we doing?"

Not enough. "What do you mean?"

"You and me." She looked up. Sea-blue eyes, surrounded by black lashes. Pale freckled skin, flush with life. "Are you and I—"

He kissed her. He had to. It was the only answer to her question.

He pulled her against his chest and felt his heart thump slowly. *Once.* Soft lips opening to his mouth. The taste of sugar and mint on her tongue. *Twice.* His hand ran from her shoulder, down her spine, over the soft curve of her hip. Three times his heart beat before he gave in and grabbed her thigh, hitching it over his hip to bring her closer. There were no words, just the sound of her breathing and her heart as it pounded. He could hear the rush of blood in her veins. Her skin flushed with heat. Kissing Natalie felt like a memory of the sun on his skin.

He reached a hand up to pull at the tie that held her hair back.

"I hate these things," he murmured between bites of her mouth. "Never wear them."

"Sometimes…" She pressed into his chest, and her arms wrapped around his waist. Her hands tucked into the waistband of his slacks, and he moaned when he felt the tickle of her fingertips against his sensitive flesh. "Sometimes, it's just the most practical thing to tie it back," she murmured between kisses.

"It's beautiful when it's loose around your face." He grabbed a handful of her hair and tugged her mouth back.

She kissed him for a long, breathless moment. "It's a mess."

"Woman," he said and kissed her more deeply, their tongues tasting and teasing, "are you arguing with me? Now?"

"Of course I am."

Baojia smiled against her lips, then he started to laugh, his nose bumping against hers as he squeezed her thigh and let his head fall to the pillow. She stared at him, her lips swollen and red from friction. Her face was flushed. Her hair was a mess. He just laughed harder. "You'll argue with me forever, won't you?"

Natalie shrugged innocently. "It's what I do."

The laughter died down and he tugged her back down to his shoulder, tucking her head under his chin as he played with a curl of her unruly, argumentative hair. The heated mood had shifted into something warmer. Plus, he could feel the house beginning to stir for the night, filling with activity as humans and vampires filled the halls. He savored the lazy indulgence of lying beside her, even if it was just for a few more minutes.

"Baojia?"

"Hmm?" Why was her heart picking up again?

"Am I more than an assignment?"

Th-thunk. His heart beat with hers for a second, and his breath caught.

"Yes."

The Italian did have an excellent library. Technically, he knew Giovanni had given the library to his wife, but he could see the years of work in its shelves. The rumors were that Giovanni Vecchio was a minor nobleman who had been turned by a very famous water vampire during the Italian Renaissance. The immortal never suspected that the urbane man would wake as a fire vampire, the most dangerous and unpredictable of their kind. Giovanni's reputation was enough to make Ernesto give him a wide berth. His marriage to Ernesto's blood relative was another.

But whatever uneasy truce Giovanni and Beatrice had with Ernesto, it had never extended to Baojia. As his father's enforcer for so many years, he had taken Ernesto's connections and alliances for granted. As a newly independent immortal, he would have to build his own.

"How are you?" Giovanni said, appearing at his side.

He tried not to react and instead looked to Natalie, Dez, and Beatrice, who were at the library table, poring over newspaper clippings while Natalie took more notes in one of her yellow legal pads. "I am well. Thank you again for opening your home and providing a safe place for Natalie."

Giovanni nodded. "You are welcome, as well. I have never forgotten your service to us in China."

He had joined in Giovanni and Beatrice's fight in China, even though it had not been part of his mission and Ernesto had not been pleased. "I failed in China."

The other man shrugged. "That depends on your definition of failure, I suppose."

He would have to think about that later. "I hope our presence does not cause problems for you with Ernesto."

Giovanni laughed arrogantly. "I do not fear Ernesto. He knows better. And I told him years ago I would willingly have you on my side again in a fight." He pushed away from the bookcases and said, "I don't know that I would say the same for him."

He watched the Italian walk away. Odd. That had to have been their most civil exchange. His ears perked when he heard Beatrice mention the word "elixir."

"What did you say?"

She looked over her shoulder. "I said that it could be this is the first evidence we've seen of Elixir in America."

"Elixir?" Natalie asked. "What's Elixir?"

He walked over to her side and perched on the edge of the table. "Isn't this what you were going after in Rome? I'd heard there was some crazy fight over it, but I thought it had all been destroyed."

Giovanni shook his head. "We thought that too, but the missing boxes of Elixir were never found. And then last year, some of our friends found it in Ireland. Apparently, whoever was making it had bigger plans than just Rome. We think it's being manufactured in more than one place now. We're not sure how it's being distributed."

"Shit," he muttered. If the rumors about the drug were true, this was a bigger problem than a few murdered humans.

"Can someone fill me in, please?" Natalie was annoyed. "What is Elixir?"

Beatrice was the one who spoke up. "It was intended to be a kind of cure. It was first made during the medieval period in the Middle East. An early chemistry experiment with vampire blood. Humans can't drink our blood. It can be used on open wounds, but unless a human is at the point of death and means to be turned, their body will reject it, making him or her sick. Elixir was intended to overcome that, to make vampire blood ingestible to humans so it could heal them the way we can heal each other."

"Okay…" Natalie was a little confused, but she was smart enough to fill in the gaps. "So it was made to be kind of a cure-all for humans. So we could heal the way you guys do. That's not a bad thing, so something must have gone wrong."

Giovanni said, "Along with curing humans, if a human drank the elixir, it made their blood…" He broke off, at a loss for how to explain it.

Baojia spoke up. "The rumors are that a human who drinks Elixir has supercharged blood. You don't have to drink much and it's like you've been fed for a year. And it tastes better than anything you've ever had." Some memory tickled the back of his mind. "But those are just rumors. I've never met anyone who's actually tasted it. I'm not going to lie, something like that would be popular, particularly with younger vampires. There were a lot of stories flying around the club in San Diego."

Beatrice shook her head. "It's like a drug, Baojia. Don't ever drink from a human who's taken it. It messes you up. It won't kill you, but vampires who have tasted Elixir blood go wrong in the head. They're really, really strong at first—"

"A quick burst of elemental power. Increased amnis," Giovanni said. "But then—"

"Totally nuts," Beatrice added. "Messes up your amnis. Weakens you."

Baojia started. "Kills you?"

"Not exactly," Giovanni said quietly. "But you'd be as good as dead. You might not even realize someone was after you. Or you might walk out into the sun without even knowing it."

Natalie said, "So, it's like any other drug. Seems amazing at first, but slowly kills you. Great. And it's for vampires?"

Giovanni nodded. "It's given to humans who the vampires drink from. And according to what we've heard, the rumors are true—Elixir blood does taste heavenly."

"Well that might explain the bite marks," Natalie said, looking up at him.

Beatrice asked, "What bite marks? What do you mean?"

"Of course." Baojia took a quick breath. "Of course. They were… high. The vampires who killed the girls. It's just like you said, Natalie. You asked Tulio and me if there was a drug, and we dismissed it. But there is a drug…" He stood up from the table when the realization hit. "Ivan's giving it to the waitresses."

Natalie stood too. "At the bar?"

He nodded. "When I went that night, I noticed a few… I almost grabbed one right then, even though I'd fed that night. They smelled *that* good. I didn't think about it at the time because I was focused on getting you out of there, but they smelled incredible."

Her mouth fell open a little. "Wow. Now I'm strangely insecure."

He broke into a quick laugh and dropped a kiss on her mouth. "Don't be. This explains everything. The women in the desert had been given Elixir. The vampires feeding from them must have lost control of their bloodlust and Ivan disposed of the bodies. And that explains the odd smell that Tulio and I noticed on the dead humans."

"What odd smell?" Beatrice and Dez asked at the same time. Funny, he'd almost forgotten they were there.

"The dead girls all smelled… sour. Not like a normal human at all. Their blood smelled fermented."

"Hmm." Giovanni leaned onto the table, eyes narrowing. "That fits with what Brigid has discovered about the smell of Elixir, too."

"The smell?" Natalie asked.

Beatrice said, "It has a distinctive smell of pomegranates—"

"Yes, that's what it was." His heart pounded. "Pomegranates. The girls smelled like pomegranates."

Beatrice and Giovanni exchanged a look. "Well, it's definitely Elixir then. We'd better call Dublin."

"Already have," piped up a voice from the couch. Baojia turned. It was Tenzin. She was putting together a puzzle that was laid out on a low table. "I sent the plane last night."

Giovanni said, "You just sent my plane to Dublin?"

She shrugged. "I sent a note."

He saw the Italian smother a smile. "You know, we could have just used the telephone, Tenzin."

Tenzin frowned. "Where's the fun in that? I'd rather see Brigid."

Baojia turned to Natalie, whose eyes were beginning to droop from exhaustion. "You might want to get some sleep. It appears there will be more vampires showing up tomorrow."

She forced out a wobbly smile. "Goody."

It was only an hour before dawn, and Baojia was paging through the notes Natalie had left out on the library table. The pieces were finally forming a clearer picture, but he still had no idea what their plan of action needed to be. And there were still too many questions. If Ivan was doing this, what was his game? Did the cartel in Mexico City know? How many humans had been infected? Baojia had been the head of Ernesto Alvarez's security and even *he* hadn't known the details of this drug. Did Ivan? Was Ivan taking it?

He felt the presence at the door and a smoky smell filled the air.

"Hello," Giovanni said. "She's very smart."

"Natalie? Yes, frighteningly so, at times. She rushes into things, following her brain with no thought to her physical safety."

"Your relationship—"

"Is private," he said quietly. "I'm sure you understand."

Giovanni nodded. "I do." He walked over and sat at the other end of the table. "Does she know what it all means? You leaving Ernesto? Being placed under your aegis?"

"No. Not entirely."

"So she doesn't know you'll have to leave?"

"We haven't talked about it." He gave up and set down the notes. "I haven't thought about it much myself, to be completely honest. I can't stay here. I have resources, but few connections outside my clan. And I cannot ask for an official introduction from Ernesto at this point." Vampire politics was tricky. In order to move to a new place, he'd need the tacit permission of whoever controlled the area, or he'd need to be in an isolated enough location that no one would pay him any mind. The problem was, he now had Natalie to consider, too.

As if reading his thoughts, Giovanni said, "Would she go with you willingly?"

"Her life is here."

"Her *old* life is here. You have to make her realize she won't be able to go back to that."

"How…" Baojia's voice was rough. "How did you tell Beatrice—?"

"I didn't. Not for five years. She moved here, and I never told her the truth of it. Not completely." The Italian gave him a rueful smile. "I wouldn't recommend that course."

"Understood." It was too complicated to solve in one night. There were too many factors to consider and too many unknown variables. His thoughts were a jumble, and his feelings for the woman were no less tangled.

"Have you thought about San Francisco?" Giovanni asked.

"San Francisco? No. Why?"

A smug smile crossed the fire vampire's lips. "You were turned there, were you not? While Katya was in power? Do you know if Ernesto had permission from her to take a human from her territory?"

"I don't." He'd never even thought about the ruler of the Pacific Northwest more than in passing or when talking with his peers on her security team when they'd arranged for business or political meetings. "You think I should reach out to her?"

"I think…" Giovanni smiled again. "I think she and Ernesto have had a friendly rivalry for many years. I think she might be *more* than happy to welcome home a former resident who has lived so long away from his mortal home. And I think she might be particularly welcoming to someone with your… unique résumé."

For the first time since he's left his sire's home in disgrace, a ray of hope seemed to break through.

Giovanni rose and nodded toward him as he made his way to the door of the library. "Rest well. And think about it. I'd be happy to write a letter."

"Finally get me out of your hair," he called to the Italian.

Giovanni only answered back with a lazy laugh that echoed down the hall.

CHAPTER FOURTEEN

"WOW," SHE MURMURED.

Dez bounced a chattering baby on her knee and said, "Yeah, that's what I was thinking."

"It's like watching a Bruce Lee movie. Only, you know, way hotter."

Natalie watched Baojia demonstrate another combination of kicks and punches for Benjamin before standing back and motioning the boy toward the wooden training dummy. She and Dez were sitting in the corner of the training studio that Beatrice, Giovanni, Tenzin, and Ben used to practice. One wall was lined with weapons, swords, spears, axes, and more weapons she could barely identify. Four fountains marked the corners of the training mats and dummies, ropes, and weights lined the other walls. It looked like a very well-equipped private gym, and currently, Baojia was giving Ben a lesson in some martial-arts technique.

His body was a subtle work of art. While he may have been average in height, there was nothing average about Baojia's body. The skin of his torso was smooth and unmarked, though his forearms and back were marked with a few pale scars. His muscles had been defined by what Natalie guessed was a mortal life filled with manual labor. Not bulky, but incredibly strong. The loose pants he wore concealed his legs, but nothing could conceal the carefully controlled strength. His movements were sharp and almost quicker than her eyes could follow.

"What's it called again?"

Beatrice said, "This particular style is known as Wing Chun. It's very fast and very precise. Designed for close-range combat. I'm pretty sure he practiced it as a human, which only made him faster as an immortal. Baojia's a bit of an anomaly. Very powerful for his age."

"Ben seems to be picking it up fast," Natalie said. The young man appeared to take the practice very seriously, watching Baojia at each turn with an intense focus.

"He's been training in various martial arts since he was about thirteen. Gio and I want him prepared for… whatever."

Baojia spun around in a blur, barely visible to the human eye.

"It's so fast." She leaned forward, fascinated and… well, completely turned on from watching him. She had seen him fight—the memory of his attack on the vampires at Bar El Ruso was painted in vivid color in her mind. But to watch him, *really* watch him, as he patiently explained each movement or stance to the boy was mesmerizing. He exhibited total efficiency of movement. There was no flourish or extravagance, only a pure economy of energy and focus.

Her mind tripped back to his kiss in her bed the night before. Focus. That was part of what made him so irresistible. As quiet and distant as he could be in front of others, when Baojia turned his focus on her, the intensity of it rocked her. He kissed her as if it was his mission in life. Just then, his eyes flicked to hers and the dark promise in them caused her face to heat.

"Oh, hello, dark and sultry look," Beatrice murmured. "Someone likes an audience."

Dez slapped at Beatrice before Natalie got a chance. "Be quiet. You're embarrassing her. And he can hear every word we say, you know."

Natalie's blush just got brighter. "Oh, right."

Obviously proving Dez's point, Baojia looked over his shoulder and gave her a quiet smile. Then he turned back to Ben, adjusting the young man's arms and pulling his elbows farther in before he practiced a punch. She could see him tell Ben something and the boy nodded, then Baojia demonstrated himself before patting Ben on the back and letting him go.

"He's a good teacher," she said.

Beatrice nodded. "The best. Even Tenzin says so. I was lucky to have him as my weapons instructor. You should ask him to show you a few things, Nat. I'm fairly positive it'll come in handy at some point."

"I'm going to hope that most of my battles are won through the whole 'Pen is mightier than the sword' philosophy, but I'll keep that in mind. Dez, can I?" She held her hands out for Carina to give her something else to focus on.

"Sure. My arms could use a break."

Carina immediately started pulling on Natalie's hair, which caused her to laugh and wince at the same time.

"She's so funny, Dez. Amazing. Do you love it?"

"It has its moments, but yes. Totally love being a mom."

Beatrice smiled and reached over, tickling the baby's tummy and eliciting a giggle. "And she's definitely the cutest member of the family. Don't tell Gio."

"Or Ben," Dez said.

Natalie watched the two women, one mortal, one immortal, tease back and forth. She watched baby Carina nibble on the vampire's hand as both women watched Ben practice the forms Baojia was teaching him, slowly speeding up with each repetition.

"This is special," she murmured. Beatrice and Dez stopped talking and looked at her. "What you guys have here? The family you've built. It's really special." She swallowed back the lump in her throat and kissed the top of the baby's head. Her whole life, she'd wanted something like what they had. Did they even realize how lucky they were? For years, it had only been Natalie and her mom and dad. Then her mom was gone and her dad... Well, he was sort of gone, too. She had friends, close ones, even. But it was nothing like what her old friends had built between them.

Beatrice smiled as if she could read Natalie's thoughts. "Human. Vampire. Family's family."

"Yeah, starting to get that." Her attention shifted when the baby pulled at her hair again, tugging Natalie's face down to her own. Carina patted her chin with one drooly hand as she grinned and babbled. At that moment, Natalie saw him from the corner of her eye, staring at her holding the baby, an odd look on his face. She looked away, suddenly realizing what had led to Baojia's unexpected confession the night before.

He was like her now. He didn't have a family either.

The moment was interrupted by a whirl of movement. A dark-haired pixie of a woman spun into the room, energy sparking around her. She flung a long, hockey-like stick toward the practice mat, yelling, "Catch, Ben!" as she did. Baojia zipped toward the incoming projectile, grabbing it before it hit anything, then he glared at the newcomer. As if by magic, she was sitting next to Beatrice and bumping her shoulder. "Hey, there. Miss me?"

Beatrice said, "Incoming."

Natalie barely caught her breath before the woman was standing again, one hand held out toward Baojia, who was baring his teeth and already had a sword in his hand. Flames burst into the strange vampire's hand and Natalie let out a yelp as a sheet of water appeared out of nowhere to flank Baojia. Carina wiggled and laughed in her lap, clapping at the sudden special effects show that had appeared before her.

"Hello," the stranger said with a smile. "Friend. Sorry, thought they would have warned you."

Baojia said nothing, a low growl rumbling from his throat as he remained in a ready stance, his eyes never leaving the fire vampire.

"Brigid," Beatrice said, "you might want to move away from the redhead with the baby."

Dez was obviously trying not to panic, even though Carina was delighted by the action. "Yeah, guys. Baby here. Teeny, tiny human."

"Oh, is that how it is? She's his?" The woman shrugged and took a step back. "Understandable, then. Sorry about that."

Natalie scooted farther away from the woman, and every foot that separated them seemed to put Baojia more at ease. Eventually, the sword was lowered and the water returned to the fountains, though his fangs remained visible in his mouth. He made no effort to hide them as he walked toward her and leaned down, rubbing his cheek along hers in a quick movement before he turned and stomped back to the practice mat where Ben had been standing and staring silently. Eventually, Ben lifted the long stick the woman had thrown.

"Is this the hurling thing?"

"Yep," Brigid called. "Also handy for bashing idiotic husbands across the back of the head, should the need arise." Everyone looked at her. "What?"

Ben said, "I'll keep that in mind, thanks." Then he and Baojia returned to the training dummy, with Baojia keeping one eye on Brigid the whole time.

Natalie finally breathed out. "So… That was interesting."

Dez whispered, "And *hot*." Beatrice was just beaming at her.

"What?" Natalie's face was red again.

Brigid smiled. "I'm Brigid, by the way. I'd shake your hand, but he'd likely amputate it at the elbow, so I'll just wave."

Natalie waved back. "I'm Natalie. And I'm not really sure what just happened."

"That's one highly possessive vampire you have," Brigid said in an amused voice, her accent obviously marking her as the Irish vampire Tenzin had sent the plane for. "He's young, eh?"

Beatrice shook her head. "Not as young as you. But she's new. Or rather, *they're* new."

"Fun." Brigid leaned back and surveyed the studio. "B, is he the one who taught you to use those crazy hook-swords I want?"

"Yep, that's Baojia. And please. You'd never give up your guns."

The vampire grinned, fangs fully on display. Like Beatrice, she had black hair and a slim figure, but Brigid was a tiny ball of pure energy. She had shockingly pale skin, even for a vampire, and close-cropped hair that suited her delicate features. Like Giovanni, heat radiated off her. Natalie could feel her from yards away. And her eyes were startlingly inhuman, brown around the pupil feathering out to a deep ash gray. Though Dez had told her the fire vampire was young, Natalie guessed she would have a hard time passing as human to a careful observer.

The baby was dozing off, no doubt a vampire schedule wreaked havoc on normal bedtime. Carina had nestled into Natalie's chest, her soft pink cheek warm against the skin of her neck and her little hand still clutching a lock of her red hair. "Hey Dez…"

"She asleep? I'd better get her home."

Reluctantly, Natalie handed over the little girl, feeling the loss of the baby's warmth as she sat back on the bench.

"Good to see you." Beatrice stood and hugged her friend goodbye. "Tomorrow night?"

"I promised Matt a human night," Dez said with a wink. "Bedtime by eleven and a real breakfast the next day."

"Daywalker," Beatrice muttered. "Fine. At least I have new friends to keep me busy." She threw an arm around Brigid.

"And cause trouble. Speaking of that…" Brigid looked around the studio and lowered her voice. "What are we waiting around here for?"

Brigid might have been lighthearted upon first meeting, but the woman was all business once they got in the car. Natalie, being the only human, was the designated driver.

"Jeez, I miss driving," Brigid moaned as they caught the 5 going south toward the border.

"I miss my bike," Beatrice added. "I need to buy an older one so I can just ride, but I miss my Triumph. By the way, where's your husband?"

They had returned to the house an hour before, Beatrice assuring Baojia that Natalie would be carefully guarded. She might have left out the current plan to drive to the border to check with one of Natalie's contacts at the Otay Mesa border crossing.

"No idea," Brigid said absently as Natalie steered the car through light traffic. "We're going to the Mexican border, right? And why there?"

"The earth vampire Baojia and I spoke to out in the desert said trucks were dumping the bodies, but the victims have all been Mexican nationals. You want trucks coming from Mexico? You go to Otay Mesa. It's the third busiest port of entry between the US and Mexico. Tons of traffic. And I know a few people who work there."

"You're a newspaper reporter, then?" Brigid asked. "Very cool. I was horrible at writing in university."

"Brigid was studying to be a criminologist when life got interesting. Now she does security for the vampire who runs Dublin."

"Along with a bit of… consulting, we'll call it."

It felt weird to have them in the backseat. Natalie felt like a chauffeur. She was reminded of poor Luis in San Diego. What would happen to him now that Baojia wasn't working for Ernesto? What would happen to Baojia's things? Did he own his house in San Diego? Suddenly, her stomach dropped. Would he be able to move back or would he disappear into the night when this was all over?

Beatrice piped up from the back. "Why are you so upset, Nat? Your heart is racing."

Natalie cleared her throat. "I'm… I'm not. Don't listen to my heart, B."

"It's pounding out of your chest," Brigid said. "And you smell of nerves."

"God!" Her breath exploded. "Is it always like this with you people? You can smell everything! Hear everything. Baojia never—"

"He probably doesn't mention that stuff because he knows it makes you nervous," Brigid said. "Humans who don't grow up around our sort tend to be jittery."

She bit back an angry retort, feeling like a fish out of water. She felt a hand patting her shoulder from the back seat.

"It's fine," Beatrice said. "You're doing great, Nat. And the good thing is, Baojia's not so old he doesn't remember what it's like to be human, you know? You'll be fine."

She hoped so. *Not* being fine wasn't really an option at this point. She might not have super powers or combat skills, but she knew she'd have to figure out some way to survive if she was going to live in this crazy new world.

Brigid asked, "So tell me more about this Ivan fellow. Your man's quite sure he's the one behind this?"

"Baojia said that the waitresses at the club smelled amazing. Like pomegranate. Very hard to resist."

"Yep." Brigid sighed. "That sounds like Elixir. Poor things. They're dying and they don't even know it."

By the time they'd pulled into the port of entry, Natalie was getting nervous about the dawn again. It had to be almost two in the morning and it had taken them over two hours to get there. She'd already called her contact at Customs to ask her if she was working, but Natalie was still worried about the sun.

"Are we going to have enough time?"

Beatrice didn't seem concerned. "We'll worry about that. You just find your friend."

It turned out she didn't even need to look for Sandra. Almost as soon as she parked the car, she saw a flash of a familiar face.

"No freaking way..." she muttered. They couldn't be that lucky. "Beatrice, Brigid, back in the car."

The two vampires spun around in almost choreographed movement.

"Back in the car! We have to follow that truck."

To their credit, neither hesitated; they just jumped back in the car as Natalie started the engine and slammed it into reverse, hoping to catch up to the nondescript container truck that was already heading north.

"Natalie, what are we doing?"

"There's a vampire in that truck, and I recognize the bastard. He almost bit me in Mexico, but Baojia put a knife through his throat. His name's Tio."

Brigid grinned. "Well, that's a stroke of luck!"

"So we're chasing one of Ivan's men?" Beatrice groaned. "Oh shit. He's going to be pissed."

"Nonsense," Brigid said. "This is far more fun than asking questions."

By the time they reached their destination, Natalie already had a sinking feeling in the pit of her stomach.

"I know this place," she said as she pulled into the mostly empty parking lot. She found a spot a few rows away from the truck and they stopped, rolling down their windows. The same electronic noise filled the air as the last time she'd been here. Tio and the driver were already jumping out and walking into the casino. "This is Ernesto's casino. I came here with Baojia."

Beatrice was the first out of the car. "This is my grandfather's?" She kicked a rock, which sailed over the dumpsters and into the black desert. "Shit. Shit! What the hell is going on? There's no way he could be involved. I don't trust him completely, but he'd never get mixed up in something to do with Elixir."

"I don't know your grandfather, but I say we have a look at that truck," Brigid said. "If there are humans inside—"

"They're not likely to be alive, if there are," Natalie interrupted her. "But we should still check it out. Someone needs to call the police."

"No police," Brigid said.

Natalie felt her temper heat. "If women have been murdered—"

"Just wait, Nat," Beatrice said. "Let's check it out first before we start arguing. I'll go listen, but if there's no one alive, I say we wait and watch for now."

Brigid smiled smugly as Natalie glared and Beatrice darted away.

She wanted to scream in frustration. The journalist in her said that the people—no matter who they were—deserved a proper investigation if they had been killed. Those women didn't deserve to be pawns in some vampire chess game. She wanted to call the police. She wanted to open the truck door and take pictures of the atrocities these creatures had committed and plaster their deeds on the front page of every newspaper in the world. She wanted to shine a glaring light on the guilty and make them burn.

But as she considered it, Baojia's voice echoed in her mind:

Those girls deserve nothing. They are dead. They are past caring. And if you publish a story that exposes our kind to the world, then you will be dead, too. You will be ridiculed by your own press and then someone, somewhere, will come and kill you. I am not threatening; I am predicting. And you cannot die. It is not acceptable.

Her own fear shamed her, because she didn't want to die. And she knew, as much as she hated it, that Baojia had spoken the truth. So she shoved back her indignation and waited in the car. Beatrice only shook her head when she returned, slipping silently into the backseat as Natalie's instincts throbbed.

They waited for only ten minutes before they saw him again. The driver was nowhere to be seen, but Tio was exiting the casino and heading toward the back with a woman on his arm. She stumbled, either drunk or intoxicated by his amnis; there was no way of knowing. Brigid and Beatrice didn't even hesitate.

"Oh no, this isn't going to happen." Her old friend's voice was a grim promise. "Asshole."

Brigid leaned over and shoved what looked like a flare gun in her hand. "Taser. You ever shoot one of these before?"

Natalie felt the panic start to well up. "No, never."

"Well, crash course, then." Brigid pulled her out of the car, following Beatrice, who had already sped toward Tio. "Point, shoot. You've got about twenty feet with this model. Try not to hit anything friendly."

"Wouldn't it be better if I stayed in the car?" she whispered.

"And leave you there unprotected? Not likely. Just follow me."

Natalie hoped Beatrice had already incapacitated Tio, but by the time they rounded the corner, her hopes were dashed.

Five figures struggled in the dim lights behind the casino. Natalie could spot one with long hair, swirling and kicking in an almost elegant fight. Brigid grinned. "Elixired vampires. So much more fun. Stay here. These bastards tend to be strong."

With a snap, Brigid brought two balls of fire to her hands and strode toward a vampire who charged her. The creature only had a split second before he was engulfed in flames. The others spotted him and ran into the night, Brigid and Beatrice hot on their trail. Natalie heard a muffled sob from the corner. It was the woman, huddled against the wall.

"That… What the hell was that?" She wasn't in good shape. Natalie tried to lift her to her feet, but the woman pulled away. "Oh shit, you're one of them, aren't you?" She pointed at the stun gun in Natalie's hand.

"What?" She looked at it, holding her hand up in surrender. "No, no. Let me help—"

"Get back, bitch!" The woman scrambled to her feet, still sobbing. "Help!" she cried into the night. "Help me!"

Natalie was about to run after her when a dark shape swooped in from the night, grabbing the woman and clamping a hand over her mouth as the creature latched on to her neck. The woman went still, and Natalie froze at the sight of her nightmare, watching helplessly as Tio drained the human dry. She opened her mouth to scream, but no sound escaped. Tio kept his eyes on her, black gaze staring madly over the woman's neck as the blood dripped on the ground. Without a word, Natalie turned and ran.

CHAPTER FIFTEEN

HE STALKED HER. Panic pumped through her blood, and the acrid tang of adrenaline kicked in the air.

Faster.

He could hear her scrambling through the brush and the rocks. The smell of blood cut through the dry night and he knew she was bleeding.

Faster.

A low snarl ripped from his throat when he sensed her other pursuer. There was no time to lose. He heard her heart racing, faster than the beat of birds' wings and just as fragile.

The tremor of breath caught and held. A small cry escaped her throat.

Faster. Faster. Faster.

He was almost on her.

Not fast enough.

Baojia felt the sting of a thousand blades when he reached the rise of the hill to see Tio closing in on Natalie. She had stumbled in a gully, splayed on her back, her legs twisted beneath her as she raised her hands, holding something in front of her in the low light of the moon. No cry rose in the night when she reached out toward the monster that hungered for her. There was a spike of energy scenting the breeze, then a blue flash as the blur of the immortal's body stilled, arched, and flew back from Natalie's raised hands. Baojia was already on top of him when he felt the quake. The rush of energy mushroomed out from the prone immortal as the earth beneath his feet groaned and shuddered.

He reached out, slicing off Tio's head with one clean stroke as the ground opened up and a chasm appeared in the desert sand. He heard Natalie cry out as she disappeared into the dark slash of earth. Baojia roared as his enemy's body fell lifeless onto the sand, blood soaking the earth that was still shifting and rolling.

"Natalie!" He looked for her, but saw nothing. The ground around where she had been lying was an open wound, sand and rock pouring into it. He dove after her.

Landing in a roll, he spotted her crouched in an odd cavern that seemed to bloom beneath the desert floor. The earth around them still quaked, but though the sand and rock rained down, the cave appeared stable. In the blink of an eye, he bent over her and wrapped his arms around her body, shielding her from the falling debris until the earth stilled. She trembled underneath him, and he could smell the blood that stained her skin from cuts and scrapes.

He said nothing when the earth finally stopped moving, uncurling from around her body to clear the sand and hair from her face. His senses reached out, searching for any threat, but no energy reached him. The gash where they had fallen had caved in and was covered by tumbled sandstone. The cavern narrowed into a small passageway that led into the unknown. Was it a mine shaft? An old tunnel?

Baojia could hear her heart beating furiously, so he lifted her in his arms and carried her toward the narrow opening that led farther down. It was pitch-black, but he sensed a familiar energy, a trace of scent and amnis that still lingered under the earth. Tulio. This passage, whatever it was, must have belonged to the old hermit.

She began coughing, and he could smell the salt of her tears and the teasing metallic scent of her blood. He followed Tulio's scent farther into the black, but could feel nothing and no one else. They were utterly alone beneath the earth.

Eventually, he could feel the air grow fresher and the sound of his steps echoed as he entered a wider part of the passageway. From the right, he caught the distinct smell of wax. Carefully, he set Natalie on her feet, reaching out until he could feel a niche in the wall. A stack of candles lay there, next to a box of matches. With steady hands, he lit one and looked around the room, carefully keeping his eyes on anything but the woman who was shaking only a few feet away.

He lit another, then another, placing them at intervals around a room lined with small alcoves. It had to have been an old hiding place. Or maybe the earth vampire kept many passages such as this one. Burrows carved from the earth to make for easy escape or shelter.

Whatever it was, it was safe.

The floor was dusty, but wool rugs were scattered over it, and a soft pallet sat in one corner. Wordlessly, Baojia picked up Natalie and laid her on it, carefully surveying her for wounds as his tension shifted from survival to anger.

"Where are we?" Her voice was scratchy and hoarse. "Is there anyone else down here?"

"No."

He ran careful hands over her legs first, checking her ankles for twists or breaks. He bent and rotated the joints, carefully watching for signs of pain. There was a cut in her right calf but it wasn't deep. He quickly ripped the lower part of her jeans away and bent down, piercing his tongue to clean and heal the wound before he checked her knees.

"Baojia—"

"Be quiet," he muttered as he continued his examination. Her arms were next. He performed another cursory examination of her wrists. The right appeared to be slightly swollen, but not broken or seriously sprained. Another cut marked her left forearm. He ripped away the sleeve of her shirt and healed that wound as well.

"Are you going to talk to me?"

He still didn't speak, just pushed her back on the pallet to gently run hands over her torso and ribs. Though there were more scrapes, particularly on her lower back and left shoulder from where she must have fallen, there appeared to be no sign of internal injuries or broken bones. He could hear her start to sniff.

"Will you say something? Please?"

"That would not be wise."

Finally, he looked up. Placing his hands on her head, he gently probed her skull and neck, still searching for signs of trauma. He ignored her wet blue eyes. He brushed the hair away from her forehead and bent down, his lips inches away from a red scrape on her forehead. She was crying silently, tears running down her face as she pushed him away. She started to tremble again, but he could tell this time it was from anger.

"Say something."

He refused, the quiet rage forcing him back on his heels as he crouched next to her, stubbornly looking anywhere but her eyes. He could feel the blood start to pulse in his veins as her anger mounted. He bit down, tasting the blood from where his own fangs pierced the inside of his lip.

"Say anything!"

He caught her outstretched hand a fraction away from his face as she tried to slap him. He held her wrist, barely containing his raw fury. Finally, his eyes lifted to hers.

Anger. Relief. Desperation. He saw every emotion he had locked away spilling from her eyes.

"I returned to the house to find you gone," he said, barely above a whisper. "I had to wake Matt in the middle of the night to activate the GPS tracking on my car. I flew down here with Tenzin, convinced I would find your body drained in the desert."

"I was with Beatrice and Brigid—"

A swift hand covered her mouth as he continued in a deadly soft voice. "He was seconds away from killing you. You were moments from death."

She peeled his fingers from her mouth, grasping his hand in hers as she sat up slowly. "I had the Taser. I shocked him. I would have had time to—"

"You can die, Natalie."

"I know that."

"You can *die*."

"I know!"

"You almost did." The wall of anger that had masked his fear began to crumble. The sheer terror of the previous two hours began to slash at his throat.

"Baojia—" She tried to lean closer, but he put a hand on her shoulder, halting her.

"You can die," he said again. "And you would be gone. And I would have nothing."

He heard her tears again, felt them against his skin when she pressed his hand to her cheek, but she had no response.

"Do you even understand how fragile you are?"

"Tell me I'm not an assignment," she whispered as he drew closer, brushing the hair from her temple and framing her face with his hands. Slowly, he leaned forward and kissed the scrape on her forehead, licking the blood from his lips. "Tell me this is real."

"I would have nothing," he whispered, kissing her again. He lowered his head and kissed the delicate skin of her eyelids, tasting her tears. "Do you understand?" He still held her face, and her hands came up to cover his as he kissed the rise of one cheek, then the other. "Tell me."

He thought he felt her nod as he captured her lips. Fear gave way to need, and he pulled her closer. She grabbed at his shoulders and tugged, knocking him off-balance as she pulled his body over hers. He crawled up the pallet, carefully moving her body under his. Her legs parted and he moved closer, their lips still fused in a desperate kiss.

Alive. Alive. Alive.

She was alive, and she wanted him.

Bracing himself over her, Baojia pulled away a fraction of an inch, staring into deep blue eyes.

"I need you," he said softly. "I need—"

"Yes," she breathed out her answer, then reached up and pulled his mouth down to hers.

Need. Desire. Ache. He ached for her. He felt her hands ripping at his shirt as he tore at hers, desperate to feel the pulse of her heart against his chest. Desperate to hear her blood. Desperate to hear her call his name. Natalie's quick fingers slipped down the front of his slacks where his flesh, roused by anger and desire, leapt beneath her fingertips.

"Aah!" He arched up, fangs dropping as the ecstasy of her touch ignited him. His eyes sought hers, locking on to her hungry gaze as he sat back on his heels, stripping the jeans down her legs, fumbling with the shoes she finally kicked off. His hands ran up the inside of her legs, lingering behind her knees when he heard the quick intake of breath. He reached up and pulled at the blue panties she still wore. They were torn at the corner, from her fall or his hands, he didn't know. He didn't care. He rid himself of his own clothes before he bent down.

Baojia breathed in, letting his senses fill with her scent as his fangs scraped along the inside of her thigh. "I want to bite you." He licked at her flesh. "Here."

Her heart was racing. In excitement or fear? "It won't hurt?"

Baojia's mouth moved along her shivering skin before he looked up to meet her wide blue eyes. "I'm going to bite you here, put my mouth on your flesh, and suck. I'm going to let my amnis flood your senses until the only thing you can feel is fire in your veins. You will experience the most intense pleasure imaginable. You will come. And you will want more."

What do you know? He'd finally rendered her speechless. All she could do was nod.

He fluttered his tongue along the artery, sucking until her skin was red and swollen under his mouth. At the same time, his fingers stroked along her belly, up and over her breasts, finally running down the length of her arms until he had linked their hands, palm to palm. And everywhere his hands went, his cool energy went, too. He could feel her react, her body flush with life, her skin prickling in awareness. And when she started to pant, he bit.

"Baojia!" she cried out as he drank from her, swallowing thick gulps of her rich blood until her back arched and she came with a violent shudder. He immediately sealed off the wound, then he slid up her body and inside with one smooth movement, capturing her cries in his mouth as he thrust. His hand ran down over her thigh to grip and lift it higher. He listened for her pulse, timing his steady strokes to the beat of her heart as the air around him became laden with the scent of her pleasure and blood and sweat and life.

She was alive. In that moment, she was everything.

And when he felt her come around his flesh, felt the heady rush of pleasure course through her again, Baojia let go and surrendered.

Natalie was curled into his side, still naked. She was so warm, he wanted to drape her over his body like a cloak. His hands teased through her hair, pulling out tiny pieces of rock and debris from her run through the desert. He could feel his senses slowing. Sunlight was near.

"Natalie?"

She was drowsy, too, nuzzling into the skin of his chest. He could feel her tongue flick out occasionally to taste his skin. Her lips closed over one nipple and bit lightly as his eyes rolled back in his head.

"Hmm?" she purred.

"Dawn is coming."

That brought her up short. She looked around the room. "Are we safe here?"

"I don't feel anyone around, and anything truly dangerous will be sleeping soon. Reach into my pants on the floor. Sewn into the front of them is a weapon."

"You could definitely say that."

He closed his eyes and laughed. "No, a sword."

"That's certainly one name for it."

"Woman—" He reached down and pinched her backside. "An actual sword. I'm going to pass out in a few minutes. I'll be asleep until nightfall. Keep the sword out, just in case."

Her voice was suddenly insecure. "I thought you said we were alone down here."

"We are. I'm just being cautious."

"I've never used any weapon like that before."

"We've got to start training you," he mumbled. "You have… good balance and coordination. You should pick up the basics well enough until I can put together a proper training regimen for you."

"Baojia…" All the playfulness was gone from her voice. He looked down to see her hiding her eyes from him. Not good.

"We'll talk more tonight." He reached down and tilted her chin up so she was forced to meet his eyes. "Okay?"

She nodded, uncertainty still etched on her features.

"When I fall asleep… I don't breathe, Natalie. I don't have to, except as habit and to sense the air around me, so when I'm asleep, I don't breathe at all. And you know my skin is cooler, so—"

"You're going to feel…" She gulped. "To look kind of…"

"Dead," Baojia said. Her heart sped up. He could tell she was afraid. "Think of it more like a coma. It's just a very deep sleep. When I am older, I will be able to wake from it; right now I can't. But I will wake at nightfall. Don't forget that. I will wake and be just as I am now."

She nodded, and he could feel the heaviness descending on his limbs. A cloud started to fog his mind.

"Grab the sword," he said.

"Okay." She reached down and got one of his short swords from his pants. "Okay. I'm not going to freak out."

"Good girl," he whispered. "Your turn… to guard me."

Her tentative smile was the last thing he saw before his eyes closed.

Her scent was the first thing he smelled upon waking. It was the scent of skin and blood. Their scent together, mingling in a pleasing way. He wanted her by the ocean, outside in the water with the fog blanketing them. Maybe a hot tub. That had definite possibilities. Of course—he felt a rock beneath the pallet on the cavern floor—just a bed would be an improvement.

Cave in the desert. Bed near the ocean. He just wanted her.

Baojia's fangs lengthened instinctually as his eyes flickered open. Natalie was not next to him. Candles still lit the room, and he heard a rustle of movement from the corner. His eyes darted over to the disturbance. It was her, rifling through a low cabinet that appeared to need a good dusting. The whole cave looked like it hadn't been used in years. She must have heard movement, because she spun around, sword raised.

"Hi." He held up his hands. "I surrender."

A lingering trace of fear haunted that stare, but she threw the sword down and leapt onto the bed, kissing his face and holding him tightly.

"Oh, that was weird. I'm not going to lie, the way you just go out is kinda freaky, George. I maybe had a little minor panic attack at one point, but then the whole crazy night caught up with me and I fell asleep. I just woke up a little bit ago, so I was looking for some water. There's a cabinet over there, but I—"

He pulled her down and shut her up with a kiss. She talked too much for just waking up. Of course, when she didn't talk it bothered him more. Natalie's natural state was chatty. He'd learn to live with it.

"Hi," she finally whispered when he released her lips. "How did you sleep?"

"I sleep. There's no variable. I'm awake, then I'm gone."

"Yeah, I noticed that. You don't toss or turn. You really are kind of… comatose. We'll call it that."

He smiled. "Whatever you can live with." There it was again, that doubt. It leapt to her eyes any time he mentioned the future. "Can I ask you something?"

"Sure. What?"

He tucked a curl of hair behind her ear. She was wearing what was left of his shirt and the panties he'd left in tatters. It must have been something about the crazy, panicked night; he wasn't usually such a barbarian. "I know you feel unsure about... us. About all this."

"Yeah?" She squirmed.

"Give it a chance. Us. This." He swallowed the odd lump in his throat. "Whatever it is, it's new for me too."

She bit her lip and sat cross-legged on the bed. "We're so different, Baojia."

"Yes, we are." He knew she was thinking about her mortality. So was he. More and more every night. "But nothing in life is certain. Not in human life. Not in immortal life. Just remember that."

Slowly, she nodded. "I'll try."

"And do not *ever* do something like this again, Natalie."

He saw her eyes start to narrow. "Don't. Don't lecture me. You're not my father."

"I most certainly am not."

"So don't think—"

"My name is Chen Bao Jia," he said quietly, sitting up next to her in the bed. "Sired to water in 1884 by Don Ernesto Alvarez." He reached out and tilted her chin up so she met his eyes. "Protector of a family that no longer wants me. Subject to no clan." Her eyes filled with tears as he continued in a soft, urgent voice. "I offer you my protection, Natalie Ellis. Will you accept it?"

She blinked back her tears and lifted her chin proudly, but he put a single finger over her mouth.

"I offer you my protection. Do you understand what I am saying?"

Natalie paused and then she whispered, "Yes."

Elizabeth Hunter

Chapter Sixteen

"THIS WOULD HAVE BEEN a lot easier if you hadn't taken my phone, you know." She was holding a candle while he dug a tunnel out of the cave. The wax kept dripping onto her hand. "Ouch!"

"Lift it up a little higher."

Her shirt had been ripped beyond repair during the fight, so he'd given her his. Baojia only wore a pair of pants while he dug through the sandstone rubble. She had to admit, the view was nice. Well, what she could see of it, anyway.

"You have super strength, right?" She watched as he hefted a boulder the size of a Saint Bernard out of the way. "Shouldn't this be going faster?"

He turned, frustration evident on his dark features. He pointed to his chest. "Water vampire." Then he spread out his arms. "Desert!"

Natalie bit her lip and tried not to smile. "You're really cute when you're angry, George."

He blinked, obviously not expecting her answer. Then she saw him try to suppress the smile. "Just… hold the light. I'm almost through the biggest pieces and the smaller will go fast. We'll be out of here soon."

"Can I help?"

"You can hold the light, Natalie."

"Don't you have super night vision, oh elemental creature of the dark?"

He spun and walked toward her. "I have excellent night vision when there is some natural light." He grabbed the candle and set it on a rock nearby. "Moon. Stars." He grabbed her and pulled her to his chest. "But there is no light down here. None."

He bent down and kissed her, his lips hard with anger, then softening when she melted. He did this to her. In his arms, she felt like the center of the world. She reached up to hold his shoulders, because her knees actually felt weak. Finally, he pulled away. "Now be quiet and hold the light." Then he shoved the candle back in her hand and went back to work.

She swayed a little, leaning against a boulder to regain her balance. "Okay."

How, how, how had this happened? She'd fallen. Hard. Natalie had thought she was going to die the night before. No matter how she had protested, she'd run through the desert searching for Brigid and Beatrice with no thought of leaving alive. She'd had the Taser, at least. And then Baojia had come. Furious. She'd seen him cut off the head of her attacker with one stroke. It was… otherworldly. *He* was otherworldly. And then he wasn't. He was a man, angry with her for risking herself. Desperate to feel alive. Giving her…

Do you understand?

He hadn't said it with words. Watching the strong, silent man she was falling in love with, Natalie realized he might never give her words. But she could probably live with that, because she had a feeling he would give her everything else.

Do you understand?

She understood. Now she just had to decide if she could live with the rest of it.

The muscles of his back flexed effortlessly as he moved the enormous rocks that had fallen in, blocking the cave. No sweat marked his skin in the flickering candlelight. He didn't breathe harder because he didn't need to breathe. When she'd lain next to him through the day, he had appeared, for all intents and purposes, dead, though his skin had retained the same soft tan color, and she could feel his energy humming every time she touched him. So Natalie had closed her eyes and laid her hand on his arm when she fell asleep, comforting herself with the single sign of life his body exhibited. But he hadn't turned to her in her sleep and held her close, because he couldn't.

Tell me you understand…

He might give her everything, but could it be enough?

"Why are you upset?"

157

She blinked back the tears that had started gathering in her eyes. "How did you—"

"Your scent changes when you get upset. And I can smell your tears. Are you afraid?" He turned, carefully walking over to her. "We are almost out. I can smell the fresh air now."

"No." She cleared her throat. "Just… thinking."

He frowned, as if he could guess what had been on her mind. "Oh."

"Can vampires have kids?" She flushed immediately, cursing internally for blurting that out.

Baojia's mouth had dropped open a little. "No. We can sire other vampires, but we can't… it's not possible to—"

"Oh." She nodded and looked at the candle. "Okay. I was just curious."

"You want children." It wasn't a question.

The flush she'd been trying to control came back. "Not right now. It's kind of a 'someday' thing. You know, someday I want kids. Not now. I mean, I work too much. And I travel a lot. So kids now would be… And I'm single, so—"

"No, you're not." He had stepped closer, and his voice dropped to a low growl. "Whatever this is… you are not single. You're not unattached as far as I'm concerned."

Her back straightened instinctually. "And what about you?"

"You think I would pursue someone else while I am with you?" His frown grew fiercer. "Is that what you think of me?"

"No!" She was making a mess of this. And really, they needed to get out of this stinking cave. The air was getting practically claustrophobic. "I just… Are you going to bite other people? I mean… It feels really good and if you—"

"I will feed from donated blood if you insist, though it would make me weaker. I don't need to drink very often, only a couple of times a week, depending on my physical activity. It would be too much to take from only you, and I would not want to see you weak. And yes, bloodlust and physical lust often go hand in hand, but not exclusively."

Natalie decided that her face was just going to stay a weird tomato red for the rest of her life. But, on the bright side, Baojia could only see her at night, so that was good. She'd just have to stay in dimly lit rooms when they were together. He stepped closer. She could see his lean musculature covered with sand and dust. He was mouthwatering. He was beautiful. And he would always be that way.

"Natalie," he asked, "is that acceptable?"

"Yeah." She nodded, crossing her arms and still holding the dripping candle. "I mean… I guess that was a stupid question."

"No, it wasn't." He tucked that irritating lock of hair behind her ear again. "These are good questions." He was smiling, his fangs peeking from the corners of his mouth. She could barely see him in the candlelight, but he was smiling, so she smiled, too.

"We should probably get out of here."

"Mmmhmm." He stood there, his hand soft on her neck as his fingers traced the edge of her jaw. "The sooner we get out of here, the sooner I can kill Brigid and Beatrice for bringing you out here and leaving you in the middle of a fight."

"Ugh!" She shoved his hand away. "You can't kill them."

He rolled his eyes and walked back to the pile of rocks. "I'm thinking about it." He tossed them over his shoulder at vampire speed, careful not to aim any in her direction.

"It would create an international vampire incident. Or something."

"Everybody hates me anyway. Not much would change."

"Not everyone hates you."

"Close. Close to everyone. I think Isadora still likes me, which must piss my father off."

"Dez and Matt like you. Beatrice and Gio like you." She kept going, even when he snorted. "And I like you. A lot."

In a blink, he was back in front of her, bending down to capture her lips. "Do you?" he murmured with a smile. "You like me a lot? Only a lot?"

She tried to roll her eyes, but it was hard to be annoyed when he was doing that thing with his tongue and his hands… "I like you… the most, George."

"Good." Baojia stepped forward, snugging his hips against hers and running his hands down her back to squeeze her waist. "Am I your favorite vampire?"

"Eh…" She tried to play it cool, but the memory of his bite from the night before assaulted her. "You're probably my favorite."

"Probably?" His hands. And his arms. Natalie bit his lower lip and his arms tightened around her.

"I might need more convincing." She broke away and took a deep breath. "And a shower. And an actual bed. So…"

He stepped back. "Out of the cave."

"Out of the cave."

She watched him walk away, and it took more than a little self-control to let him. But within minutes, Natalie was glad she had because the rush of cool night air filled the cramped tunnel and before she knew it, Baojia was reaching a hand down to pull her up. They walked back toward the casino, hand in hand. He led, making sure to steer her around any brush or rocks that might trip her up or scratch at her; his eyes constantly swept their surroundings.

"Baojia." She tugged at his hand to get his attention.

"Yes?"

Natalie kissed him. A sweet press of her lips to his with her hands reaching up to frame his smooth cheeks. "Thank you for rescuing me."

He smiled. "Again."

"Wow." Her hands dropped. "You really had to go there, huh?"

"Second time, Natalie. This is the second time you've put yourself in danger."

She started walking again and muttered, "And it won't be the last."

"I heard that."

"Of course you did."

He didn't kill Brigid and Beatrice, but he didn't talk to them either. Both vampires were waiting at the back of the casino, near where Tio had shown up and scared Natalie after they'd first run off. Both were covered in sand and dust. Natalie had a feeling she'd gotten the better end of day accommodations.

"Tenzin?" she asked, remembering that Baojia had said the wind vampire had flown him down to the desert.

Brigid said, "Already took off. Wouldn't take either of us with her."

Baojia tucked her under his arm and started walking toward the Camaro, holding his hand out in silent request for the keys.

"So, he's a *silent* angry type, eh?" Brigid asked.

"Apparently," Beatrice said, following after him. "Listen, we were right behind you. She was supposed to stay at the casino and shock anyone who —"

Baojia spun around, holding up a hand. "Don't speak. Don't speak right now."

Beatrice's eyes popped open and she bared her teeth. "Oh no. You don't get to talk to me like that. Natalie knew what she was doing coming down here. And she's not some weak-kneed little—"

"She's human," he growled through gritted teeth. She could see his fangs low in his mouth as he shoved her behind his body and stepped forward in an aggressive stance. "Has it been so long that you have forgotten how vulnerable she is? You risked her needlessly, Beatrice. You call yourself her friend, but she could have died." He paused a moment, trying to keep control. "I cannot stress to you how unacceptable it is to put her in harm's way."

Natalie wanted to speak up, but she was afraid her voice would come out as a squeak. Barely restrained violence was pouring off him. She looked around Baojia's body to see something shift in Beatrice's face. The other vampire's stance shifted and she stepped back, glancing at Natalie with a softer expression. "You're right. I'm sorry." She held up her hands. "Brigid's sorry, too."

"Hey!" The tiny brunette piped up. "I'll speak for—"

"We both got excited about a fight and we were thinking about taking these guys down," Beatrice said, glaring at Brigid, "and we didn't think about her."

"Apologize to your friend," he said.

"Baojia." Natalie shoved at his back, finally speaking up. "That's enough. She apologized. I'm fine. The bad guys are dead—" She looked to Brigid. "The bad guys are dead, right?"

Brigid nodded. "Ashes. And I hope you didn't get any of that vampire's blood on you, Baojia. We're not sure if Elixir can spread vampire to vampire, but no use taking chances."

"I didn't." She could see his shoulders start to relax. "They were all elixired? How many of them?"

"Five." Brigid started walking toward the car, all business. Natalie was relieved that someone still seemed immune to all the vampire posturing that was flying around. "Which makes them harder to kill. The humans they'd been feeding on were already dead. Three humans. Tio was just joining the crowd with the other. She didn't smell drugged, so she must have just been a snack."

Natalie's stomach churned. They were talking about human beings like they were food. She could feel Baojia tighten a firm arm around her to steady her as she crossed the parking lot.

"The truck?" she asked. "Any sign of the truck?"

Brigid shook her head. "Must have gone wherever it went during the day today."

"We'll head back tonight," he said, "but I want to come down here and speak to Tulio again."

Beatrice said, "Big silent earth vampire who came for the girls' bodies? He said he was a friend of yours, but we kept our distance."

"That's smart. He's very strong and he knows this desert better than anyone. I want to know where these girls are coming from, and I have a feeling he might have discovered more."

They got to the car and Baojia slipped into the driver's seat. He started the car and reached for Natalie's hand. "Sleep if you can. We'll be back in LA within a few hours."

She wanted to talk more. About the girls. About the vampires who had been killed. But the fight and the restless day were finally catching up to her, and Natalie felt her eyes slip closed.

When she woke, she was in yet another room she didn't recognize. But at least this one smelled familiar.

Baojia.

She was carefully tucked into a large king-sized bed in a room with no windows. A door to the side was open to a lit room she assumed was the bathroom. Her duffel bag was on the dresser, and a plate of food was on a small table in the corner, along with a note. She stood up, rubbing her eyes so she could read it.

Sleep as long as you wish. I'll be in the library until dawn. The code for the room is your birthday.

She blinked. Apparently, someone had moved her in. Or he didn't trust her out of his sight. It might have been a little of both. She took a long drink of water and began to pick at the fruit and cheese on the plate before her. After a few minutes, she realized she wanted company more than food, so she left the room and walked down the hall. It led to a staircase going up, and Natalie realized the hallway full of vampire rooms was just below where she'd been staying. Well, that was convenient; she knew where everything was. Heading toward the library, the house was almost eerily silent until she got near the second floor.

"—suspicious of your own family."

"You are not my family any longer."

"Do you think because you and Father fight I no longer consider you a brother?"

His sister. Baojia had a vampire sister, and they were arguing. Natalie didn't go any closer, but she couldn't manage to tear herself away.

"I don't want to put you in an awkward position. But I cannot deny I am worried about Ernesto. He tied my hands. I couldn't protect him. I couldn't protect you or Rory. I was stuck in San Diego doing nothing while my sire and his territory were being threatened. I had no choice."

"You made the choice. You chose that woman and the humans over us. If you had stayed—"

His voice was clipped and impatient. "If I had stayed, he would have kept ignoring it and then I would have lived with the guilt of knowing something was going wrong and not being able to do anything about it, Paula! How can you not see that? And how can Rory ignore this? He must know what's going on."

"It is a human problem, Baojia. A serial killer like the one in Juarez. It is for the human police to investigate. Not our problem. Not *your* problem."

"We found a girl who had come directly from Ivan's bar. Do you think that is coincidence? Natalie was attacked by one of Ivan's thugs last night. Is that a coincidence?"

"Natalie? Is that the reporter's name?"

She shrank against the wall.

"This is not about her."

"This is completely about her. Take your amusement, *hermanito*, but why do you abandon your family for this human? She is here today and a memory in fifty years. We are your *family*. Go to Father. Ask forgiveness."

"It will not happen." His voice broke. "And it does not matter if she is human. I have sworn my protection over her. She is under my personal aegis. Do not think to attack her or send someone who might. Attacking her is the same as attacking me." The soft voice grew hard. "And will be dealt with in the same manner. Do you understand?"

The other vampire's voice was acid. "I understand you have lost your reason. I only hope you come to your senses before this has gone too far."

She heard footsteps approaching and darted into a coat closet she'd just passed. She heard the steps slow, then speed up, a low female voice muttering in Spanish about what, she couldn't understand. A second set of feet approached and the door creaked open.

"She could smell you in here, you know." He parted the coats she'd hidden behind. "She could sense you on the stairs."

"Did you leave your family because of me?"

Baojia held out a hand. "How did you sleep?"

"Answer me, please."

He sighed and leaned against the doorjamb. "It was for a number of reasons. You were part of it, but not the whole. Can we leave the coat closet now?"

Natalie brushed past him, unsure of how she was feeling. Worried. Elated. Nervous. Grateful.

"You show everything and nothing on your face," he called to her back.

Natalie spun around. "I could say the same thing about you."

"Are you hungry?"

"No."

He stepped closer. "Thirsty?"

"I drank some water in your room. Which looks an awful lot like *our* room now."

Baojia sped to her side, making her eyes swim as he rubbed her shoulders. "I don't particularly want you out of my sight."

"How very caveman of you."

He grinned. "Still thinking about that cave, aren't you?"

She blushed and saw his fangs lengthen in his mouth. His eyes watched her with predatory awareness.

"Baojia?"

"Are your human needs met?"

"Yes, but—"

"Then we can talk later." He picked her up and ran so fast she thought she was going to throw up.

"Okay, motion sickness is not sexy, George."

He laughed and slowed down a little as they reached the bottom staircase. Within seconds, they were at the door and he was kissing her again, making her head spin for a whole new reason.

"Baojia—"

He wouldn't let her talk. He just kept at her mouth. Then her neck. She felt his fangs scrape against her skin as he laid her down on the bed and went to secure the door with a combination of way more numbers than just her birthday.

"Did you... did you just change the code?"

"Yes. We'll have to think of a new password every dawn." He moved back toward her, intent clear as he pulled off his shirt. "I will not take any chances with your security, but I do not want to keep you prisoner during the day." He lay down next to her, shirt gone, playing with the edge of her T-shirt. "You've had quite enough of that, am I right?"

She pulled off her T-shirt. "But not enough of you. I should take a shower."

The smile dropped from his face and he dove toward the newly revealed skin. Her green bra turned into a scrap of lace when his teeth encountered it. The now-familiar sensation of his amnis flowing over her skin caused her to moan.

"Later," he whispered, his mouth already busy on her breast. "Much later."

Much *much* later, after Natalie had discovered just how entertaining showers could be with someone who controlled water, they lay in bed. It was still an hour or so before dawn. His cool fingers ran over her still-flushed skin, and his other hand played with the red hair splayed over his chest.

"I am very..." He spoke softly.

"What?"

"Content. I am very content, Natalie."

She smiled against his chest. "I'm glad. I'm sorry you fought with your sister."

"She is not my sister anymore."

Pulling back a little, she looked into his eyes. "Yes, she is. Feelings don't just disappear because you fight."

"She brought me to him. When I was human, it was Paula who found me and took me to Ernesto."

"But you said you weren't forced to become a vampire."

"No." He took a deep breath. "I was willing."

"Why?"

Frowning, he rolled to the side and then turned her over so she could meet his eyes. "You have to understand what was expected of me. My family was in China. I was sent here to work. For them. So they could eventually pay passage and move, too. There was no future in China, my father said. He was, in his own way, very American." Baojia smiled. "He thought our family could have a better life here. There were so many rumors of gold, but also regular jobs. On the railroads. On farms. Shops. Just *jobs*, which were scarce in my village. I was sent over and worked on the railroad at first. Then for a mining company. Every place I could. I sent a little bit home, but mostly I saved it. I slept in the cheapest lodging I could. I bought nothing for myself. I would have been able to do it. I had over half the money for their passage saved already."

"What happened?"

"In 1882, Congress passed the Chinese Exclusion Act. No Chinese immigrants were allowed. They said it would be for ten years. I had been here working, had saved up so much... But it didn't matter. No matter what I did, they would not have been able to come. There were smugglers, but I could not afford to pay them. And there were no guarantees they wouldn't take my money and leave my parents in their village anyway."

"That's horrible."

Baojia shrugged. "It was reality. But I became very depressed. I considered going back to China, but my parents wrote me and told me that I should stay. They needed me to continue sending money for them, and there were no jobs in the village that paid what I was making. I was... angry. I felt very alone. And there were very few women here—no Chinese women, anyway—who would want to marry a laborer like me. So I had no hope of a family or children. I was an income to them. That was all."

Her heart ached for him. He had wanted a normal life. Wanted a family and a future. But instead...

"They didn't deserve you."

"I'm sure they didn't see it that way. They were doing what they needed to survive. I can't blame them for that."

She could. No one should be taken for granted the way he had been. But she dropped it and asked, "Why did you become a vampire?"

"Ernesto had ships. He did trade in China. And he wanted me to be his guard." Baojia shrugged. "So, he offered to make sure my parents and brother and sister had safe passage to San Francisco and the start of a new life if I would become his child. It was a trade. I didn't have to say yes."

Natalie had her own doubts about that, but she let Baojia speak.

"I agreed. He paid for my family's passage and gave them the money I had saved, and I became his vampire. He was certain I would be very powerful because of my speed and skill as a human. He was correct."

"And your human family?" She reached out and stroked his face. He leaned into her touch, closing his eyes in pleasure.

"They still live in San Francisco. There are many of them now." He opened proud eyes. "They have been very successful."

"Do they know about you?"

He shook his head. "No. I have monitored them through the years, but not closely. It would not be wise."

"You sacrificed a lot for them."

"Yes." He narrowed his eyes. "But don't make me a martyr. It was difficult at first, but I like being a vampire. I like the power, Natalie. Even if there are costs. And I like being feared by my enemies. Being feared means those I protect are safer. I would not want to be anything else."

She shivered at his words but didn't look away. "I know."

"Do you?" He moved over her, locking his eyes with hers as his fangs grew long. His knee spread her legs and he settled against her, letting his amnis tease over her skin until she thought she could burst from a single touch. Baojia had barely moved, and she was already panting. "I am not a good man. I have not been one for a very long time."

"I don't agree."

"You're still getting to know me."

Her chin lifted and she reached up to bite his chin as he growled low in his throat. "I know enough."

"Are you sure?"

There was desire in his eyes, but even more, there was challenge, and for the second time in as many nights, Natalie said yes.

CHAPTER SEVENTEEN

BAOJIA WOKE with the instinctual knowledge that she was not near him. Her scent lingered, but it was faint. She had been gone for hours. He sat up and quickly and pulled on his weapons. Knives strapped to worn holsters at his thighs. A thin knife went into the waistband of the pants he pulled on, along with another at his ankle. His dress shirt was black, loose enough for movement, and tailored specifically for his body. He grimaced when he buttoned it. He'd have to find a new tailor in… wherever he ended up going. Giovanni's offer of an introduction to Katya in San Francisco teased the back of his brain.

The thought of returning to Northern California appealed to him. He preferred the cooler, misty weather along the northern coast, as well as the quieter feel of the population. Southern California had been his home for over 120 years, but it had never quite fit.

She had a father in Northern California; they didn't speak. He needed to find out why.

He picked up a pencil and punched in the code he'd programmed the night before, then took the note he'd left for Natalie with the numbers. He'd have to burn it before dawn and program another. Part of him wished he could take her to his own place downtown, with its familiar surroundings and ironclad security, but he knew it wasn't possible. He'd have to arrange for his things to be brought from San Diego and stored somewhere until he knew where to go. He'd already called his personal banker to confirm that his domestic and offshore accounts were secure and had not been tampered with. He didn't think Ernesto would try anything, but then his sire hadn't been behaving normally, had he?

So many details…

As if on cue, Caspar appeared at the end of the corridor.

"Ah, Baojia. How are you this evening?"

He nodded at the older gentleman. "I am well. Thank you, Caspar. And how are you and Isadora? I've been meaning to ask, has she had any further problems with her heart? I know it was an issue last year."

Caspar smiled graciously. "The new medication seems to have solved the blood pressure problem. Thank you for asking. And if I may..."

He frowned. "Yes?"

"May I be of any assistance to you? I don't know all the details, but I am aware that you'll be making some changes. I have a full roster of trusted human contacts who might be able to facilitate some of the more... practical details."

It was as if an angel had appeared in front of him with graying hair and a Savile Row suit. "Caspar, I cannot tell you how helpful that would be. I have a home in Coronado I need to empty and another downtown. The downtown house will be more problematic. And I'll need to arrange for storage."

The old man nodded. "We have some available here on the property, or I would be happy to arrange something more private."

"Private, please." A weight had been lifted off his shoulders just by the offer. "Caspar, thank you. Very much."

"Please." He held up his hand. "You have always been generous to Isadora and myself, far beyond what was required of you. It is the least I can do."

"I won't forget this."

Suddenly Caspar smiled. "And I should inform you that Desiree and Matt Kirby are here for the evening. I believe the ladies have all gone to the pool room. Giovanni and Matt are hiding in the library."

"Oh?"

"The ladies took several bottles of wine."

"Ah." The library it was, then. He'd check on Natalie, but he didn't want to intrude on whatever female bonding rituals the wine stimulated. Then again... Caspar had said pool room. Natalie in a bathing suit would not be something to miss. He bid the man goodbye and walked toward the smell of salt water.

Leaning against the door that opened to the underground pool, Baojia smiled. All the women were there. Beatrice and Dez were laughing about something as they sat on the steps. Brigid, the odd fire vampire, was sitting off to the edge, separate, but seemingly at ease and chiming in with the occasional witty remark. He liked the woman's sense of humor, though her carelessness with Natalie's safety still left something to be desired. In the water, Natalie turned and flipped, as comfortable as a fish.

Or a mermaid. The thought made him smile as he watched her. She was wearing a tiny white bathing suit that showed off her creamy skin and freckles. The same skin he could make flush with a whisper or a kiss. His fangs grew long at the thought.

She would make an excellent vampire. She had the intelligence and practicality necessary for their kind, and a humor that would serve her well in immortality. He could see her born to water. Her fair skin grew paler in his mind. Her red hair more vibrant in contrast. Her rosy lips fell open as her fangs dropped. He realized, rather shockingly, that he wanted her to bite him. Wanted the feel of her teeth in his neck.

Ridiculous. It would make her ill to taste his blood.

He willed his fangs to retract as he silently approached. Natalie was doing flips in the shallow end, alternately joking and drinking a glass of white wine. Beatrice and Dez saw him enter; Natalie did not. Stepping to the edge, he reached out with his amnis and called the water to himself. It sang and danced, wrapping around Natalie and pulling her toward the corner where he stood as she yelped in protest.

"Hey! What the—? B, are you—?"

Beatrice held up her hands. "Don't look at me. And hey, leave some water in the pool, will ya?"

He was smiling when the waves whipped her around, bringing her up and toward him as he bent over slightly. Her lips were parted in shock when he leaned down to kiss her.

"Good evening," he said quietly. "I don't want to intrude. I just wanted to check on you."

"Am I going to fall?" Her face was flushed and strands of wet hair curled along her neck. "I feel like I'm going to fall."

He shook his head. "Never." Tucking the hair back, he placed another quick kiss on her mouth before he stepped away from the edge of the pool. "Apparently, I'll be in the library if you need me."

"Oh, I'm fine, we're just—" Her mouth fell open and she looked down to the water that held her. Her cheeks were suddenly rosy again. "Oh, hi. Neat trick."

Baojia released the water he'd been directing over her body and lifted one eyebrow. "In the library if you need me. For anything."

She gulped and nodded. "I'll let you know."

The corner of his mouth turned up as he walked away. "You do that."

"Bye."

"And don't leave the house without me."

"Spoilsport!"

He continued down the hall and up the back stairs toward the smell of fire. The damn Italian always smelled like smoke. He supposed it was instinct that set his fangs on edge. He could also hear Matt Kirby's low voice coming from the room. When he entered, the two men were drinking scotch and leaning over the library table, which was full of Natalie's notes. They had arrived two nights before, just about the time he'd flown off to the desert with Tenzin.

Baojia frowned and cleared his throat, but Giovanni only waved him closer, still concentrating on a map in front of him. "Welcome. I'm assuming you found Natalie already. Please, help yourself to a drink."

He frowned and walked closer. "What are we doing?"

"We're looking over Nat's notes," Matt said with a smile. "And avoiding the girls."

Giovanni frowned at one of Natalie's yellow legal pads. "Apparently, they went over all the files this afternoon while we were sleeping. They're taking a break and…" The scowl deepened. "Comparing notes."

Male alarm bells began to clamor. "About what?"

"Who knows?" Matt shrugged. "All I know is I finally got my mom to babysit Carina, and Dez wanted to come over here." He looked at Baojia and Giovanni. "No offense guys, but you're not that cute."

"None taken," Baojia said. "And did they mention anything specific?"

Matt said, "About us? Or Natalie's notes?"

He honestly wasn't sure which answer he wanted. He decided to stick with murder and political manipulation. "The notes?"

"Beatrice noticed a pattern in the locations the bodies were dropped in. All the locations were within a few miles of Highway 8."

Baojia nodded. "That fits with a big rig coming from Mexico."

"And most of the women—the ones they've identified anyway—have been poor girls who came to Ensenada looking for work."

"Waitresses?"

Giovanni said, "A lot of the families didn't seem to know what the girls did. Or the police didn't ask. She only has the reports they took. But most of them are from around Ensenada."

"Easy prey for Ivan," he muttered. An idea struck him as he looked at the map of the city. "If these girls are from the country, chances are many of them are devout. Is your priest friend coming? Why didn't he come with his wife?"

He saw Giovanni smother a smile. "There might have been a fight. Or five. I sent the plane back for Carwyn almost immediately. He won't be happy about traveling on it, but he'll come if Brigid's here."

Baojia made a mental note to stay out of the way when that reunion occurred. He knew the reputation of the earth vampire who had left the priesthood. He didn't want to stand between the immortal and his fire vampire of a wife if they were in disagreement.

"Why?" Giovanni asked. "What are you thinking?"

"There is a priest…" He pointed to a small church near the downtown area. "Here. He has a shelter for women. Abused. Prostitutes. Homeless. Anyone who struggles, really. I'm almost certain he knows about our kind. It would be suspicious for me to go speak to him now, but if your friend could, he might be able to learn something about these girls. If they were from the country, they might have gone to this church. And the priest might know what their situation was. Were they being coerced? Did their behavior seem odd? I don't know if he would know anything about the elixir, but if girls are disappearing, he probably would have noticed."

"Good idea. I'll have Carwyn get in contact with him when he arrives. I'll be going through the rest of these to see if I can spot anything she missed. What is your plan for tonight?"

How perceptive for the fire vampire to realize he would grow restless poring over pieces of paper. "I am going to trail Rory. It's ridiculous to think he knows nothing about this."

Matt asked, "Do you think Ernesto knows?"

"I don't think so, but he can be… careless." Baojia shifted, uneasy about speaking of his sire in any unflattering way. "He's an excellent politician, but he depends on others too much. When it was me giving him information, he could trust it. But Rory is not me."

"Caspar mentioned Paula came last night," Giovanni said.

"Yes." He flipped through another pad of Natalie's notes.

"Do you think—?"

"I don't know what to think of my sister. I do not believe she would betray our sire. Neither would she choose to be suspicious of her mate."

"And Ernesto?" Giovanni asked. "Does he know about this? Or is he turning a blind eye?"

"Ernesto will do what is good for Ernesto and those under his aegis. He's no philanthropist to the general human population, but he doesn't want to lose face, either. If he was getting the right information, he would see how bad this looks for him. Which is why I think he must be in the dark."

"So… Rory?"

He gave a quick nod. "Rory. I'll trail him tonight. Try to get a feel for what he's doing with me gone."

Matt said, "Be careful."

"I will. Don't tell Natalie where I've gone, and don't let her leave the house."

Matt looked like he'd be avoiding Natalie for the rest of the evening, based on his uncomfortable expression. Giovanni just shrugged and said, "No problem."

Baojia nodded in approval. Maybe the Italian wasn't so bad after all.

He was reassured to find that, other than household security, most of his protocols were still being followed. The businesses and clubs he'd been in charge of in LA still seemed to have the same guards stationed as he trailed Rory in the borrowed Mustang. He grimaced when he realized who Rory's driver was. It looked like poor Luis had been demoted from running the club. He'd have to find a way to make it up to the young man.

Overall, his brother-in-law didn't seem to be doing anything suspicious. It was the same boring routine Baojia had been in charge of for years. He made the rounds, collected the cash, and dealt with whatever minor problems the managers mentioned to him. He made one trip up to

Malibu to rough up a marijuana grower who hadn't paid Ernesto a distribution fee he owed, then he headed down PCH toward Long Beach.

Opening the windows, Baojia followed at a comfortable distance, knowing that Rory was probably heading to Ernesto's yacht. He enjoyed the crisp ocean air whipping through the car and thought about what Natalie had said at the bar.

I miss fog sometimes. Miss the smell of the ocean. It smells like the ocean here, but not the right way. That probably doesn't make much sense.

It made perfect sense to him. The ocean held a million scents. He remembered the smell of the ship he'd taken to America. Even though the human memory was old, it was vivid. He remembered the smell of the fog off San Francisco Bay, and the first memory of waking as an immortal. He'd been near the ocean, and the smell of it—the kelp and crab, cold northern currents, and cypress-scented fog—clung to his mind like some persistent ache.

What if he could go back? What if she went with him? His mind kept circling back to her as he drove. Her intelligence. Her humor. She made him laugh at himself, and no one did that. When he was with her, he felt alive. By the time he arrived in Long Beach, Baojia was ready to jump in the Pacific to distract himself.

Which was fortunate, because he'd have to swim if he wanted to reach Ernesto's boat. He didn't want to attract attention by stealing a smaller craft, so he parked in a dark corner, slipped off his clothes, and swam out to the *Esmerelda*, Ernesto's favorite—and most luxurious—craft. As he approached the boat, he could hear his family dining on the deck near the bow. He clung to the hull and let the wind carry their voices to him.

"—delighted if she would come for a visit. She's a darling girl. And I adore the French."

"Beatrice promised an introduction, but no more. I do not want some silly child boring me with her chatter."

"She's over seventy years old, not a child."

"Desmarais dotes on her—" The wind stole the words from his ears. "—we shall see."

"It would be a good connection to have. Oh, did you see the new film that is opening next week? We must go, Papa. Rory doesn't want to go because it has subtitles."

"It shouldn't be that much work to watch a damn movie, Paula."

"Whatever you like, *querida*..."

They chattered on, the familiar banter of those who had once called him brother and son. Baojia tried not to care. If he were honest with himself, he had never fit in. Not completely. Paula was Ernesto's favorite and always had been. Rory was Paula's mate. And Baojia...

He worked. He made sure things ran smoothly and no one was hurt. He had the sudden realization that his human family and his vampire family were startlingly similar.

"Do you see? They are settled now. Your father has his own shop, and your brother has a future. Your mother mends clothes, but soon, she will not even have to do this and will be comfortable in her old age." Ernesto leaned toward him, whispering into his ear as they stood in the dark alley in Chinatown, so near where he had first encountered the strange creature. The familiar, comforting lilt of his native tongue filled the air as Ernesto continued in English. "Your sister will make the finest of marriages. She is a good girl from a respectable family. She will have her pick of husbands."

Baojia watched from across the road as his mother swept the dusty front step and his father counted the new money at the counter. His brother was now as tall as he was; they had once looked like twins. But his brother still had the slight frame of a young man and the pale complexion of a clerk, unlike Baojia's ruddy skin and thicker shoulders. He craned his neck to see his little sister, now grown into a young woman. Beautiful. She was beautiful.

He blinked back tears. It had been worth it. A fair bargain with the monster.

His family would be safe. They would never see him again, but Baojia would know they were safe in their new life. They had a shop his money had helped pay for, along with a contribution from the vampire who would sire him. They had a prosperous future ahead of them. It was the best he could give.

"Are you ready now?"

He slowly nodded. "Yes, Father. I am ready."

Baojia shoved back the unexpected memory. He hadn't checked on his human family in years. Perhaps it was time. His brother had married and had three children. His sister had raised even more. Some of their grandchildren were now among the wealthiest in the city. The Chen family had respect and long ties in the Chinese-American community in San Francisco. And they had no idea who he was.

I like you the most, George.

He smiled at the memory of her voice, despite the cold water and the feeling of isolation. He glanced up at the lights on the deck, shining over the harbor as he hid in the shadows.

They didn't deserve you...

Baojia looked for the moon, finding it lower than he had expected. How long had he been gone? He dropped back in the water and swam for shore. Suddenly, returning to Natalie seemed far more important than eavesdropping on a family that had never really been his.

Was it only desire? He desired her deeply, but Natalie wasn't the most beautiful woman he'd ever enjoyed as a lover. Was it her humor? Her intelligence? For some reason, he knew it had become far more than the commitment he'd made to keep her safe.

By the time he reached the house, Baojia's mind had conjured up forty-seven different scenarios that all ended with Natalie in mortal danger. Had she managed to sneak away without someone spotting her? Had Ivan's people somehow slipped past the Italian's guard? Had one of the other enemies he'd gained over one hundred years of violence tracked him down and taken her? Had she hit her head on the edge of the pool? Had she tripped and fallen down the stairs?

His mind was on the edge of exploding with all the ways the human could die. It was exasperating. Infuriating. She was ridiculously vulnerable. He parked the car in the driveway and rushed through the kitchen door. Beatrice was sitting at the kitchen table, sipping what smelled like coffee.

"Where is Natalie?" he asked in a clipped voice.

She lifted one eyebrow. "Hello to you, too. Been swimming in Long Beach?"

"Where is she?"

"Sheesh!" She curled her lip. "Relax. She turned in about an hour ago. Had a little too much wine and got tired of waiting up for you. She's nuts about you, by the way. I'm only telling you this because she's conflicted about it, and I'm pretty sure you're in love with her because you're doing that panicky, protective thing Gio did when I was still human."

He ignored Beatrice's presumptuous statement and asked, "Why is she conflicted?"

"Men." She shook her head. "All idiots. Why do you think, *vampire*? She's human. She's spent her whole life thinking her happily ever after is going to involve finding someone to love and grow old with. Have kids and maybe a dog."

Baojia forced himself to relax and stepped closer. "I don't have a problem with dogs. I'll get her a dog."

"That's not..." Beatrice shook her head. "That's not the point. She's adjusting to the new reality, you know? She's had, what? A couple of weeks? It took me months to get used to the idea with Gio. Years, really."

Baojia smirked and sat across from her. "I remember. It was kind of fun to see you put him through the wringer."

"Yes, I'm sure you enjoyed that." Beatrice set down the coffee and reached for his hand. "You were a good friend to me, even when I didn't know it. And... if there hadn't have been Gio—"

"Don't. There was. There always was. And it's not the same." He looked toward the door. "Nothing is the same with her."

"I'd like to see you happy."

"I am," he said, somewhat surprised. "I think... I am."

She smiled. "Then run along." She picked up her coffee again and sipped. "And don't mess it up."

Baojia rose and walked toward the door that would take him back to her. He paused at the threshold. "Beatrice?"

"Hmm?"

He turned and leaned against the wall. "Do you ever wonder?"

"About..." She raised an eyebrow.

"Yeah."

She grinned. "When he's pissing me off? Sure."

Baojia broke into a grin and started to laugh as he walked down the hall and toward the lower floors. He punched in the code and slipped into the dark room where Natalie was already sleeping. As he reprogrammed the lock, he noticed she had left on the light in the bathroom and had pulled his pillow under her face, clutching it as she slept.

"Natalie?" He laid his clothes carefully over the chair in the corner when he undressed. He'd hang them the next night. "Natalie?" he whispered again as he slid into bed behind her.

"Hmm?"

"I'm back."

She was still sleeping, but she snuggled up next to him, tucking her back into his chest and fitting their bodies together like two pieces of a puzzle.

"Hey. Cold."

"Sorry about that. I was swimming."

"Gonna talk tomorrow, mister."

No doubt she'd have an opinion about him taking off without her. Baojia smiled. "I'll put it on the schedule."

"Hmm," she sighed. "Going back to sleep. Missed you."

Murder. Betrayal. An uncertain future. And despite it all, he was happy.

"I missed you, too."

CHAPTER EIGHTEEN

NATALIE WAS TRYING to take her first *tai chi* lesson seriously. Really. She was. But the feel of Baojia moving her arms and legs into various positions, then standing really close to move her from form to form was more than a little distracting.

"You should really put on a shirt if you want me to concentrate."

He moved in front of her and tilted her chin up as she stood with arms stretched out and legs half-bent. "I don't have many clothes here, and I'm not going to ruin my nice shirts practicing. Now focus."

She muttered, "Kind of hard to do after that thing you did an hour ago."

A lift at the corner of his mouth was the only reaction she got.

They were in Beatrice and Tenzin's studio again, but this time it was just the two of them in the empty practice room. She focused on moving her limbs slowly. Deliberately. Her breath moved in and out of her body at a steady rate. She'd never been athletic, but she had practiced yoga with her mother her whole childhood. Though she'd stopped after Mallory Ellis's death, the breathing exercises were like riding a bike.

Baojia moved around her, sometimes demonstrating, sometimes correcting. Always very... present. Even when he didn't say a word, she was intensely aware of him.

"Soften your arm. Keep it relaxed, but strong."

She frowned. "I'm not sure what that means. And this seems so slow. Why are we—?"

"The purpose of teaching you this self-defense technique is to teach you to respond to an opponent with more physical strength than you. You will not be able to counter with an equal opposing force, so you must learn to yield to it." He stepped forward, moving one of his arms as if to punch her. She tried not to flinch when he grabbed her arm and moved it to block his. Her balance shifted without thought. "Yield to it, then counter. The best fighters know how to avoid a fight if they can. Never waste energy on an unnecessary struggle. It will leave your resources drained when you might need them later. *Avoid* the punch." He moved her arm across his, directing it to the side so that it passed her body, leaving them in an odd embrace. "See? You will do this slowly, then the movements will become very natural. Your balance is excellent. You have a good awareness of how to move in response to me already."

She couldn't hide the smile. "You've mentioned that."

Natalie felt his chest move in silent laughter. Then his arm reached back and around her waist, pulling her closer. "I'm teaching. Pay attention."

She felt the flush rise in her face when her skin pressed against his. "Trust me. I'm paying attention."

His energy hummed under her fingers. Touching Baojia was like putting her hand over an electrical wire. His skin contained him, but just barely. It was as if power vibrated under her fingertips. Keeping her close, he moved into another position.

"Try this—no wait, I'll demonstrate first."

He pulled away and showed her another form, then moved back and helped her position herself correctly. They practiced for another hour like that. Natalie could tell he was a great teacher, but if he wanted her to learn self-defense, she had a feeling there were other, faster, methods.

"How long does it take to learn this?"

"The proper practice of tai chi takes years to master. But it is an excellent martial art." He paused to let her get a drink. The slow practice had been unexpectedly tiring and her muscles already felt it. "You will be able to practice this your whole life."

Her whole life? See, it was phrases like that she simply couldn't brush off. Because *her* whole life and *his* were vastly different. Turning away from him, she stared at the fountain in the corner. "What the hell are we doing?"

She heard him, felt him, come to her side. She was starting to get used to the speed, but other things, like his complete stillness when he was unsure of a situation, still kind of freaked her out. He was still as a statue when she turned back to him.

"What do you mean? We're practicing. You're learning self-defense."

She set the water bottle down on the bench and threw a towel around her neck to have something to hold on to. "You're teaching me something that takes years to master."

"Yes."

She remained silent, waiting for him to speak. Surprisingly, she didn't have to wait long.

"You're under my aegis, Natalie." His face was doing that whole closed-off thing it did. She couldn't read him at all. "That means I am responsible for your safety."

"Does it mean I belong to you in some weird vampire way?" He paused long enough for her to guess the answer. She felt her temper rise. "Dammit, Baojia, I'm not a… possession. I have a life of my own. Whatever we're doing here doesn't change that."

He stepped closer and she saw the flash in his eyes. "You're right. What *we're* doing doesn't change that. It changed the minute you walked into Ivan's bar and became a human on his radar. Don't think you can avoid this."

"I'm not trying to avoid anything!"

"You're trying to avoid the reality that *you* are the one who walked into this, Natalie. I didn't pull you in. You walked in. And you can't just walk out without consequences."

Her stomach dropped. "Is that a threat?"

His eyes closed and he shook his head. "As if I would threaten you. As if… Natalie, I am the *last* person on earth who would ever hurt you. But you have to realize that others will. If I'm not there—"

"You weren't here last night." Her anger spiked. "You took off without me to go tail Rory, and you didn't even tell me."

She saw his fangs fall. "Is that what this is about? You're pissed off that I went somewhere without you?"

"This is *my* story. I should be there if you're going to—"

His control snapped. "It's not a fucking story! It's a deadly game that someone is playing with consequences you don't even want to imagine. And you put yourself on the board. I tried—" He grabbed her shoulders. She thought about pushing him away, but didn't. "I tried to keep you out of it, but I couldn't. You wouldn't let me. And now…" His hands softened and he took a calming breath. "You're more than just an innocent bystander. You're more than Dez's friend. You're…"

She stood, trembling with anger, but also with fear. Because he looked afraid. And if Baojia was afraid of anything, then it was something to take seriously. "I'm what?"

His hand left her shoulder and pressed against her chest right over her heart. It pounded at his touch.

"You're so vulnerable. A thousand different things can kill you in the space of a heartbeat. I'm trying. I'm *trying*, but I would sincerely like to lock you in a padded room until I can kill every vampire who looks sideways at you. Maybe then we could have a rational conversation about this. Right now, all I can think of is all the ways you could be killed, and I wouldn't be fast enough to save you."

How could he be so frightening and so sweet, all at the same time? "A padded room?" she said hoarsely. "I'm not *that* nuts, George."

Baojia pulled her into his arms and she let him. He pressed her against his chest and just held her. "You are completely nuts," he said. "But for some reason, I like it."

She wrapped her arms around his waist and hugged him back. "I'm getting attached to your overly protective, control-freak self, too." Getting attached? She was half in love with him. It had happened so fast she was still reeling.

"I'm teaching you this because I need you to be alive, Natalie. Do you understand?"

She hugged him tighter and sighed. "But it takes years to learn."

"I have time if you do."

"I know." She blinked back tears, hoping he couldn't feel them on his skin. "I know you do."

They were driving down to the desert in his old Camaro again, but by this time, Natalie found the lack of lit-up switches and dials soothing rather than disturbing. She was starting to see the unexpected benefits of a life without as much technology. Her eyes were more sensitive to changes in light and movement in the dark interior of the car. Her ears weren't distracted by anything but the hum of the wheels as they sped over the cracked asphalt.

She still missed her iPhone, though.

"Hey, when am I getting a phone? You owe me one."

He glanced over. "We can go tomorrow and get you one. Will you lose anything from your old one?"

"I had it synched up with my laptop, so not much. Still not apologizing for taking it, huh?"

He smiled. "Nope."

Typical. He probably didn't apologize for much. At least when he did, she'd know it was sincere. "I need to call Kristy and let her know where I am. And I don't even want to think about what she's going to tell me about work." She sighed. "I'll be amazed if they haven't fired me already."

"You told me you had sick days."

"Yeah, I'm pretty much to the end of those. And how long is this going to take before I can get back to work?" And, as suspected, he had no response to that. She decided to change the subject. "So, Rory, huh?"

"His involvement makes sense and it doesn't. He's either clueless—a definite possibility—or he's letting Ivan dump his victims on Ernesto's property. According to Brigid and Gio, most of the major water vampires on the Atlantic have had challenges to their authority recently. If this is connected to the spread or distribution of Elixir—"

"Which everyone seems to think is likely."

"—then we need to be prepared for Ernesto to be challenged, too. But at the same time, what's in it for Rory if Ernesto is challenged? He's got a pretty easy life right now. Well, not as much now that I'm gone, but he still has a lot of status. Ernesto has always been generous with him and Paula. So changing the status quo makes no sense."

"One, you're asking almost as many questions as me now; I'm so proud. And two, sometimes people's motivations for crime don't make sense. Sometimes…" Her voice fell. "…they can seem downright crazy. Or there is no purpose. No reason. I've seen that, too. You really think these murders are linked to some big conspiracy?"

"They're either linked, or it's a hell of a coincidence. Elixir just happens to show up in Mexico, and Ivan just happens to lose a waitress who's been taking it, who just happens to show up dead near my sire's casino? I don't believe in coincidences like that. Hopefully, we'll find out more tonight."

She had forced him to take her when she heard he was going out to the casino again. It was time for the regular monthly meeting that Rory would have with the manager, and since Baojia wanted to talk to Tulio again, he thought they could investigate Rory's involvement and speak to Tulio with one trip. Well, originally he had thought to do all that by *himself*, but she'd shown him the error of his ways and badgered him into taking her, too.

"...and you're not going to wander off anywhere without me. No matter what you hear. Or see. Or suspect."

"Yes, Commander George."

"I like you so much when you're cooperative, I'm going to ignore the sarcasm."

She snickered. "You like the sarcasm."

He didn't say anything for a few moments, then he finally muttered, "Fine. I like the sarcasm."

They arrived at the casino only minutes behind Rory, judging by the still-warm engine of his car. The driver was nowhere in sight. Baojia pulled a beanie onto his head and grabbed her hand. "Let's go."

Natalie tried not to laugh. He was wearing clothes he'd borrowed from Ben, of all people. The young man was tall for his age and between his wardrobe and Matt's they had managed to make Baojia look much younger and more casual. He was wearing jeans and a tight grey T-shirt with skulls on it. A brown leather jacket and beanie completed the look of a young man out with his girlfriend for an evening of gambling and fun.

"You look so much younger without the badass black dress clothes."

He tugged her hand and grinned. "I know. You're such a cradle robber."

Natalie threw her head back and laughed. "Thanks, George. It's a good thing I'm a confident woman."

He pulled her back and laid a heart-pounding kiss on her lips as Natalie tried to remain standing. He might have looked different, but his lips didn't feel any less intense. His desire didn't feel any different. She let out a soft sigh when he finally pulled away.

"You have every reason to be confident."

"Good to know."

His smiled dropped. "Now stay close. I doubt anyone is going to recognize me dressed like this, but I don't want you out of my sight if we need to run."

They walked in, and Natalie was immediately assaulted by the casino smell. The smoke wasn't as bad as it used to be, but there was still the stale air and pervasive smell of cheap liquor and beer that seemed to seep from every surface of the building.

She heard him mutter, "I hate this place."

"Too loud? You used to run a club."

"And I hated it. Loud. Smelly. Too many people in one place."

"Grumpy old man."

His eyes narrowed on something she couldn't see. "The grumpiest. I see Rory. And Luis. Poor kid. We'll have to avoid him—he'll recognize me."

Baojia steered her toward the left, deftly avoiding the crowds as he made his way back toward a staff entrance. From his pocket, he pulled out a thick wallet and opened it. "Top card on the left side. Let's hope they haven't changed the codes."

She pulled the card from the thick paper envelope that encased it. No doubt, the wallet and envelope were both necessary to protect the magnetic strip from the vampire's natural electrical current. She quickly slid it into the lock and pulled the door open when the light lit green. Without a backward look, he slipped inside and she followed him, keeping her head up while glancing from the corner of her eye at the cameras which were sure to be following them.

"You've done this before," he said softly, walking at the same confident pace she was.

"Breaking and entering? Half the trick is just looking like you're not trying to hide what you're doing. I wish I'd been able to get ahold of a waitress's outfit."

He shook his head. "No waitstaff allowed back here. Admin only." He turned right, gently nudging her to follow him. "Hold on." He stopped and waited near a water fountain. After a few moments, she saw him push the button and grab a handful of water, snaking it between his fingers in what almost looked like a nervous gesture.

"What are we—?"

"We'll stop here. I can hear them. We're close enough to the office now."

"But *I* can't hear them." She tried to go farther, but he grabbed her.

"No. You'll just have to trust my ears."

She glanced between his hard eyes and the length of the hallway. Sighing, she gave up. She'd never get past him, and he was probably right. If he could hear, then it would be far safer to remain closer to the exit if they should happen to get caught.

"Fine, but what are they—"

"Shh." He was already listening. Natalie crossed her arms and leaned against the wall, watching him. His face was a picture of concentration, his eyes narrowed, his forehead furrowed. The water continued to slip over and under his fingers before circling his wrist and traveling back to his palm as they stood idly in the hallway while Rory and the manager had their meeting. It was mesmerizing. She hardly noticed when a fine thread of it reached out and touched the end of her finger. Then she felt the sting of a small shock, like a burst of static electricity.

"Ow! How did you do that?"

"Pay attention," he whispered with a grin.

"What are they talking about?"

He shook his head. "Nothing out of the ordinary. They're almost finished. I doubted the casino manager would be involved in anything shady. He's human and he really likes his job."

"What's the next step?"

He tossed the water back in the fountain, then nudged her back down the hall. "Let's go play the slots."

Natalie frowned. "You mean… you really want to gamble?"

"No, but the nickel slots have a good view of where Rory will exit. And I want to know if he meets with anyone else before he leaves."

They left the staff hallway with no questions asked and wandered over to the slot machines until Baojia spotted two stools in the right location. He nodded toward them, but she pulled him back. "They're occupied."

"No, they're not." He walked over and laid a hand on the retired couple that looked like slot machines were their second career. Both leaned toward him a second, then abruptly stood to leave, taking their giant cups of coins with them. Natalie just shook her head and went to a change machine nearby.

"What are you doing?" he asked from the now free machines.

"Getting nickels. Nickel slots are the luckiest."

She waited for the machine to spit out a ticket, then walked over to the machine and sat down.

"You know the odds on these, right? None of them are actually lucky."

"Oh, be quiet and let me dream, George. I'm gonna hit it big on the nickel slots while we surveil the bad guys. I feel lucky tonight."

He laughed but let her start to play without any other comment, his eyes already sweeping the room.

"So, the thing you did with the people sitting here? Kinda creepy."

"I avoid using amnis to manipulate humans, but sometimes it is necessary. And most humans aren't like you; they would rather be oblivious."

She pulled the lever on the machine, hoping to make her twenty dollars last longer. "You did that to me?"

"Sort of." He shook his head at the approaching cocktail waitress, and the woman walked away. "You had a much stronger reaction than they did."

"You mean I tried to kiss you? Bet you're glad that didn't happen with those two."

She heard him laugh as she played. She looked around, too. But other than Luis, who she spotted near the door Rory had gone in earlier, she didn't recognize anyone. She couldn't even spot any vampires. If they were enjoying the games, they blended in well. But then again, even with their slightly paler skin, they definitely could in this lighting.

Baojia sat next to her, ignoring the slot machine in front of him but running an absent hand up and down the small of her back. She tried not to melt into a puddle. He probably didn't realize the effect he had on her. Slow, steady, she wanted to take that hand and put it someplace far less appropriate, but she also didn't want to get kicked out and arrested for public indecency, so her back was probably safer. She did, however, feel him tense when he recognized someone. She bit her lip and forced herself to remain looking at the slot machine.

"Who is it?" she asked under her breath. "Who did you see?"

"Well, isn't that interesting?"

"Dammit, Baojia, what are you—"

"Told you I don't believe in coincidences."

Natalie looked up to see Rory shaking hands with a man she recognized from Bar El Ruso, and the smiling manager was ushering them over to a dark-paneled door.

"That's not Ivan. Is that—?"

"Carlos. Now why on earth would my dear brother-in-law be having a meeting with Ivan's right-hand monster?"

Chapter Nineteen

RORY, RORY. What are you doing?

Baojia reached for Natalie's hand and slid around the slot machines, trailing his brother-in-law and Ivan's most trusted employee. Carlos was the one Ivan sent when he couldn't meet personally but needed someone smart and loyal. Baojia had no idea why Carlos was so devoted to his boss, but they may have been related some way he wasn't aware of. The two vampires headed for one of the private rooms in the back of the casino, closing the door just as Baojia turned the last corner.

Shit.

"There's no way I'm getting in there."

Natalie looked around. "Want me to find a waitress's uniform?"

He felt his fangs fall at the idea. The insane way this woman was willing to run toward danger unnerved him. "Natalie, the only humans in that room aren't going to be serving drinks. They'll *be* the drinks. No. You're staying with me."

"Don't get your panties in a bunch." She pulled her hand away and leaned against the wall. "It was just a suggestion."

"You have no sense of self-preservation." He took her hand again and started toward the exit.

"That's what I have you for. Preservation. Where are we going?"

"Back to the parking lot. I want to see what Carlos is driving and if anyone is with him."

The casino was like a maze. A buzzing, flashing, clanging maze. How humans could stay in one for hours on end, he had never understood. They were walking down one long aisle of slot machines when Baojia saw

Luis heading straight for them. In one smooth movement, he turned, pushed Natalie against the side of a machine, and kissed her.

Baojia let himself get lost for a moment. The taste of her, that faint taste of vanilla and mint from the gum she chewed, hit him. His fangs lengthened, throbbing with the need to bite, take, possess. She didn't push him away but pulled him closer, tugging on the lapels of his jacket as she met his desire with her own. One of his hands reached for the tangle of hair that drove him crazy. He grasped the red waves in his fingers and tugged, pleased to hear her breath catch as he felt her body react.

She met him, kiss for kiss. Touch for touch. She was perfect under his hands. A flash of her body rising to meet his was all he allowed before he pulled away, glancing over his right shoulder to make sure Luis had passed by the anonymous couple kissing in the casino.

"Did he see us?" Her voice was just a little breathy. Baojia turned back to her and smiled.

"How do you know I wasn't just overcome with desire and had to kiss you right this minute?"

Natalie snorted and pushed on his chest, smiling as she started walking toward the exit again. "You? I don't think you're overcome by anything, Mr. Cool and Confident."

"You might be surprised." He reached over and took her hand again, acknowledging the indulgence to himself. He liked holding it, plus he knew she wasn't wandering away from him when he did, so he could allow himself to enjoy it.

As they passed through the dark glass doors, he reached out with his senses to detect any stray trails of energy. Just like humans left a scent trail as they shed minute particles of skin and hair, vampires left a trail of their own. Each vampire had his or her own unique fingerprint that their amnis left. He didn't know why or how, but he often thought if those trails were visible, they would each glow or reflect light at slightly different wavelengths. For now, he could focus on one signature. Carlos.

Knowing his target made it easier. Baojia had met so many immortals in his 129 years that it would be impossible to remember them all, even with the faster cognitive function vampires enjoyed. But knowing it was Carlos, whose trail he'd just caught in the casino, made following him much easier. Now to determine which vehicle in the sea of cars was his.

"Follow me, but don't talk. I need to concentrate."

Natalie trailed after him, quiet as a mouse. As silly as she pretended to be, at times, when her professional instincts were triggered, she was all business. He found the juxtaposition of Serious Natalie and Fun Natalie intriguing. She was highly intelligent but down-to-earth. He admired her determination even though it exasperated him. She believed in justice and right and wrong; that the good guys should win and the bad guys... serve a long and fair prison sentence in a humane facility of the state's choosing. He couldn't help but smile. She was so much of what he once was before a hundred years of politics and pragmatism had worn him down.

He stopped and let her catch up to him.

"Did you find it?" she asked as he turned toward her.

"I understand."

She frowned, obviously confused. "What? You understand what?"

"Why you are hesitant about us. I'm not human. I haven't been in a long time. And you love humanity." He reached up and trailed his finger along her warm cheek. "You are its champion. I admire that."

She looked away. "That's not it. Not really. And you believe in justice, too. And loyalty. But you're so..."

"Immortal." Her impermanence had eaten him up for nights. "And you are not."

"I'm not."

"We should talk more." He nodded, still stroking along her cheek. "But right now, I should keep looking."

"What are you looking for?" The deep voice rang from the shadowed edge of the parking lot, causing Natalie to jump. Baojia smiled and took her hand again, turning toward Tulio. He'd detected the old vampire on the edges of the desert but didn't know how old the trail was. Apparently, not that old.

"I'm looking for the car Ivan's man was driving."

The big vampire stepped forward. "Who cares? I have something more interesting to show you." He waved them over and Baojia followed.

"Where are we going?" she asked.

"Underground," Tulio said.

She hesitated, but he pulled her along. "Again?"

Tulio chuckled. "Now you'll really see the way to travel, human."

Baojia saw it ahead of them, the black mouth where the sandstone and rock had opened for the earth vampire. Baojia suspected that Tulio had tunnels all through the desert that he used to move around undetected. It was even possible that, like the oldest of their kind, he could stay awake through much of the day, which meant the underground was a safe place to be.

Natalie hesitated. "Wait, we're going down *there*?"

"Baojia, it's a long, fairly straight passage. It goes deeper and shallower, but doesn't twist and turn too much."

"Got it." He let go of Natalie's hand and turned his back toward her. "Hop on."

"You want to give me a piggyback ride?"

Baojia turned to Tulio. "How long to where we're going?"

The other vampire shrugged. "Forty, fifty miles, maybe?"

Baojia asked her, "You want to run to keep up with us for forty miles?"

She was on his back with a leap. "Hope I can hang on."

He reached back and hitched his hands under her knees as she wrapped her arms around his shoulders. "Just close your eyes; I've got you. Try not to worry."

Natalie placed a kiss on the back of his neck, just behind his ear. "I'll try."

The passage was dark as a moonless night. Baojia followed Tulio's trail more like a bat than a vampire, listening for the slight echoes and sounds of the immortal running ahead of him, following the trail of amnis left in his wake. And for forty miles, he didn't breathe as Natalie gripped his neck so tightly she might have been trying to kill him if that was possible. Every now and then, he heard her squeak when a tangle of roots brushed against them or some debris fell from overhead. But she held on. Finally, he felt Tulio begin to slow down and a light glowed farther up the passageway.

When Tulio slowed to a walk, Baojia paused and patted her knee. "You okay?"

"Are we there?"

"I don't know." He brushed the sand from her face and looked for their guide. "Tulio?"

"Here." Just ahead, there was a glowing break in the tunnel. He crept up to it, making sure Natalie was near him.

"What are we looking at?"

Tulio nodded toward the opening. "Look for yourself."

They scooted closer, crawling on their bellies to be able to see out of the crease. When he finally reached the gap, Baojia looked around. It was a moonlit valley, sparse and dry, with similar vegetation to the desert farther north. "Where are we?"

"Northern edge of the cartel's territory. Ivan's territory. Just south of the border."

His thoughts immediately turned to the woman at his side. "It's not safe here."

The vampire shrugged. "We're fine. They'd be foolish to try to best me. This is my desert." Tulio lifted a hand and the earth sighed as it moved for him, widening the opening so they could see more.

"These vampires, they are stronger," Baojia said. "There is a drug we haven't told you about, and it makes them more powerful."

"I was wondering about that. Something seemed different." Tulio lifted one eyebrow. "It makes them stronger. Does it make them crazy?"

"Yes," Natalie said. "It's called Elixir, and it affects your amnis. Also, it smells like pomegranates, so don't drink anyone who smells that way."

He huffed and nodded toward the valley. "That explains a few things."

Baojia squinted. "Is that... are those...?"

"People. Humans." There were nine or ten huddled shapes darting around the floor of the small valley. Ducking behind rocks and tumbleweeds. A few seemed to be trying to climb out.

"What are they doing?"

Tulio's eyes narrowed. "Hiding. Before they come. They get an hour. Or the last group did."

"An hour?" Natalie's voice rose. Alarmed. "An hour for what?"

Baojia let out a long breath. "An hour to hide, Natalie. Before they are hunted."

It was barbaric. An old game most civilized leaders had outlawed before he'd been sired. He'd heard the stories, of course, but he'd never seen an organized hunt. Ernesto, even as indifferent to most humans as he was, would never have allowed it.

It was simple, really. His kind were hunters by nature. Long ago, they'd hidden from the sun and humanity had been scarce. They'd used their wiles and hunted discreetly, careful not to take too much from a community lest their presence be suspected. Vampires were, after all, still vulnerable during the day. Others lived apart in large communities like Penglai Island, where the eight immortal leaders of China made their home, keeping a stable of healthy blood donors at their convenience. But for many, the hunting urge was too strong, especially when young or absent the fear of a powerful leader.

And so they hunted. Humans didn't prove much of a challenge unless there were other enticements. Wagering was popular. Setting down rules about speed. Giving the humans weapons to fend the vampires off. All these things prolonged the hunt and added extra amusement. But the practice had almost become taboo with the explosion of the human population. It was considered too risky. Too blatant. And no respectable leader would allow it.

But then, Ivan had always been fond of breaking the rules.

A whiff of enticing blood reached Baojia's nose. There was a human close. A woman. And she had Elixir in her system.

"Ah," Tulio said. "I smell the pomegranate now. This drug, it makes the humans stronger?"

"No, it kills them," Natalie said. "Eventually."

"It makes the vampires stronger at first," Baojia said through gritted teeth. The human was coming closer. "Then it weakens the amnis and causes confusion. It attacks the mind. Eventually, it will drive you mad."

"That would explain their behavior," Tulio muttered. "They seem to hunt the girls in packs. They even fight with each other like dogs. The humans can try to run away, but out here?" Tulio shrugged. "We're miles from anything. Even if they lasted till the morning, they'd die of heatstroke and thirst before anyone found them."

"So Ivan's arranging these hunts?"

Tulio said, "I think so. I haven't seen him, but I recognize some of his men. They don't take part in the hunts, just watch. The vampires hunting are strangers. Lots of languages. Lots of accents."

Baojia sensed it before he saw it. A vibration in the wind or the earth. Something tipped him off that others of his kind were approaching.

"Time's up," Tulio whispered. "We should go now."

"What are you doing?" Natalie said. "We can't just let them kill these girls."

Tulio glared at her. "There will be ten or more vampires, woman. If what you say is true and they are stronger than average, we don't want to confront them. Besides, officially, we are on their territory. They would be within their rights to attack us."

"Baojia!" Her indignant voice tore at him. "You can't let them."

He turned over to look at her. "What would you have me do? Take humans from another's territory? It would start a war. It's likely Ivan or one of his people has fed from all these women before. They are under his aegis to do with as he pleases." He saw her face drain of color. "Natalie, we are not prepared to fight them tonight."

"But… you can't." Her hollow eyes turned toward the women scrambling in the valley. "You're going to just let them die?" He caught her a moment before she made for the opening of the tunnel.

"No." He held her without amnis, restraining her arms and legs as she struggled.

"You… you monster! They're going to kill them!"

Tulio said, "If they don't kill those girls out there, they'll kill someone else tonight. They come in bloodlust. We cannot prevent this."

She was sobbing by then. "You're a bastard. They're going to die and you're not going to help them."

"If we tried to, it would cause more deaths than theirs. Now is not the time."

Tulio said, "Someone is going to hear her. Knock her out."

"No," he whispered, bending down to her ear. "Natalie, you have to calm down. You're putting us all in danger."

"I hate you."

"I don't hate you. And I understand why you're angry." He was angry with himself. The humans did not deserve death. But neither was he prepared to tackle ten elixired vampires that night. He doubted Tulio would help, and Natalie's safety was his first priority. Not to mention, he had no idea if he could control himself around ten women who all smelled as tantalizing as the woman who was scrambling toward their tunnel.

"*Ayúdame*," she cried out in Spanish. "*¡Cristo, ayúdame!*"

Baojia closed his eyes when he heard her.

"She's going to die," Natalie whispered, limp in his arms. "You could help her, but you're letting her die."

What would he do with the human if he did save her? Her sobs grew louder, and Baojia heard the car doors open and close. Then the snarling began as the vampires began to hunt.

"We need to leave," Tulio said. "You don't want her here."

"¡*Ayuda!*" the pitiful human called again. Her blood was redolent with the smell of ripe fruit and sunlight. His fangs lengthened in his mouth and he clutched Natalie closer. She was crying just like the woman outside the tunnel.

"Baojia, please." Her quiet plea did him in. He rolled over and shoved Natalie toward Tulio.

"You carry her. I'll get the woman."

Tulio gaped at him. "What are you doing?"

"Maybe we can't save all of them, but we can take her." He scrambled for some reason to justify his actions. "We'll question her. Find out where they're bringing the humans from. See if she knows the schedule of the hunts. She could be useful."

Tulio lifted an eyebrow, clearly not convinced by his reasoning. Finally, the vampire shrugged and pushed Natalie back toward Baojia. "You carry your woman. I'll bring the girl. I'm older, and her scent won't be as tempting to me."

Natalie clutched at the front of his jacket. "Thank you," she whispered. "Thank you, Baojia."

"Don't thank me yet. You're still not safe."

Baojia saw Tulio widen the tunnel opening, and he could finally see the girl. She was no more than sixteen or seventeen. Her wardrobe didn't say cocktail waitress, it said farming village. He was disgusted with them. Disgusted with himself that he couldn't save more. That he wanted her blood even as Tulio snuck up behind her and put the girl to sleep with *amnis*, lifting her in his arms and turning back to the tunnel.

The old vampire didn't even see it coming.

The wind walker fell with a gust that lifted the dust around him. He snarled, his fangs dripping blood from a previous kill. Baojia shoved Natalie back and scrambled out of the tunnel.

"Behind you!" He reached into his open pockets and grabbed the twin short swords, pulling them out as he launched himself toward the attacking vampire. Tulio had already dropped the girl and turned at Baojia's warning. The wind vampire shot into the air, spreading his arms like some mad bird of prey. He hissed and swooped in the air, angling himself toward the girl lying on the ground.

Baojia stopped and watched him for a second. This creature was already half out of its mind with bloodlust, forgetting the twin threats of two other immortals, his eyes locked on the human. He dove from the air, arms outstretched toward her as Baojia leapt. The elixired blood had captured the vampire and he saw nothing else.

Reaching out, Baojia slashed at the vampire, the cut throwing his opponent to the ground as he reached out for any strength the dry desert air offered him. There was little to be had, so he gripped his sword and threw himself toward the mad immortal who had taken to the air again, his eyes still following the unconscious girl.

"Get her out of here," Baojia hissed. "Get my woman and the girl out of here."

"You'll take care of him?"

Another swoop downward and another slash at the soft midsection of his attacker. "I'll be fine. Go."

The wind vampire's eyes darted away from them and toward more cries out in the desert. The sounds of the hunt were everywhere. Women screamed. Vampires snarled. The scent of blood drifted on the wind. Baojia had to end the fight before he lost control of his own lust or attracted more attention.

Leaping up, he flipped over his opponent as the vampire dove after the retreating Tulio. Baojia landed on the monster's back. The creature was strong but distracted. He tossed one weapon to the ground and grabbed for his opponent's long hair, pulling it back to reveal his soft, vulnerable throat. His enemy had just started to let out a frustrated scream when Baojia sliced his sword back, taking off the vampire's head with a clean stroke. He tossed it over the rise of a hill and kicked the body to the side before he reached down and grabbed his sword. He took only a second to clean the blade on the dead vampire's shirt before he walked back toward the tunnel. Tulio and Natalie were still there with the unconscious girl. Natalie's eyes were glued to the blood that had sprayed over his chest.

"I couldn't get her to leave you here," Tulio complained. "She's far more stubborn than mine."

He didn't say a word, just tore his borrowed pants a little more at the thighs and sheathed his blades before he turned his back to Natalie. After a second of hesitation, she hopped on and wrapped her legs around his waist. Baojia grabbed on and said, "Let's go."

CHAPTER TWENTY

SHE WATCHED HIM wash in the small basin Cirilda had provided when they returned to Tulio's cave. The girl was still unconscious but safely stowed in a locked room that only Tulio and Cirilda could enter. Baojia had taken Natalie by the arm and led her to his own chamber before leaving to return with a basin of clear water to wash up. He had let her wash first before stripping off the borrowed clothes, still silently stewing about something.

"Are you brooding?"

"No," he said quietly. "I am thinking. I don't brood."

The drip and splash of the water echoed off the smooth walls. He dipped the washcloth in, then covered his face, wiping away the grime that had accumulated as they traveled under the earth. He wet the cloth again, and Natalie rose from the bed in the corner. Cirilda had loaned her one of Tulio's shirts, which fell to her knees. She padded over to Baojia and reached around to grab the washcloth from his hands, trying to ignore the red stains from the blood he washed away.

"I'll get your back."

"Thank you."

The tense muscles began to relax under her fingers as she smoothed the washcloth over his shoulders. "What are you thinking about?"

He was silent for a few more minutes, standing still as she rinsed out the cloth to wash around his neck and the backs of his ears. "I am thinking… those women did not deserve to die."

Natalie bit her lip to keep from crying. "We saved one."

"Yes. But not the others. This has to end. I cannot bring it to Ernesto at this point, but it has to end. Too many have already died, and I have done nothing to prevent it. I think my own brother may be involved, and I didn't see it. This should not have gone on as long as it has."

She had a vision of him, flying out of the cave toward Tulio and the girl, leaping in the air to slash at the monstrous creature that had come after them. The thing had scarcely looked human, and it had moved so fast, Natalie could barely see it. She hadn't seen much of the fight, it was dark and they moved too fast, but she had seen Baojia end it, ruthlessly cutting off the head of the monster and tossing it aside as he used the dead vampire's shirt to clean the blade that had killed him.

And yet, here he stood, thinking not about the girl he had rescued, but the ones he had not.

"I think you're much harder on yourself than anyone else." She lifted an arm to clean along his side.

"I don't compare myself to others. That's useless."

"But you expect more—"

"I expect," he said, spinning around, "to protect those I am responsible for. To cause as little harm as is possible for one of my kind. And I expect you to take off that shirt because it smells like Tulio and, as much as I like the man, I do not want his scent on your body."

She blinked and looked down at the shirt. "Are you serious?"

"Very."

"I don't have anything else to sleep in."

"I don't care." Then a smile touched his lips. "And it's hardly necessary, is it? I've seen every freckle."

She rolled her eyes. "I'm not being modest. It's cold down here."

"The shirt, Natalie."

"Fine." She was already blushing when she pulled it over her head and tossed it in the corner. "Happy?" Her face was on fire.

"Yes." He gave her a smug look before turning around again. "Could you get between my shoulders now?"

"You ass!" She laughed and slapped at him with the washcloth, happy that he seemed to be coming out of his mood. She pressed against his back and let one hand trail down his stomach as she dipped into the basin again. "Between your shoulders, huh?"

His breath hitched at the feel of her fingers. "Among other places."

She smiled against his back. His skin was alive. The hair on her arm rose simply by touching him.

"You're a good man," she whispered. "I won't believe otherwise."

"Natalie—"

"Shhh." She saw his head fall forward and heard him groan as her hand slid beneath his waistband. "Let me take care of you for once."

Natalie was lying in his arms, drifting off to sleep after their very long night, when she heard him.

"Natalie?"

Her eyes were closed, but she answered, "Hmm?"

"Talk to me about your job."

She pulled away from the hypnotic feel of his skin and rubbed her eyes. "Well, I'm going to run out of personal days soon. I was supposed to be following this story on my own time, with the backing of the paper, but still on my own time. I have court cases to report on. Regular crimes. Local politics. Stuff like that. I'm sure Kristy's probably pissed at me, but she can't do anything about it because I have so much personal time saved up."

He trailed a finger up and down her arm. "And what about when it runs out?"

She had a feeling he wasn't really all that interested in her job. "What do you really want to know, Baojia?"

He reached for her and pulled her to lie on his chest. "You are under my personal aegis," he said quietly. "But I cannot stay in Southern California. Not while my sire rules here."

She froze. Natalie knew he had quit his position in his father's business, or organization, or whatever it was. But she hadn't realized he would have to leave.

"So what does that mean? Explain it to me."

"It means I am responsible for you. Both for your actions and your safety. But you live here. And I cannot stay here."

"You're saying if I did something any vampire considered a threat that *you* would be the one responsible?" She looked away. "That's... medieval."

"Yes." He pressed gentle fingers to her face so that she was forced to look at him again. "Some of my kind would use amnis to make a human go where they wanted. I could do that, but that's not what I want."

Natalie forced back the tears. She didn't want to cry while she was looking at him, but the crushing sense of loss was almost overwhelming. Once again, she felt like she was losing everything. "What are you asking me, Baojia?"

The insistent fingers on her cheek turned soft and soothing. "You have family in Northern California. Could you—"

"I don't talk to my dad. Maybe once a year."

"Why?"

She rolled away from him. He tried to grab her, but she pushed him away. "Don't."

His voice held an irritated edge. "What do you want to know about my life that I haven't told you? Ask me, right now, and I'll answer."

She closed her eyes and took a deep breath. He was right. As many questions as she had asked, he had been forthcoming about his past. And he knew nothing about her.

"Your father is a police officer."

Her eyes flew to his. "How did you—"

"Guesswork, mostly. At the bar, the way the retired officers talked to you... It made sense."

"Yeah." Somehow, it made it easier that he already knew part of it. "He was a detective in Oakland. That's where I grew up."

"I remember. And your mother?"

"My mom was not a cop." She took a deep breath and forced out a rueful laugh. "She was a mom, mostly. And a writer. A poet. She'd been published a few times. She and my dad were complete opposites. He was the strict cop, she was the hippy poet who did yoga and wore caftans to PTA meetings."

His voice softened and he moved closer. "You loved her."

"We both adored her." She tried not to tense when he touched her shoulder. "My parents had a great marriage. We had a good life."

"What happened? Your mother is dead?"

"There was... this homeless man in our neighborhood. Well, there were lots of homeless people, but she always took Oscar food because he usually stayed around our corner. She helped him find a shelter when it got cold. Tried to help him find work here and there. He was a vet, I think." Natalie frowned. "He had a lot of... issues he never got the right help for. But Mom always said we were all someone's child and some people just needed an extra hand sometimes. That's the way she was."

"She sounds like a very fine woman."

"She was. She was the best."

"This Oscar…" His voice was soft and coaxing. "Did he hurt her?"

"He was harmless, mostly. Everyone in the neighborhood knew him. Helped him out a little. But he adored my mom. Called her his angel."

"What happened?" Baojia had moved behind her and put his hands on her shoulders, slowly drawing her back to his chest and covering her with one of the blankets on the bed.

"She would let him in the house to take a shower when he got really dirty. Dad told her not to do that, but I know she did when he needed it and couldn't find room at a shelter. One day, my dad picked me up from school and we went home." She started trembling. "And… Dad went in the kitchen. She was there. He had killed her with a kitchen knife."

"Oh, Natalie." He whispered her name and rocked her back and forth. She felt numb, relating the story as if it was just another she was reporting. She put her hands on his arms as they held her.

"My dad… he kind of lost it. He, uh, he left me with a neighbor to call 911 and went looking for Oscar, but the thing was, Oscar wasn't even trying to hide. He was sitting on the corner covered in her blood, sleeping. A hundred people must have walked past him, but no one asked why he was covered in blood. And when Dad picked him up and shoved him against the wall, screaming, he didn't even know why. Mr. Pak, who had the market across the street, told me Oscar kept saying, 'Where's my angel, Mr. Ellis? You seen my angel today?'"

"He didn't know he'd killed her?"

She shrugged. "The doctors think he had a psychotic break. He hadn't taken his medication in a while and he had no idea what he'd done. Had no memory of it. When the police finally got there and put him in the car, he was sobbing. They put him on suicide watch, but he killed himself a few months later."

Baojia had his arms wrapped so tightly around her that she was beginning to wonder if breathing would become an issue.

"And your father?"

"He just… broke. We moved out of Oakland. Left the city. He commuted in for work, and I switched schools. But mostly he disappeared unless he was lecturing me about my safety. He got super-protective. I'm sure he was worried about losing me to something random, too."

"How old were you?"

"I was fifteen when she died. As you can imagine, teenage Natalie was a huge fan of all the new rules."

He let up the pressure on her ribcage and ran a hand over her hair. "I'm sure you drove him crazy."

"Well, I was looking for a reaction." The pressure around her heart eased a little with his touch. "And I got it." She finally turned to him. "You say I can be reckless, but the thing is, there is evil in this world. It's a broken, broken place sometimes. It can be obvious, like Ivan. But sometimes it doesn't even know it's evil. Sometimes it's random and no matter what you do, it will find you. So I don't want to live my life worrying about my safety. I can't, Baojia, because even if I do everything right, even if I followed every one of my dad's rules, or your rules, or any rules… the bad might still find me like it found my mom. That girl you rescued tonight probably wasn't looking for trouble, but it found her. I want to live my life fearlessly and help other people without worrying about myself, because even after what happened to her, I think that's what my mom would have wanted. Does that make sense?"

He was frowning, staring at her hard, as if he was memorizing her face. "It does make sense. Even if I don't like it."

She forced out a wobbly smile. "Be scared. Live anyway."

Baojia drew her back toward the pillows and she could feel him start to slow down. "Rest with me. Sleep. I'm sorry I asked you to share all this tonight. It's already been upsetting enough."

"It's okay." Strangely, it was. Lying at his side, Natalie felt peace. She felt safe with him, safer than she'd felt in many, many years. "It happened a long time ago. I can remember the good things now."

"I'm sorry you don't speak with your father," he whispered. "You should have been a comfort to each other."

"The dad I grew up with left at fifteen when my mom was killed. He never really came back from that kitchen after he went in. I escaped as soon as I could. Southern California was as far away as I could handle."

"And you'd never consider going back?"

"To Oakland?" She shook her head, remembering the streets of her hometown like she'd been there yesterday. "No, I don't want to. I don't want to live with ghosts. Dad moved back, eventually. But I couldn't."

"What about somewhere else? Somewhere north?"

She paused, trying to measure his intent. "What are you saying?"

"I promised to keep you safe, Natalie."

"So I'm just supposed to follow you?" Her heart rate began to pick up again. Was it fear? Excitement? A combination of both? "I'm just supposed to leave my whole life here and follow—"

"Who said you would follow me?" he offered casually. His voice was drowsy as dawn approached. "I could follow you. There's a possibility that a move to Northern California or the Pacific Northwest would be an option for me. Even welcome."

"But—"

"I'm just asking you to think about it."

Think about it. She could do that. Sure, she'd only known him for a few weeks, so why didn't that seem insane?

"I'll think about it." She settled down at his side as he squeezed her shoulders, her eyes already feeling heavy. "But if I can't—"

"Natalie, when I offered my loyalty, it was not with conditions. Now sleep."

"But—"

"Sleep."

The events of the night started to ambush her, and she felt her eyes droop. "Bossy."

"You love it."

Natalie sighed and closed her eyes. "Yeah, George. I think I might."

The girl was named Rosa and she was frightened, looking to Cirilda for reassurance as Baojia and Natalie questioned her. Baojia's Spanish was better than hers, but with over a hundred years to practice, she'd be kind of annoyed if it wasn't.

"Where did you come from?" he asked.

"It's a small town near Ensenada," Rosa said. "No one has ever heard of it."

Natalie saw his nose twitch and knew he was scenting the girl's blood, even though he'd taken hers at nightfall.

"Do you remember what happened?"

She shook her head, then frowned. "Maybe a little? I remember walking at night to my grandmother's house. I was taking her and my mother food because my grandmother has been sick. So I cooked dinner for my brothers and then took some food to my mother and grandmother."

"But you didn't get there?"

"I woke up in a room. I could hear very loud music, like the radio, but much louder. And it was coming from above me."

"The club in Ensenada," Natalie murmured in English. "There had to have been a basement of some kind where they kept the girls."

Baojia nodded, then turned back to the girl. "Did they feed you, Rosa?"

"Yes. They didn't beat me or hurt me. I was fed twice a day, along with the others."

Natalie and Baojia exchanged a look. "How many others?"

"Six. They were all in the truck with me when we went out to the desert last night. Along with some others." Tears filled her eyes. "What happened to them? It sounded like there were animals. Are they dead?" The girl began to sniff.

"Yes, they are probably dead," Baojia replied as Natalie slapped his arm. "What?" He switched to English. "They are. I'm not going to lie to her."

"She's crying!"

"I will not give her some kind of false hope." He lowered his voice to a whisper. "And if she's taken Elixir, then she is probably dying, too. Just more slowly."

Natalie wanted to throw up. This girl, this innocent girl walking to her grandmother's house, had been taken, held captive and fed poison. Solely to make her blood more intoxicating to the vampires who wanted to hunt her. These monsters had to be stopped. And they had to find some kind of help for her.

Baojia continued while Cirilda comforted Rosa. "So, they took you and held you somewhere with loud music. Did you see anyone else? Anyone besides the other girls?"

"Well, there was one man who came in at night, but he never spoke. And…" Her forehead furrowed in concentration. "I don't remember him clearly, but I think he came in every night. I can't remember him now. How strange."

A vampire. Was it Ivan? Carlos? One of the other, nameless monsters that Ivan employed? It didn't even matter. They weren't getting her back, that was for sure.

"Then I remember waking up in the truck heading out to the desert. It was like a delivery truck. And it dropped us off. Some of the girls were crying, trying to ask the driver to take them back, but I could tell he wouldn't, so I didn't bother. Then you found me." She smiled at Natalie.

"We're going to make sure you're safe, Rosa," Natalie said. "We'll get you back to your family."

Baojia's hand darted out to Rosa's and the girl's eyes swirled, then winked shut before he turned to Natalie. "What are you saying? Don't say that."

She frowned. "We're going to get rid of these guys and then send her back, right? I mean, she's innocent. She doesn't even know anything about vampires."

"She has taken Elixir, Natalie. She's walking poison."

Tulio grunted from the corner. "And an appetizing one, too. Any vampire who smelled that blood would want to have a taste."

Temper raised its head. "So what? Are you going to kill her when she's not useful anymore?" She rose to her feet.

Baojia grabbed her hand and pulled her back. "Of course we're not going to kill her."

"I would if it were up to me," Tulio muttered. Cirilda sneered and said something that sounded insulting in her own tongue. Tulio shrugged. "According to you, she'll die anyway."

"Then we have to find a way to help her," Natalie said. "There has to be something we can do."

She sat when Baojia pulled her down. "We'll figure something out. According to Dez, they've been trying to find the right doctor to study this formula. Hopefully someone immortal with experience in medieval alchemy. Maybe having a live… patient will help whoever they find. But she can't go back. Not as she is right now. You can ask your friends—she'll die within months without treatment."

Natalie sat, irritated with Tulio's callous regard for the girl and heartbroken over the situation. "It's not her fault."

"Of course it isn't," he said. "But would you have her spread it to others? What if this is a blood-borne disease and anyone who touches her blood or comes in contact with it is also infected? What if they also spread it? Not only vampires, but humans are in danger until we know more."

She nodded. "Fine. But what are we going to do with her? You think it's a good idea to take her to Gio and Beatrice's House of a Thousand Vampires?"

"Probably not."

"We will keep her," Cirilda spoke in heavily accented English.

"I knew you could speak English!" Natalie almost shouted while Cirilda smirked.

"Woman, you do not consult with me on this?" Tulio asked gruffly.

"We'll take her and keep her until you can find a more permanent solution," Cirilda said, ignoring Tulio. "She'll be safe here. And he won't touch her blood. He only likes mine anyway."

"He only drinks from you? Is that safe?" She blurted out the question before her brain caught up with her mouth. "Sorry, none of my business."

Cirilda stood and walked toward Tulio, patting his cheek as she left the room. "Don't let his face fool you. He is an old, old man. I'll get some clean clothes for the girl and some food for you. You should eat before you leave."

CHAPTER TWENTY-ONE

THE ROAD WAS BLACK and empty on the way to Los Angeles as Natalie and Baojia tossed ideas back and forth.

"You mentioned something about a priest who might know some of the missing girls," she said. "Was it Father Andrade?"

"Yes, how do you—?"

"The first time I worked with my friend Manuel it was on a drug-mule case and he was a source." He saw her eyes drift to the window. "That was a good story. Well, not good, but it had good results."

"These girls, they're a little like drug mules if you think about it."

"Yeah, I guess so." She turned back to him, frowning. "So, Father Andrade? You want someone to go to the mission? I know who he is. I could go down during the day and—"

"Too close to Ivan's club. Even during the day, he could have people watching and they might know who you are. If Brigid's husband comes, he'd be the best person."

"I still think if it was during the day—"

"No, Natalie."

He saw her eyes narrow, but she changed the subject. "Brigid's husband was a priest?"

Baojia nodded. "He's left the Church—well, the priesthood, I guess—and works mostly with Brigid now. But I've been told he still maintains a close relationship with the Vatican. He's an earth vampire. I don't know him that well, but I know he has a huge clan. From what I can tell, he and Brigid have been quietly investigating Elixir ever since it showed up in Dublin, where they live. They have a lot of contacts and if Father Andrade knows something, he'd be more likely to confide in someone connected to the Church."

She was silent again, and Baojia could almost hear her brain spinning as she stared out the window. Finally, she said, "I wonder how long Rosa was kept."

"I was wondering the same thing. Does it take time to work into a human's system? How much do they give them? Does Elixir make the blood more appealing the longer they've been on it?"

Her eyes were lit with wild curiosity. "And why? What's the point of all this? Pure amusement? Or are they inviting people who might not know what the drug does? Political enemies? People they want to weaken? How would they convince them to come? How much do Ivan's people even know about it? You said yourself you'd only heard rumors."

It was a question that had been swirling around ever since they'd made the connection between the missing girls and the Elixir. "It's entirely possible that they know very little about the lasting effects of the drug. I had heard rumors, but only about the benefits. No one mentioned the downsides."

"Big surprise there."

"And Paula doesn't seem to know anything about it. Rory?" he muttered. "I don't know what to think about Rory. When did the first bodies show up in the desert around here?"

"According to what I could find, the first ones were found on the south side of the border about three months ago. No one made any connection between them at first. It seemed random. Then a month later, they started showing up on the American side. It was a cop down in El Centro who tipped me off. I did some investigating on my own before I made the connection with Juarez."

"I don't know if there is any *real* connection with Juarez, Natalie. The more we find out, the more I think that Ivan or whoever is orchestrating this is using that situation as a convenient scapegoat to cover his actions. He makes it *look* like Juarez and no one will see what's really going on. That's why they're dumping the bodies how they are."

"Why not make them disappear? There's no need to dump the bodies. Where they're hunting, they could easily bury them and they'd never be found."

"But they'd still be missing. If too many girls just disappeared, someone might listen to their families. If they're murdered…"

She nodded. "They could be the victim of random violence because they worked in the city. Or they could be the victim of whoever is killing in Juarez and moving west."

"Or victims of smugglers who took advantage of them," he added. "Isn't that what the police think now? If I were Ivan and wanted to cover my tracks, I'd copycat a human killer. Everyone would be looking the other direction, including his bosses in Mexico City."

"But why?" she asked again. "Is this some horrible game? Or is there a plan behind it?"

"I don't know. I didn't recognize the vampire I killed. I'd never seen him before. He could have been a new vampire of Ivan's, but I think Tulio is right. These are strangers he's brought in. The one I killed was stronger because of the Elixir, but normally, I don't think he would have been a challenge. He didn't feel old."

He saw a slight shudder pass over her frame. He wondered if she was bothered by him killing the air vampire or whether her more primitive survival instincts were finally kicking in. They would. The longer she remained in his world, the more they would have to. He didn't live in the kind of polite society where trials and jails happened. And neither did Natalie. She just didn't realize it yet. He was trying to break her in to the idea slowly, but he honestly couldn't see her returning to her old life. She knew too much. She had already been flirting at the edges of vampire attention, being close friends with Beatrice and Dez. She was fully on the radar now.

You need me. He found himself reaching across the car to take her hand. *More than you know.*

She squeezed it as she continued talking. "If we think the first hunts happened around three months ago, it could be that the negative effects of the drug are just becoming known. According to Beatrice, her friend Lucien started feeling strange about three to four months after he had fed from a human who'd taken it. So if they didn't know about it before, they're going to start figuring it out now." She sighed. "Why do I feel like a lot more innocent people are going to die, human and vampire, before this is over?"

Natalie fell silent again, but Baojia couldn't stop thinking about her mother. It explained so much. She was reckless not because she was foolish, but because she'd experienced loss. He found humans—and vampires—who had lost those close to them tended to live either far more cautiously or with less regard for safety than ever. For Natalie, that meant taking chances. No wonder her father worried about her. One night ago, she'd witnessed a monstrous game that made humans into prey, and yet she still offered herself up to go back to the lion's den and talk to the priest.

He had to keep her out of this. She was too fragile. She had no combat training. None. Training her satisfactorily would take years he didn't have. The inevitable confrontation would happen well before she was ready. He wondered if Matt and Dez Kirby might be his best chance at keeping her out of the actual fight. He could knock her out with amnis and lock her up. He didn't want to do it, but he might if it came down to it. She could hate him later—she probably would—but she'd be alive. He'd have time to ask forgiveness.

"What are you thinking?" Her voice jolted him out of his musings.

"What?"

Her suspicious eyes narrowed on him. "You're trying to figure out a way to keep me out of this, aren't you?"

"Absolutely." And he wasn't going to lie about it.

"Forget it. Not going to happen." She crossed her arms and slumped a little. "I'm not a helpless little girl."

"No. From a physical perspective, you're a helpless grown woman. You have no natural defenses against these vampires, and you're a target."

Her jaw was clenched when she said, "Point taken, but you're not leaving me out of it."

Irritated at her willful disregard for her own safety, he gripped the wheel but kept his voice carefully even. "Tell me something, Natalie. When you did that drug-mule story, were the police involved?"

"Eventually."

"And were there arrests made? Were they taken to your human jails?"

"Yes. What does this have to do—?"

His quiet voice rose. "And did you, the intrepid reporter, actually go along *with the police* when they made those arrests?" She was silent.

Fuming. "Did you? Or did you let the police do their job after you had done yours?"

"It's not the same!"

"It's exactly the same!" he exploded, pulling the car over to the side of the road and turning to face her. "And these vampires are far more dangerous than human gangs. These vampires are the people that human gangs run away from!"

She pushed her car door open and walked outside, but he followed her.

"Natalie, don't walk away. You need to think about—"

She spun. "It's not the same! It might not seem logical to you, but I didn't *know* those police. They weren't my friends. And it's my friends I've brought into this. It's my friends who could be in danger because of something that I pulled them into. I can't just stand by while you all—"

"You are not going into any vampire fight. I will not allow it."

"What are you going to do? Knock me out? Lock me in a room while you go fight this?"

Yes. That was exactly what he had planned on doing. Perceptive human. He only crossed his arms and stared at her impassively.

She could read his expression. "Bad idea, Baojia! Bad. Idea. The jury's still out on you, mister. I haven't decided whether you're safe or not, and shit like this is not helping!"

Baojia took a step back, unexpectedly stunned by her words. She didn't know if he was safe? He allowed her—a human he had known for a matter of weeks—to lay by his side while he slept. Utterly trusting that she would do him no harm while he was at his most vulnerable. But she didn't trust him?

It hurt, but that hurt quickly turned to anger.

"You can't trust me?"

Her face fell. "That's not what I meant."

"You said you didn't know if I was safe or not." He stepped forward as she took a step back. It only angered him more. "What have I done to harm you, Natalie? How have I not protected you?"

The color drained from her face. "Baojia—"

"I have done—I would do anything to keep you safe! *Anything*. And yet you say—"

"I don't know if it's safe to fall in love with you!" she shouted, tears falling from her eyes. "And I am. I'm falling in love with you, and it scares me to death."

He halted, standing stock-still as her words reached him.

I'm falling in love with you.

In love. With him?

Her words reached him. Filled him. Soothed him. Excited him.

She was still talking. "And part of me still thinks this is nuts. It *is* nuts! And I have this tiny idea of what your world is, but mostly I feel blind. I'm stumbling into a life I can't see the end of, but you're the only thing that makes me feel the slightest bit sane. And *that's* not sane. You're not human. When you killed that vampire—you cut off his head! You. Cut. Off. His. Head. And you did it like you were taking out the trash. And part of me screamed, 'That's not normal!' while the other part was just happy that it was him and not you. I was *relieved*!"

He stepped closer, put his hands on her shoulders, and drew her near.

"I would be giving up everything to love you," she said under her breath. "I wanted a family. I wanted a normal life. I wanted what my parents had, no matter how it ended, but I've never—" She choked, and he pulled her closer. "I've never felt like this about anyone. I feel crazy, but nothing else makes sense."

He kissed her forehead, holding her as if she was something fine. Breakable. She was.

"Natalie."

"What?"

"No one, in my very long life, has ever told me they loved me."

She sniffed again, and he cupped her cheeks, kissing the angry tears that had fallen.

"Do you realize…" she whispered. "Do you know what loving you would mean for me? For my life?"

"Yes." He kissed her lips gently, then he whispered in her ear, "Love me anyway."

"Baojia," she groaned, trying to pull away. He wouldn't let her. He wanted it—he wanted her—with a desperate kind of longing he'd never allowed before.

"Be afraid," he pressed her. "Be angry. Love me anyway. I promise you won't regret it."

"You can't promise that."

"But I will." He held her as she stood motionless in his arms. "I will, Natalie."

He was afraid to breathe until her eyes lifted to his, defiant again. "Then I do."

Baojia backed her up against the black car. "Tell me."

"I love you."

She said nothing else, because he kissed her with a lifetime's worth of longing. She was his. However she might protest, however they might fight. She was his from that point until the end of her days. His mouth ravaged hers. His fangs fell, cutting the edge of her tongue, but he only sucked it into his mouth, tasting the blood that flowed from the cut. Natalie grabbed his hair, yanking him closer as he lifted her to sit on the edge of the car so they were face-to-face.

"I'm still angry with you," she panted. "Even though I love you."

"I can deal with angry." He yanked her hips to his and she wrapped her legs around him. "I want to bite you. And not because I'm hungry."

"Why—?"

"Do you crave it yet?" He licked up the side of her neck until he could bite the lobe of her ear. "Do you crave my bite like I crave your taste, Natalie?"

Her only answer was a breathy moan. Her head fell to the side, exposing her throat to him. He grabbed the nape of her neck and forced her eyes back to his.

"If you were a vampire, I would take your blood every night. I would give you mine." He grabbed the edge of her shirt, yanking it up and over her head so he could feel the heat of her skin on his. "I would feel your teeth pierce my neck. I would live in your body as you live in mine."

Just then, she leaned over, sinking her dull teeth into the skin of his neck, biting down possessively as her lips sucked.

Baojia roared, his hand slamming into the hood of the car as her mouth pulled. She hadn't broken the skin, but her teeth held him. A thousand nights flashed in his mind. A thousand years of her love. He had to have it. He had been empty until she filled him. With a snarl, he ripped her mouth away, baring his teeth at the drop of blood that lingered at the corner of her lips.

Her eyes held a kind of madness that mirrored his own. She fumbled with his pants, so he quickly shoved them down, then tossed up the skirt she had borrowed. His fingers slid up the heat of her thighs. Hot. She was burning for him, like a fire in the black desert night. The moon shone down on her pale skin as she lay back on the hood of his car, the metal still holding the warmth of the engine. The only sound around them was the whistle of the wind rustling the brush. She glowed. The single bright spot of light in the blackness that surrounded them. No light, except the moon and the stars that dotted the blackness like the spray of freckles along her pale skin.

Suddenly gentle, he trailed his fingers lightly over her delicate collarbone, over the curves of her breasts, the dip of her waist. "You are lovely beyond words," he whispered in Chinese. "For no words deserve you."

She only breathed out, "Please."

Baojia hooked her leg up and slid inside. Her heat surrounded him as he leaned over her body, pressing his mouth to her navel. The ripple of her ribs and the freckles that marked the swell of her breasts. He lifted her arm, drawing it over her head to anchor her as he moved faster.

"Yes," she moaned.

"Yes, what?" One hand locked around her wrist as the other shoved her leg higher, changing the angle as her body bowed up.

"I want it. Your bite." She swallowed hard, the tears teasing the corners of her eyes.

"Then say it." He bit back on his control, slowing down deliberately when he felt her pleasure mounting.

"Bite me, Baojia." Her body arched, trying to move closer to him as he held her down.

"Not that." He pulled her closer to the edge. "That's not what I want to hear."

She blinked in confusion until her eyes met his, then the blue softened as they glittered in the low light of the moon.

Natalie whispered, "I love you."

He let out a harsh breath, leaned down, and bit.

Baojia thought they probably looked like refugees from some post-apocalyptic zombie film when they pulled up to the house in Pasadena. He looked over at Natalie with her torn shirt and dusty skirt. His pants were already ripped at the pockets from having to draw his swords the night before. His shirt was history, and his hair was almost as tangled as hers. They had not been gentle with each other out in the desert, and the dent on the hood of the car... Well, that had been worth it.

He cocked his head, frowning at her. "You know, once upon a time, I would have taken you out and charmed you. There would have been nice dinners and theater tickets. Maybe the opera."

"Do you like the opera?"

He nodded. "I do, actually."

"Then we should go to the opera sometime." She glanced down. "We might want to change clothes."

"San Francisco has an excellent opera."

Her smile was shy, but not forced. "I've heard."

"Just a thought." He got out of the car and zipped around to her door before she could open it.

"My knight in dusty armor," she said, brushing at the tatters of his clothes. Then she glanced at the rather large, hand-shaped dent in the hood of the Camaro. "I almost feel sorry about that."

"Don't. It was dented for a worthy cause." He caught her glancing at the spot on his neck that had already healed, and she blushed. He was about to give the neighbors another show when he heard the motorcycle coming up the street. Baojia turned, recognizing the old amnis of the immortal riding it. The priest had arrived.

The gates swung open as someone spotted him from the house, and the motorcycle pulled up beside Baojia's car. The giant of a vampire set a foot down and the earth trembled a little. He felt Natalie step closer to him and his guard went up, even though he knew the other immortal was an ally. The man pulled off his black helmet to reveal a shock of unruly red hair and a hard face. He swung his leg over the bike and stalked toward them.

Natalie blinked. "Carwyn?"

The vampire ignored her and growled, "Is my wife here?"

Baojia said, "We've just arrived, but I believe so."

Natalie whispered, "Wait, B's goofy friend *Carwyn* is Brigid's husband? How many vampires do I know?"

"Apparently, more than either of us realized."

"What kind of vampire wears hideous Hawaiian shirts?"

He had to smile. "That one."

Grumbling under his breath in some language Baojia didn't speak, Carwyn ap Bryn, earth vampire, former priest, and currently pissed-off husband stomped up to Giovanni and Beatrice's home, only to be met at the door by his host. Giovanni raised his hands. "She's here, but if you catch anything on fire, you're paying for it. And no structural damage to the house, please."

Carwyn exploded. "One fight and she takes off on your bloody plane, Gio! She's gone! Out of the country!"

"Don't yell at me, I'm not the one who married her."

Carwyn let loose with another string of unintelligible ranting as he rushed in the house. Baojia escorted Natalie up the walk.

"Well, this should be interesting."

"I've never seen him that angry before. He was always the life of the party when he visited B at school."

"We don't want to miss this, then." He nodded at Giovanni as they passed him in the hall. The fire vampire also looked amused. "We'll pop popcorn. It's not the show the opera would be, but it should still be pretty good."

Her eyes widened. "But is it going to be safe for spectators? That's the real question."

"I thought you liked living on the edge."

"I think I've been a bad influence on you, George."

CHAPTER TWENTY-TWO

"SO YOU DECIDED leaving the country was the best response? Really, Brigid?"

The fire vampire's reply was muffled by the walls outside the pool room, but it must have been intelligible to those with immortal ears, because Giovanni's mouth dropped open in shock and Beatrice let out a very unladylike snort.

Tenzin frowned as she reached for a kernel of popcorn from the bowl sitting in the middle of the hall. "I don't think that's physically possible."

They were sitting on the floor outside the pool room, eavesdropping shamelessly as the two vampires fought.

"All I know is that if I had to listen to another one of your smug apologies—"

Natalie heard a splash. *"At least I apologize, Brigid!"*

"Stop shoving me in the pool!"

"You were starting to smoke!"

She leaned into Baojia's shoulder, newly clean and recently fed. She was happy in a way she hadn't experienced in more years than she could count. Baojia's arm draped across her shoulders as he leaned against the wood-paneled wall. She loved him. And she was fairly certain he loved her too, even if he hadn't said it. It wasn't the kind of love she'd experienced in the past. There was no giddy excitement. No rush of hormones. What Natalie had, instead, was a bone-deep sense of being exactly where she was supposed to be. Next to him, for however long they had.

Baojia gave a low chuckle. "They enjoy this."

"What, fighting?" Giovanni rolled his eyes. "Yes. Almost as much as they enjoy making up."

Beatrice shrugged. "Carwyn does say really stupid stuff sometimes."

"Spending a thousand years celibate will do that to you." Tenzin grabbed more popcorn from the rapidly emptying bowl. Most of it, Natalie could admit, she had consumed. She kept forgetting to eat hanging around with all these vampires. "We're running out." Tenzin reached behind her and tossed another bag to Giovanni. "More."

Giovanni grumbled. "We do have a microwave, you know."

"No, we don't," Beatrice said. "Brigid broke it last night. Kaboom."

As if on cue, the ground shifted slightly. Natalie's eyes widened as she looked around, but no one else seemed to be concerned. "Uh…"

"Earth vampire," Baojia said. "Don't worry—the house has been retrofitted for quakes. This is one of the safest places because this wing of the house is modern construction."

Tenzin said, "More popcorn, my boy."

Giovanni ripped the plastic bag open and held the paper bag. "This is ridiculous. I'm not a kitchen appliance."

Tenzin clapped in delight when the kernels slowly started to pop in his hands.

After a few minutes, Beatrice grabbed the bag. "Not too much. And it's convenient, not ridiculous." She kissed his cheek as Natalie heard Baojia laugh quietly.

Giovanni glared. "Not a word from you, water boy."

"I bet you're the most popular guy at the Fourth of July barbecue."

"I'm good at lighting all sorts of things on fire. Want me to show you?"

Beatrice hit Giovanni's leg. "Stop it. Both of you."

Natalie stifled a smile. "I bet you keep a lot of fire extinguishers around here, don't you?"

"I have no idea," Giovanni said.

Baojia said, "There are thirty-six."

Carwyn and Brigid were still arguing in the background. *"How am I supposed to make this right when you leave the country? Should I thank you for at least leaving me a note?"*

"Maybe you should thank me for speaking to you after what you said to Deirdre."

"It was a joke!"

"She's my sire! Do I look like I'm laughing?" The ground shifted again and there was another splash.

"How long do you think this will go on?" Natalie asked. "Has anyone talked to him about visiting the priest in Ensenada yet?"

"We probably won't get anything more done tonight," Beatrice said as she grabbed a handful of popcorn. "And the night's half over anyway. We should start fresh tomorrow. Natalie, you look dead on your feet."

"Told you." Baojia tugged on a lock of her hair. "Refugees from a zombie movie."

"Well, before you fall asleep, I want to hear more about these hunts," Tenzin said. She looked at Giovanni. "Am I the only one who remembers Siberia?"

"Are you talking about Oleg's sire?" Giovanni asked quietly. "I'd forgotten about that. He was a nasty one; I didn't mind killing him."

"No, and the money was good, too."

She felt Baojia's hand press into hers, trying to negate the instinctive tension. She was still getting accustomed to the casual way life and death were mentioned by these seemingly civilized people. She forced her voice to remain calm. "So this has happened before?"

Tenzin nodded. "At times. The situation in Siberia was more clear-cut. And our work was a contract. There was a vampire who invited others over and they hunted humans who had been let loose out in the woods. Like animals in a nature preserve. It was purely for sport. And feeding, of course. We were hired to kill him by one of the many vampires he'd pissed off."

Her stomach turned. "But this is different."

Giovanni nodded. "This has more political implications. As much as it may disgust you, the vampire we killed didn't see himself doing anything wrong, so he wasn't trying to hide it. We were hired for business reasons. Oleg's sire saw hunting humans the same way that human hunters go after deer or any other game animal. Brutal to our modern sensibilities, but he wasn't modern. He was hunting humans from his own territory on his own land. In his mind, he had every right to do it. Whoever is running these hunts on the southern side of the border, they're keeping it concealed. Which they should, as no modern immortal leader would condone that behavior anymore."

"Good to know," she muttered.

"It's not humanitarianism," Baojia said. "Killing humans like that would be too conspicuous. There are more of you than there are of us. We're still very vulnerable if our secrets get out. Plus, every immortal leader needs humans to operate in the modern world. Human employees aren't usually keen to work for someone who views them as animals."

"At least not openly," Beatrice said. "And then there's the Elixir problem."

Baojia shook his head. "I don't think they realize what it does. Not really."

The loud fighting had ceased behind the door, and a low urgent voice drifted down the hall. Natalie raised an eyebrow. The voice did not sound angry.

Beatrice stood. "And that would be our cue to leave. Show's over."

Tenzin pouted. "I wanted them to fight more. They're funny when they fight."

Sounds of passion were quickly overtaking any fighting in volume. Natalie's face turned bright red. "Yeah, I think we should go."

They all walked toward the library. Quickly. "So the Elixir complicates things because whoever is giving it to the humans wants the vampires who hunt them to die? Or do they not realize that's what happens?"

"I don't know," Baojia said. "Ivan is not easily fooled. But he is greedy and he likes power. It's possible that he's even doing this without the cartel's knowledge. And I can almost promise you he's not taking it himself. He's too smart for that."

Natalie saw Beatrice and Giovanni exchange a look. "What was that?" she asked. "That look was something."

Baojia halted and put an arm around her. "Giovanni?"

The fire vampire took a deep breath. "I was just thinking about Terry and Gemma and what happened in Spain."

Natalie was confused. "Who are Terry and Gemma?"

"The leaders of London," Baojia said. "And friends of mine. You think someone might be using Ivan like they did Leonor's child?"

She huffed in frustration. "More information, please!"

Beatrice led her over to the library table and pulled out a map. She pointed to Ireland. "A while back, Brigid and Carwyn were both taken captive by someone they trusted. He was one of the lieutenants for Patrick Murphy, the vampire leader of Dublin. He was young, ambitious, and didn't see himself rising in the ranks fast enough. He's the one who first brought Elixir to Ireland. He was giving it out in clubs. Getting other vampires to take it. It weakened them so he could manipulate them. We think he was working with a supplier. And we think that supplier is the one actually making the drug."

Giovanni walked over. "And then recently, our friends were attacked by a child of the Spanish leader, Leonor de Peña. She's very powerful, but her son defied her and tried to take out two of her longtime allies, Terrance Ramsay and Gemma Melcombe, then blame Leonor for the attack. Very risky move. We don't know for sure it had anything to do with the Elixir, but we know he was working with someone else. And again, whoever was behind it used someone relatively young and ambitious who was dissatisfied with their role in a prominent organization."

"Ivan," Baojia said quietly. "You could be describing Ivan. He's not young, but he's younger than the leadership in Mexico City. He's ambitious. Always hungry for more power. He's continually pushing the cartel's limits and then they push back. It's not a peaceful relationship."

Natalie said, "So whoever is making this drug is targeting dissatisfied people within existing power structures. Take a ruler down from within, instead of an open challenge. Smart, really." She looked up at Baojia. "Young, ambitious, and unhappy. Who does that describe in Ernesto's organization?"

The expression fell from his face. "Me. At one point, me."

Tenzin shook her head. "But you are known for your loyalty, Baojia. I don't think anyone would believe you would ever turn on Ernesto or work against him."

"You've also been gone," Beatrice said quietly. "Someone might have seen that as an opportunity."

"Rory," Natalie said, even when she felt Baojia draw back. "I know you don't want to believe it, but it makes the most sense. You were away. They needed someone unhappy. Ivan organizes these fights to infect vampires with Elixir. He and Rory dump the bodies on Ernesto's land. Mexico City looks like they can't control their vampires and Ernesto looks weak because he's letting this go on in his backyard. Everyone is pointing a finger at someone else, then the humans get involved. It makes the news. No hiding it at that point."

Giovanni gave her a smile. "Very good, Natalie."

She shrugged. "Hey, politics is politics. I've been covering stuff like this for years." She turned and looked at Baojia. He was doing the blank face again, but by this time she knew him well enough to realize it was because he was shocked. And hurt. She went over and gave him a hug, which he didn't return. "I know he's your brother, but you have to see we're right about this. What's the other explanation?"

Baojia nodded stiffly and pulled away, turning to leave the room. And with the loss of his presence, Natalie felt a hint of panic. "Baojia?"

He paused at the door. "I realize you're probably correct. Please… I'll return shortly. Just stay here."

He left, and Natalie sat down on the couch, suddenly exhausted. Giovanni and Beatrice exchanged a few words, then he and Tenzin left too while Beatrice settled next to her.

"He'll be fine. He's not mad at you, Nat."

"I told him I loved him, but he didn't say it back." She squeezed her eyes shut and wished she could take back the words. "I'm sorry. I shouldn't be talking about this right now."

"Of course you should. And I think he loves you very much. I think he loves you so much he doesn't know what to do with it yet."

She swallowed and blinked back the burning at the corners of her eyes. "So why leave?"

"He's hurting, and you want to help because you love him. I don't think he's used to that. It doesn't mean he doesn't need it, just that he's not used to it."

"Is it worth it?" she asked quietly. "Are you happier now? Did you become a vampire to be with Giovanni?"

Beatrice sighed. "I became a vampire for a lot of reasons. And yes, he was one of the main ones. But not the only one. And he didn't really want me to turn as soon as I did. I did it without him knowing. You think Brigid and Carwyn were fighting? He was furious. It doesn't even compare."

"So why—?"

"I was in this world, and I knew it was my life. I knew it. And…" She frowned a little, a crease forming in her otherwise perfect forehead. No wrinkle or line would ever mar it, Natalie realized. She was slowly aging, but her friend would not. "I didn't want to be the weakest one. I wanted to be something feared, not protected."

"Did you ever want kids?"

"No, but that's an important question. I think Gio wanted me to. I think he wanted me to have kids and then turn later—he likes kids, even though he's kind of cranky sometimes—but I didn't want that." She took a deep breath and leaned back. Natalie mirrored her movements; her eyes felt like they were weighted. "I don't think Matt or Dez would ever become vampires. They don't want that kind of life. They want a normal lifespan. To watch their kids grow up and watch each other get wrinkles. It's different for everyone. You have to make that decision for your own reasons."

"It's a lot to think about."

"I know." Beatrice leaned over and gave her shoulders a squeeze. "Love is never easy. Not the real kind, anyway. Look at Carwyn and Brigid. They fight all the time. They adore each other, but that doesn't mean they don't have problems. They'll figure it out. You and Baojia will too."

"Thanks for the vote of confidence." She wished she felt as optimistic. "I really can't go back to my old life, can I?"

Beatrice eyed her cautiously. "Harsh truth?"

"Harsh truth."

Her friend slowly shook her head. "No. You're a reporter, Natalie. No vampire would believe you'd never write anything about our kind. I can protect you some, but unless you want to be under my personal aegis, which means I'd drink from you and you'd basically live here, I can't truly keep you safe. If you went back to San Diego, Ernesto would take you. He'd try to wipe your memories. If that didn't work, I don't know what he'd do."

"He's your great-grandfather."

"Doesn't mean I trust him." The look in her eyes was grim. "He's a very cunning vampire, and his interest is his own."

Her head fell against the back of the couch and tears came to her eyes. "Shit. How did I end up pulled into this?"

Beatrice said, "I'd stop trying to figure it out. There's no way of knowing. But I do believe things happen for a reason. Maybe Baojia is yours."

"My what?" she snorted. "My vampire? My… boyfriend seems like a ridiculous term. He's my what?"

"Your reason."

Natalie blinked and turned her head. "That sounds crazy." Still, she couldn't help remembering how she'd felt earlier in the evening, leaning against his side as they munched on popcorn, brainstormed about the case, and swapped jokes. She felt the most uncanny sense of peace. The look on her face must have given her away, because Beatrice gave her a knowing grin.

"Trust me, I've heard crazier."

She must have fallen asleep in the library because the next thing she remembered was strong arms lifting her from the couch. She nuzzled into Baojia's familiar scent and wrapped her arms around his neck.

"Where did you go?"

"The training studio," he said softly. "Let's get you to bed."

"Needed to hit something?"

"Yes."

"Did you?"

"Many times," he said, sounding amused. "It was highly satisfying. We need to be better about you sleeping. Your body needs more rest than you're getting. And food. You haven't been eating enough. You're getting too thin."

"I'm fine." She could feel him walking down the stairs. "Really, don't worry about me. Do you believe me about Rory?"

Natalie felt the minute hitch in his step. "I do. I did. Please don't think I doubted you. That's not why I left."

"Okay." She sighed and burrowed into his chest. "Why do you smell like smoke?"

"Long story."

She heard the door creak and the familiar scent of his room. Maybe she was becoming a vampire by osmosis. She seemed to notice how things smelled all the time. Or maybe she was just more conscious of it. Or maybe… she was exhausted and a little nuts and needed to go to sleep.

Baojia laughed. "I think sleep is a good idea."

"Did I say that out loud?"

"Yes. And I'll join you. It's almost dawn."

He stripped off her jeans and the soft shirt she was wearing, peeling back the layers until she was naked and tucked under the covers, pressed against his long, cool body as his amnis washed over her like an embrace.

"Baojia?"

"You should sleep."

"I'm sorry about your brother."

His arm reached around and hugged her. "I'm still hoping there is another explanation, but I think you're correct. I'm worried about Paula, mostly."

She hadn't even thought about that, but he had. Of course he had. It was just who he was.

"I love you," she whispered. There was silence in the room. She hadn't expected him to say it back, but it still hurt a little. The hurt was wiped away when she heard his voice.

"Thank you," he said, almost reverently. As if her love was the greatest gift she could give him. A prize beyond worth. Natalie blinked back tears when he kissed the back of her neck. "Thank you, Natalie."

Chapter Twenty-Three

THE IRRITATING FORMER PRIEST was singing—actually singing —in the car on the road to Ensenada. The fact that it wasn't off-key was somehow more annoying than less.

"You seem to be in a much better mood tonight," Baojia remarked as he steered the car south.

"I am, thanks. Being in my wife's presence tends to do that. I'm in a better mood even when I'm mad. Odd, that…" The singing stopped for a blessed moment before it started again. Baojia gritted his teeth and tried to ignore it. They were headed south to speak to Father Andrade, whom Carwyn had confirmed was part of the network of priests the Vatican used. The members of that network were well aware of the existence of vampires. The fact that the church in Rome used clergy around the globe to keep tabs on the immortal population didn't surprise Baojia in the least. It had impressed him.

Finally, a few miles south of Tijuana, he'd had enough. "Can you stop the singing, please?"

"You're more prissy than usual," Carwyn said with a gleam in his eye. "I'd have thought your lovely human companion would have loosened you up a bit."

"Natalie is none of your business. And I'd simply prefer time to think."

"You don't like being away from her, do you?" There was a smug tone in his voice. The priest continued, even though Baojia ignored him. "I met her when the girls were in school. Did you know that? She's a fun girl. Very smart. Not surprised she caught your attention."

Fun? What did fun mean? Baojia felt his lip curl up. Had the blasted priest—

"A harmless flirtation," Carwyn said with a laugh. "Nothing more. Very focused on her studies, Natalie was. And she didn't know anything about our sort, of course."

"No." He tried to will his fangs to retract. "She was completely unaware until she was pulled into this mess."

"She's doing all right, though." Carwyn nodded. "I like the two of you together. She's a bit wild, always has been. A bit of a crusader. Doesn't think about her own safety at all."

"I'm well aware of that, thank you." Would this trip never end? And how did he get nominated to drive Carwyn? And what was Natalie doing while he was gone? If she left the house—

"So, you've had more than a bit of change, haven't you?" Carwyn had slumped down in his seat, trying to cross his leg over his knee in the cramped car. The man was huge, well over Baojia's average height, and he seemed to fill the car. No wonder he preferred a motorcycle. "Have you had time to process all this? Thought about where you'll go? What you'll do?"

Relieved to have the subject switched from Natalie, he said, "No, not really."

"Gio mentioned Katya in passing. I've known Katya for years. She's calculating, but fair. One of my daughter's children lives near Portland. Very happy there."

It shouldn't surprise him that Carwyn knew the vampire leader of the Pacific Northwest. At over a thousand years old, the immortal knew practically everyone, at least in the Western Hemisphere. "What does she do? Your daughter's child. Does she work for Katya?"

"No no. Well out of politics. She owns vineyards. Excellent winemaker." Carwyn grinned. "Very good occupation, in my opinion."

He nodded. It was always good to hear from those not involved in politics; it gave a more balanced impression of what it was like to live in a certain immortal's territory. "And not much intrusion?" Some vampire leaders could be nosy about the others who lived on their land. Ernesto was not, and Baojia imagined he would grate under too much scrutiny.

"Practically none. Quite a hands-off kind of leader from what I can tell. She keeps to herself. Has a very close circle of confidants—not unlike your sire—but mostly leaves others alone. I've only met her socially, and she seems lovely. Been mated to a Dutch water vampire for years. Can't remember his name…"

Baojia took it all in. What would it be like to live somewhere he could make his own way? Where there would be no expectation of loyalty because of blood? He could be… an employee. Or simply a resident. The idea appealed to him. He would need some occupation to keep busy, but perhaps a real job in security consulting would be entertaining. Perhaps he could even lure Luis away from Ernesto. The human had been an excellent assistant. And any of the major cities would have newspapers where Natalie could work. Yes, an introduction to Katya would be worth asking the Italian for a favor.

"Thinking about taking Natalie with you?"

"She can't remain in Southern California. She's not safe here."

Carwyn chuckled. "Does she know that?"

"I think she's figuring it out."

"Best of luck. I have faith you'll work everything out. After all, if Brigid and I can learn to live with each other, then you two should be able to manage. You seem quite well-suited."

Baojia tried not to squirm. It wouldn't do for the other immortal to see how uncomfortable the topic made him. His feelings for Natalie were clear in his own mind. She belonged with him. She had even said she loved him. But it was no one's business but their own. He tried to change the subject.

"This priest, Father Andrade, his church is located very near the clubs and bars in Ensenada. Many of the girls who come to the city from the country don't do well. He and his church help many of them. If there are girls who have gone missing, he is likely to have noticed. I wouldn't be surprised if he's aware of what's going on, or at least suspicious."

Carwyn nodded. "I doubt he'd be aware of the Elixir, though. Most vampires don't even know what it does. But if any of the girls have had it and they *haven't* been killed—"

"Would they be sick?"

"It depends on when they started taking it. From what Brigid and I have found, it puts a human in excellent health for a few months, even up to a year. It varies from person to person. But inevitably, they seem to fall ill with a wasting disease. Doctors have no idea how to treat it. We don't know much more than that. I've been trying to get Lucien Thrax involved."

"The physician?" Lucien Thrax was an extremely old vampire—rumored to be the son of one of the ancients—and a noted scientist. If he had studied the formula for the Elixir, he might be able to find a cure for the humans who had been affected.

"He had it, you know?" Carwyn noticed Baojia's widened eyes. "A couple of years ago. He drank from an infected human. Was ill for months. His sire is still alive and could heal him, but he lost a human who was dear to him. He's been recovering in North Africa for some time, but Beatrice and I have been trying to tempt him to join us. We need someone who has the scientific knowledge—and the knowledge of alchemy—that he has. Maybe this will motivate him."

"So the cure for vampires is blood from their sire?"

"Or enough of their direct line. But a sire's blood is best."

Good to know. Considering his relationship with Ernesto, he'd better avoid elixired blood.

"But no known cure for humans?"

"None that we've found so far."

Baojia's thoughts swirled around the human Tulio was protecting. Rosa. He was young enough to remember the confusion she must be feeling. Thrust into a world that made no sense. Fearful of everything and everyone. And he knew Natalie must still be feeling as Rosa did at times. And yet, she was brave enough to love him. Her courage floored Baojia.

Carwyn said, "So, you're no longer under Ernesto's aegis."

"I'm not." And it still stung. Just a little.

"If you were..." The priest stared straight ahead at the passing lights. "How would you handle this situation? If you were still the head of security in Los Angeles—had all his resources—how would you handle this?"

"I'd take six or seven of my best people, along with three humans, and go down to Mexico. Stake out the hunting grounds and kill them. I'd need at least one earth vampire and preferably one wind."

"You've thought about this more than a bit."

"Yes." He'd been thinking about it for days.

"Only seven people?"

"The less the better, in this case. There are too many political implications. We wouldn't want to alert the Mexican cartel of our movements. My guess is they don't know what Ivan is doing. We don't want to start a war, we just want to take care of a problem. I'd go down with the equivalent of a special forces team."

"Why the humans?"

"Whoever is coming is going to be expecting them. Maybe they're already mad with bloodlust when they get there—they certainly seemed that way from what I saw—but you still need some humans there. If they don't catch the scent, they'll know something is wrong."

"So you definitely need a few humans," Carwyn muttered.

"I'd stake out the hunt and remove the drugged women after they've been dropped off. Tulio said they left them for an hour. More than enough time to hide them somewhere. That's only one of the reasons I'd need an earth vampire. After the elixired girls are gone, I'd put my own human security in place, then wait for the ambush. As long as you had the element of surprise, it would work with minimal risk. Not none, of course, no operation is risk free, but it would be manageable."

"And no one would be the wiser."

"We'd make a very quiet statement. Everyone would know what had happened, but no one could prove anything. It would be a good show of power on Ernesto's part—others would know not to cause trouble along his borders—but we wouldn't make a public statement, so the cartel could ignore it and not be forced to retaliate."

"That's a well-thought-out plan."

Of course it was. "Thank you."

"Ernesto was foolish to have fired you."

His heart beat. "I am the one who asked to leave his aegis. He refused to listen to my warnings and…" He glanced over at Carwyn once. The vampire was staring at him intently. "He wanted Natalie. I would not allow it."

Carwyn said nothing as they took the exit that would lead them to the small church only a few blocks from the lively tourist district. The night was lit up. Humans filled the streets, and music blared from the clubs. A cruise ship must have been in port.

The former priest scanned the sidewalks as they drove. Then he said softly, "You must love her very much."

Baojia stared into the traffic as he thought about what the priest had said. *Love* Natalie?

Well… of course he did.

Father Andrade seemed to have been expecting them. The gray-haired priest shook hands with Carwyn and led both vampires back to the kitchen in the small house behind the church. It was a modest home, decorated with pictures of saints and a few children's drawings. The father was obviously loved by the people he ministered to. He put a kettle of water on to heat and joined them at the scarred table.

"I have been expecting one of you people, but I didn't know if it would be to help me or kill me."

Carwyn said, "Why would anyone kill you, Father?"

The priest shrugged. "I see many things I'm not supposed to see. No one pays attention to old men."

"What have you seen lately?" Baojia asked. "Anything unusual?"

"I've seen more girls going than coming," he said. "Girls who have disappeared. There's always some of that—most of them go back to their families or move along when they realize the city isn't all they want—but there's more now. More missing girls. And some of the regular girls… the ones who know about your sort, they look worried."

He was hiding something. The old man was telling them part of the story, but not all. Carwyn must have sensed it, too.

"Father Andrade, I hope you know that many of our kind have no quarrel with you or your work. In fact, Arturo Leon gave me your name if I ever needed help in this area."

Baojia didn't recognize the name, but Father Andrade must have, because the priest's face suddenly relaxed and his shoulders slumped.

"I have no idea what do to for her," he said. "She came to me months ago. Begged me not to take her to the hospital. She says it won't help anyway. I've called doctors to the house. Prayed for guidance…"

Baojia leaned forward. "Who? Who are you talking about?"

Father Andrade said, "Constantina Rosales. Ivan's former mistress."

Baojia stopped breathing. He'd thought the man harbored some affection for the human. He'd been wrong.

Where's Constantina?

Some ridiculous illness. Not sure. You know how they complain.

Constantina wasn't sick. Ivan had given his own mistress the Elixir. "Where is she?"

She was lying on a narrow bed in the basement. No cords or monitors were hooked up to her, though she obviously needed to be in a hospital. The stunning woman who had dazzled all of Ivan's associates lay wasting away, the formerly lush curves of her body nowhere in evidence.

"Constantina," Baojia said softly, kneeling down next to her as her eyes flickered open. "Do you remember me?"

"Ernesto's man, Baojia." She smiled weakly and put a hand up to his lips. He could smell the sickness radiating off her skin. "All the girls loved having you visit. I heard rumors about that mouth for years. Sorry you have to see me like this."

"What happened? Was this Ivan?"

Her eyes rolled back and her body arched in pain for a moment. Father Andrade knelt beside her, placing a tablet between her lips and offering her a sip of water. "She goes in and out. The doctor who came said it looks like she is starving to death, but even a feeding tube didn't help her. We tried."

Her blood held none of the sweetness of the other girls. It smelled of fermented fruit baked too long in the sun, pungent and on the way to sour. "Constantina, did Ivan give you a formula? An elixir of some kind?"

"The Elixir of Life…," she whispered. "He didn't drink from me after that, even though I could tell he wanted to. He stayed away. Said it was too soon. If it worked, he would be able to keep me for much longer." Her smile was bitter. "I was aging. He couldn't have a wrinkled mistress to introduce to his guests. Ivan was too proud for that."

"Who gave him the Elixir, Constantina?"

She gave a weak shrug. "I don't know. I always thought I would die very quickly or all alone. Even if I survived him, he'd shove me off somewhere when I became too old." The thin woman sighed. "And I had peace about it. I loved him. Stupid, I know. But I did. And I enjoyed the power and attention I had, for a time." She reached for Father Andrade's hand. "But the wages of sin are death, aren't they, Father?"

"Please, Constantina." The old man had tears in his eyes. "Let me take you to the hospital. Let me find you proper care, my dear. You are too young to waste away like this."

"It won't help. I could tell by the look on his face when I first started to lose weight." She looked straight into Baojia's eyes. "He knew. Ivan knew what was happening."

"Who else did he give it to?" he asked.

"Some of the waitresses. And he told some of his men—not the good ones, the stupid ones. Told them to drink from the girls. They became… addicted. Those girls were the most popular at the club. All the men wanted to drink from them. Ivan let many of them, but not all. That's when I knew that it was a poison for your kind, too. Then the girls started disappearing, but no one noticed at first. There were always more girls. I noticed the ones who had taken the same drug I had disappeared after only a few months. More showed up in their place. They would pick a few and give them the drink."

"New girls?"

"Or annoying ones," she said with a weak smile.

"How long ago was it?" Baojia was still trying to figure out a timeline. Were the effects immediate? If a girl was taken by Ivan's people, how long did she have? They had to know how much time they had before another hunt would take place. "How long did it take the waitress's blood to become affected?"

She frowned. "Only two or three days, I think. So…"

"So if a girl was taken—"

"If they gave her the drug right away, she'd only have to wait a couple of days before she'd become everyone's favorite drink." Constantina's lip curled in disdain. "I was *only* Ivan's woman. No one else drank from me. These other girls… they fed anyone who asked. *Putanas.* I left around the time the lock showed up on the basement door. He was keeping women down there. I didn't want to know why. I left." Her eyes flickered closed. "No one came after me."

Father Andrade said, "When she came here, I tried to take her to a hospital, but she refused. Constantina, please let me call someone. I beg you."

Baojia had a feeling that there was nothing the human doctors could do. Carwyn only confirmed it.

"Just make her comfortable, Father." He sat in a chair next to the woman and brushed a bit of hair from her forehead, looking down on her sadly. "There is nothing the human doctors can do for her. We are still trying to find a cure ourselves."

She had fallen asleep, and in that rest, Baojia saw a shadow of the beautiful woman who had charmed so many. Had Ivan intended to kill his favorite mistress? Somehow, he doubted it. But the vampire seemed to have no hesitation about using the knowledge he had gained to further his own ambitions. He was not mourning his woman or seeking a cure, he was spreading it for his own benefit, whatever that might be. Perhaps he had truly intended for it to be good, to keep her young and at his side. Perhaps. But he had still used Constantina as a test subject. He hadn't fed from her, and that told him Ivan knew the drug could be harmful.

"Father Andrade, does she have any family?"

"No one."

Baojia rose from his knees. The sick woman rested uneasily, her eyes jerking under her lids as she dreamed. Baojia backed out of the room, certain he would not see her alive again. They climbed the stairs and took their leave of the priest, exchanging phone numbers so Father Andrade could call them if any more useful information became known. As they were leaving the house, a teenage girl came running up the walk.

"I can't find her, Father!"

"Carmen?" The priest's eyes widened in alarm. "You can't find Carmen?"

Carwyn walked over to the girl's side. "Who is this?"

Words tumbled out of the girl's mouth. "I told her not to take that job. I told her—" She eyed Carwyn suspiciously. "I told her they weren't like us. That they couldn't be trusted. But the money was too good. She needed the money. That's the only reason she went there. We have to find her!"

"Lena, I don't know—"

"Who is Carmen?" Baojia asked, keeping his distance from the distraught child.

"My sister!" she sobbed. "Carmen is my sister!"

Father Andrade said, "Both Lena and Carmen have been in my church since their parents died. They support themselves." He patted her shoulder. "They are very hard workers. Carmen went to Bar El Ruso to take a job. We both told her it was a bad idea, but she ignored us. She's been working there for two months now. She keeps to herself and hasn't had any problems, but Lena has been checking on her every night. Every night, they meet each other. To be safe."

"But she wasn't there. I snuck in the club. The other girls said she didn't show up tonight, but I know she went to work." The girl was sobbing, fat tears running down her face.

"Has the truck been there?"

"I don't see it."

Carwyn asked, "What truck?"

"There is a truck that shows up sometimes," Father Andrade explained. "It doesn't deliver anything, just sits outside the club for a time, then is gone again. There are no markings on it."

Baojia and Carwyn exchanged worried looks.

"How long?" Baojia asked. "How long does the truck stay behind the club before it leaves?"

"Sometimes one or two nights. Never more than that."

"We need you to call us, Father." Baojia stepped closer. "As soon as a truck shows up, you will call this number. Do you understand?"

"Yes." The old priest nodded, gathering the crying girl under his stooped shoulder. "I can do that."

If there was a delivery truck behind Ivan's club, then another hunt was likely only two or three nights away.

"We have to get back to Los Angeles," Carwyn said.

Baojia headed for the car. A truck could show up even as they left the city. Could they make it out to Ivan's hunting grounds in time?

CHAPTER TWENTY-FOUR

NATALIE WOKE in the dark room to the feel of soft lips against her neck and steady arms turning her over in bed. She was drawn to a hard, familiar chest and the smell of the ocean. Her eyes were still closed and part of her wondered whether she was still dreaming.

"Natalie?"

"Hmm?" she murmured as she burrowed toward his scent. The bed was warm and her arms felt too heavy for her body.

"I'm back."

"Hey." Her eyes fluttered open. "What time is it?"

Baojia kissed her forehead. "Don't wake up. It's almost dawn. Sleep more. I'm going to rest soon, too."

"Okay." She sighed and closed her eyes again, feeling herself drift as she was tucked into his chest. "Goodnight. Or… day. Whatever."

She felt him playing with a lock of her hair, twisting it around his finger as he liked to do. His voice came as if in a dream.

"If I were human… would you want to marry me? Have children with me?"

Was he serious? She'd never met anyone more devoted to family, even one that didn't appreciate him.

"Course, silly." She sighed and snuggled closer. "You'd be an amazing father."

The heavy press of sleep bore down on her, and she couldn't seem to fight it off. Baojia's hands ran up and down her arms, soothing her. Protecting… always protecting. Natalie hadn't felt so safe or loved since her world came crashing down when her mother died. It didn't matter if he gave her the words or not—she'd known it after the first time they'd made love—he'd give her everything else.

When she woke again, it was still dark, but the clock on the phone by her bed told her it was four in the afternoon. She blinked and untangled herself from Baojia's limp arms. His complete stillness no longer seemed inhuman or frightening. It was just how he slept. The solid weight of him behind her was comforting, not strange. Again, she shook her head at how quickly and drastically her life had changed. It was only a matter of weeks, but everything she had planned for the future had been thrown in the air by the startling, unexpected man who lay before her.

Would you want to marry me? Have children with me?

Had she been dreaming? She really didn't know. Natalie showered and dressed, locking the room carefully behind her before she walked upstairs. She stopped by the kitchen and made a sandwich before following the low voices into the den. Ben was there, along with Carwyn. The vampire looked groggy, but was still fairly awake. She smiled and plopped down next to him.

"Hey, stranger."

He grinned. They'd flirted shamelessly the few times they'd met when Beatrice was in school, but Natalie had known it was just for fun.

"If it isn't my other favorite redhead." He tugged on her hair. "How are you, Nat?"

"Good. Feeling a little more rested finally." She took a bite of her sandwich. "You were holding out on me, mister. A priest?"

His low laugh rumbled across the room. "As if that was the worst of it. It was up to B to decide who knew what. Don't blame me. Is your man still sleeping? He's a young one, eh?"

"Young? Riiiight. How are you awake?"

Ben piped up. "Because he's old. Really, really old."

"I can still beat your ass at *Mario Kart*, boy." But Carwyn winked at her. "It's true though. Brigid's a young one, too. She has to have a full day's rest."

"But Beatrice can be up during the day?" Natalie frowned. "How's that work?"

"She's had Tenzin's blood in a roundabout way," Carwyn said. "Makes her a daywalker. Not unheard of, but rare. Not that desirable, to tell you the truth. We all crave sleep. Let our brains rest. As old as I am, I still sleep most of the day. Baojia will too. At least for another few hundred years."

She must have paled, because he patted her knee. "You'll get used to it."

Natalie heard Ben leave the room, mumbling something about a snack. She cleared her throat. "I… uh, I don't know that I will, to be honest. It's pretty hard to wrap your mind around, even when you…"

"You love him." It wasn't a question, but she nodded anyway. "Then you'll figure it out. Brigid and I, we didn't have the easiest go of it. Still don't. But we do our best. You don't have to be perfect, you just have to try and don't quit."

Try and don't quit. She could probably do that. Natalie tried to smile again. "Sorry. I'm being silly."

"No, it's a whole new world for you. Nothing to be embarrassed about." He patted her hand and sat up a little straighter. "Tell me everything. I used to be a priest, and I have four daughters. I've probably heard it all at this point."

She blinked in surprise. "You have… *what*? Four daughters?"

"Eleven children all together. And more in my human life." Carwyn grinned. "I enjoy mayhem. Nothing says fun like immortal family dysfunction."

Natalie snorted. "Wow, so… Wow! You have a family?"

"Course I do. Did you think that wasn't going to be part of the picture?" He frowned. "Is that what's been bothering you?"

She shrugged. "Kind of. I just… I always wanted a family. My mom and dad were really great, and I always figured that would be part of my life, you know? Eventually anyway. Husband, kids. I hated being an only child. I wanted a big crazy family the same as you, I guess. Well, maybe not *exactly* the same."

"So what's the problem?" Carwyn asked with a laugh. "There are ways —especially in this modern world—for you to have the family you want. I can see him wanting that, too. He's one of the most loyal fellows I know. Trust me, I've known a few. And he's crazy about you."

The corner of her mouth lifted. "Yeah?"

"In his own quiet, try-to-guess-what-I'm-thinking, mysterious way, yes." Carwyn's eyes crinkled at the corners. "It's completely obvious."

She shook her head. "Oh yeah. He wears his heart on his sleeve."

"He loves you, Natalie. Very much." Suddenly Carwyn's merry face turned serious. "He's going to try to keep you out of this. Are you going to let him?"

She leaned back into the couch. "What do you think?"

"I'm going to say no." He sighed. "Ah, Nat. I wish you would. I know I'm banging my head against the wall, but this thing is so dangerous."

"I can't believe you're even asking," she said. "With *your* wife?"

"It's got nothin' to do with doubting you." He nodded toward the hall again. "That one? Drives me out of my mind. Love her like mad. And she's a frightening creature, Natalie. Powerful. Focused. Has a mind like a blade. Did as a human and she's even sharper as a vampire. Bloody woman is a force to be reckoned with."

"So you should know better than to—"

"And I'd wrap her up in tissue paper in the blink of an eye if she'd let me." He smiled ruefully.

Natalie's mouth dropped open. "You wouldn't!"

"I would. She'd never let me and I'd probably be a fool to try, but if I had my way…" He shook his head. "Has nothing to do with doubting her, love. It has everything to do with my own fear. The fear of losing her makes me weak. When you've found your mate in this life, the thought of losing her—living the rest of this eternal night alone—it can lead you to a very dark place, Natalie. So don't be too hard on him. He's just found you, after all."

"And, uh…" She took a deep breath. "If I don't want to become a vampire? What then?"

Carwyn's smile was wistful. "Then the time only becomes more precious, doesn't it?"

She felt a sinking feeling in the pit of her stomach. "I'll keep that in mind."

He winked. "You do that."

She watched him later that night, a map spread on the table in the library. He was pointing out the area where the hunt had been to

Giovanni and Tenzin. Tenzin's head was cocked to the side, studying the map intently, chiming in with a question in Chinese every now and then. Natalie didn't think she even realized she was doing it. She asked and Baojia answered. Natalie made a mental note to learn Chinese.

"So this area is completely deserted?"

"I asked Beatrice to find satellite photos last night. It appears to be clear of any real development for approximately thirty miles in every direction. There's an old mining road that leads to about here." He pointed at the map. "Then the road ends. You'd have to have the right truck, but you could access this. The terrain is rugged, but passable. They must be knocking out the girls with amnis, transporting them out there, then dumping them—"

"Is that an old crater?" Giovanni asked.

"It looks like it. There's a natural depression of some kind, but the tunnels Tulio dug seemed solid."

Giovanni and Tenzin both nodded. "So this plan of yours—"

"Won't work." Baojia shook his head. "I'd need seven or eight vampires. We have no way of knowing how many will come, or if Ivan will be with them. Probably not. I don't expect you to go down there. I'll just have to figure something else out. Maybe if I go down alone—"

"What?" Natalie sat up straight. "No way! You can't go alone. With all those other vampires?"

He gave her a warning look. "I'm not going to risk anyone else to do this. And don't even think—"

"I'll go," Tenzin said quietly. "Between the two of us, we should be able to take out the rest."

"We'll tag along," Carwyn called from the door, his hand on the small of Brigid's back as the two walked toward the table. "We've been looking for some fun."

Brigid added, "And if all of these vampires have taken elixired blood, they'll be stronger than average. There's no need to take chances with the two of you." She nodded at Baojia. "Carwyn told me your plan. It's a good one. We're in."

Giovanni said, "Beatrice and I—"

"Can provide a distraction," Baojia said quickly. "See if Ernesto wants to meet for dinner tomorrow night. The last thing we need is for the two of you to become involved in a political problem. If you meet with him, it provides both you and Ernesto with cover should this turn messy and the cartel raise a fuss later."

"Are you sure?"

He nodded. "I'm sure. It'll be a relief to know that this isn't going to come back and cause more problems down the road for either you or my sire. All I want is to stop Ivan."

"Only if you're sure, Baojia."

"I'm sure."

Natalie watched the quick exchange with mounting anxiety. The plan seemed to be that Baojia and the other vampires would go down to the desert and stake out the hunting grounds where the women would be taken. Then, when all the vampires were there, he'd launch a surprise attack and kill them with no one in Ensenada or Los Angeles the wiser.

Brigid looked at her. "We're going to need some humans. If you want to get the women out of there, we're going to need someone to replace them. The first thing they'll notice when they get there is scent. If it doesn't smell like humans, they'll know something is wrong."

"I'll go," she said. "It's my story. I'll go."

"No," Baojia said quietly. "Not acceptable."

Tenzin ignored him and spoke to Natalie. "Ben has already offered to help. He's well-trained. With us providing cover, he'll be able to guard you while we handle the vampires. You'll be safe with him."

"No," Baojia said again, slightly louder. "She's not trained. She's staying here."

Tenzin cocked her head. "She has to go. We need her. Ben's presence will not be enough. And he's male. They're expecting women. If you want to save these girls—"

"I'm not saving them by putting her at risk," Baojia said, stepping closer to Tenzin. "It's not an option."

Both vampires broke into a sudden flurry of Chinese that looked seconds away from turning into blows. Tenzin's voice was raised and she gestured toward Ben, who had been sitting quietly on the couch by the fire, seemingly at ease with the angry voices. Baojia looked furious, biting out words and baring his fangs at the small woman who would not back down.

Finally, Natalie stood and shouted, "I'm going, okay?" They both stopped and stared at her. "I'm going." She looked pointedly at Baojia. "You knew I was going to. Don't try to stop me."

His nostrils flared while Tenzin simply nodded. "Good. So, we will leave at dusk tomorrow. We will stake out the crater and wait for the women to arrive. When they do, Carwyn can tunnel under the crater and hide them while we leave Ben and Natalie as bait for the other vampires. Ben will cover Natalie while Baojia, Brigid, and I kill the vampires who come to hunt the women. Will Ivan be with them?"

Baojia's fangs were still down, and he was still glaring at her. "We don't know."

"So how are we going to make sure this doesn't happen again?" Tenzin looked cross, but Natalie was still focused on Baojia, who had not taken his eyes off her.

He said, "Because if he is not with them, then I will hunt him down and kill him myself."

"Oh," Natalie muttered. "But *I'm* the reckless one."

He slammed his hand on the table, spun around, and stormed out of the library. Natalie watched him go but did not rise to follow him. She raised her chin and looked at Tenzin. "I want a stun gun. Two of them would be better."

Tenzin smirked and nodded toward Brigid. "She'll get you set up. You'll be with Ben. Tell him not to worry."

Giovanni murmured, "Oh yes. Obviously that's going to ease his mind." He winced when Tenzin kicked him under the table. "What?"

Carwyn squeezed Natalie's shoulder. "Go talk to him," he said quietly. "You know why he's angry."

She rose and walked out the door. When she got to the foot of the stairs, Caspar was there, nodding toward the French doors that led out to the back garden. She followed the lit path that led toward the pool at the back of the house. He was there, pacing around the deck, the water following him as he walked, creating a churning whirlpool that matched the stormy look on his face. He only glanced at her once before he turned his eyes back to the water.

"Well, you got what you wanted," he said.

"I didn't want you mad at me."

"Are you surprised?" he bit out.

She sighed and crossed her arms. "I guess not."

"He's a teenage boy. You're going to be guarded by a teenage boy while I'm dealing with the rest of them."

"Tenzin told me you once took on over a dozen trained soldiers yourself and killed every one."

"And I almost died!" he stopped, spinning toward her. "I had two swords at my neck." He took his finger and traced a line. "And they cut halfway through it. I was inches away from death, Natalie. If I was human, I wouldn't have survived. Plus, I was by a river. I was *strong* there." He kept walking and she forced herself to remain where she was. His fangs were down, his black eyes glittered. He was still furious. "I was as strong as I can be on land, and I still almost died."

"Baojia—"

"But *we're* going out to the desert! There is no water around for miles except a few irrigation canals. Nothing. I will not be at my strongest, there are going to be an unknown number of vampires there hopped up on some drug that makes them super-strong and crazed by the scent of human blood." He stopped a few inches from her face. "And you are putting yourself in the middle of all that out of some insane need to save the world!"

"You need me there for this to work. I'm the only one—"

"Yes!" He grasped the back of her neck and pulled her face to his. "You are the only one. The *only* one. Why don't you understand?"

She grabbed the collar of his shirt and pulled his mouth to hers. Their kiss was hard and angry. Desperate and needy. "I do understand."

"Then don't do this."

"I have to!" she cried, tears in her eyes. "Why can't you—"

"I love you," he breathed out, the words caressing her cheeks as he held her. "Can't you see? I love you, and I can't see you die." He captured her lips again, wrapping his arms around her, almost cutting off her breath with the ferocity of his embrace. "I can't, Natalie."

"I'm going to die someday," she said, the tears welling up in her eyes. Her heart soared at his words. Her mind raged at the thought of the danger they both faced. "Everyone dies someday."

"Unacceptable," he breathed out, tilting her head to the side. His fangs scraped along her collar. His hand grasped the nape of her neck almost painfully, but she reveled in it. She had never felt more alive. "When we live through this, I'm leaving this place, and you're coming with me."

He spun her around, pressing her back against the wall of the house as he kissed her again and again. Natalie could feel the water drawn from the pool lapping at her feet, drawn to him as the energy crackled around him. She could only gasp as he continued the relentless assault on her senses.

"Vampire or not," he hissed against her skin, "you are my mate. I will not be without you."

Natalie gasped, "I am your mate."

"And you will never do anything this dangerous again."

"Baojia!" He took her breath away. His fingers pressed into the small of her back, and he shoved his thigh between her legs. He growled low in his throat when her fingers sank into his hair and gripped. She couldn't get close enough. She felt wild. Feral. A creature of instinct and sense. Her mind was blurred by the hum of his energy, the scent of his skin, and the feel of his fangs as they pierced her neck. Natalie cried out when she felt the pull of his lips. Taking. Claiming. She was his. The waves of pleasure crashed over her as the water reached for him, soaking her legs as he held her against the wall.

"Say it, Natalie."

"I love you."

His hoarse groan echoed in the night as the waves came harder, buffeting against the wall, lapping against her skin and causing her to shiver. He reached for her pants, pushing them away as he moved her farther into the shadows. Natalie tugged at his clothes frantically, desperate to touch him. Desperate to feel. To remind herself that, whatever happened later, in that moment, she was alive. He was her reason, and he loved her.

"I love you," he whispered again as he entered her, holding her gaze as firmly as he held her heart. Her back scraped against the wall, but Natalie only held him closer. "Don't make me live without you."

She ignored the tears that slid down her cheeks. "I won't. I promise."

His thrusts were hard, still holding an edge of anger. "You can't promise me that."

She cried out, biting into his shoulder to suppress the scream as he drove them both. Pleasure coursed through her body, but his fear pierced her heart.

"I promise," she finally panted as he arched back in release and she came apart in his arms. "I promise you, Baojia."

He held her close, both of them soaked to the skin, and Natalie clutched him tighter, praying she'd made a promise she could keep.

CHAPTER TWENTY-FIVE

HE LISTENED as they drove south, the night growing lighter as the waxing moon rose and traveled the sky. The lights of Tijuana were in the rearview mirror, and Ben sat next to him, eyes focused on the cracked asphalt they followed into the desert.

"The main difference between a stun gun and a Taser is proximity." Brigid was lecturing in the backseat as they drove, a duffel bag of weapons open on the seat between her and Natalie. "To use a Taser, the ideal distance is around ten to fifteen feet. But you're dealing with vampires who are far faster than anything human. So if you see one, point and shoot even if they're farther away. These all have laser sights built in. By the time it fires, they'll probably be within a few feet of you."

"Lovely. And the stun gun?"

"Very effective, but you'll have to be in direct contact—"

Baojia growled in the front seat, and Brigid narrowed her eyes at him.

"Hey," Natalie said. "No growling."

"Obviously," Brigid muttered, "direct contact is not the ideal. So try to use the Taser. I packed a few of them for you."

"I'm counting at least twenty, Brigid."

"You can never have too many weapons. And this model can be used as a stun gun for about half a minute after it's fired. But you shouldn't need any of this. It's purely a precautionary measure. We will be engaging the vampires at the perimeter, and you and Ben will create a defensive position in the center of the crater."

Natalie nodded vigorously. "I remember there were some rocks and trees and stuff we can use to hide."

"They shouldn't even get near you."

Brigid was obviously young, Baojia mused as he drove the old car, dodging potholes before he turned onto the dirt track that had been used as a mining road. Battle plans—even his own—rarely went as planned. The only constant was the *un*planned factor. There was always something unpredictable, and it usually happened at the most inopportune time.

He had tried again when they woke that evening to dissuade Natalie, but she was determined. He had used all his powers of persuasion, thrown every logical argument in her face, before he finally conceded humans were an integral part of the plan, and if they didn't use her, they'd have to use someone else. After that, all arguments were moot. She wouldn't stand to have anyone else put at risk. He briefly considered knocking her out anyway, but at that moment, Tenzin had pounded on the door and told them to stop having sex and get in the car. Which was doubly annoying because they weren't actually having sex.

He had to fall in love with the stubborn one, didn't he? The stubborn, beautiful, defenseless human with no sense of self-preservation and a hero complex.

"And make sure you don't ever use a Taser on a fire vampire, or you're toast."

Baojia gritted his teeth and glanced in the rear view mirror at Natalie's wide blue eyes.

"How will I know if it's a fire vampire?"

Brigid said, "You'll know. But chances are, it won't be. There's not that many of us, to be honest. Meeting two like you have is fairly extraordinary. The most common type of vampire is Earth, with Wind and Water rounding things out. Fire is very uncommon."

"It's like a recessive gene," Ben said from the front seat.

"Okay, and I'm assuming that they'll burst into flames if shocked or something?"

He saw Brigid nod. "Our amnis is nothing more than an enhanced electrical current. That's why vampires short out electronic equipment so easily. It also seems to be what connects us to our element, so when we're shocked, our systems react by loosing an incredible amount of elemental power. Carwyn would create a large earthquake. Baojia would draw all the water around to him."

"Except we're in the desert, where there's no water," he muttered, still highly annoyed at the handicap.

"Well, yes. Try to make the best of it," Brigid said. "Tenzin is air, but I'm not sure what it would do. I've never shocked an air vampire before."

Ben said, "Can I try? Please?"

Baojia said, "The fact that you're still alive is truly amazing sometimes."

"Eh…" The boy shrugged. "She has a soft spot for me."

That much was obvious, but it had been to the boy's benefit. He was one of the most well-trained mortals Baojia had ever met, even just shy of his eighteenth birthday. Ben was proficient in judo and jujitsu, could fire various weapons with accuracy, had a good command of hand-to-hand combat with knives, and could even handle a blade passably well. Added to that were the instincts he could only have been born with. The boy was incredibly sharp. If Baojia had enough time with him, he'd have him a master by the time he turned immortal. If he turned.

He glanced in the rearview mirror again. *If she turned.*

What if she didn't want it? What if she *never* wanted it?

"What other weapons did you bring?"

Ben's voice broke into his ruminations. Baojia glanced down at the twin short swords that were strapped to his thighs. "I have a few other swords in the trunk. A *dao* and a new *katana* I bought last year, but I probably won't bring them."

"Are those going to be enough?"

He nodded.

"They're kind of…"

Baojia smirked, knowing exactly what the boy was thinking. "Kind of…?"

"Short."

"Are you saying that size matters, Benjamin?"

The teenager snorted. "I just mean that your reach with those—"

"These are fourteen-inch twin butterfly swords. Handmade and balanced within ten grams of each other. They are also perfect for the way I fight." He glanced at the boy. "One thing you will learn is that every fighter is different, and this is important to know. We all have our strengths. What is your aunt's favorite weapon?"

"*Shang gou.* The hook swords. You trained her on them; you know."

"I picked those for her because her sense of balance and flexibility makes them ideal for her. One of her strengths as a fighter has always been balance and knowing how to use her opponents' weaknesses against them. She needed reach and heft. The hook swords were perfect for her."

Ben muttered, "And they're really cool."

"No, Ben. They're really *fucking* cool." For the first time that night, he felt a real smile cross his face. "But I have different strengths, first of which is speed. I'm much faster than your aunt or your uncle."

"Yeah, I noticed." Ben rubbed his ribs where Baojia had given him a good punch the other night while they were practicing.

"Good. And so a long sword like a *dao* or a *katana* or the *shang gou* is not ideal for me. Short swords are faster. Besides, I don't try to keep my opponents at bay. I draw them close and then attack. It's the way my father taught me, and still the most effective way for me to fight."

"Ernesto taught you that?"

Baojia paused, his breath catching a little at the flood of memories. A man—almost a mirror image of himself—practicing *wing chun* forms in a small garden. Watching. Baojia was always watching. Then he was the one practicing. He could hear the man's murmured instructions as he gently corrected the small boy. The evening sunlight pouring over them as the smell of food drifted from the outdoor kitchen where his mother sang.

"No," he said. "My human father taught me to fight."

"He must have been good."

"He was."

Natalie and Brigid were silent in the backseat. He glanced in the mirror to see her watching him. Then he felt the brush of her warm fingers at his neck, and he turned his eyes back to the road.

"You are young. Your body is still developing, and your frame is still filling out. You won't truly settle into a fighting style for a few years. But all the preparation you're doing is good. And if there has to be a human guarding Natalie…" He glanced at her again, only to find her sticking her tongue out at him. He smiled. "I'm relatively satisfied that it's you."

"Stop with the gushing praise; I'm going to think you have a crush on me."

"Don't push it."

Ben laughed as he reached into the duffel bag at his feet. "I have backup. It's me, Smith & Wesson, Sig Sauer, and my darling Miss Kimber."

"Good to know you brought friends. That won't kill them, you know."

"A .45 still packs a hell of a punch, my friend."

"Aim for the neck."

A wicked glint came to Ben's eye. "Always."

They had to hike the last five miles to the hunting grounds. Baojia gave Natalie a piggyback ride. Brigid offered to carry Ben, but he refused with red ears and ran to keep up. Carwyn and Tenzin were already at the crater, bickering.

"Stop calling me fat. Just because I'm not as light as a fifteen-year-old girl—"

"I was older than fifteen when I turned, you idiot."

"Then stop acting like a whiny little schoolgirl. It's not like you're not strong enough. You could carry ten of me and not feel it, so stop bitching. Did you feed tonight?"

"Just bagged blood. I didn't have time to hunt."

Carwyn grunted. "No wonder."

"You two fight like siblings," Baojia said as he set Natalie down.

"Always." Ben went over and threw an arm around Tenzin's shoulders. "Stop picking on Tiny, Carwyn."

"Picking on—?" Carwyn threw his head back and laughed. "Good one. Ah, there's my lovely girl." Brigid went over to him and tilted her face up for a kiss, but Carwyn lifted her in his massive arms and swung her around, greeting his wife far more enthusiastically than he had only two nights before. "Mmmm, my lovely, lovely girl… There are caves around here. I've already scouted them out."

"One-track mind," Brigid muttered as Carwyn coaxed her away from the group.

Baojia rolled his eyes at the pair and turned to Tenzin, who was brushing off Ben's arm. "Stop calling me Tiny."

"It just fits."

He broke in before they could start arguing. "No truck, I take it."

She shook her head. "Going to sniff around? We just got here. We stopped by Tulio's place—Carwyn knows him, of course—and let him know what the plan was. He says we can use that tunnel you mentioned to get the girls out. Says it's safe and he'll be watching for them. The one human he has is still tucked away."

"Good. That will help." He looked around, really examining the hunting ground for the first time. Leaving Natalie with Tenzin and Ben, he walked the perimeter. It was a natural crater, no doubt formed hundreds or thousands of years ago by something massive hitting the ground. The depression was almost perfectly round, and little grew in it except a copse of trees that had sprung up from the middle and a few tumbleweeds. He toed his shoes off and sank his feet into the sand, but could sense no water.

His eyes darted around, taking in bits and pieces. The more he looked, the more subtle evidence of violence he saw. Cracked branches and bloodstains. A pile of rocks had tumbled down the side of the crater where it looked like someone had tried to run up quickly. Though the wind had carried the scent of fresh human blood far away, brown smudges still remained on the sandstone rocks that lay scattered around. And the scent of the predators was everywhere. The traces of energy were old—he guessed no one had been back since the hunt they had witnessed days before, but they were numerous and varied. It wasn't the same vampires hunting over and over. Though a few signatures seemed familiar, most were unknown and belonged to unique individuals.

"Hunting parties," he murmured. Why was Ivan doing it? For amusement? To make money? It was the type of thing responsible immortal leaders had outlawed to avoid exposure to humans, but in this part of the world—where no one was watching, using girls that no one cared about—it certainly wouldn't be unheard of. Were the other vampires paying him? Did they know they were getting a poison as well as a fresh meal? Somehow, Baojia didn't think that was on the brochure.

He felt Natalie approach.

"What are you thinking?" she asked.

"I'm thinking… I still wish you weren't here."

"Can we stop now, please? I'm here. Talk to me about the plan."

He closed his eyes and took a deep breath, letting it out as she slid her hand in his. "We'll all hide in Tulio's tunnel today. Obviously, it's not happening tonight. It might not happen for days. We only know the girl, Carmen, was taken two nights ago. According to what we can tell, it takes anywhere from two to three days to collect the girls and infect them with Elixir. Was Carmen the first they grabbed for this hunt? The last? It might be tomorrow night; it might be a week from now. Hopefully it's not a week, but we did bring provisions for you and Ben, and Father Andrade has Ben's phone number to call us when the truck shows up at the club."

"And when they do get here?"

She knew this already. They'd gone over it seven times, by his count. She was asking to let him process it in his own mind again, searching for any loose ends.

"After they drop off the girls, the count starts. An hour, according to Tulio. We'll have to gather them up and get them headed toward Tulio's. Or we might just knock them out with amnis and hide them in Tulio's caverns." He frowned. "Yes, I think that would be better. Safer."

"Okay." She nodded. "Then Ben and I take position."

He tensed instinctually. "Yes. Carwyn, Tenzin, Brigid, and I will have to remain in the tunnel until they come back, but you and Ben will be in the center of the crater. In that stand of trees there. No use giving them a clear target. There's no shower here, so your scent will already be heightened, which will draw them."

"Wonderful. I won't smell like Elixir, though."

He shook his head. "I don't think it will matter. From what I could tell last time, they came already high on the drug. They'd already fed—this was just an added experience. To make it all more exciting." She shivered at his words and Baojia drew her closer. "I wonder... he doses the humans at the club with it. When they start to get sick, is this their last stop? If Constantina hadn't run, would she have ended up out here?"

"But Rosa didn't seem sick."

"Good point." He cocked his head, thinking. "Maybe they're running out of waitresses. Running out of time. They don't want to wait for healthy girls to get sick. Healthy prey would be more fun to hunt anyway, so why wait for girls to get sick? In fact, find girls who can run and fight back a little. It would make them a bit more of a challenge if they can fight back." He rubbed his cheek against her hair, taking comfort in her touch, her scent, her warmth. She had wrapped her arms around his waist as they spoke.

He heard her gulp. "It makes a twisted kind of sense, I guess."

"Yes, it does." He took a deep breath. "Natalie?"

"What?"

"This is a very sick world," he whispered. "And sometimes I feel like I have lived in it too long."

"No," she said. "Just long enough. Long enough for me to find you. Long enough for me to love you."

The wind whistled past as he felt Tenzin fly overhead. Carwyn and Ben had started a small fire near the mouth of the tunnel where he had killed the air vampire and rescued Rosa. He pulled Natalie down to sit next to him on a large piece of sandstone.

"When this is finished, I want to move north. I think we can live in the Northwest and be safe. I have lots of money. You can find whatever work you want. I don't want to live like this anymore."

"Then we won't." She laid her head on his shoulder. "Kristy called yesterday. She tried to hold them off, but she and Dan got chewed out by our big boss. I didn't want her to get in trouble, so I called the *Tribune* and quit. Officially."

He looked at her, startled. "You didn't tell me this when I woke tonight?"

"Didn't seem all that important at the time." Natalie gave him a rueful smile. "And I knew going back wasn't really an option. I'll manage, I guess. Maybe I'll publish online. Lots of writers do."

"Then you can work from anywhere."

She nodded. "Mmhmm. Even the Northwest."

Despite everything, he smiled. "I like this plan."

"And if I work from home, you won't have to worry about me getting hit by a bus crossing the street or being struck down by a meteor or choking on a donut or anything." She elbowed him. "So much safer. Well, maybe not from donuts, but definitely buses."

"Approximately four thousand pedestrians are killed every year, you know."

"Why doesn't it surprise me that you know that?"

Because she was his world now. And everything he could do to make her safe, he would. As much as she would let him, anyway.

"I want to marry you, Natalie. I want you to have children like you want. Our children." The vision of his father in the courtyard came back to him. "I will protect them. I can teach them how to fight."

"You could teach them a lot of things," she said, her voice hoarse. He looked down to see tears in her eyes. "How to fight. How to play. How to break my cell phone…"

"Yes." He smiled. "All of those things. I believe I would be a good father."

"I think you'd be a great father. It wouldn't bother you? That you can't —"

"There are humans who cannot father children, aren't there?" He shrugged. "We will do whatever they do. It won't make them any less mine." He looked down. "If that is what you want."

"Maybe not right away, but…" She smiled. "That's definitely what I want."

"Then that's what we'll do."

"Okay." Natalie heaved a sigh and settled close to him again. "After we kill all the bad guys."

"After *I* kill all the bad guys, and you keep your head down."

"That's what I meant."

Ivan's men didn't come that night. They didn't come the next night, either. By the third night, everyone was getting restless. Carwyn had dug more caves off of Tulio's original tunnel just so they could avoid each other. Brigid and Baojia were both thirsty; Baojia only took a little blood from Natalie, not wanting her weak. It had caused yet another argument. Which he lost, so he drank again.

When he woke on the fourth night, it was with a distinct sense of foreboding. He left Natalie in her sleeping bag and went outside. Tenzin was crouched at the mouth of the cave, eyeing the horizon.

"They're coming tonight," she said.

"Are you sure? The priest hasn't called."

She cocked her head to the side, like a bird examining an insect. "Fairly sure."

He lowered his voice. "Tenzin… If Natalie is injured in this fight, I do not want to lose her."

She raised an eyebrow. "You ask this of me? Do you trust me so much, Dragon?"

"No."

She grinned, her curving fangs glinting in the moonlight. "Good. You shouldn't. So why ask me?"

"I would bargain with you, and your blood is powerful."

"So is the priest's."

Baojia stopped as Ben crawled out of the cave, grumbling about the heat and muttering something about clean water. He walked away from them, no doubt looking for somewhere to relieve himself, and Baojia saw Tenzin watching him with an amused smile.

"Perhaps," he said, "I think you would understand my wish to not lose a human so valuable to me."

Tenzin's eyes cut toward him, narrowing.

"Perhaps," Baojia said, leaning closer, "you would do the same, even if it was not that human's wish."

"Perhaps you're right." She stood, brushing off the dust. "I'm going to look around and see what's coming."

"Is that a yes?"

"I would say... *perhaps*." Tenzin took to the air, disappearing into the black night.

Baojia sighed and stretched, enjoying the feel of his muscles working. He took off his shirt, folding it neatly and laying it on a rock before he centered himself and faced the darkening western sky.

Perhaps.

He closed his eyes and swept a leg out, crossing his arms, then pulling them away from his body before he brought them back to center and flexed his shoulders.

Perhaps.

Baojia practiced his forms as the moon rose and the others gave him the gift of their silence. They all knew what the plan was; they simply needed the enemy to arrive.

Perhaps?

He breathed deeply, sensing a welcome—but unexpected—gift on the breeze. His amnis jumped when he felt it. *It couldn't be...* His eyes flew open, searching the sky just as Tenzin landed.

"There is good news and bad news, as they say," she said, walking toward him.

"Bad news?"

"Four SUVs are heading this way, following the delivery truck that will be here within a few minutes."

Four. With three or four immortals in each SUV, that would mean anywhere between twelve and sixteen opponents. And four of them. Normally, he could handle that many on his own, but with the Elixir involved, the odds were unknown.

"And the good news?"

She grinned wide. "There's a storm coming."

CHAPTER TWENTY-SIX

ONE MINUTE, she was sitting quietly, watching him practice his martial arts forms in that steady, meditative rhythm, the next, everything happened at once. Baojia spun around and picked her up in one swoop, carrying her to the tunnel so fast the world around her blurred. He was speaking to Tenzin in rapid Chinese as they raced toward Tulio's cavern.

"Stop!" she finally yelled. "English, please! I don't know what's going on!"

"They're on their way. The girls are in a large delivery truck and they'll be here in a few minutes. We have to hide and hope they don't sniff too closely. I didn't think about the danger of us camping here. Our scents could be everywhere. If the driver is a vampire—"

Carwyn broke in. "Father Andrade mentioned a human driver to me. So did the girl. I think we'll be fine, but we need to get everyone inside so we're not seen. How long do we have after the women are dropped off?"

"Tulio said an hour, but I don't know. His sense of time is not all that accurate."

Natalie was dumped in the tunnel while the others raced around, tidying up their little camp and trying to erase any evidence of their existence.

"Too lax," she heard Baojia mutter once when he dropped off a shirt Brigid had draped over a bush to air out. "I have been too lax."

Everything around her turned into a blur.

Vampires were coming. Fast, inhumanly strong vampires, hopped up on some vampire drug that made them irrational and bloodthirsty. And those vampires were going to kill Natalie, Baojia, Ben, Tenzin, Carwyn, and Brigid unless they killed them first. Everyone around her was pulling out swords and guns, strapping them to arms and waists and thighs in strange holsters that curled around their bodies like deadly ribbon. Even the teenager, Ben, had more weapons than the average SWAT officer. And Natalie had… a stun gun.

What the *hell* had she been thinking?

She was desperately trying not to throw up when Baojia—the vampire who, two nights before, had basically proposed to her—pulled her hand and tugged her farther into a deserted alcove off the main cave. He straightened her shoulders and Natalie stared at his chest, still bare and exposed to the night air. There was a light sheen across it, almost as if he'd been sweating. She frowned. He didn't sweat.

"You're scared," he said.

"Yep. Terrified."

He nodded. "Good. Be scared. Use it. It'll make you more aware. Don't take chances. And make sure you stay with Ben."

"Okay."

"And when we get out of here, we're getting serious about your self-defense lessons."

"Okay."

"And we're going to get out of here." He tipped her chin up so she was forced to look at his dark eyes. "Do you understand me?" He was all calm and cool collection in that moment. Confident. Sure. The only rock-solid thing in this pile of crazy she'd landed in weeks ago.

Only weeks? It seemed like a lifetime.

"I love you, George." Her voice broke. "I'm really happy all this happened. No matter what."

He shook his head. "Don't act like that. We're going to be fine. You're going to be fine. Stay with Ben and trust me."

She nodded, trying to smile. "Okay."

"You have your guns?"

She nodded, patting the holster Brigid had brought for her. She wore two and had a small duffel with the rest that she'd take with her.

"Natalie?"

"Uh huh?"

He paused for a moment, looking nervous for the first time that evening. "We only have a few minutes before the girls get here. I can hear the truck. I need to know… You shouldn't be hurt. I have every

confidence you won't be, but if you are... I need to know if... if you want
—"

"Want what?" Her heart began to pound. "For you to make me a vampire?"

He shook his head. "Not me. If I did—"

"I don't want you to!"

"I won't." He swallowed. "But someone else... someone else could."

The heart that had pounded now felt like it would fly out of her chest. "I don't know!"

"You have to know."

She felt the tears prick the corners of her eyes. "But I don't." She blinked them away. "I don't know, Baojia. How can I know that?"

He looked away, toward the flurry of action at the mouth of the cave. "I can't lose you."

"Then don't let them get me." Forcing a calm face, she took a deep breath and tried to stop the shivers that wanted to take over. "Don't let them get me, Baojia. Give me that time."

He gave her a quick nod, then leaned down, pressing his lips to hers in a toe-curling kiss before he pulled away and put his arm around her, guiding her back to the others.

The drivers were human. There were two drivers and twelve girls, leading Baojia to speculate that the SUVs carrying the hunters would hold twelve vampires. Good. Twelve was better than sixteen. The drivers forced the crying girls to the center of the crater at gunpoint. Some of them screamed. Some wailed. Others begged. But a few stood stoically, arms crossed as they glared at the humans who backed away and spun out, leaving the girls alone in the middle of the desert night.

The smell was overwhelming.

The sweet, heady scent of blood washed up the edge of the crater and down the tunnel, carried on the breeze that was growing ever more laden with moisture as the storm approached. He heard a high, whining sound and turned to see Brigid biting her arm. Carwyn stroked her short cap of hair back, soothing his mate as she forced herself to remain still. Carwyn's eyes met Baojia's in the darkness. He glanced at Natalie.

"They're going to know."

Baojia nodded. There was no question. When the hunt started, the vampires were going to know something was wrong. There was no mistaking the smell of the girls. If anything, they smelled even more appetizing than the ones at Bar El Ruso had.

"What the hell are they putting in that Elixir?" he muttered, trying not to breathe through his nose.

"We have to keep at least a few of them there. Taking away the majority of them will still decrease the distractions we have to deal with and probably some of the bloodlust, especially for Brigid, but we have to have some of them there or they're going to know."

Natalie, finally catching on to what they were talking about, butted in. "But those girls are innocent! We have to get them out of there. They're not bait."

Carwyn snorted. "That's exactly what they are, Nat. And you've volunteered to take their place, but you don't smell like them. We need at least a hint of their scent in order for the hunters not to immediately guess that something is wrong."

Brigid forced her head up, blood staining her mouth. "Keep to the plan. Pick a few of the more defiant girls and give them stun guns. Leave them there with Natalie and Ben. It will be enough to draw the vampires without distracting all of us. The rest need to get as far up this tunnel as possible, or they're just going to throw us off."

Baojia nodded. "I was thinking the same thing." He glanced toward the dark crater. The truck was no more than a retreating rumble in the night. "Let's start rounding them up. Brigid, pick the girls you want to have stay."

She forced a nod and started out of the tunnel, Carwyn close on her heels. Baojia stood and Natalie followed him, dogging his steps.

"You can't let them use these girls as bait, Baojia. It's not fair. They've already been—"

"Abducted. Kidnapped. Poisoned. Probably abused in other ways, too." He kept walking, watching the girls cry out and run as they saw the shapes in the darkness. But there were two who didn't run, and he turned toward them. "I realize all that. I'm not even going to mention that you forced me to let you use *yourself* as bait."

"It was my choice!"

"And it will be theirs, as well." He approached one girl who looked vaguely familiar. She was staring at him with furious eyes, chin up and mouth screwed into a sneer. "You!" he called in Spanish. "Is your name Carmen?" She looked like the girl who had come to the church. Enough alike to be sisters.

At the mention of her name, the sneer fell. "Who are you?"

"We're friends of Father Andrade's. And we're trying to save your life."

She shook her head. "Nothing is going to save my life. I saw what happened to Constantina. I know what's going to happen to me."

"Want to give Ivan's men a surprise?" Baojia grabbed at one of the stun guns on Natalie's belt and held it out. "You stay, you get a chance to hurt them."

Carmen grabbed the gun. "I'll take it."

"And help us round up the girls."

She gave him a quick nod and started running toward a group of girls Carwyn was trying to calm. Just then, Tenzin landed on a rock nearby.

"They're close. Get these girls in the tunnel."

He cursed under his breath. "That wasn't an hour."

"Nope. Looks like someone's impatient." She flew off toward Carwyn. Between the two vampires and Carmen, most of the girls headed toward the tunnel, with three others standing with Brigid as she gave them a quick lesson on stun guns, which Ben translated. Baojia turned to Natalie, who had been silent the whole exchange.

"Time for you to get in position," he said.

She nodded, then reached for him. He let her pull his face down, and she kissed him hard as she gripped the hair at his nape. He breathed her in, memorizing her scent and taste, wishing she was a thousand miles away. Finally, she broke the kiss and patted his chest, right over his heart.

"I love you," she said. "I'll see you later."

He swallowed, unable to say anything for a second. "Get a... get another stun gun from Brigid. Make sure you have two."

She gave him a thumbs-up as she walked away. "I'm on it, George."

Fucking hell. If the last time she ever spoke to him was to call him George, he was going to be pissed.

She and Ben were crouched in the center of the crater, backs to a large sandstone boulder that was sheltered by some scrubby trees. The stars had slowly begun to disappear as unexpected clouds rolled in.

"Clouds." She turned to Ben. "Clouds are good, right? Clouds mean rain, and Baojia—"

"Isn't the only water vampire in the world, unfortunately," Ben said. "But yes, better he has it as a weapon. We can just hope none of the bad guys are water vamps, too. Of course, it also means that Brigid is going to be screwed."

"Shit. I hadn't thought about that. Fire vampires get doused, huh?"

"There's always a trade-off, Natalie." Ben gave her a crooked grin. "To everything. And why do you call Baojia 'George?'"

"Long story." She glanced to her left and right where the three Mexican girls sat, new Tasers held out in front of them like shields. "Are they ready?"

Ben shrugged. "Point it this way. Fire it at anything with fangs. Let's just hope they don't shoot any of our people. It was the best we could do with the time we had."

She took a deep breath. "You been in anything like this before?"

"Not exactly."

"What are our odds?"

He shrugged. "Tenzin says you should never try to calculate odds in a fight. Just win. That's all that matters."

Natalie let out a slow breath. "Win. Got it."

He heard them approaching as they crouched in the tunnel. The vampires must have left the cars at the end of the mining road. He looked at Tenzin, who was closing her eyes and listening intently. After a moment, she looked up, then held up ten fingers, then three.

Thirteen? So someone wasn't hunting. Carwyn and Brigid had tunneled around to the other side of the crater to lie in wait so they could attack from front and back. The idea was for Brigid and Carwyn to attack from one side as Baojia did from the other, Tenzin taking to the air to catch any stragglers or air vampires who could fly. Also, she said she'd try to pull as much of the storm toward them as possible. Baojia had doubts about how much the small vampire—even as powerful as she was—could manipulate the clouds. Still, the steadily increasing moisture fed his strength. Once the rain was falling, he'd be even stronger.

He glanced toward the crouched figures at the center of the crater.

Don't let them get me. Give me time.

He'd give her as much time as he could. But he sure as hell hoped that Tenzin held up her end of the bargain if time ran out.

Shit, shit, shit. Natalie's heart beat a staccato rhythm. She could hear growls and laughter on the air. They were coming. She crouched as she heard a swooping sound overhead, like a dark bird on the night air. Drops of rain began to fall and she gripped her gun closer. Ben held one weapon in his hands, another was ready at his waist, and still another was strapped to his thigh.

Natalie said, "You're kind of frightening for a teenager, you know?"

Ben only grinned. "Aren't you glad I'm on your side?"

She nodded as the growls came closer.

"Wait, Natalie," he said in a soothing voice. "Nothing's going to happen to you."

She gave a jerky nod a second before she heard the collision midair. There was a popping sound, then a hoarse scream was cut short. A second later came a quiet thud as a blond head landed only inches from their feet. Its bright blue eyes stared at Natalie as its mouth fell open in an eternal snarl. She slapped a hand over her mouth to hold in the scream, then all hell broke loose.

CHAPTER TWENTY-SEVEN

BAOJIA SAW TENZIN swoop down to intercept the wind vampire who had spotted the humans in the center. The enemy vampire dove for his prey, only to be interrupted by the fearsome woman who grabbed him by the neck and flew him up toward the clouds. With a quick twist, his neck was broken. With a swipe from her ancient scimitar, he was dead. The head fell to the ground as she tossed his body toward Baojia's hiding place. Just then, dark shapes crested the hill.

He slunk out of the mouth of the tunnel, drawing his right sword as he crept toward the shadows. The hunters were taking their time, not being quiet. They wanted to elicit fear by toying with what they thought were defenseless humans in the center of the crater. Snarling and laughing as they came closer, none of them noticed the loss of their friend.

What they did notice was the sudden silence when two of their number fell through the earth. Baojia grinned.

Playtime was over.

Three down, ten to go. He raced around the perimeter, arm sweeping out to take the head of one shocked vampire before he was even spotted. A grab of the hair. A quick slice. Another thud. The body slumped to the ground and he tossed the head over his shoulder as the crazed vampires began to realize they had walked into a trap. Their attention immediately diverted from the humans in the center of the circle, all nine vampires suddenly went on alert. One took to the air and was out of his sight. One began to run, only to have his feet sink into the earth as Brigid burst from the ground and used what little time she had to turn the screaming vampire to ash.

The rain was falling harder. He felt a heavy sheet hit his back and reveled in the feel of it, cool against his skin.

Baojia took a deep breath and let out an angry roar as every eye turned toward him.

Two more dead. Only seven now.

Another headless body thudded to the ground.

Make that six, plus the driver.

His first real attack came as he heard Carwyn exclaiming from across the crater and two gunshots fired. The vampire ran toward him, hands out, directing a sheet of water at him as he tried to knock Baojia off his feet. Damn. His breath rushed out. These creatures—high on whatever Ivan had been feeding them—*were* stronger.

The drops turned to tiny blades under the other water vampire's command. Baojia didn't halt, though he felt his flesh break open in a hundred places from the impact of the driving rain. He ducked to the side to dodge another watery attack before he reached out with his amnis and grabbed the water, turning it on his attacker to slice into his face as the vampire screamed.

The immortal was dark-haired. Possibly Mexican, but not certainly. Baojia ran at him, letting his enemy get close enough to grab an outstretched arm, drawing him toward his body as Baojia ducked his head, bracing his neck as he rammed his forehead into the vulnerable underside of his opponent's jaw. The vampire's head slammed back as Baojia grabbed him by the hair and held, bringing his blade up to sever the spine with one efficient slice. He dropped the body and looked for the next opponent.

There was a blond vampire trying to run away. Too damn bad. His fangs long and gleaming, Baojia ran after him, jumping over scrub and ignoring the sting of cactus as he raced to catch him. He caught up with him a few hundred feet from the crater. Not wanting to waste time, Baojia pounced on the other man's back. A young one, he guessed, from the level of amnis. He was an earth vampire and tried to let the ground swallow him. Baojia was halfway sunk in the ground before a jerk and a swipe ended his enemy's life.

Natalie.

He was too far away from her. He left the body where he'd killed it and raced back. Carwyn was ripping into another vampire only a few feet away as he heard more shots, but not from where Ben was still sitting. Natalie was still crouched next to the boy. Still clutching her stun gun as if her life depended on it, but happily isolated from the bloodshed around her.

"Who's shooting?" he yelled.

Carwyn twisted a scrambling immortal's head under his arm, reached down to grab at the man's arm, and pulled, holding him as his neck was detached and the scrambling stopped. Then Carwyn looked over at Baojia and grinned. "That'd be my girl. She does love her weapons. A few shots to incapacitate, then a quick slice to the spine to end things quickly."

"How kind." Baojia tried not to shiver. He'd never liked guns. He glanced at the still-unmolested humans at the center of the fight. "How many left?"

"Tenzin's had two or three. I think. I've had three. Brigid two. You?"

"Three."

Two more, and where were they? He fell silent. Everything was silent. Then he saw him.

The vampire had snuck down from the other side of the crater. He'd been able to flee from the initial surprise attack, but instead of running, he'd come back, drawn like an addict to the smell of the girls' blood. Baojia spread his arms, gathering the driving rain that pelted his back and turning it toward the vampire. Within seconds, a bridge of water formed in the air as he sent a rush of amnis through the element he commanded. The vampire exploded in pain as Baojia's energy hit, reeling back with bared fangs as Tenzin fell on him and cut off his head, snarling into his face as he still reached for the women.

"Pathetic," she muttered as blood dripped down her chin. Then she turned to Baojia. "There's one I can't find. I looked in the desert, but I can't spot him."

Baojia frowned as he looked around, then his eyes landed on Carwyn and he yelled, "The ground!"

A second later, the center of the crater caved in, taking Natalie, Ben, and the women with it.

CHAPTER TWENTY-EIGHT

SHE ACHED. EVERYTHING HURT. Her head. Her body. She felt as if she'd been run over by a truck. One second she was watching the brutal fight around her as if she was caught in some otherworldly action movie, the next, everything was dark and she heard a scream. Then quiet. Another scream.

More quiet. There was a scrambling sound as blood and sand filled her mouth. Water fell on her face as she blinked her eyes open and saw him.

She knew him. Where did she know him from?

A clanging sound. The casino? Flashing lights and a bitter aftertaste in her mouth.

Carlos. His name was Carlos and he was Ivan's right hand.

Ivan's right hand who was apparently killing the evidence of his boss's guilt.

"Natalie?" She heard Baojia's voice from above.

No Ben. Where was Ben? The young man had kept her centered and calm as the fight around them had raged.

"She's over here, Baojia! I've got her."

There he was. It made her smile to hear Ben's voice.

"Carlos?" she whispered.

Natalie turned toward a scuffling sound. Carlos was barely visible in the dim light, holding a girl by the hair as she wailed. But within seconds, the girl's eyes had gone dead, no doubt calmed by the same power all vampires wielded.

"Put the girl down," Baojia said. "It's over."

"No," Carlos said. "It's not. You have no idea. This has just begun."

"Nat," Ben whispered, "we have to dig you out of here. Just hang on. I'm going to get Carwyn."

"Okay."

Baojia was yelling at Carlos. "This wasn't you! You don't do anything without Ivan's permission. Put the girl down. There's no need to kill her."

"She's dead already!" Carlos laughed. "Don't you realize? You're saving these girls so they can die anyway. You think he's going to stop? He'll just set up somewhere else. Somewhere you don't know about. He made so much money, Baojia. More than he ever made through the cartel. They came from everywhere to get a taste of these worthless girls." Carlos's bitter laugh churned her gut. "He was only doing it here and dumping the bodies on your land to fuck with you."

"Why?" Baojia moved farther into the cave. His chest was soaking wet and his pants were, too. His hair dripped around his face, the water pouring over him from the crater above. Natalie could feel it, sloshing around her feet as she lay in a crumbled heap on the dirt floor. "Why was Ivan baiting me?"

"It wasn't his idea," Carlos said in defeat. "It was Rory's. Rory wanted you gone. As long as you were in San Diego, you could always go back to LA, but if you fucked up something down here? He figured Ernesto would just get rid of you. Everyone knows how you two fight. Rory wanted you out of the way. He found out what Ivan was doing and came to us."

The pain had stopped and a dull ache was crawling up her side toward her neck. Her feet were cold. Was it from the water?

Carlos had dropped the girl and raised his hands. "You know what? Kill me. I've killed your woman anyway. I deserve it. I'm sorry, Baojia. You were always honest with me. I don't want to be a part of this anymore anyway. It was too much."

Baojia snarled and looked her direction. His eyes widened in alarm just as Carmen sat up and reached for the Taser. She raised it toward Carlos, who was still holding the hair of one of the girls.

Oops. Guess Ben had skipped that part of the lesson.

"Carmen, no!"

"*¡Pinche cabrón!*" she screamed a second before she fired.

Carlos arched back and dropped the girl when the shock hit him. There was a second that time seemed to stand still as Baojia leapt toward her, then the earth around her exploded and everything went black.

CHAPTER TWENTY-NINE

"NO!" BAOJIA SCREAMED into the night as Carwyn carried Natalie's body out of the cave. They were still digging up Carmen and the other girls. "No. You promised, Natalie. You can't die. *Tenzin!*"

Carwyn laid her gently on the ground. Her pulse was weak and irregular, her face pale. A root had pierced her side and hot blood spilled onto the ground. Tenzin knelt beside her and pressed a cloth to her side.

"She can be saved," the wind immortal said, looking at Baojia. "I can get her to the healers, and they can save her life."

"Are you sure?" He bared his fangs as he spoke.

"Nothing is sure."

"Then change her. Turn her now."

Tenzin shook her head. "She does not want this. I know she doesn't."

"I tried to give her time, but she doesn't have it. Turn her." He felt Carwyn put a hand on his shoulder. "Do it, Tenzin!"

"Baojia," the priest said quietly, "she does not want this. Let Tenzin take her to a hospital. Let the doctors save her mortal life."

"She is not your woman!" he roared, punching Carwyn back as he knelt beside Natalie and took her hand. His eyes met Tenzin's over the limp form of the human woman who had become the center of his world. He bit his lip and made the bargain that had been teasing the back of his mind. The deal he knew the other vampire would never pass up.

"Take her to the hospital, Tenzin. As fast as you can. And let them heal her." Tenzin moved to go, but he grabbed her wrist. "But if they cannot…"

Tenzin raised one eyebrow in curiosity. "What?"

271

"I will not live without her. You and your friends face something far larger than any of this. If she lives—however she lives—I am yours in any fight. I give you my word. You will call on me, and I will answer you. But know this." His voice dropped to a low growl. "I *will not* live without her."

He saw Tenzin's mouth quirk up and the dark satisfaction gleam in her eyes. Then she lifted Natalie from the ground and disappeared into the night.

A cold resolve filled Baojia's chest as he stood and walked toward the tunnel where he had kissed Natalie the last time. Where she had lain in his arms. Where she had been safe. For a little while, he had made her safe.

"Where are you going?" Carwyn ran after him.

"The keys to the car are in my backpack. Get out of here and get all of them to safety. Use your amnis to get across the border, but leave Mexico as quickly as you can. The cartel cannot know we were here. The bodies will burn up in the morning, so don't worry about that. They can think what they like about the cars. Take the girls to Tulio's. Beatrice will know how to find him."

"Baojia!"

He stopped for a moment, but did not turn. The rain poured over his skin, but it brought no comfort. "Or destroy my car. Sink it in the desert if you want and tunnel north. But leave quickly."

"Where are you going? She's going to live. I've seen many injuries of that kind, and I know—"

"I really can't talk, Carwyn." He wiped the mud from his face, enjoying the scrape of grit as it raised blood along his cheek. It made him feel—just for a second—not quite as dead inside. "I need to go kill my brother now."

The rain might have been pouring, but the casino was still busy, even at two in the morning. Baojia left the tunnel Tulio had dug and walked across the parking lot, past the tour buses and pickup trucks. He walked into the entry, not pausing when the human security guards came toward him. He saw them speaking into their headsets in mild panic, but they did not try to stop him. He did not stop at the odd looks the patrons gave the shirtless man, dripping with mud and traces of blood painted across his chest. They backed away but said nothing. Baojia looked up at each and every security camera he passed, willing the machines he had installed to transmit his image to the vampire he had come to kill. Willing the cold terror to enter his brother's heart.

He walked past the slot machines. Past the bar. Past each and every human, not caring what they thought. Were his fangs visible?

He didn't care about that, either. That, he decided, was Rory's mess. Not that Rory was going to be alive to clean it up.

The electronic door lock shorted out as soon as he touched it, then patrons finally began screaming and running for the exits when he reared back and punched it in.

One punch. One kick. Another punch and a roar as the humans scrambled for the doors, then he was in.

The hallway was dead already, deserted except for the flickering fluorescent lights that guided him toward his brother's office.

"You comin' to kill me, brother?" The voice came from the speakers above.

Baojia looked into the nearest camera and said, "Yes." He kept walking.

"Gonna kill your sister, you know? To lose her mate. Sure you want to do that?"

Baojia paused. Thought. "Yes, I am." He turned right and a girl in a casino uniform darted into a room. He heard the lock turn behind her.

"Does Paula know what's going on?" Baojia called out, not caring who heard.

"I'm trying to make things better for us. That's all. You know how hard she works for that old man?"

"Yes, I do." He turned left and lifted his eyes to the round camera mounted to the ceiling. "I used to work just as hard for him. And I did it gladly. *She* does it gladly."

"She shouldn't have to!"

He shook his head. "She knew about none of this, did she?"

"She'll forgive me when she's the one in power."

"No, she won't, you stupid man. Rory, Rory…" He turned right again, slowly getting closer to the security room where he was fairly certain Rory was holed up. "Always looking for the jackpot. Never the one willing to do the heavy lifting. Paula's too good for you. She always was."

"She should be running that city. She *does* run that city. He's just a figurehead."

"There's a lot you don't know. Not that I care. You're going to be dead soon."

"You don't even work for him anymore. What difference does it make?"

He paused and closed his eyes at the rush of pain. "Your actions, Rory. You took something of mine. Not my job. Something far more precious."

His brother's voice was harsh when it came over the line. "So you finally fell for a girl, huh? That human? Ivan get her? I... I didn't want that to happen, Baojia."

"It doesn't matter what you wanted. Results matter, not intentions. Not that your intentions were any good to begin with. I'm going to kill you. But I won't torture you. I'll give my sister that."

"It's a big casino." The sadness was gone from Rory's voice. "Figure you can find me in here? I'm not in my office."

Baojia looked up into the nearest camera. "I can find you." Then he ducked into a closet.

He was in the original section of the casino. The original bingo hall the tribe had put up before Ernesto's millions made them all rich. The dropped ceilings had always been a problem from a security standpoint, but there was no way of getting around them as Ernesto didn't want to waste the money on a low-priority, low-risk venture like an Indian casino. None of the money was kept anywhere near the old section. Who would try to break in?

Baojia braced his hands on the walls and climbed up, silently lifting the panel from above and reaching into the blackness to the old pipes that were just strong enough to hold his weight. He shimmied into the void, reaching back to put the panel into place, removing evidence of his passage. Then he silently moved toward the security office. As he reached the air-conditioning vents, he paused to listen. He could hear Rory somewhere, talking over a radio to guards, no doubt wondering where he had disappeared to. The echo of the guard's reply told him that his brother was exactly where Baojia thought he'd be—the fortified guard room with one reinforced door. It was light-tight. A panic room, in a sense. Rory could hole up in there for days if he wanted. Only, it was primarily used for guards, and human guards wanted air-conditioning when they worked in the desert.

He swung from the old pipes and into the ductwork, still listening for Rory's voice, for any indication that his brother suspected he was being stalked.

It was almost too easy.

Baojia slid through the ducts, navigating the byzantine network until he was staring at the back of his brother's head, listening to him yell at the guards, who still couldn't find the intruder. The panel was screwed on. It would have been hard for someone who was trying to avoid detection. But at that point, Baojia knew it was only a matter of seconds before his brother sensed him. They did, after all, share a bloodline. But Rory was no longer his family, and Baojia's mission was very clear.

He kicked open the vent and slid into the room in one movement, drawing his sword as he did. Rory spun, the knowledge already clouding his features. Then Baojia reached up and grabbed Rory's face in his hand, crushing it between his fingers as his sword relieved the old cowboy of his head.

Rory's body crumbled to the ground, his head still clasped in his brother's hand, mouth gaping open in shock.

Baojia had found a shirt by the time he made it back to his house in Coronado. He didn't know where else to go, and the car he'd stolen from the casino parking lot didn't look like it would make it far. Logic said that Tenzin would take Natalie somewhere in San Diego, but he had no idea where. Nor did he have any idea whether Natalie still lived at all. He thought Tenzin would hold up her end of the bargain, but he couldn't be certain. The low, gnawing pain in his belly wouldn't go away until he saw her alive. Human. Vampire. He didn't care.

The house in Coronado was just as he'd left it, including Luis sleeping on the couch downstairs as if he'd been waiting for him. At the sound of the slamming door, the human woke.

"Boss?" he rubbed his eyes. "That crazy vampire was right. And you look like shit."

"Which crazy vampire?"

"I don't know. She didn't give me her name. Just called the club, yelling into the phone, asking for your human."

"That would be Tenzin."

"Anyway. She said to get back here and wait for you. Gave me a number to call when you got here. Why the hell are you here? Are you supposed to be?"

He tried not to scream. "The number, Luis."

"Holy shit, this night is crazy. What time is it?"

He didn't even know. Baojia glanced at the wall. "It's four a.m. The number."

The human handed him a slip of paper, which he took to the office, punching the number into the phone. He pressed the button for speaker mode and began to pace.

It was Dez Kirby who picked up. "Baojia?"

"Dez." He hated that his voice broke, but he couldn't seem to control it. "Where is she?"

"She's at UC Medical Center. Matt and I are here with her. They have her stable. Both her legs were broken, and she lost a lot of blood, but they're worried about head trauma right now. They induced a coma until the swelling goes down."

"Is she going to live?" There was enough of a pause that he punched a wall. "Dez!"

"They think so, okay! There's no way of knowing if she has any brain damage right now. We just have to wait. They think, if everything happens like they're hoping, that she'll be significantly better by tomorrow."

"I'm coming to the hospital."

"She's just sleeping. And you'll have to leave in like an hour."

"I don't care." He was already pulling on a new shirt. "I'll be there."

She wasn't awake, but she wasn't dead, either. And Baojia sat there, holding her limp hand until he was forced to leave before dawn. Carwyn had explained to the doctors about the horrible rockslide while they were hiking, and a brush of Tenzin's amnis made any lingering questions go away. Dez and Matt would stay during the day while Baojia could not. He returned to Coronado.

He had no place else to go.

The next night, he was holding Natalie's hand, trying to keep his distance from the hospital equipment, when his sire slid into the room.

Ernesto pulled up a chair and sat across from Baojia, cocking his head to the side as he looked down on the sick woman. "Will she live?"

Baojia ignored the leap in his chest and tried to make his voice as calm as possible. "They are optimistic. The swelling has gone down the way the doctors were hoping for. They were very pleased when I arrived tonight."

They both fell silent, the only sound was the beeping from the monitors, which filled the room.

"You killed your brother last night," Ernesto finally said under his breath.

"I did."

"Because of this?"

"Because he was conspiring with Ivan to hold human hunts and implicate you in the deaths of the victims. Because he was dumping human bodies in your territory in an attempt to make you look weak. And yes, because his actions led to the injury of my mate."

"She is not your mate." Ernesto smiled indulgently. "She is not a vampire."

"That makes her no less my mate. Not to me."

Ernesto's eyes never left Baojia's face. The vivid green took on an eerie quality in the fluorescent lights of the hospital. "You are in love with her."

"Yes."

"Why didn't one of your friends turn her after she was injured?" Ernesto looked over his shoulder toward the hall where Carwyn and Beatrice waited with Dez and Matt. "Perhaps they are not friends at all, but those who want to use you?"

He clenched his teeth. "Like you did?"

"I am your sire. I gave you this life. Without me, you would have never met your lovely human. You would be dead in an unmarked grave, or buried in a mine that caved in. Perhaps part of the railroad you helped to build, stuffed under the tracks like garbage."

Baojia looked away from him and began to count the freckles on the back of Natalie's hand. "I know you are my sire."

"I am your family."

"No," he said firmly. "You are not."

277

Ernesto frowned. "You sister is devastated."

His chest ached for Paula. "I am devastated for her."

"Did she have any knowledge of Rory's actions?"

"No."

"How can I be sure?" Ernesto shrugged. "Unless you come back to my aegis, how can I be sure who to trust, Baojia?"

He blinked. Ernesto wanted him *back*? Impossible. Unless…

"Who has been inquiring after me? You must have heard some rumor. Someone else has been showing interest in me, or you would not want me back."

He knew it was true the moment he said it. Ernesto's gaze narrowed, but he didn't speak.

"Is it Katya?" As soon as the name of his old rival was spoken, Ernesto's amnis spiked. The monitors near Natalie began to go wild and the nurses rushed in. Baojia stood and backed against the wall, smiling at his sire as the nurses ushered Ernesto out. "I see."

"You see nothing, my son."

"I am not your son," he said quietly, glancing at the sleeping woman with wild red hair and everything he needed. "I know who my family is. Goodbye, Ernesto. Don't bother us. You may question my friends, but I do not. Nor do I question Natalie's." Beatrice was already at the door, along with Carwyn, waiting with worried eyes to see what the commotion was.

Ernesto looked away from Baojia and toward Beatrice, smiling kindly before he patted his granddaughter's cheek and murmured, "I wish the best for your friend, *cariña*. I'm sure she'll be fine. The doctors here are unparalleled."

"Thank you, Grandfather." Beatrice's voice was carefully neutral. "I'm just so glad she has such a fervent protector." She glanced toward Baojia with a smile. "She's in very good hands."

"So she is." The old vampire's smile was tight when he turned to Baojia and said, "Good luck."

CHAPTER THIRTY

SOUND WAS MUFFLED, almost as if she was listening from the bottom of a pool. Gradually, Natalie began to sift through her murky senses.

Beeping—a low, steady beeping. Her eyes were closed, and flashes of memory darted through her mind. A rumbling sound and the taste of blood in her mouth. Dark eyes turning toward hers in horrified surprise. Panic. He was shouting her name.

Natalie!

Hurt. She ached all over; her body was stiff with pain, and she somehow knew she had not moved in days. At the very edge of her senses, there he was. A cool hand stroking along her fingers, running up and down each one before he traced her palm. She could feel the brush of his hair along her arm as he lifted her hand to kiss the knuckles. And more, his buzzing energy, his amnis. Spreading over her skin and warming her, coaxing her toward consciousness.

Magic, she thought again. His touch was magic. He could explain it away with whatever science he chose, but he was magic. His love. His devotion. The fullness of who he was and all that they could be together washed over her as she focused on the feeling of his fingers tracing her skin. Magic.

Voices joined the beeping.

"Her lips moved. Did you see? I'm sure of it. Natalie?"

She didn't want to wake. She knew it was going to hurt more. Some instinct told her that wherever she was, it was safe. She didn't want to mess that up. But the magic that coursed over her skin spread upward, teasing deeper into her mind.

Wake up. You need to wake up.

No. Waking up was going to hurt.

Wake. Open your eyes.

She didn't hear the words, but the press of his influence pushed against her mind. There was a sense of urgency behind it.

Wake. Wake. Wake.

"You're so bossy," she croaked.

With that, the floodgates seemed to break. Natalie forced her eyes open when she heard the relieved laughter around the room. Beatrice and Dez started talking, but she didn't really listen. Carwyn was at the foot of her bed, grinning like a madman. Natalie forced her head to the left.

There he was.

She felt the corners of her mouth turn up when she saw him, her lips cracked a little as she smiled.

"There you are," he whispered through the cacophony of joyful chatter that had begun to fill the room. More voices joined in. Giovanni, Ben, even Tenzin's low voice could be heard asking questions, laughing, trying to get her attention. But she couldn't take her eyes off him.

He was sitting in a chair to her left. He wore a black T-shirt and his hair looked like he'd been running his hands through it for hours. It stuck out at odd angles, telling her he hadn't looked in a mirror in a while. And his eyes were so tired. Baojia let out a long breath and squeezed her hand a little. Then he took another breath and brought his other hand up to his face, covering his eyes for a few moments before he shook his head and let out another shaky breath.

She whispered, "Nothing but trouble, right?"

He leaned forward, taking her hand in both of his and bending over, placing his forehead to her wrist and kissing the palm of her hand before he looked back up. What do you know? Vampires cried pink. He blinked his red-rimmed eyes at her and managed a small smile.

"Nothing but trouble," he whispered back.

"Where am I? I had a really bad dream. I'm sorry." The voices were beginning to irritate her, but she focused on the feel of his hand holding hers.

"Why are you sorry? You're alive. Don't be sorry."

He couldn't seem to stop touching her. He brushed the hair back from her face and kissed her cheek. He ran his hands over her arms and pressed another kiss to her forehead. The look in his eyes was fierce, almost desperate.

"How do you feel? Are you in pain? What's the last thing you remember?" Then he looked around the room. "Is the doctor on the way? Where's the nurse?"

Dez rushed to reassure him as the monitors went wild. He must have gotten too close to the equipment.

"Chill, Baojia. You're stressing her out. They're coming right now."

Natalie tugged at the thing on her arm, but a nurse was suddenly there, pushing her hands away.

"What is all this?" she said. "I want to go home. Baojia, take me home."

"Not quite yet." He brushed her hair back again, coaxing her head to the side so he could put her hair in a ponytail. "Let the nurse check you. You're in the hospital in San Diego."

Dez said, "You scared us to death, Nat. They stopped the medication for the coma hours ago, and you were supposed to wake up and then you didn't. They told us not to worry, but—"

"I want to go home," she rasped. "I want…" She didn't know what she wanted. The nurse was poking at her and tugging on things. She hurt everywhere. And there were tubes and wires and beeping and too many people who were all happy, but she wanted to go home, and she wasn't quite sure where home was, or where *she* was, or why she was even here.

Baojia suddenly let go of her hand and stood up. "Okay, everyone out. It's too much. Thank you all for being here, but you need to leave now."

The cacophony stopped in seconds. Natalie closed her eyes and took a deep breath as murmuring well-wishers fled the room.

"Sorry, Natalie."

"We'll wait outside."

"She smells very strange. It must be all the chemicals." That had to be Tenzin.

When all the voices were gone, she opened her eyes again and it was just her and Baojia with a nurse smiling and making notes on a chart.

"The doctor will be here in just a second, hon," she said. "Everything looks good, but he'll want to examine you. I'm going to get you some water and something for your lips. Is there anything else you need right now?"

Natalie realized she couldn't move her legs. They felt heavy and hot. Her toes itched, but she couldn't move them. "What's wrong with my legs?" She started to panic and tried to sit up, but Baojia pushed her back.

"You broke both your legs in the rockslide," he said. "They're in casts right now. But they're going to be fine."

"Am I paralyzed?" Her heart was racing, and the monitors went crazy again. He took her hand and she immediately calmed down.

"No," he said in a steady voice. "There was no damage to your spine. You are not paralyzed."

He continued soothing her when the doctor came, holding her hand as the man outlined what her body had gone through. Three broken bones. Brain swelling. Trauma to her right side, accompanied by massive blood loss. She'd been in a medically induced coma for three days, and she'd be in the hospital recovering longer.

Finally, she said, "I guess I'm pretty lucky to be alive."

The doctor smiled. "Very lucky. Quite frankly, you're a miracle. If your friend hadn't driven you to the hospital so fast…" He smiled. "It's a good thing she broke some traffic laws."

Natalie frowned and looked at Baojia. He cleared his throat and glanced at the doctor before meeting her eyes.

"Tenzin was with you and Carwyn on the hike, remember? She's the one who brought you."

"Ah. Got it." Natalie was a little disappointed. She didn't even remember her first vampire-flight. "So my noggin is fine, and my side is repaired." She stretched a little and groaned. "But that's still gonna hurt for a while. I broke both my legs, but they're clean breaks—"

"And with proper physical therapy, you should be able to walk with no lasting problems. There will be pain while you're healing and possibly afterward for some time. Luckily, we didn't have to do surgery, but physical therapy will be very important."

She looked at Baojia. "I think I know a good physical therapist," she said. "I'll be fine."

Baojia finally gave her a real smile. "Yes, you will."

"There, there, *theeeeeere…*" Natalie threw her head back and groaned. "Oh, that feels amazing."

"Who knew chopsticks had so many uses?" Baojia smirked and leaned back, throwing his arm around her as she lay in the hospital bed. The blessed chopstick was placed on the side table for the next time the itching in her left cast became unbearable. They both turned their heads when they heard the faint tapping on the door.

"Hey." Kristy smiled when she walked in. "For a minute there, I thought I was interrupting something."

"The itching," she said. "The rocks didn't kill me, but the itching from these damn casts might."

She'd been in the hospital for almost two weeks. The doctors had been worried about her head for a while. Baojia had just smiled and said it was good someone was finally examining it. Natalie tried to be mad at him, but he was so happy she was alive it was hard to be irritated. Then they were worried because she had a fever and they thought the wound in her side had become infected. Baojia fussed because he couldn't heal it completely while she was still being observed by the doctors and nurses. He might have used a bit of his blood to heal the worst of the surface injuries so she wouldn't scar. Then he made a face when he tasted her and said he'd be grateful when she tasted right again.

Vampires.

Natalie couldn't decide if vampires would make wonderful or horrible doctors. She was leaning toward horrible.

But he was there every night. No one seemed to question why her husband—because that's what they had told the hospital—only came when the sun went down. Dez or Kristy were there during most of each day. Natalie was grateful for all the caring company, but mostly she wanted to go somewhere that nurses didn't wake her up every three hours.

"Be grateful you itch," Baojia said. "That means you're alive and your nerves are in excellent health."

Kristy sat on the other side of the bed. "Is he always so logical?"

Natalie nodded. "Yes. It's a good thing he's cute, too."

Baojia frowned and stood up. "I'll leave you two to talk. I'm going to find something to drink."

"Hey, can you bring me back a soda?"

He turned at the door. "Are you allowed to have soda?"

Kristy looked over her shoulder. "She's a big girl. Bring her a soda. But no caffeine."

Natalie shook her head. "You're as bad as he is."

Baojia sighed. "No caffeine still leaves me with too many choices."

"Oooh," Natalie said with a grin. "See if they have that *blood* orange." She wiggled her eyebrows. "I love that one."

He tried to stifle a smile as he left her room, but she heard him chuckle as he walked down the hall.

Kristy turned back around and slumped in her seat. "So you're really leaving?"

She nodded. "Yep."

"And you're really marrying a guy you met in a bar a few weeks ago?"

"It's been... almost two months." It probably did sound crazy to someone who didn't know the whole story.

Kristy shook her head. "Part of that time you were unconscious."

"And he was there the whole time," she said quietly. "I know... I know it probably seems crazy, but it's not. We're not. I've never been more sure of anything in my life."

"Well..." Kristy looked over her shoulder again. "He's totally nuts about you, that much is obvious. And I'm glad I know his real name now. Baojia is not that strange. Trust me, I knew a guy named Tam. And you know why he was named Tam? Because his real name had so many syllables you needed a weekend to say it..."

She had to smile. She'd told Kristy as much as she could, but not everything. And to Natalie's surprise, she felt okay about that. She'd come to realize that while knowledge was power, that power wasn't always necessary for everyone to have. And if spreading the truth about vampires would hurt Baojia... Well, the public didn't really need to know everything, did they? Besides, keeping secrets was part of her job, too. If it meant protecting a source, her lips were sealed. And if it meant protecting the vampire she loved?

"You're not telling me everything, Natalie," Kristy said, narrowing her eyes. "I'm not dumb. Spill."

Spill the truth about immortal beings who lived in a shadow society? Spill the truth about a dangerous drug that seemed to be spreading, no matter what they did to combat it? Spill the truth about the girls who had died? The ones still in danger from ingesting Elixir? Would speaking the truth help or hurt more?

"He saved my life, Kristy. That's the truth. And I think... I think I might have saved his, too. In a way." She grabbed her friend's hand. "I love him like crazy, but there's nothing crazy about it. He's the best man I've ever known."

She saw Kristy's eyes well up with unshed tears. "Where will you go? Why can't you guys stay here? If you went and apologized to the *Tribune*, they might—"

"I think we're going north," she said. "Not sure yet. We're both kind of... unemployed right now. But we're good. We'll be fine."

"Are you sure?"

She saw him coming down the hall, scanning the surroundings in that cautious way he had, carrying three sodas because he probably couldn't decide which one she would like best. Constantly watching. Constantly guarding. Always aware. Her bodyguard. Her lover. And maybe... her eternity. She still didn't know. But as he entered the room and bent down to kiss her cheek, she turned to Kristy and said, "Yeah, I'm sure."

"She wants to meet with both of us," Baojia said again, wheeling her toward the downstairs living room in Giovanni and Beatrice's house. They had been staying there, at Giovanni and Beatrice's insistence, since she'd left the hospital. Caspar and Isadora—the whole household, in fact—had spent most of her recovery fussing over her and hovering. She loved it. She kind of hated it, too. "Katya didn't say why she wanted to meet us together, but I'm assuming it's to be polite. For a human, you have quite a high profile in our world now. You're friends with Beatrice De Novo and Carwyn ap Bryn. Tenzin saved your life. According to rumors, I left my sire's aegis so that we could be together. I'm sure she's curious."

"She's a really, really powerful vampire who rules Northern California, Oregon, and Washington." She swatted at his hand in annoyance. "I'm an unemployed writer. What on earth are we going to talk about?"

"I don't know. But you are also my mate and she has been in talks with Carwyn and Brigid about something for weeks now. Something to do with both of us, I suspect. So just be pleasant and try not to interrogate her if you get curious."

"I wouldn't interrogate her!"

He laughed. "Yes, you would."

"Questioning is not interrogating."

"So you say, my love."

"Don't…" She held up a finger. He'd been doing that—calling her "my love" and something in Chinese she didn't understand, which probably meant "my perpetual headache" or something equally endearing. It didn't matter. When he said it in that low, sexy voice she melted every time. "Don't call me 'my love' just so you can—What are you doing?"

He had stopped a few feet down the hall from the living room, before kneeling in front of her and framing her face with his hands. "I'm proposing to you."

Despite her annoyance, she blushed. "W…what? Here?"

"Yes." He reached in his pocket.

Her voice squeaked. "Now?"

"Whatever happens in that room," he said, pulling out a ring from his pocket, "I do not want anyone to question my commitment to you. You are not just a human under my aegis. Vampire or not, I consider you my mate. And I am asking you to be my wife. Officially."

They'd talked about it. Natalie had even assumed it, but seeing him down on one knee, ring in hand, made her fall in love with him all over again. This startling creature, this inhuman marvel, wanted her to spend the rest of her life with him. And more. She knew he wanted more, but he was patient. As different as they were, they were perfect together.

"Yes," she said simply. "Of course yes. I would be honored to be your wife."

She knew she'd said the right thing when his face lit with a joy she'd never seen from him, spilling out of his eyes, his smile. He lit up from within as he slid a simple solitaire over her finger. Not a diamond, a light blue stone. Blue, like the water he commanded.

"It's the color of your eyes," he said quietly. "Is it—"

"It's perfect," she said. "I love it." She pulled his collar and kissed him, claiming his mouth, claiming everything he was for her own. Her body hummed in awareness of his. Weeks recuperating had led to one very frustrated Natalie. She didn't want to go to a meeting; she wanted him alone. Her body missed his, and she was not very good at being patient.

"Natalie," he growled, pulling away with regret. "Soon."

"Soon." She closed her eyes and took a deep breath, wishing they could escape as she gathered her nerves and said, "Okay, let's go meet the new vampire."

He stood and started pushing her chair again. "You'll be fine. Just be polite. Respectful. Don't interrogate."

"I told you—" She broke off when Brigid pushed the door open, obviously hearing them in the hall. When Natalie entered, she was surprised by how young the powerful Katya looked. The vampire looked as if she'd been turned when she was around eighteen. She was small, blond, and lovely, with warm brown eyes and angelic features. Despite her seeming innocence, Natalie could spot the keen intelligence behind her gaze.

"Natalie, Baojia," she said, rising to her feet. She was dressed casually in a pair of jeans and a sweater that seemed at odds with the formal room, but somehow, she still commanded it. "May I be the first to offer my congratulations?"

"Oh, right." Natalie realized Katya had heard everything from down the hall and tried to remember if she'd said anything adoringly stupid. "Thanks."

"Thank you, Katya," Baojia said more formally. "It is very nice to see you. I hope your visit to Los Angeles has been productive."

Her eyes sparkled with interest. "Very. So many interesting things have been happening lately. I almost feel as if I've missed out on the fun."

Baojia wheeled Natalie over next to an armchair and everyone sat at once. Carwyn and Brigid were on the sofa, facing the fireplace. Katya sat casually across from Baojia and Natalie.

"Baojia, I want to offer you a job," she said directly. "I think you have been underutilized, and I have a particular position I think you'd be perfect for."

After a few shocked seconds, he spoke. "May I ask what it is?"

Katya looked to Carwyn, who had been silent up till then.

"The girls…," he said. "The ones affected by the Elixir—we've been debating what to do with them. There are eleven still alive. They can't go home and risk poisoning another human or a vampire, but we don't want to kill them, obviously."

"Obviously," Natalie muttered.

"I have called in a favor," Katya said with a smile. "Several, actually. Lucien Thrax has agreed to come to a facility I own in Northern California, only an hour from San Francisco. He has agreed to work with my pharmaceutical company to discover more about this Elixir. If we can discover a cure, it would be beneficial for everyone."

"And profitable," Natalie said quietly.

Katya smiled at her. "Of course. Profitable as well." She returned her attention to Baojia. "The girls will live there. We are building a comfortable house right now. A home where they can live and be looked after. They will be prisoners, of a sort. That is unavoidable. But their time is limited, and we will offer as much protection and treatment as we can. We have decided this is best for them."

The superior tone put Natalie's instincts on edge. "Who has decided?"

"I have," Carwyn said. "And Brigid. This was our idea, Nat. We've seen what humans go through with this illness. Unless we find a cure, it's a slow and painful death."

Brigid said, "My closest human friend died of Elixir poisoning." Her strange eyes met Natalie's. "I wouldn't wish it on anyone. And we don't know who might come after these girls. Whoever Ivan was working with —whoever is making this drug—would kill them without a thought."

"If you take my offer, I don't believe it will come to that," Katya said. "Lucien is brilliant, but he is a man of science. And these girls will be targets. They're loose ends that need to be protected." She looked at Baojia. "That is what I want you to do. I want to hire you to run the security for this facility and everyone—human or vampire—who works there."

Natalie looked at Baojia, then at Katya, then back to Baojia. He wanted to say yes, she could tell. But he didn't want to answer without asking her. She could tell by the way his grip on her hand tightened.

"Yes," she said quietly, looking at him. "It's too important to let anyone else handle it. Yes."

He turned toward her and murmured, "I said I would follow you. You don't have to—"

"There is a job waiting for Natalie as well," Katya said. "If she'd like to work for the *Chronicle*. I have been assured they would be very flexible about her schedule and most happy to have her on staff or as a contributor."

Natalie turned toward Katya, lifting her chin. "Are you offering this just so he'll come work for you?"

The vampire cocked her pretty blond head. "Yes. But you'll only keep the job if you're good." Then she smiled at Carwyn. "I like her."

Natalie let out a burst of sharp laughter, trying to come up with an objection. She still had questions—plenty of them—but as far as plans went, it seemed like a good one. She looked at Baojia, recognizing the gleam of anticipation in his eyes. She thought about the girls who were sick and would only grow sicker without help. No one would protect them like he could.

"I'll take it." She nodded. "We'll go."

Baojia squeezed her hand, but she could see he was pleased. "Only if you're sure."

"George," she said, throwing her arm around his shoulders as he groaned, "I'm sure of you. Everything else, we'll figure out along the way."

CHAPTER THIRTY-ONE

"THIS ISN'T A GOOD idea, Boss."

Baojia considered the young man's words from the back of the black Cadillac that his new employer had bought for him. The streets of Ensenada flew past; Luis still drove too fast.

"You worry too much," he said as the driver pulled up to the side door of the club. He slapped Luis on the back before he slid out. "Stay with the car. I won't be long."

Luis only sighed and said, "Okay. But this is still—"

The slam of the car door shut him up. Baojia raised an eyebrow. The sedan had excellent soundproofing. He'd have to remember that. He walked to the doors of the club where the vampire guard eyed him cautiously.

"Is he expecting you?" the stocky man asked.

"No."

The guard gave a nod, spoke to a human standing at his shoulder, then smiled at Baojia patiently. A few moments later, the human came back and nodded, and the guard waved him in.

"Welcome to Bar El Ruso."

"Thank you."

The flashing lights still annoyed him, and he was glad he hadn't needed to spend time in their presence for over six months. The house he and Natalie lived in north of San Francisco faced the ocean and was set on top of sweeping cliffs with a secluded beach below. It had enough light for her and dark for him. Plus, it connected underground to the facility where he spent most of his nights. The infected girls had been brought from the desert four months earlier—much to Tulio's relief—and most seemed comfortable so far. Security renovations on the facility were well under way, and Natalie was healing as quickly as she could. Though pain was still an issue, it was less and less every night.

Baojia climbed the stairs to the VIP lounge, nodding at the vampire guarding the entrance. He spotted Ivan holding court in his corner sofa as soon as he entered. The vampire watched him with a curious smile as he strolled over.

"My friend," Ivan said graciously, though he didn't stand. "What a pleasant surprise. What brings you to my city? Please, have a seat."

He sat across from the wily earth vampire, as casually as he could when he was surrounded by six of Ivan's guards. No sign of Carlos, of course. Carlos's dust was scattered in the desert, along with Ivan's old customers. "I'm only here for the night. I came to pay my respects to an old acquaintance."

"Oh?"

He watched Ivan carefully for his reaction. "It is a beautiful monument, Ivan. Constantina would have been honored."

A slight tic above his right eye was the only indication that the words had surprised Ivan. "I'm sure she would have," he said. "And how is your woman?"

"She is well. Thank you for asking."

"I heard she was in a rather bad accident." Ivan leaned back, spreading his arms across the back of the sofa. "So unfortunately fragile, aren't they? I trust the human doctors were able to repair her."

Baojia smiled. "It was very bad, but she has recovered."

Silence fell between the two immortals; even the guards surrounding them seemed to sense that they were intruding.

"I hear you are working for Katya now." Ivan leaned forward, reaching for a red cocktail in a martini glass.

"I am." It was the only reason Ivan was still living. If Baojia had not been connected to an organization, the vampire would be dead already.

"How very fortunate," Ivan said with a smile. "For both of us."

"I suppose that's a matter of perspective," he said under his breath so Ivan's guards couldn't hear.

Ivan only laughed. Despite everything he had done, the immortal was still clever. He knew, just as Baojia did, that both of them represented powerful organizations. An open attack on either would have grave consequences, so Ivan and Baojia could parlay in relative peace.

"Some in Mexico City were surprised by your move, but not me."

Baojia folded his hands in his lap. "No?"

Ivan took a sip and smiled. "Some might say you have behaved… very out of character over the last year. I am not one of them."

"You know me so well."

The other vampire smirked. "I know you better than you might think. We're not so unalike, you know."

"I can think of a few important differences."

"I'm sure you think you can." Then a glint of anger entered Ivan's eyes. "I'd be curious how far you would go if something of yours was threatened. Hypothetically."

"I believe…" Baojia leaned forward. "There might be no limit to what I would do. *Hypothetically.*"

"Then we understand each other better than most, don't you think?"

And suddenly he did.

Constantina. The lavish tomb in the rich cemetery was not something one did for an obligation. It was the tomb of an honored lover. Ivan *had* loved Constantina. Perhaps he had brought the Elixir to Mexico, thinking it would allow the human to live with him forever. Perhaps the truth had been as much of a shock to him as anyone else. But despite that, when Ivan had learned the reality, he had sought profit and power. He hadn't cared for his lover in her final, painful days. That job had gone to another.

"I may understand you, Ivan. But don't think we are the same," he said quietly.

"I would never make that mistake, my friend."

"Did the cartel know?"

Ivan smiled demurely. "Know what?"

Carlos had disappeared. Rory was gone. He hadn't caught a whiff of any tempting waitresses on the way in. Ivan had indeed learned a lesson in caution.

"You were operating right under their nose, but they didn't even get a cut. Plausible deniability? Or were they truly unaware?"

Ivan's smile grew wider. "*If* I was conducting any business without their permission… hypothetically…"

"Of course."

"Then I'd hardly worry about them listening to rumors, would I? Things could get..." He winced dramatically. "So complicated. No one would want that. Why, then they'd have to find someone else to run this territory and clean up their messes, wouldn't they? And they'd have to admit that someone was more clever than them."

"Hypothetically."

Ivan raised both eyebrows innocently. "Of course."

"And Juarez?"

Ivan shrugged. "Such an odd situation. Who knows what is happening there? It could be any number of things. So often, people make assumptions. Especially humans."

So Ivan *had* used the Juarez murders as a cover. And the human police were still looking for the connection between the two. As far as Baojia was concerned, they could keep looking. He was confident they would find nothing pointing to either Ivan or himself.

Ivan said, "It's so strange how things work out sometimes, isn't it?"

"How so?"

"*If* I were involved with something as hypothetically damaging as murdered women—"

"And human hunts?"

"So you say. And *if* someone were to clean up all the loose ends for me... Kill everyone involved, for instance. Whoever did that would be doing me a favor." Ivan's friendly gaze grew keen. "No one to spread lies. It would leave me... quite blameless. Hypothetically."

Baojia leaned forward. "Wherever has Carlos run off to?"

Ivan shook his head sadly. "I'm afraid my first might have been involved with some rather unsavory characters. I've already reported it to my sire. I do hope he can be found, but I'm not terribly optimistic."

"Such a shame to lose valuable people."

"I'm sure your sire thinks the same thing."

Baojia leveled his gaze at Ivan. "I'm sure my sire will be fine. He is already shoring up his defenses with all the activity happening along the border. Nicolas is taking over my position since I am moving."

"How very fortunate for Ernesto. He's a good man."

Ivan didn't look pleased, which was exactly what Baojia was hoping for. He'd used Beatrice's influence over Ernesto to put his chosen successor in a more powerful position. As much as he wanted to cut ties with his sire, he could not, in good conscience, leave the southern border unguarded. He'd trained Nicolas himself.

Warning Ivan off Ernesto's people was only part of the reason he'd come down for a visit. He was also following up with Father Andrade. The priest, despite their fears, was still healthy and helping the poorest in Ensenada. Carwyn had been worried when the man hadn't called, but in the end, it appeared a simple wrong number had led to the mix-up.

It was always the most unexpected things.

Ivan took a deep breath. "The last few months have been rather messy, haven't they?"

"Nothing we're not used to." He scooted forward. He'd found out the truth about Juarez—as far as Ivan was concerned. He'd warned the cartel that Ernesto's people would be well guarded. And he'd checked on the priest for Carwyn. Baojia was ready to leave.

A hint of temper lit Ivan's gaze. "Does it bother you to go to work for someone else who will just expect you to clean up their messes?"

Baojia paused. "I work for whom I choose. I do not have your ambition, Ivan."

Ivan shrugged. "There are some who might see ambition as a virtue. They might appreciate immortals with talent, such as ourselves."

"Because we're so much alike?"

The vampire turned a seductive grin on Baojia. "We're more alike than different. Whether you'll admit it or not."

Baojia smiled and stood. "So you say. I need to go now. It was interesting to see you." Both vampires stood, neither holding out a friendly hand to shake. Baojia began walking away.

"Baojia?" Ivan called.

"Yes?"

"When you get tired of other people's problems, let me know."

"We're not alike, Ivan. Don't fool yourself." *And I have promised to kill you myself. It won't be tonight, but I do not break my promises.*

Ivan only smiled, as if he could hear the challenge in Baojia's thoughts. "I'll see you soon."

He turned and looked over his shoulder. Ivan was still standing, hands in pockets, face in a mask of polite deference. Perhaps they *were* more alike than he'd thought before, because Baojia doubted most would recognize the anger and pain that burned beneath Ivan's piercing stare.

"Yes," he said quietly. "I'll see you soon."

Baojia left. He walked down the stairs and out the door without a single look back. He listened for his car's distinctive pitch and followed it, tapping on the window so Luis would unlock it. Then he ducked in and relaxed into the seat, letting out a long, relieved breath.

"Take me home, Luis."

Epilogue

Six months later...

THE DOCTOR HELD the stethoscope to her heart, then lower, smiling as he did. He couldn't use the more modern equipment his nurses could, but with his keen immortal senses, Lucien Thrax could diagnose illness or catch medical problems with inhuman skill. Because, well... he wasn't human.

The quiet vampire straightened Natalie's gown and smiled. "Everything sounds wonderful. We'll wait for your blood work, but so far, it looks like a totally normal pregnancy."

She couldn't hold back the grin. "Cool." She sat up, arranging the clumsy hospital gown around her on the table. Despite the exterior, the house on the Northern Coast was a functioning hospital on the inside, complete with exam rooms, labs, and research facilities she didn't truly understand. She still grilled Lucien about his work on the Elixir every time they met, much to the earth vampire's frustration. But that afternoon, the focus was on *her* newest project, not his. It was her three-month checkup, and so far, everything looked good.

"How are your legs?"

She nodded. "All right. The right one seems fine, though there's pain when the weather changes, and the left is getting better every day."

"Keep up with your physical therapy."

"Trust me, my physical therapist is a slave driver."

Lucien smiled. "With your best interests at heart, I'm sure."

"That's what he keeps saying," she said with a frown. "I have my doubts."

She finally got Lucien to laugh. No mean feat for the quiet immortal with sad eyes. She'd known him for almost a year, but Lucien Thrax was still a mystery. He could be awake for most of the day, so Natalie guessed he was old—very old. He was tall, with a lean face that looked older the longer you looked at it. She wanted to hand him a pair of very old-fashioned eyeglasses even though she knew his eyes didn't need them.

Her instincts told her Lucien had suffered loss like she couldn't really imagine. And yet he was one of the kindest men she'd ever met. Unfailingly calm with his often unruly patients. Brilliant beyond her understanding, yet always ready to explain some point of research to her. But there was a sorrow that lived behind his eyes, giving Lucien a stern gravity despite his young face. She was glad he and Baojia were becoming friends.

Lucien said, "There's no reason you shouldn't have full use of both legs eventually, though the pregnancy will increase your body's stress."

"I know. Baojia said the same thing, but I didn't want to wait."

"Impatient girl." He shook his head. "You can get dressed now. Did you want me to leave?"

She nodded toward the curtain in the corner. "You're fine. I have a couple questions for you."

"Of course you do." Lucien smiled and sat in his chair as Natalie went to pull on her clothes.

"So, what I'm wondering is, if I decide to change at some point in the future—and that's still an *if*—would my legs heal completely? How does that work?"

She heard him sigh. No doubt this was another one of those questions with a way longer answer than she wanted. She smiled when he started to answer anyway.

"It's hard to say. Unfortunately, there doesn't seem to be any hard and fast rules about some things. It's a bit like human genetics, to be honest. No one knows what characteristics a baby will be born with. He or she could be the spitting image of one parent, a combination of both, or look nothing like either, but some very distant relative. There are some general rules, but not hard and fast ones, except for our elemental strength, which I liken to blood type."

"So, it might heal and it might not?" Well, that wasn't helpful. She was still debating the issue. She liked being human. She liked it a lot. And being a vampire had a lot of drawbacks. Some benefits to be sure, but drawbacks too. The biggest benefit was still sleeping in their room because the sun hadn't gone down yet.

"It would be most accurate to predict that function would improve, but not perfectly. That's why it's very important to get your body into peak physical condition before a change, if it is planned. Becoming vampire increases the strengths you already have, which is why Baojia is so strong, even though he is relatively young for our kind."

"Got it." She buttoned up her jeans. They were snug; she'd have to get new ones soon. The thought made her smile.

There was a long pause until Lucien finally said, "Can I ask… are you leaning toward yes? After you've had your children?"

She took a deep breath and stepped from behind the curtain. "I don't know. To be completely honest, some days I watch the sunset and think… how could I spend an eternity without this? And then I see him when he wakes up and think, how could I ever say goodbye? How could I ask him to live the rest of his life without me? To watch our children—our grandchildren maybe—without me? Is this too cruel?"

"He wants this child as much as you do." Lucien smiled. "Maybe more."

She blinked back tears. "So every night I lean a little more toward that compromise. But I don't know; I still have doubts. What do you think, Doc?"

She saw Lucien look toward the window that had been blacked out with shutters. A faint glow of afternoon sunlight peeked through. "I don't want to influence your decision, Natalie."

"But?"

He looked back at her with a rueful smile. "I had to say goodbye. And I didn't want to live afterward. You have nights you still debate living as a vampire? Well… so do I. So I'm probably biased."

Her heart broke for him; she walked over and kissed his forehead. "We'd miss you if you were gone."

"I'm sure he'd say the same thing." Lucien squeezed her hand. "Better get out of here if you want to catch that sunset. You can take a picture for me."

"You got it." She patted the phone in her pocket. It was new. Baojia broke them every six weeks or so. It was a good thing the guy was loaded.

Natalie left the hospital, walking into the afternoon sun and down the path leading toward the ocean. Her new home rested on top of the cliffs with a winding path that led down to the beach. She was still working on making that walk by herself without a cane or a helping hand, but she'd get there eventually. For now, she sat down on a clump of rocks that overlooked the Pacific and watched the scarlet sun set into the water. She took a few pictures to show Lucien later, and she waited.

The salt spray rushed up the rocks as the tide came in, tickling her nose with the scent of the living water. The ocean here smelled exactly right. She worked as much as she wanted to and had a new life growing in her. Change was good. Change was living. And the world was always changing. What wonders would she see if she lived as long as Lucien? Would the world still excite her? Could she ever grow bored? An eternity stretched in front of her if she wanted it. An eternity with Baojia by her side. An eternity to watch him change. Watch herself change.

Natalie heard the door to the house close just after the sun slipped below the horizon. The sky was growing dim, but it was still lit with a last wash of glorious color when Baojia settled behind her, wrapping his arms around her belly and laying his cheek on her shoulder. He placed teasing kisses on her neck, brushing her hair to the side and pulling her closer.

"How is everything?" he asked quietly.

"Good. Everything looks good and normal and no problems."

"Excellent."

She knew her short response wouldn't satisfy him, and he'd seek out Lucien later for a full report. He was thorough that way. The thought only made her smile.

He craned his neck around. "What is that smile for?"

"You. You make me smile."

"That's good news." His hands teased under the shirt the wind was blowing up. "I'm hungry."

"Lucien says you're stuck with donor blood until my labs come back. He wants to make sure I'm not anemic."

"Not that kind of hungry," he growled.

"Oh." She blushed. "Got it."

"I love that you still blush."

"I'm glad one of us thinks it's funny."

He turned her in his arms and kissed her, worshiping her mouth as his hands held back her unruly hair and the breeze whipped around them. She felt her body responding to him as he pulled her closer. His lips teased along her collar, then up to her ear, whispering promises of what he would do to make her blush more. She could feel his smile against her skin. A year. Ten years. An eternity. She didn't think she'd ever stop wanting him.

"Why don't you go for your swim, and I'll go in the house?" she said.

"Why don't you do that?" He kissed her once more, then stood, walking toward the edge of the cliff and pulling off his shirt as he walked. He turned at the edge of the rocks, smiling and beautiful. Startling creature that he was. He was incandescent against the dying day. He ran the last few feet and leapt off the edge of the cliff. She gasped in delight as she watched him. He soared over the water as it rushed up to greet him. The wave caught him in midair and pulled him toward the churning ocean, welcoming him as he laughed.

Baojia *laughed*. The deep, joyful sound rushed up the cliff and spread on the breeze, causing her own smile to bloom when she saw him dive deep. His happiness only fed her own.

"How could I say goodbye to that?" she whispered. Then Natalie turned and walked home.

THE END

ABOUT THE AUTHOR

ELIZABETH HUNTER is a contemporary fantasy, paranormal romance, and contemporary romance author. She is a graduate of the University of Houston Honors College and a former English teacher. She once substitute taught a kindergarten class, but decided that middle school was far less frightening. Thankfully, people now pay her to write books and eighth-graders everywhere rejoice.

She currently lives in Central California with an eight-year-old ninja who claims to be her child. She enjoys music, writing, travel, and bowling (despite the fact that she's not very good at it). Someday, she plans to learn how to scuba dive. And maybe hang glide… but that looks like a lot of running.

She is the author of the Elemental Mysteries and Elemental World series, the Cambio Springs series, and other works of fiction.

Website: ElizabethHunterWrites.com

Elemental Mysteries fan site: ElementalMysteries.com.

E-mail: elizabethhunterwrites@gmail.com.

Twitter: @E_Hunter

Find me on Facebook!

Made in the USA
Las Vegas, NV
20 March 2024